I0569807

BAD DAY FOR A ROAD TRIP
BOOK TWO OF THE BAD DAY SERIES

JASON OFFUTT

SEVERED PRESS
HOBART TASMANIA

BAD DAY FOR A ROAD TRIP

Copyright © 2018 Jason Offutt

WWW.SEVEREDPRESS.COM

All rights reserved. No part of this book may be
reproduced or transmitted in any form or by any
electronic or mechanical means, including
photocopying, recording or by any information and
retrieval system, without the written permission of
the publisher and author, except where permitted by law.
This novel is a work of fiction. Names,
characters, places and incidents are the product of
the author's imagination, or are used fictitiously.
Any resemblance to actual events, locales or persons,
living or dead, is purely coincidental.

ISBN: 978-1-925711-96-7

All rights reserved.

PART ONE: THE GOOD LANDS

CHAPTER 1

Leaf blades raked Matty's face as he ran, his white polo stained by red dirt and sweat in the July heat. Tiny cuts from the sharp dry corn leaves covered his exposed skin, but he didn't have time to notice. The monsters were back there, somewhere.

Matt Senior's RV, a sleek gray toy with a fully-stocked bar, was far behind, its gas tank as dry as the dehydrated brown stalks in this field. *Who the fuck plants corn in Oklahoma?* ran through Matty's head as he pounded over the dry dirt between the rows, his once ash gray Chuck Taylors the color of rust. He hadn't wanted to go into the corn. Hell, he didn't want to get off the highway, but Matty had pointed the dead RV toward a tall sawtooth oak tree and crawled it underneath the shade before the vehicle's momentum died like its engine. According to the vehicle's GPS, he was still three miles from Muskogee. Three miles from a gas station that probably didn't work anymore. Three miles from the possibility of people.

"What the hell, man?" he'd said, his words loud in an afternoon devoid of sound.

When the engine coughed at the sudden lack of fuel, Matty resigned himself to the reality that he was only temporarily screwed. Three miles wasn't far to walk for gas. The walk back to Senior's RV might be a little less fun, but doable. Before he set off, Matty just wanted to climb on the roof of his dad's RV and have a couple of beers in the shade while he watched for something cool to happen, but something cool didn't happen. Something uncool happened. *Totally fucking uncool.* He was only half-way into his second can of Elk Valley Pale Ale when the cornfield on the south side of the rural highway began to move.

What the hell?

The day was hot and dead; not a hint of breeze to cool him or his sweaty beer and sure as hell not enough wind to whip through a cornfield like that. He lowered the yellow and black can into his lap and squinted through the bright Oklahoma day into the corn to the south of the road. As far as he could see, the field swayed, not like it was caught by a wind that didn't have the decency to cool Matty, but like waves at the beach in Galveston. Not that he'd seen the beach with his parents. Oh, no. Senior "worked too damn hard" and was too fucking cheap for a family vacation. Matty went for spring break, blowing his scholarship money. He'd been

1

drunk, but he remembered the waves; the waves moved just like the cornfield.

Then he saw the birds.

A line of black grew over the far reaches of the field, shifting within itself, flowing like it was alive. The beer slipped out of his hand and landed on the roof with a thunk. The can tipped onto its side, spilling craft beer over his legs. Matty didn't notice the wet creeping into his khakis because he now knew what was coming toward him through the field.

Monsters had found him.

"Shit," he whispered and climbed down the ladder on the back door of Senior's RV. He ran across the road and disappeared into the cornfield on the opposite side of the road, hoping it wasn't filled with monsters, too.

***

It wasn't. At least not yet. Matty pulled up after about twenty yards, a stitch stabbing his side, breath coming in painful gasps. It had been four years since he'd last run cross country for the Gore, Oklahoma, High School Pirates, three of those years spent at Cameron University in Lawton, throwing back beers at the Railhead Saloon with his buddies. The last year he spent at home on academic suspension, frequently unemployed, a disappointment.

Matty pulled an arm across his face, trying and failing to wipe sweat out of his eyes. The damn sun didn't help; the yellow ball poured heat over Matty, making the beer he'd just sucked down seem to boil in his stomach. He stood slowly, feeling out the pain; after too long, his breath came more easily. *Okay, Matty. You're okay. Just keep moving. Keep moving.*

He stood silently for a moment, just a moment. The crunch of more feet than he could count beat out a cadence in the afternoon. It was soft now, like the alien creaking of far-off cicadas, but he knew if he stood there any longer it would get louder – much louder. Matty turned and looked the way he'd come, the top of the RV still visible above the corn.

What? "That's all? That's as far as–" His voice caught in his throat – the birds had come back into view, a dark cloud covering the southern sky. "No," Matty moaned, turned and broke into a jog.

***

The end of the world happened slowly. So slowly Matty didn't know anything was wrong at first. His no-bullshit Middle Eastern boss Ahmud had just fired him from the Kum & Go convenience store, his on-again-off-again stopped returning his texts – again – and his father was an asshole. Perfectly normal. So, when Matt Sr. pulled an enormous RV into the driveway of their Gore home, he wasn't surprised. Everything was as it always was.

"This here is finer than the *Starship Enterprise*," Matt Sr. said when he and Mary climbed out of the thirty-seven-foot, eleven-inch-long recreational vehicle when they drove it home from the dealership; the dealer sticker still in the front passenger window. Matty waited for them on the front steps drinking a Dr Pepper mixed with Southern Comfort. Sure, that was Mom's drink, but Senior's single malt Laphroaig Scotch gave Matt a stomachache. Senior gave Matt a stomachache, too.

"Want to take it out for a spin, son?" Senior asked, the smile on his face wide as the ass end of that RV. "Well tough shit." He leaned toward Mary and squeezed her left butt cheek. "You can come in and take a look some time, but don't open that door if there's a necktie on the knob. It'll be occ-u-poddo."

Mary slapped her husband's hand away, the frown on her face nearly audible. "Don't be an asshole in front of Junior," she said, the words flat, emotionless. Her eyes moved to meet her son's, her face sad. "This stupid thing cost more than our first house," she told Matty, pulling a soft pack of Pall Mall's from her purse and tapping one out. "I'm afraid we're going to have to put up with your father being stupid for a while."

She stepped away from Senior and walked passed Matty to the front door, lighting the cigarette as she pulled open the screen. Matty stood and took a drink, the sweetness almost overwhelming. "Don't worry, Dad," he said through a piece of mostly-melted ice. "I won't mess with the Fritomobile. I'm too busy with my career."

Senior had been a manager at the Frito Lay plant as long as Matty could remember, overseeing the production of crunchy fried corn snack sodium bombs. The Berning house was never short on Chili Cheese Fritos, no-siree. Frito-Lay had given the Berning's a nice house, nice cars and Matty an exciting education in accounting for three years before he flunked his way home to face the fact he'd never be good enough for his father.

Matty downed what little was left in his cup and followed his mother inside where he knew she'd have already poured herself a drink and turned on the living room TV to watch whatever she'd TiVo'd. "The Great British Baking Show," or some shit that goes well with a plastic convenience store cup full of booze and a bowl of chocolate chips.

"I earned this, goddamnit," Senior shouted as Matty disappeared into the house.

Trouble is, Matty knew his father was right. It wasn't until everybody around them started to die that he realized it wasn't his problem.

***

A dog lay in a bald patch in the cornfield, the tall stalks giving way to stunted ones with shriveled leaves, like the plants had just given up. Matty jogged into the dusty spot and froze, the monsters behind him momentarily forgotten. He'd never owned a dog; Senior wouldn't allow it. 'They bring fleas in the house and piss on the furniture,' he'd told a fourteen-year-old Matty, who stood in the yard holding a stray black Labrador puppy he'd found in a vacant lot by the Smith house. 'Some things just are. And our just are is no fucking pets.' Senior walked his son back to the lot and they left the dog there. Matty hadn't thought about it in years. The dog was probably dead, like everything else.

Matty stepped closer to the dog in the corn, but it didn't move. It was a mongrel, maybe with some shepherd in it, but Matty couldn't really tell. He stared at the mutt, the poor creature's stomach bloated like it was pregnant, or like those starving children in a late-night TV commercial.

"Sorry, buddy," he said, tensing to push his muscles back into action when the dog's chest quivered, then fell still again. Matty didn't move; his breath caught in his throat.

Alive?

"Hey," he said a little more loudly. "Are you still with me, buddy?" Matty hadn't seen anything decent alive since his parents died; no deer, no armadillos, no people. Only those fucking black birds that seemed to be everywhere now. Scavengers in a dying world.

The dog didn't move again. Matty squatted and stared at the beast, its black and white fur matted and dotted with fat, white ticks and cockleburs. The monsters in the corn behind him were momentarily forgotten; he hadn't realized how much he needed something to talk to. *Come on, little guy,* he thought, his brain, his emotions dredging the puppy from the vacant lot across his mind. He blinked, trying to hold back tears.

"Are you—" he started, but the words froze. The dog's stomach shook, violently this time. Matty rose to his feet and took a wobbly step backward.

The dog's abdomen swelled further and a squeak split the air, like air escaping from an overfilled balloon. *What the hell?* The dog's chest grew visibly round, then exploded sending jagged, shattered ribs through the skin. A stem, thick as the neck of a beer bottle, pushed itself into the air from the cavity, a bulb attached to the end. The stalk stood tall and straight, streaked with the dog's blood, then the bulb began to turn like it knew Matty was there.

"Oh my god," spilled from his lips. It was just like the thing in his mother.

Matthew Berning Jr. bolted from the bald patch and vanished back into the corn.

***

It all happened the day Senior came home from the American Legion Hall with a runny nose, the RV two weeks old; Senior and Mary's first trip to San Antonio a month away. "Just a cold, Junior," he said, pouring a scotch – like he hadn't already had enough at the Legion Hall. "Takes more than a cold to knock Matthew Berning off his feet."

It did. Senior didn't have a cold. Blood began to leak from his nose during dinner, dripping onto his plate of pot roast, potatoes and carrots. By 8 p.m., he was in bed. Mary Berning walked from the bedroom, a Southern Comfort and Dr Pepper in her hand, a pill bottle in the other. "He'll be okay, Matty," she said, her voice weak, strained. "I gave him some aspirin."

Aspirin. Matty watched the news; he knew about the Piper, the deadly illness conspiracy theorists claimed was caused by the new anti-depressant Ophiocordon. The pharmaceutical gurus said that was bullshit, but whatever it was, aspirin sure as fuck wouldn't help.

The next morning, his parents didn't wake up.

Matty sat his empty bowl in the kitchen sink, a few stray milky corn flakes stuck to the side and walked to their bedroom.

"Mom?" Matty said through the flimsy press-board door. No answer. No sound of movement. No coughing. Nothing. "Dad?"

Matty pressed his ear against the smooth surface and closed his eyes, concentrating on any sound. Any sound at all. Then he heard it. A soft whine, like when he tried to let a fart out slowly.

"Dad?" he said again. The noise had stopped.

Come on, Matty. Something's wrong. Man up and look in there. What's the worst you could see? Mom and Dad doing it? He looked, there wasn't a tie hanging from the doorknob.

He swallowed and twisted the knob. The mechanism clicked and the bolt slid free of the door fame. Matty took a deep breath and let it out slowly before pushing the door open into his parents' room.

Matty didn't understand what his eyes saw, not at first. Senior stood on Mary's side of the bed, his white wife-beater shirt stained red with blood. *That nosebleed is terrible,* ran through Matty's head before he saw the thing – the thing that stood from Mary's chest like the stalk of an enormous mushroom. He'd seen it before, on television – the fungus. The Ophiocordon fungus. *Oh, my god. This is it. The Piper. My parents have the fucking Piper.*

The wonder drug turned hell on earth.

"Shit," Matty shouted and Senior's eyes turned on him, the baby blues wild and bloodshot. A strip of flesh hung from Senior's dripping red lips. It took Matty a few seconds to realize that skin had once been part of his mother's face.

Senior growled like an animal and lunged across the bed toward him. Matty slammed the door and ran toward the kitchen.

***

The corn opened suddenly and a gravel road cut across Matty's path in an L-shape. The dusty lane to his left probably went to the highway; the one ahead had to go to Muskogee. It just had to. He turned and looked behind him for a second, only second. The sky had grown darker with what he was certain were those wretched crows, but they weren't close enough for him to make sure, at least not yet. The monsters were still there, although he couldn't tell how far they were behind him, or how close. He was sure he could outdistance them; he was alive, after all. It was just, well, the fucking birds that bothered him. Crows were scavengers. *Why are there so many crows?*

Matty turned from the corn and something red caught his eye – the back end of a pickup that sat off the road at the corner of the L where two fields met. It was a red Ford F-250 pickup about thirty yards away facing west, its back windshield clouded by red dust. Matty hated to leave Senior's RV behind – it's a bus, it's a house, it's a bar, it's a bathroom, it's everything at once – but here was another means of transportation away from the crows and away from the hungry, once-human creatures that followed them. He briefly considered getting in the truck and driving back to get the RV, but the thought of driving the truck toward the creatures in the corn, creatures like Senior had become, sounded crazy.

Matty walked toward the truck. It could have been abandoned there a month, or a week, or two days. He couldn't tell. The truck hadn't stopped because of a flat tire; all four looked like they'd just come off a dusty rack. A rusty red gas can sat in a corner of the bed. Matty wrapped his fist around the handle and lifted it, but it didn't budge easily. The gas can was full. That didn't leave many options: the driver abandoned his truck, the driver was pulled out of his truck, or the driver was still inside, dead or—

"No," he whispered, then squinted into the back window of the cab. "No, man. Give me a fucking break."

Matty hadn't been able to see through the caked-on dust when he first broke onto the dirt road, but he was closer now; someone sat in the truck. A man in a ball cap was in the driver's seat; he didn't move. *He's dead,*

Matty thought, breathing in through the nose, out through the mouth. *Dead. I can do this. I can handle dead-dead. I'll just open the door, pull the body out and drive off. I'll even push in his 8-track of George Jones or some shit and listen to "He Stopped Loving Her Today" all the way to Muskogee.* He took another deep breath and let it out. *Everything's cool.*

A black shape dropped out of the sky, landed on the truck cab and cawed. Matty jumped. A crow. A black, greasy crow perched on the roof over the door, its dead, glassy eyes glared at him.

"Fuck off," Matty said, his voice wavering more than he'd like. He glanced to the south; the flock – no, the murder – of crows was closer. Much closer.

I can do this. He stepped toward the driver-side door and grabbed the handle. The crow followed his every movement, its soulless eyes never leaving him. *Oh, boy.*

Matty broke his eyes from the crow's gaze and looked through the dusty window into the cab of the truck. Farmer Joe turned his head toward him and threw himself at the window. The poor man's face slammed against the glass, the window streaked with bloody saliva. A scream burst from Matty and he lurched back, almost tumbling over his own feet. Farmer Joe began to beat the glass with his dead, blue-veined hands. The crow cawed just above Matty's head, the sudden shock dropped him backward into the dusty gravel. The winged bastard landed to the road and hopped closer, its black, lifeless eyes looked like death.

"This isn't fucking fair," Matty screamed before he pushed himself to his feet and ran down the road.

***

The fire had just started to show as Matty sat on the roof of Senior's Moe-Bile Ree-Tirement home. He'd always liked high places; they made him feel safe, away from everything that could harm him, like Senior's disappointment. Matty took another bite of a Ding Dong and watched tongues of flame lick the windows of his parents' house. He popped the last bite into his mouth and chewed, sort of. Ding Dongs didn't require much chewing. The clear cellophane wrappers that once kept the chocolate spongey hockey pucks fresh for twenty-five days on a store shelf sat in a pile between his legs sprinkled with crumbs. He held up the box and shook; two more cakes fell out. Oh, well. There were lots more out there, all for the taking. One of the benefits of almost everyone else dying. Matty wondered if Ahmud was still at the Kum & Go. He'd stop by that dump later; the shelves were stocked with Hostess cakes.

The living room window glass shattered onto the lawn that had begun to get shaggy. Mowing the lawn was Matty's job, the only one he'd been able to keep for more than a couple of months. Nine years of steady lawn-mowing employment a half-hour at a time wasn't bad, he figured, even though Senior paid in phrases like, "Stop complainin'," and "You eat, doncha?" *Lawn looks like shit; sorry to disappoint you again, Pops.*

Smoke rolled from the house into the Oklahoma sky. The box of Ding Dongs and a couple cans of Armour chili were the only food Senior had moved into his new RV, although he'd stocked the bar, apparently on the way home from the sales lot. Three days. Matty had lived in the RV for three days and had nothing but Ding Dongs and chili straight from the can. Mom made meatloaf full of onions and covered in ketchup before she died because it was Matty's favorite, but the leftovers and the other real food were in the kitchen and Matt knew he sure as hell wasn't going back into the house. The change had hit Senior and Matty knew he was safer outside.

Senior had broken through the flimsy bedroom door a day ago, maybe two. Matty saw him through the big front windows, blindly bumping into furniture, his clothes soaked in Mary's blood. Oh, no. He wasn't going into the house, but he wasn't going to leave Senior like that, either. Senior might break out of the house like he did the bedroom and eat someone else. Matty wouldn't have that, he wouldn't have that at all.

The bottle of Laphroaig was easy to decide on, Senior's choice of scotch gave Matty gut rot. He pulled his handkerchief from his back pocket and walked to the side of the house where he soaked it with the liquor.

The windows were triple pane energy savers Senior ordered last spring. Too thick to chance throwing the bottle through it. Matty fetched Mom's concrete yard gnome from beneath a bush below the front window, ducking low to keep Senior from sensing him and walked to where he'd left the whisky. The window shattered all the way through on the first throw; the gnome, with its pointed red hat and sunflower yellow tunic disappeared into the house. Senior growled from somewhere inside, but had no idea where the sound had come from.

"Sorry, Mom," he said as he stuffed one end of the liquor-soaked handkerchief into the whisky bottle and lit it with a lighter Mom had left in the glove box along with an emergency box of Pall Malls. "Nothing personal." He pulled his arm back and tossed the bottle through the broken window.

A whoosh told Matty the fire had spread as the bottle hit the floor.

That had been about a half-hour or so ago; Matty didn't know and he didn't care. Time didn't mean much anymore. The only thing that mattered to him right then, as he sat on the roof of the RV, were the Ding Dongs. The interior of the house was completely engulfed when Matty decided he needed to leave. He didn't want to watch his childhood home go up in flame. He didn't want to set his parents on fire, either. Well, at least not his mother, but his mother was dead and the monster in the house wasn't his father anymore.

***

Matty had to stop again, his breath gone. He knew he shouldn't have sprinted; his body wasn't used to that anymore. It was used to Southern Comfort. He knew a jog may have easily kept the distance between him and the two-legged creatures moving through the cornfields, but Farmer Joe was too much, just too much. *Keep it calm, Matty. You're going to get through this.* Sure, the crows could keep up with him, hell they could pass him, but Matty wasn't afraid of birds. The crow behind him cawed, then once more; too quickly for it to be from the same bird. *Was that one? Or two? Shit.* He looked up, his breath still coming hard. The dusty country road took a slight left in between the fields. How many miles had he gone? One? Two? None?

He sucked in as much air as he could, his lungs burning. A sudden rustling to his right brought his head around, but that was it, just his head; the stitch in his side still stabbed at him. The crow landed at his feet and the fat bird looked up at him with its dead eyes.

"Shoo," he wheezed.

The bird cocked its head at the words like it was trying to make sense of this two-legged thing before it.

"Shoo," he said again, stronger this time. "Get out of here, bird."

"Caw," the slick, greasy thing squawked.

What the hell?

"People are scary, bird," Matty said, staring the creature in the eyes. "Why don't you shoo?"

The bird clicked its beak open and shut, the clacking sound threatening. *Wha—?* started to cross Matty's mind when the crow slammed its beak into his shin; pain lanced through his leg.

"Hey, goddammit," he shouted, pushing himself straight. Something trickled down his shin. Blood. *Blood?* "You made me bleed, you little bastard."

A rustling from behind froze Matty, his stomach clenched, the pain in his leg and in his chest forgotten. He turned slowly. At least a half-dozen black birds sat in the corn, staring at him.

***

The drive north was a no-brainer. South? What hell was south? Dallas? What was in Dallas? Cowboys fans. Senior was a Cowboys fan, so Matty became a Packer's fan early. From Sequoyah County, the closest big city was Muskogee, population about 40,000, a lot bigger than Gore's 977. Gore was dead; the streets empty, the air silent. Even Mom's land-line telephone she insisted on keeping had fallen quiet, her gossip partners as dead as she was. So Matty climbed down from the roof and hefted himself into the driver's seat of the RV. He stared at the house for a moment, but only a moment. Senior walked by the window covered in dancing orange flame and Matty started the vehicle, backing from the driveway, not even bothering to look behind him. He didn't need to; no one was there.

***

Matty couldn't feel his legs anymore, they simply moved underneath him. His head swam, his chest was on fire. The sky had grown dark behind him, the air filled with flapping wings, but Matty knew better than to turn to look. The cloud of crows was closer, but so were the monsters in the corn. He had to keep moving.

The road turned to the left and emerged from between cornfields. Matty limped across the gravel as the city of Muskogee, Oklahoma, appeared in front of him, the long, white form of a Motel 6 the closest building. Between Matty and the motel were a cemetery and a highway. *Gonna make it. Gonna make it.* He pulled open a gate in the cast-iron fence that surrounded the cemetery and nearly fell inside, slamming the gate behind him in a clang. *Oh, shit.* The sky behind him was thick with birds and the cornfields shook with movement of the once-human monsters inside. He released the gate and hurried through the graveyard, the tops of tombstones uncomfortably black with gathering crows.

"Fuck you," he rasped, stumbling through the tall unkempt grass between the stones, the bird's attention following him as he moved by.

Caws barked around Matty. Something was wrong here, something different than these damned birds and the creatures pursuing him in the field. He grew closer to the motel, the streetlights popping on in the growing darkness under the approaching blanket of birds. Matty's feet slowed, his head understanding what he saw. A fence. A twelve-foot-tall chain-link fence rose from the ground, splitting the cemetery in two. It continued as far as Matty could see to the east. He swung his head to the west and the nearby highway; the fence continued, aluminum poles embedded in the asphalt, the fence keeping him from the motel, from safety.

"What the hell?" he whispered, the words soft, weak.

The gate rattled behind him. Creatures that used to be people pressed against it; the decorative fence tilted forward.

Fuck.

Matty lurched to the chain-link fence and wrapped his fingers into it. *Climb, Matty. Climb. Up high, where you're safe.* "Come on, man." He tried to pull himself up, but his breath and strength were gone. The flimsy barrier that surrounded this resting home of the dead groaned and collapsed, the growls of the monsters grew louder. *Fuck, fuck, fuck.* He tried to shove the toes of his Chuck Taylors between the links, but they were too big. *Fuck.* Matty stepped on the heel of his right shoe and pulled up with a shaking leg. The shoe came free. He pulled off his left shoe, stuck his toes into the links and pushed up. It hurt, the quarter-inch galvanized wire dug into the soft balls of his feet, but he thought being eaten would hurt worse.

Sweat ran down his forehead and into his eyes, but the stinging didn't matter, he couldn't wipe it out anyway. Matty pulled himself upward with shaky arms and moved his right foot to gain a higher purchase. *Come on, Matty. Come on.* He struggled to suck air into his burning lungs and reached upward, hoisting his body higher inches at a time. The guttural roar of the monsters was clear now, an underscore in the symphony of crows.

His fingers and toes kept pulling, the pain in his feet deadened now, but the wires cut into his feet and his socks were wet with blood. Four feet, six feet, eight feet. *You got this, baby. You got this.*

A voice came from nowhere, propelled across Matty's eardrums from a megaphone, or a loudspeaker. He didn't know where it originated, he just knew he could deal with that later, when he was on the other side of the fence, away from the monsters, hopefully sitting in a hot tub sipping something cold and foamy.

"Citizen," was all the voice said.

Citizen? Matty kept his arms and legs moving slowly, painfully upward, the guttural sounds of the creatures closing on him now louder than the cawing of crows.

The voice said something else, but a nearby crow drowned it out.

"What?" Matty said, his voice too soft to reach anywhere.

The voice came back. "Citizen. Back away from the fence," the woman said.

No. No, no, no.

"It's cool," he tried to yell, but it came out as a rush of air. "I'm cool." Eight feet, nine. The top was near his grasp.

"Please remove yourself from the fence," the woman said, the voice tinny through the speaker. "Remove yourself immediately."

Immediately? Crows had already begun to perch on the fence just feet above him, the birds' caws drummed in his ears.

"Help," he yelled, his face pressed into the metal links, sweat, tears and snot glistened on his face. "Help me."

The first of the Piper monsters grew close enough for Matty to hear its individual groan; his fingers wrapped tighter around the thick wire, strength quickly leaving his limbs. *I'm not going to make it. Shit, man. I'm not going to make it.*

He forced in a breath deeper than he thought he could take and screamed through the fence. "Hey, asshole. I need help, here." A crow screeched above Matty's head, the sound drowning out his words. *Fucking help me.*

Something as hard as a baseball slammed into the top of Matty's head, pushing his face hard into the wire. Claws dug into his scalp. "Help," he screamed. A crow had landed atop his head, it punched its beak into Matty's temple, blood gushed down his face.

The voice came back, emotionless, cold. "I'm sorry," she said. "I truly am, but I have my orders. You are in violation of United States Army Code No. 45986B. For the survival of the human race, no one is to cross the Southern Border of the United States. Trespassers will be shot on sight. Now, please, remove yourself from the fence."

Matty's head swam. The bird's beak cracked his forehead, searching for his eyes. He shook his head, but the crow wouldn't budge. The fence began to shake beneath him; the monsters were here.

"Please, help me." The words came in a whisper.

JULY 28: I-80, WESTERN NEBRASKA

CHAPTER 2

Smoke. Screams. Fire. Blackness. Smoke. Screams. Gravelyman. Fire. Blackness. Smoke. Hot dogs. Fire. Blackness. Always blackness. Doug stirred in the eternal night. He'd been in the blackness too long; something in his mind knew he needed to come out, to come out of the blackness now, or he might stay there.

The eerie silence of the B-2 overhead dropping unguided Mk 82 bombs down onto the Community, a fenced-in hell the government locked anyone it thought had been exposed to – what? A disease? No, the Piper. Yeah, the Piper. The antidepressant some lab genius created out of a Southeast Asian fungus that turned ants into zombies and used the ants to spread their spores through the jungle. Why didn't the science guy think it would do the same to people? Explosions. Blackness. The Gravelyman, the coughing man from the bus lying in a puddle of his own blood. The bus. The bus had taken Doug and friends with faces but no names to the Community after they were picked up in, where? Des Moines? No. Omaha. Omaha, Nebraska. Shit, is my ankle broken? Dear God, it hurts. Explosions. Fire. Screams. Hot dogs.

Hot dogs?

The warm smell of roasting hot dogs flooded his thoughts. Were they real hot dogs? Or memory hot dogs? One of his memory friends loved hot dogs. He cooked them in a barn near Platte City, Missouri, even though Doug told him not to, they might be caught. By whom? He couldn't remember. But, wait. That was wrong. His friend cooked bratwurst in the barn; he'd had a hot dog with Johnnyball at the stadium.

Smoke. Screams. Fire. Blackness. No, not quite blackness anymore. Grayness. Doug stirred in the grayness.

"Well," a voice, a familiar voice, said from far away. Or was it close by? "Good morning, sleeping beauty. You kept us worrying long enough."

The voice was from his friend who liked hot dogs. Terry. His name was Terry and Terry was okay. Doug's eyes fluttered and the grayness got brighter, driving the last of the velvet black from his eyes. Shapes formed slowly, the light, what light there was, stung his eyes.

"Doug," a different voice, a softer voice said. He knew this voice, too. He was intimate with this voice. "Doug, honey. Wake up. I was so worried about you."

Something wet and warm pressed against his forehead. Lips. Her lips. Jenna's lips. Oh, lord, Jenna. Jenna was alive, too. Doug opened and closed his eyes a few times, the lids heavy. The shapes slowly came into focus. Jenna. Yes, Jenna, her face smudged and her once bouncy auburn hair flat, but she still looked beautiful to him. And Terry, grinning like he'd just won $10 on a scratcher's ticket. Doug had seen the scratcher's ticket grin before. And there was someone else, dark hair, Nikki. Nikki from the electric house. Doug smiled, although he didn't know if that smile grew on his face, or just inside. He wanted to tell everyone he loved them. He wanted to tell them he needed a drink of water and some food, but blackness returned and the world disappeared once again.

***

When Doug fully came to, he felt hungover. A dull ache filled his head, his mouth was a desert that tasted like dirty socks. The world was still gray. From the yellow light that streamed in from his left and the growing shadows to his right, the day might be nearing dusk. The gray was concrete with square corners. It looked like – *A box culvert? What the hell am I doing in a box culvert?*

"Hey, Doug's awake again," Jenna called toward the dusk entrance to the short concrete tunnel that probably ran under a highway. *What highway?* She sat next to him on a cardboard box marked, what was that? Spotted Dick? She's sitting on a box of Spotted Dick? What the hell is Spotted Dick? Something squeezed him. Where? His hand. Jenna was holding his hand. How long had she been doing that? Jenna turned her face back toward him; the dirt on her face washed away, her hair clean. "I was so scared, Doug. I was worried you weren't coming back."

Almost didn't, flashed across his mind, but didn't make it to his lips. He didn't know if he could talk through all that cotton. "Water," came out of him in a soft hiss.

Jenna leaned closer to his mouth. "What?"

Doug closed his eyes and focused on his thought reaching his mouth. "Water," he said, louder. "I need water." He opened his eyes to see Jenna smiling. She pulled a bottle of Aquafina from below Doug's line of sight and twisted off the cap, then gently slid a warm hand under his head and tilted it toward the bottle.

"Here you go," she said and splashed some into his mouth. Dear God, it tasted like champagne on New Year's Eve. "More?"

Doug nodded slightly and she fed him more.

"Hey, boss. Good to see your eyes open."

14

Terry stepped into Doug's view; that scratcher's grin back. He held a can of Budweiser. Where the hell did he get a Budweiser? Well, if anyone could find beer during the end of the world, it would be Terry. Doug nodded and motioned to Jenna to give him more water. For the first time since Doug felt Terry lift him off the dirt of the Community as the government dropped bombs on the mesh of tents and Quonset huts, Doug felt like he was going to live. A smile reached his face this time as he relaxed and fell into unconsciousness.

***

It was dark when Doug came around again, the orange glow of a small fire cast long shadows in the culvert. "How long was I out?"

A laugh shot from Terry like he'd just heard the best joke of his life. "Too long, boss. We almost left you for the buzzards."

Nikki sat next to Terry on the Spotted Dick box. She punched Terry's shoulder.

"Three days." It was Jenna. He felt warm. *Had she never left my side?* Doug started to sit from, what the hell? A mattress? But his chest met Jenna's hand and it pushed him back down. When did she get so strong?

"You aren't going anywhere, mister," she said. "You've been unconscious three days, most of two of those across Terry's back and you're going to lie there until I say it's okay to move."

Three days. It had been three days since the government destroyed the Community, maybe all the Communities, wiping out everyone it thought was infected with the Piper. Anyone that might turn like the Milky Cataract Man. A panicked thought touched his mind. Maybe someone had seen them leave. Maybe someone was still looking for them.

"Where are we?"

Terry crushed an empty Budweiser can and tossed it down the dark culvert, to Doug the rattle of the can was uncomfortably loud. "We're still in western Nebraska," Terry said and cracked open another beer. "I used to like Nebraska. Had an aunt in Beatrice. She made great pies. I fucking hate this place now."

Too many thoughts pushed against each other in Doug's head. God, it hurt. "Can I have more water?"

"Sure, baby," Jenna said and lifted a bottle to his mouth, the warm liquid refreshing him with each small swallow.

Doug reached up and gently nudged the bottle away. He smiled. "Thank you." Then turned toward Terry and Nikki. "Thank you all. You could have left me. You'd be miles away from here. Heck, even states away from here." His face grew serious. "No, you should have left me."

Terry shook his head. "No dice, dude. We're doin' the apocalypse together or we're not doin' it at all."

"Damn straight." Jenna squeezed his hand. "It's the four of us."

God, three days. He'd been unconscious three days. Doug's stomach rumbled. "Did I smell hot dogs?"

Terry pulled up a box of something and sat next to Doug. "You smelled that? We all thought you were still out." He picked an empty can off the culvert floor. "Hell, yes." The red, white and blue can read, 'Ye Olde Oak American Style Hot Dogs.' "It's European or Canadian, or something. They spelled flavor with a 'u'."

"Hot dogs in a can? That's disgusting."

Terry grinned. "You want one?"

"More than anything."

"Whoa, there." Jenna pushed her hand toward Terry. "You're going to start with crackers. If you can keep those down, we'll work ourselves up to rancid meat." She grabbed an open box of Ritz from behind her and pulled out a sleeve. "Eat two crackers. If you're a good boy and keep them down, you'll get Cheez Whiz."

What? "Where'd you get all this stuff? We're in a ditch."

Terry cracked another beer. "But, we're in a ditch under I-80 that runs from New Jersey to San Francisco. It's like a fucking Walmart up there." He started checking off fingers. "There's a Nebraska Furniture Mart truck right over our heads. There's a grocery truck to some place called Continental Foods just down the road and there's a goddamned Anheuser–Busch truck about a quarter mile east. We got the crackers and Cheez Whiz from a Prius. We can just stay here for all I care."

Nikki punched him in the arm.

Jenna slid the tip of a cracker into Doug's mouth. He bit down. The taste of butter and salt flooded his senses. He closed his eyes to savor the taste. "Doug, are you okay?" Jenna asked. He grinned as he chewed.

"This is the best thing I've ever eaten," he said. "And I've had Kansas City barbecue."

"Looks like you're feeling better," Jenna said. Doug looked up at her, the flickering firelight danced in her eyes. He never thought she'd looked more pretty.

"Yeah, I am." He tried to sit up again and she pushed him back down.

"What you need to do is rest," Jenna said, the look on her face sterner than Doug had seen. He grinned, hoping to see many, many more looks. She held up another Ritz. "You're going to eat two more of these and drink more water, then you're going to sleep."

"But I've been asleep for three days," Doug protested.

"No." It was Nikki. "You've been unconscious. There's a big difference. Your head hurt?"

Doug tried to nod, but yeah, his head hurt. "Yes."

She picked up a bottle of generic acetaminophen, shook out two caplets and handed them to Jenna. "It might help him sleep if he doesn't hurt so much."

Ten minutes later, Doug was asleep.

***

He woke bathed in sweat. Milky Cataract Man was in his dream, the man at the Community, the only thing Doug had seen that looked like a zombie during the zombie apocalypse. It had screamed behind him, then moved toward him fast, its jaws working like one of those wind-up monkeys banging cymbals. The four of them ran into the nearest Quonset hut and it was filled with people dead from the Piper, their skin covered in a fine gray mold, a fungal stalk growing from their chests. The ends were swollen like an engorged penis, ready to explode and spread their spores to create new zombies. In his dream, the bulbs followed Doug and his friends like they could see them, like those things knew they were there. *Did that really happen?* Then they ran. They had to run. Run fast or become one of those things foaming at the door. Terry opened the door, the Milky Cataract Zombie Man fell in, Terry bashed in its head with a crutch and they got out. Away. But not safe. Crutch? *Maybe my ankle really is broken.*

Then he snapped fully awake.

"Doug, are you all right?" The voice was Jenna's. She let him sit up this time, his breath came in quick, heaving bursts. The pain in his head wasn't gone, but it wasn't so bad.

"Yeah," he whispered. "Bad dream. I figure I'm going to be having those for a while."

"Join the club, boss," Terry said. "I've had a couple about the zombie guy I killed with your crutch." He reached up and rested a hand on the back of his head, Terry's eyes went from cheery to tired. "You remember that?"

Yeah, I do.

When Nikki appeared from seemingly out of nowhere, Doug realized he wasn't quite ready to join the world of the living. His vision swam and she just appeared in a wavering fuzz, kind of like when somebody beamed up on *Star Trek*. "You're up early," Nikki said. "Terry and I were just ready to start breakfast. You hungry?"

Doug felt he'd never been hungrier. "Famished. If it's okay with Doctor Jenna, I think I'm ready for something more than crackers. Got any of those canned hot dogs?"

"Puke," Jenna said, sticking an index finger in her open mouth.

"Yeah, we've got a crate of those," Terry said. "But I'm going to fix us something a little bit classier for your first day back to life."

Canned ham pulled from a rooftop cargo carrier on a Toyota Prius somewhere above them, fried over an open fire, powdered eggs with a dash of onion powder scrambled in a Spam can with reconstituted milk was better than Thanksgiving dinner at Mom's. He had the best meal of his life in a culvert underneath a highway.

"I'm glad you're up and running," Terry said. He'd already cracked open a beer at whatever time of the morning it was. It didn't matter anymore, 'It's five o'clock somewhere' just became law. "But what now?"

What now?

"I don't know," Doug said. "But we can't stay here. It's too wide open. We have to find someplace secure, someplace that will keep those things out."

"Tanelorn," Jenna said. The word cut the culvert to silence. Tanelorn, the city in Michael Moorcock's Eternal Champion series where the heroes go when they die, retire, or get fed up with saving everyone. It's what the Marstens named their summer home, a virtual survivalist bunker in Western Nebraska, filled with food, medicine, weapons, its own well, solar power and a twelve-foot high electrified chain-link fence to keep out whatever baddie the apocalypse sent calling. The Marstens might not have expected zombies, but they were ready for them. Just like at home. Doug, Terry, Jenna and Arnold (poor Arnold) found Nikki by accident at the Marstens' house in the tiny Northwest Missouri town of Barton. Together they discovered its stash of Winchester SX3 shotguns, M4 carbine rifles, several M27 light machine guns and enough beer to keep Terry happy for months. Doug discovered Tanelorn on the Marstens' computer and printed out a map to this safe haven, electricity still running through the house from solar power.

"Yeah, boss. It was in Western Nebraska, in Western Nebraska."

A can cracked. Nikki sat on the crate of Spotted Dick and took a drink of warm Pepsi. "That's where we were going when Herman Munster jumped out of the back of the truck," she said. Herman, the bloody man that came to the Marstens' door. The man they left the Marstens' sanctuary to save. The man who almost got them killed.

Doug slowly shook his head. "Map's gone. The military took it when they put us to the hospital. I know it was somewhere near Alliance, but that's it. I couldn't get us there for anything." He put his makeshift plate of ham and eggs on the mattress beside him, the eggs churning in his stomach; he'd suddenly remembered how he'd broken his ankle. The bear, its eyes glazed and milky shoved its face against the glass of the truck, slamming the closing door against Doug's ankle. He remembered screaming and that was it. Then he was in a hospital surrounded by soldiers. "We gotta find someplace new."

"That asshole Corson's probably planning on keeping it as a summer house," Nikki said, then poured the Pepsi onto the dusty concrete floor of the culvert. She didn't want it anymore.

Doug motioned to Jenna to help him up; she smiled and shook her head. "Anyway, you said there are vehicles up on the highway, right?"

Terry nodded. "Yeah, the closest ones are the furniture truck and that Prius. Then the Bud truck and the one with the foreign food."

"Yeah, what the hell is Spotted Dick, anyway?"

Nikki reached under her and pulled a can from the box. "It's kind of like sponge cake with bits of dried fruit. It's not bad. Want some?"

Doug's stomach turned again. He pinched his eyes tight and focused on keeping down his breakfast. If he'd been out for three days, he needed to keep it in there. The feeling passed. "No, thanks," he said, pulling open his eyes. They felt strangely heavy. Is this what a concussion feels like? "Have you tried to start any of them?"

Terry shook his head. "No. The couple in the Prius is dead on the highway. The drivers are still in the Bud truck and the food wagon. The stalk growing out of the Bud man painted the inside of the cab with that yellow spore stuff. The food guy is a friendly fellow. He pawed at the window at us as we walked by; I think he wanted to eat us."

Zombie. Doug hated to think of that word. What the fuck is this? A movie? But that's what they were. The military guys told Jenna. The disease was called HG-17, a mutation of the fungal infection brought on by the antidepressant Ophiocordon. The goddamned Piper did this. The infection causes a stem to grow from the infected's chest, then the stem explodes, sending its spores looking for a host. When the spores find one, the doctor had said, HG-17 'shuts down the higher functions of the central nervous system, meaning the thought process and leaves everything else to take care of the body's last two functions. To feed and to reproduce. It's highly contagious.'

There really are zombies.

"Have you seen any more?"

"No," Jenna said. She sat on the mattress next to him and slipped an arm around his shoulders. It felt soft and strong at the same time. Some of that strength seemed to flow into Doug.

"That's good, but we're totally defenseless here. We have to find someplace safe."

Jenna squeezed. "You're in no condition to travel."

"I think we should go, too," Nikki said. "I'm scared here. There's nothing to keep one of those things from walking right in here and killing us in our sleep."

Terry popped another beer, the crack unusually loud in the still morning. "Have you all forgotten we're in the middle of freakin' Nowhere, Nebraska? We don't have anything to worry ab–"

Terry froze.

Somewhere in the distance a car alarm wailed.

"Oh, hell."

***

Doug's dark place hadn't been empty; Milky Cataract Man had been there, too. Doug swam in the dead silence of the dark, this world of nothingness, when the snarling thing came to a door. What door, he couldn't see, but he knew it was the door to the Quonset hut, the hut that held rows of dead bodies, stalks of fungus rising from their chests like they'd been impaled. But he couldn't see them; he couldn't see anything. He could just hear the growl of the once-human thing as it got closer, then thumped on the door in slow, methodic slaps. Doug screamed in his dark place, though he knew no one could hear him, no one could help him. He had to face this monster on his own. This monster with foam spewing from its angry, hungry mouth, its eyes grown over with a white film. Doug couldn't see it in his dark place, but he knew what the thing looked like, because he'd seen it, seen it with his own eyes and it terrified him. The car alarm could only mean one thing; it was coming for him.

"That's a long way off," Terry said, his words to Doug sounding like he, too, was a long way off. "Hey, boss. You okay?"

Doug opened his sore eyes and looked up at Terry, Nikki and Jenna. Sweet, sweet Jenna. He had to protect her. He had to protect all of them.

"What's the closest vehicle that's the best bet for us to get the hell out of here now, right now?" he said, his voice a whisper.

"The Prius," Nikki said, standing from the box of Spotted Dick cans. "I'm with Doug. Let's go."

Jenna squeezed Doug's hand. "Let me help you up."

The crisp crack of a Budweiser can snapping open pulled everyone's head toward Terry, who leaned against the side of the culvert and took a sip. Hadn't he just opened a beer? "We don't even know what set that alarm off. Could be anything."

Nikki rested her fists on hips. "Like what, Mr. Wizard?"

Terry took another swig of beer and grinned. Doug wondered how many Terry'd had already this morning. "A person. Maybe there's somebody else out there lost and scared and afraid—"

Nikki interrupted. "Scared and afraid are the same thing."

"Or maybe a buck saw its reflection in the window and went after it. Some of those alarms are pretty sensitive. Maybe a bird shit on it just right." Terry drained the can and tossed it down the culvert, the flat tinging of aluminum rattling across concrete made the others wince with each bounce. "I'll go up there and check."

Nikki leaned close and kissed his cheek. "I hope you're right."

***

Terry's right boot hit a loose spot of soil and he slipped a foot down the embankment, sending a small cloud of dust into the dry Nebraska air. "Bunch of little girls," he mumbled, too low for anyone in the culvert to hear. "Scared of every little thing." Halfway up the incline he grabbed a two-by-four, about three feet long, from a patch of weeds where it had lain since it hit the ground months ago, probably out of the bed of some guy's pickup. He noticed the board yesterday, the morning after they stumbled out of the darkness, exhausted and dirty, and crawled into the hole under the highway. The board looked solid when Terry nearly stepped on it as he braved the highway that afternoon to get food from the Continental Foods truck, jimmying open the back door with a piece of rebar. He saw it again when he went to the Nebraska Furniture Mart truck looking for something comfortable for unconscious Doug. As he hefted the piece of pine in his hand, he knew he'd been saving the wood for this.

Terry pushed himself up the last few feet and stood on the shoulder of I-80, pausing to rest his hands on his knees. His breaths came too heavily for his taste. He hadn't carried Doug like Jenna had said; they'd found a long piece of cardboard from a food drop that hit outside the Community fence and they all took turns dragging him. *Thought I'd get in shape during the apocalypse. Hell, maybe the next one.* He took as deep a breath as he could and rose to full height. On either side of the highway, tall fields of green corn that would become fallow next planting season with no farmers to tend them, stood still in the windless July morning. To his left the furniture truck cast a short shadow onto the road as the sun climbed higher in the empty, azure sky. It was already hot and it was only somedamno'clock in the morning. Sweat pooled under Terry's arms and he ran his hand through his hair that had already started to mat. *Another steamer.* If the end of the world showed Terry anything, it was that he really hated the Midwest. A man of his size needed someplace that never got hot, like Canada, or the Colorado Rockies. He stood in the shade cast by the white truck with green lettering that held unassembled furniture made by a company that no longer existed and looked to the west, toward the sound of the car alarm.

The alarm was louder out of the culvert; not much, but a little. Terry wiped the sweat from his forehead with a shirtsleeve and waited. The sound came from beyond the Continental Foods truck. Probably from the pale-yellow Caddie they'd walked by in the dark, full moonlight showing the windows coated with yellow spores that may have matched the interior, but even with the moon it was too dark to tell. The sound couldn't have come from the driver; he'd been dead for weeks, maybe months. Not undead dead, but dead dead. As Terry leaned against the side of the furniture truck, the two-by-four in his left hand hung by his side, he realized something was wrong with the sky.

A black cloud slowly moved over the westward highway that stretched to the Rocky Mountains and eventually to California. It didn't just move, it moved towards him. Hell, Terry could see its shadow ripple over the tops of abandoned cars as far as he could see. Yeah, it was moving and fast, but how? Unless there was a serious undetected gale just over Terry's head, the only wind this morning was still working its way through his colon. The black cloud seemed to flow like water, rolling over itself, like it was fighting to break free and flood the sky.

"Aw, shit." Terry stepped forward, just a step, just a little step. But that's all he needed. The dark spot on the sky wasn't a cloud; it was birds. A movement dragged his eyes down from the sky. Under that cloud of black birds marched a host of those undead fuckers.

"Zombies," Terry whispered, the word dying as it left his lips. One stood from behind the piss-yellow Caddie from the spot where it had fallen, bumped the car and set off the alarm. It looked toward Terry and he couldn't drag his eyes away as his brown ones met the thing's milky-white ones. It screamed. The two-by-four slid from Terry's shaky hand and rattled on the pavement. The beast lurched forward. It was close; too close. The mob was at least three quarters of a mile away. Good God, how many were there? And what the fuck's up with the birds?

The zombie thing, lurching like a ball player with a pulled hamstring, came toward him faster than should be possible. Terry just watched it come; his feet seemed soaked in concrete. It wasn't because it was a zombie. Hell, he'd bashed the Milky Cataract Man with Doug's crutch like he'd bashed zombies every day of his life. This was different. This one had a murder of crows coming in hard and on the ground it had backup. Terry swallowed and bent to pick up the board. He knew he

22

didn't have time to run, time to warn the others before this slathering asshole in a black T-shirt was on him, but he could save them all if he just—

The monster, spittle flying from the corners of its snarling mouth, was suddenly upon him. Terry rose, swinging the board, pushing with his legs like his high school baseball coach had hammered into his head, "your power comes from below your waist. Push and swing, baby. Push and swing." The two-by-four struck the zombie on the jaw with a dull thud; its head lurched awkwardly to one side, its mouth moving like a kid hitting a PEZ dispenser over and over and over. As it fell against the open trailer of the furniture truck, Terry pulled the board back and struck again, the thing's skull cracked like a box of something expensive and the zombie fell to the pavement in a splatter of its own blood. It twitched twice and lay still.

Another scream hit Terry's ears. He looked up. It was from the mob; the mob had seen him. The black shadow of birds was even closer. "Holy shit." He dropped the board and launched himself down the embankment, rolling in a dusty cloud to the bottom.

"Terry," Nikki screamed.

He looked up; dirt streaked his face. Nikki stood at the edge of the culvert holding a Budweiser. It dropped from her hand and hit the concrete, foam spewing over the dust.

"Hey, are you—" Doug tried to stand and walk toward him, but his knees buckled. Jenna grabbed him around the waist and dragged him back onto the mattress.

Nikki knelt next to Terry and grabbed his face. It was pale, ashen. "What happened, Terry?"

He opened his mouth; his words came out slowly. "They saw me."

JULY 28: MUSKOGEE, OKLAHOMA

CHAPTER 3

The sun wasn't setting; it was an hour too early for that. Andi Bakowski ("Two I's so you can see better, toots," Big Andy always told her) lay on her stomach on the dry, tarred roof of the Motel 6 in Muskogee, Oklahoma, staring at a quickly darkening sky. A black cloud had appeared on the southern horizon staining the curtain of blue that had looked like the intro to "The Simpsons" all day. The cloud seemed to have jumped straight from one of the sun-scorched cornfields on the other end of a cemetery that marked the city limits of Muskogee, a city made famous by a country singer who had never lived there.

Andi arrived at the motel before dawn with an M24 Sniper Weapon System over her shoulder, a Beretta M9 sidearm on her belt, a Pyle PMP45R megaphone in her hand, twenty rounds of ammunition, two grenades and a rucksack stuffed with four more boxes of ammo, bottled water, three MREs (one beef stew and two lemon pepper tunas. Puke) and chocolate that probably melted before 10 a.m. She'd taken a motel blanket and two rickety chairs from the room closest to the stairs, 217, and carried them to the roof, making shade from the summer sun. The makeshift tent didn't matter; she still sweat through her fatigues.

Andi didn't want to be in Muskogee, baking on the roof of a cheap motel, guarding the Good Lands from monsters and, worst of all, people stuck in the Bad Lands. President Donald Trump once promised to build a wall to keep out illegal immigrants from Mexico. The wall never happened. It took an international crisis to get up a chain-link fence crews were still stretching from coast to coast even as Andi lay on the roof, not to keep out people, but things that used to be people.

Something moved in the corn. Or did it? A trickle of sweat ran into Andi's eye just as it looked as if a line of cornstalks moved, one after the other, like someone ran through the field. When she wiped away the sweat, everything was still. Everything but the cloud. It was moving, it was moving fast.

***

That was Andi's job, to protect the Fence.

Sgt. Cotton Monroe, a big redneck from Southern Missouri, stood in the firelight the night Andi's squad broke from abbreviated boot camp, the night before deployment in their own country. Cotton held a bottle of cheap beer between the index and middle fingers of his left hand, his right hand rested on his gun belt, hooked by a thumb. *Cotton. What the hell kind of name was Cotton?* she'd wondered the first day of Basic Training. She knew it wasn't his given name. It couldn't be. What kind of parents would name their whiter-than-white baby Cotton? Given his white-blond hair cut nearly invisible in a career Army high-and-tight, maybe they did. Cotton had been a hard ass during Basic Training – at first. He didn't want the only woman in Basic to be in his squad. He told her the first day. Then he saw how she could handle a weapon. The first time at the range, she not only beat every man in Basic, she embarrassed them. Big, bad-assed Sgt. Cotton smiled at her. Just once, but that was enough. He got off her ass after that. All thanks to Big Andy who wanted a boy, but got Andi instead.

Cotton drained his beer and tossed the bottle into the fire. Cpl. Tennyson was ready with a second. Everyone but Pvt. Guthrie held a bottle. Cotton had provided enough beer to celebrate a graduation with no ceremony, but not enough for his soldiers to wake sluggish with shaky hands on their first day of active duty.

"Gentlemen," he barked, then coughed into his shoulder, slowly looking back out to the circle of ten young men and Andi. Cotton took another swig of beer, then kept the bottle close to his chest. "And lady."

Oh, shit Andi thought. *He's nervous.* She'd seen signs Cotton had feelings, like the smile that broke just slightly on his blond stubbly face the day she set the unit record on the shooting range and the time she caught him looking at her over his tray of shit-on-a-shingle in the mess tent. He saw her eyes meet his and he looked away, his face red. That's the problem with cottons, she told herself, they can't hold it in forever. He'd been married, at least according to the indentation on his left ring finger. Andi had looked. Cotton had been married less than a year ago, or the mark would have faded, but whether the marriage ended in divorce or his wife turning into one of those things, she didn't want to know. But if the mark was still on his finger, it was still in his head. That, she realized, she needed to know.

"Congratulations on passing Basic Training." His voice stronger, more in control.

He's got it together now.

The new soldiers sat around the campfire in a compound circled with military combat vehicles and big round hay bales from nearby farms, their fields fallow, the farmers long gone. The men stood and hooted. Some tried to clap, but their beer bottles got in the way. Guthrie clapped, the slaps carried through the camp when the other soldiers' cheers died down.

"Thanks." Cotton, more relaxed now, took a swig of beer. Many of the soldiers followed suit. Pvt. Mickelson stood to yell something, but whatever words came out, his heavy twang hid their meaning. Mickelson was a linebacker for the Arkansas Razorbacks before the Ophiocordon shitstorm. He was going to be a damn fine soldier, but got excited easily. Cotton held up a hand and Mickelson shut his mouth with the lip of a bottle.

"I don't know why you signed up for this man's Army," he said, his voice strong now. No trace of emotion. "But what you're doin' here is Fence duty. Y'all already know about the Piper. Fuckin' drug companies thought it would be a good idea to take some damn fungus from Southeast Asia. Offy-O-Cord-Ecepts unilater-all-is–" Cotton's voice became even slower as he rattled off the recently memorized genus and species of the fungus syllable-by-syllable. "–and they gave it to people. Then it killed your mommas, your daddies, your sisters, your girlfriends and your goddamned third grade teacher."

Cotton lowered his bottle to his side, gripping the neck like he wanted to strangle it. Maybe now, Andi thought, she knew what had happened to his wife. "But that's where we got it," he continued, his strong voice booming. "It's been turnin' people into some kinda monsters, but they're not just monsters, they're Southeast Asian monsters."

Mark Paulson, an insurance salesman from Kentucky, laughed. "Then give us weapons that shoot chop sticks, Sergeant. That'll–"

"Shut your goddamned mouth, Paulson," shot out of Cotton's mouth, cutting off the private mid-sentence. "If you're that ignorant, keep it to yourself." Cotton cleared his throat and started again, his eyes moving from soldier to soldier. "The higher ups think this is our advantage. It don't get too cold south of the Fence, but north of the Fence, this country gets hard freezes every winter." He paused and took a slow breath, trying to pick his words carefully. "Now I'm not sayin' this is gonna work, but the people tryin' to fix this problem think it might. By next Spring, two-thirds of the United States may be free of these monsters. Then we can work our way south."

"Where do we fit in Sergeant?" Bob Litton from Tennessee asked, the night suddenly dead quiet, the popping and cracking of the fire the only sound.

Cotton took another swig of beer, lowering the bottle slowly. "I'm not gonna lie to you folks. You went through Basic fast. The Army cut six weeks off your training to get you out in the field ASAP. There ain't many of us anymore; those left are ridin' the Fence. Every grunt you trained with in Basic will be lined up across that Fence watchin' for anything on two legs."

The sergeant's voice suddenly stopped and the circle of new soldiers grew still.

"Well, what are we going to do if we see one?" Guthrie asked. "What if it's human?"

Cotton drained his bottle and tossed it in the fire after his first before looking up at Guthrie. His eyes betrayed no emotion. "These are your orders, son. Shoot it in the head."

***

Andi's world shifted from normal to now quickly. She often thought of the day she realized nothing would ever be the same again.

Big Andy stood in the doorway, wiping one of Grandma Bakowski's blue and white plates with a dish towel. He wore red flannel over an AC/DC T-shirt; "Stiff Upper Lip," the last concert he ever went to. A quiet smile broke across his lips when Andi looked up from her book, "Bridge to Terabithia," the line of a tear visible on her cheek.

"You at that one part?" Big Andy asked, his voice big, but gentle at the same time.

Andi nodded and wiped the tear away with the back of her pajama sleeve before looking up from the dog-eared paperback she'd had since middle school. A soft glow from the kitchen framed his head in yellow light.

"How many times have you read that thing?"

She tucked her thumb in between the pages and folded the book on her lap. She forced a smile. "I don't know. I can't count that high."

Big Andy coughed a short laugh and tossed the towel over his shoulder, the hand holding one of Grandma's hand-me-down plates slowly dropped to his side. He stared at Andi's bedroom floor for a moment before bringing his eyes up to meet hers. "Dinner okay?"

Andi nodded again. Soupy boxed mac and cheese. Deer burgers scorched on the outside, still cold in the middle. She wished he'd let her cook, but Big Andy didn't want her to change anything. She had a job at the local grocery store. She had college. She had a plan for her life and he wasn't going to let the Amazing Disappearing Carrie Bakowski interfere with any of it.

"I'm sorry," he said. "I did everything I could to keep your mom here. I—"

Andi threw up a hand to cut him off. "I know." Three days ago, while Andi was asleep and Big Andy was out playing D&D with his nerd friends like they had every Monday night for the past twenty years, her mother had walked out with a carry-on bag, locked the door behind her and vanished into the darkness. Andi wasn't sad anymore and she wasn't confused, she was angry. "This isn't on you, Dad. This is Mom's fault."

"Hey," Big Andy said, his voice came out in a bark. He swallowed and ran his free hand over his stubbly chin. "Please don't. You love your mom and your mom loves you. Don't you ever tell yourself different."

No. No, damn it. "Then—" She stopped. Big Andy had pulled the dish towel off his shoulder and wiped it across his eyes. *Dad?* She had never seen her father cry before. "Dad?"

He flipped the dish towel back over his shoulder and reached into the pocket of his flannel shirt. He pulled out an orange prescription medicine bottle. "I found this when I was taking out the garbage. If your mom didn't insist on buying those damn cheap garbage bags, it probably wouldn't have ripped and spilled out."

Pills? Mom's pills? "Is it—" Andi paused, not sure what to say. *Ophiocordon? That would explain so much.* "Is it the Piper drug?"

Big Andy nodded. "I didn't know she was taking it," he said, his voice shaky. "But it fills in some blanks about the last month. We both knew she was depressed. She finally agreed to go see Dr. Jane about it. Then she seemed better, you know, but she got better fast. Way too fast. She seemed—"

"Like old Mom?" Andi finished for him.

"Yeah." His eyes glanced over at Andi's Pink Floyd poster; his daughter's taste in music always made him proud. He stared for a few seconds before he looked back at Andi. "She said she was okay, that Doctor Jane just talked her through her problems. But that was a lie. She didn't tell me Dr. Jane had prescribed anything." He swallowed before he spoke again, his voice like Andi had never heard it. He sounded old. "I think she left because she had the Piper Andi. She had the Piper and when all that shit went down, when people started dying, she didn't want anything to happen to us."

The Piper's calling you to join him. Going by the book, her mom had felt euphoric at first, then had the symptoms of a cold, then a bloody nose, then she'd die and stand back up. If she was lucky, the fungus would eat away her insides and she'd fall back into a rotting pile. If she was unlucky, the spores destroying her mind would make her hungry – for people.

"Mom didn't leave us?" she asked.

A smile that wasn't a smile appeared and faded quickly. "No, Toots. I think she left *for* us."

"Bridge to Terabithia" fell from Andi's hand and thumped onto the thinly carpeted floor. Tears ran like they had the day she woke and her mother was gone. "Is she—?"

Big Andy shook his head. "I don't know, baby," her father said. He gripped the orange medicine bottle, burying it in his big right hand; the white child-proof cap was all that showed. "I don't have a good-bye note, a phone number, or a letter in Dear Abby. This is all she left and she didn't mean for me to find it."

"But—"

"Hey," he said, the words poured out loud and fast. "You want to go hunting tomorrow? Squirrel's in season."

Squirrel? She smiled. "You know I hate squirrel."

"Yeah. I just thought me and you could, you know—" His voice trailed off.

Hunting. That was what they did together, their thing, ever since she was big enough to hold a rifle. "Sure, Dad," she said, picking the book off the floor. "Just as long as you let me cook whatever we bring in."

Less than a week later, her university closed its doors, at least temporarily. Temporarily with no idea when they'd open again. A week after that Big Andy got sick. He drove her to the Army recruitment center set up in her old high school gym, but he didn't hug her good-bye. His nose was already bleeding. A month and a half after that she was a state away lying on the roof of a motel cradling a sniper rifle like a teddy bear. She knew her father was dead, although she didn't know when, or where. All she knew was she was alone.

***

The black cloud seemed to grow from the cornfields. *What the heck is that thing?*

It moved in waves, undulating as if it were a great, living beast. It could be a flock of birds, but that's what threw her off – it was too big to be a flock of birds, way too big. It covered the entire southern sky like this was Bodega Bay, California, or something. Andi eased the Leupold Mk IV scope up to her eye and aimed at the cloud.

"Holy shit," hissed from between her lips. It was birds, black birds. Millions of them. She lowered the weapon and looked at the enormous flock with her bare eyes. In those few seconds, it had grown bigger, more ominous, closer. "What—" she started, but stopped herself. The what wasn't important. It was the why. Why was a cloud of birds that stretched across the horizon coming toward Muskogee?

The corn moved again; something made its way in a single line toward the cemetery across the highway. She lifted the weapon up to her eye and drew a bead on whatever it was. Seconds later a man wearing a dirty white polo broke from the corn and fell against the iron fence that surrounded the cemetery. He paused for a second, panting, then threw open the gate and slammed it behind him.

"Shit."

'Shoot it in the head,' echoed through her mind. *Goddamn you Cotton.*

The man pushed himself away from the gate and staggered through the cemetery. Crows landed atop the tombstones around him as if they guided him. She moved the M24 back into position. The man's head bobbed slightly in the scope, but never moved from her crosshairs. Andi was steady, a rock; and when Andi pulled a trigger she never missed.

***

"Hey, Bakowski," a voice called from outside Andi's tent the night before. She lay on her cot on top of a sleeping bag in her government-issue underwear; July was too hot in Oklahoma for much else. Her pulse jumped as adrenaline hit her bloodstream; the voice belonged to Cotton.

Shit. Andi was off the cot in a second, pulling on her fatigues.

"Wait a sec," she said, her voice rushed. *What is he doing here?* There was something about Cotton that made her heart jump. Was it his laid-back demeanor? His backwoods drawl? His square chin? She didn't know. She just hoped it wasn't the fact that he was the first and closest authority figure in her life since Big Andy dropped her off at the recruitment center on his way to die. *That'd just be weird.*

She opened the flap and stepped out, ducking under the low door. Cotton stood on wobbly feet, another beer in his hand. The "don't wake up sluggish with shaky hands" rule obviously didn't apply to him. She swallowed hard, trying to dislodge the lump in her throat. It didn't work.

"Yes, Sergeant?" she said, trying and failing to keep her voice steady.

His eyes, hazel in the daylight, but flat gray now, met hers. For just the second time since she met him, she saw Cotton smile.

"You're a good soldier, Bakowski," came out slower than usual. "Best shot I've ever seen." His voice fell silent and the two stood in the darkness, uncomfortable.

"Thank you, Sergeant."

He waved the hand holding the beer bottle. The liquid foamed in the moonlight. "No," he said, his voice louder than he'd probably intended. "Don't do that. There's no sergeant, no private. This is just me and you here now."

What does that mean?

He took a drink of beer and lowered the bottle. "I didn't want you here before. I don't want you here now. Reason's diffr'nt though."

Andi realized her breath had become shallow. She inhaled deeply, trying to keep it steady.

"It's pretty much safe here," he said, "in camp. You could stay here. Or I could probably get you a desk job someplace close." He looked up at the nearly full moon, the blond stubble visible in the light. "What I'm trying to say is I don't want you to go out and get killed." His eyes dropped back down to hers. "Them ain't people out there no more. Those things you're goin' against—" He waved his beer bottle toward the other tents set apart from Andi's, "—those things ya'll are goin' against, might look like people, they might even look like someone you know, but they're monsters. Goddamned flesh-eatin' monsters."

Andi felt her heart beating hard under her shirt. *He wants to protect me. He—* No. She couldn't have that. She wouldn't have that. "Thank you, but I can't. I'm here because my parents probably turned into those things." She paused and stared at him until his eyes came back to hers. "I couldn't protect them, Cotton, but I'm going to do what I can to protect everyone else." His mouth opened to say something, but she shook her head and it closed again. "You said I was the best shot you'd ever seen. I'll be fine."

He glared at her with glassy eyes. It was a long time before he spoke and when he did Andi wished he hadn't. "You ever shot a man, Bakowski?"

Andi had shot deer, turkey, rabbit, squirrel, pheasant, but no. Shooting another human being had always been shoved way in the back of her head, reserved only for self-defense. She shook her head. "No, Cotton. I haven't."

He looked back up into the sky. "It's different. The person on the end of your sights, they got family, maybe kids. They probably got a job, people countin' on them." He dropped his eyes back to hers, his face stiff with unexpected sobriety "This ain't nothin' you want to do. This ain't nothin' you ever want to do."

They stood in silence before Cotton turned and walked back toward his tent.

Andi didn't see Cotton again. Cpl. Tennyson gave deployment assignments in the morning, one soldier for every mile. After two days, they'd move to another section of the Fence. Two days another. They'd be back to base in a month. Maybe things would be different then.

***

Polo Man paused at the Fence and looked up. Andi was convinced this person wasn't one of those things with the Piper. He was exhausted and running from something. She broke from the scope and looked at the world with just her eyes. The black cloud of birds was closer, covering half the sky; the beat of their wings was audible now, a drumbeat tattoo she heard over everything. Then she saw what Polo Man was running from; it wasn't the birds.

The cornfield shook. She put the scope back to her eye and looked more deeply into the dry, brown stalks.

"Oh, my god."

Piper monsters. Hundreds of them moved through the corn, their rotting gaunt faces streaked with blood, their bodies covered in mold. They weren't coming for the man in the polo, but he was in their way.

The man kicked off his shoes and made as if to climb the Fence. "No, no," Andi said under her breath. "Get out of there. You can still get out of there."

Andi's fingers fumbled with the megaphone before she found the handle and moved it to her mouth. Her mind suddenly grew blank. *Words. Damn. Damn, damn. What are the words?* Her squad's training wasn't just to shoot, it was to detain. Shoot the infected, but delay a possible clean human long enough to send them toward a way station near Lawton. This guy didn't look infected. She tried to relax, but the birds' wingbeats pounded her ears. One of them, a crow, landed on the roof about ten feet from her and cawed. She knew she'd have go inside the motel soon, away from those birds, but not now. Not yet. The man hooked his fingers and toes into the chain links and pulled himself up, the two-legged monsters closing in fast.

Citizen. That's what she was looking for.

"Citizen," she said, the megaphone belching the word. "Citizen. Back away from the Fence."

The man said something, but Andi couldn't hear what. 'What are we going to do if we see one?' Guthrie had asked Cotton last night. Andi knew Cotton's response too well.

"Citizen," she said again. "There is a safe zone near Lawton. It's just to the west. Please disengage from the Fence and move west."

A crow settled on the top of the Fence near his head. The man kept climbing.

Can he hear me? She looked at the settings on the megaphone; the volume was set to maximum. "Please remove yourself from the fence. Remove yourself immediately," she said, louder this time.

He said something else Andi couldn't hear before he reached over his head and grabbed more of the Fence. A crow flew straight at the man. Andi saw it coming. The big bird dipped from the cloud and struck him in the head. He teetered and almost fell, just as the Piper monsters reached the Fence below him. They wrapped their moldy hands into the chain links and shook, seemingly oblivious to the man above them.

"Goddammit," she hissed. His window to escape had vanished. *Shoot it in the head.* "Damn you, Cotton."

I can do this. I'm a soldier and I can do this. "I'm sorry," Andi said through the machine. "I truly am, but I have my orders. You are in violation of United States Army Code 45986B. For the survival of the human race, no one is to cross the Southern Border of the Good Lands of the United States of America. Trespassers will be shot on sight. Now, please, remove yourself from the Fence."

Please, God, please move away from the Fence.

The bird attached itself to the man's head and began to peck. The monsters below Polo Man noticed him, reaching upward like he was an apple on a tree.

"Citizen." Her voice trailed to nearly nothing. Her words didn't matter. "Shit."

Andi threw the megaphone. It skittered across the rooftop and sent the crow flapping into the air. The man was as good as dead. "Damn it," Andi said, her voice inaudible from the pounding in her ears. Tears didn't come. *The person on the end of your sights, they got family, maybe kids. They probably got a job, people countin' on them.*

The butt of the M24 SWS nestled firmly against her shoulder. Polo Man was an easy shot; he barely moved, but Andi's hands hook. This was a person. *You ever shot a man, Bakowski?* "I'm sorry," she whispered and gently, evenly pulled back the trigger. A crack split the air a half-thought before the bullet punched into the man's right shoulder, throwing him backward from the fence. His left hand dangled his spent body over the growing sea of slathering human monsters beneath him. The crow clung to his head like an awkward hat.

Shit. Shit, shit.

She pulled back the bolt and shoved it into place, slamming another round into the chamber as one of the Piper monsters saw what was happening just above it and grabbed Polo Man's right foot. Her second shot exploded the back of his head. Polo Man was dead before he fell onto the waiting wall of monsters.

***

Andi left the sniper weapon lying on the Motel 6 roof. There was no need to hurry, at least not now. After Polo Man disappeared into a cluster of the human-shaped monsters, the rest of the Piper things stood milling at the Fence, seemingly befuddled by it. The cloud of crows settled in the cornfield, contented to pick at the crop no one would ever harvest.

She vomited on the motel roof before she descended the ladder through the trap door, Army-issued mac and cheese splattering over the sniper rifle. The man was dead, she'd killed him. *But I saved him from being awake for that. He would have felt being eaten alive.* She dropped to the floor and walked down the dusty hallway to the stairs. *I should have asked Cotton if that's how you get past it.*

Her Humvee sat in the parking lot over two spaces like it was a Mercedes she hadn't wanted to get scratched.

There was enough water and food in the vehicle for a week, enough ammunition for her sidearm and the M4 Carbine that sat in the passenger seat to take over a small town and enough gasoline to get her far enough north the Army might forget about her. The tears finally came when she pulled herself into the four-wheel drive truck and shut the door. Polo Man. He might have had a family. He might have been a priest, or a teacher, or he might have had the cure for all this. *Shoot them in the head.* Polo Man might as well have been Big Andy, wherever he was.

Andi started the Humvee and put it in gear. She drove north, sticking to the side streets in case she encountered another military vehicle; she wasn't going back. Uh-uh. The Army had been a mistake. She could shoot but wasn't ready for what she was required to pull the trigger for.

The city was empty, desolate. Andi stopped at a convenience store at the north end of town and picked up Sun Chips and a case of Bud Light. Maybe, she hoped, she'd meet up with Cotton after the world stopped sucking so much.

CHAPTER 4

Nikki hated running. In high school, she tried out for track, not because she wanted to run, but because she wanted Thickie Nikki to go away. "I'm ugly, Dad," she told her father, Gene Holleran, the morning he found her crying on the toilet. Doors meant nothing in the Holleran house.

"You're a beautiful girl," he said. "You've always been a beautiful girl."

"But I'm a fatty," she whispered between sobs. "They call me Thickie Nikki."

Gene Holleran smiled and kissed his daughter on the head. "High schoolers are mean people, baby girl." His voice was soothing. "Don't worry about it. Just be who you are and be happy with that. Nicknames come and go. If these jerks see it doesn't bother you, it'll go soon enough."

She pulled off a line of toilet paper and wiped her eyes. "Did you have a nickname in high school?"

Gene Holleran nodded, a grin playing at the corner of his mouth. "Yeah. They called me Mean Gene."

A short laugh escaped her mouth. "Mean Gene? Dad, you're a teddy bear. How did you get that?"

Gene leaned against the sink and crossed his arms. "I kind of punched the biology teacher."

Nikki's hand instinctively went to her mouth. "Oh, Dad. A teacher?"

"I wasn't aiming at the teacher," he said. "The guy I was supposed to hit had it coming to him, he just didn't get it. Mr. Mackenzie did." Gene flipped on the bathroom fan and started out the door. "Now finish up in here. I'm fixing eggs and toast. You don't want to be late for school."

Nikki didn't lose weight on the track team because she didn't make the track team; she could almost walk faster than she could run. Thickie Nikki lasted for three more semesters until graduation when Nikki went to a community college where there were enough Thickies she could hide in a crowd. Nikki looked good now, though. Firm legs and a flat stomach. The apocalypse was apparently great for weight loss.

But Nikki had to run again.

When Terry rolled down the embankment toward the culvert, Nikki knew he didn't fall by accident; the look on his face wasn't pain, it was terror. The kind of terror that gripped you in steely claws and would not let go. 'They saw me,' he'd said. Nikki didn't know who "they" were, but she had a good guess. "We have to get out of here," she said, helping Terry to his feet.

He nodded, "Now."

"But Doug can't move that fast," Jenna said, her voice trembling.

Terry turned to Jenna. "We don't have time for that. They're coming in hard."

"Leave me," Doug said. "My ankle's broken and my head's—. Well, my head's fucked up. I'll slow you down."

"Jenna, you and me grab Doug–"

"Leave me," he said again. "You'll be faster that way."

"–Nikki, you go get the doors open on that Toyota."

Nikki nodded and scrambled up the embankment. Terry rushed to Doug and he and Jenna hoisted him to his feet. "Sorry to disappoint you, boss, but we're going to try and keep you alive today. Let's go."

***

When she reached the highway, Nikki looked to the west and her legs nearly buckled. The sky was black with birds and the highway teemed with zombies. She didn't know what else to call them anymore; they shambled toward her straight from the set of a Romero movie. And they were close, too close. Where the hell did they come from? *Move, Holleran. Move your ass.* But her legs were frozen. *My God, the noise.* The thunder of wings was deafening.

"Nikki," Terry yelled, his shaggy head popping up on the side of the road, followed closely by Doug and Jenna. "The doors."

Doors. Right. She lurched toward the Prius, the luggage shell on top of the vehicle lay open, the owners on the roadside beside the car, their bodies baked dry by the Nebraska summer. The driver's side door swung open easily in her hand, as did the passenger door, but the back doors were locked. Nikki reached in and manually opened them. When Terry and Jenna finally topped the embankment and stepped onto the pavement, the car was ready.

"Hurry," she screamed. No need to be quiet, the zombies already knew where they were. Their snarls and moans grew louder by the second, the flapping wings turned her world into a horror movie she couldn't turn off.

The horde of maybe twenty growling monsters that used to be teachers, or farmers, or accountants, reached the furniture truck when Terry and Jenna slid Doug into the back seat and Jenna squirmed in beside him. Terry jumped into the driver's seat. "Now let's see if this baby starts, or this is going to be the shortest escape ever." He took a breath and punched the ignition button on the dash. Nothing happened. "Shit."

"What's wrong?" Nikki hated the sound of her voice at that moment. It sounded panicked, weak.

Terry opened the car door and stepped out, the thunder of the approaching wave of birds vibrated the air; a blanket of black stretched along the highway. "No keys. Get behind the wheel, honey and shut the door." Nikki scooted into the driver's seat and watched the man she'd fallen in love with turn to face the monsters.

***

Damn Hipsters and their damn Prius. Terry hated hybrid cars; not because of the cars themselves, it was because of the assholes who drove them. 'I'm doing my part to save the planet,' a young bearded man wearing a hat out of a gangster movie told him one day while Terry fixed the brakes on his Prius. Horse shit. Then why are you standing here in Doug's Muffler and Brakes in your leather shoes, drinking coffee that's growing demand has caused damage to the ecosystems of small countries – and out of a Styrofoam cup, no less?

A crow cawed at Terry from the electric wires that paralleled the highway as he knelt next to the Hipster corpses; the day growing darker as the wall of birds covered the sun. "Come on, man." He pushed his hand into the right front pocket of the Hipster's jeans that were probably once tight, but now hung loose over the dried flesh. The man's eyeless face stared at Terry from behind horn-rimmed glasses. Terry's hand closed on something metal; he pulled it out. "Change? Who the fuck keeps change in their right pocket?" *Lefties.* Two quarters, three dimes and six pennies rattled on the dusty asphalt as Terry rolled the almost weightless, wood-like body onto its face and shoved his hand in the left pocket. Keys. The Prius didn't need a key in the ignition to start, but it needed the electronic keychain in the car, or it wouldn't budge.

"Terry," Nikki screamed. He swung his head away from the corpse. A zombie, a good twenty feet ahead of the horde, its eyes white, its blue dress shirt stained with spittle like a teething infant, ran toward him fast. *Fuck.* He couldn't reach the car before it got to him. Terry glanced around him, the end of a pipe stuck from the dried grass of the roadside. *Holy shit, Adopt-A-Highway needs to step up its game.* Terry reached forward and wrapped his fingers tightly around the sun-warmed metal. He stood fast, swinging the four-foot long section of three-quarter inch pipe in a wide arc. The pipe hit the foaming zombie on the forehead with a sickening crunch, a piece of its skull flew off the side of the road and the thing fell to the asphalt.

A bird flew by Terry's head; its wing clipped his ear. "Shit." He let the pipe fall to the pavement and ran to the Prius, flopping into the passenger seat and dropping the key ring in the cup holder.

"Where does the key fit?" Nikki screamed.

Terry pushed a button on the dash. The Prius started.

"How did you know how to do that?"

"I'm a mechanic."

Something slapped against the rear window and Jenna screamed; the bloodied body of a fat crow lay on the trunk. The sky was now black; the cloud of birds moved like a storm front. "Go," Jenna yelled, pounding the back of the front seat. "Go."

The first zombie, a man in a wrinkled black business suit slammed its face against Nikki's window, wiping a stream of drool and snot across the glass as it tried to gnaw the window. Another monster pounded the trunk. Jenna screamed again. Nikki slammed the shiny blue gearshift into Drive and punched the accelerator. Regardless of reputation, the 2012 Toyota Prius can go zero to sixty in ten-point-two seconds.

The Toyota shot away from the snarling mob. "Stop here. Stop here," Terry hollered.

"Are you crazy?" Nikki spat.

"No. No. Just stop."

Nikki slid the Toyota to a screeching halt next to the Budweiser truck. Terry jumped out of the car and looked to the west, slapping his ass at the approaching zombies. He pulled two cases of Budweiser out of the open door of the beer truck, the same door he'd pulled open yesterday and climbed back into the car with the beer on his lap.

"You've got to be shitting me, Terry," Jenna screamed at him.

"It could be forever the next time we find a beer truck."

"Unbelievable," Nikki said under her breath and hit the accelerator again; the Prius moved silently away from the beer truck and the pack of walking death.

Terry pulled a beer out of a case and held it toward the back seat. "Anybody interested?"

Jenna snatched the can from his hand. "Fuck you, Terry. Just fuck you."

***

"Where do you think they came from?" Nikki asked. She sat on the hood of the Prius with Jenna, sipping a warm Budweiser; Doug and Terry sat in law chairs on either side of them. Doug held a bottle of water; a pile of empty beer cans lay at Terry's feet. Nikki pulled the Prius off the highway once the sky cleared and the terror was behind them and drove up Trail Road, a country road off the intersection of Interstates 80 and 76, near the Colorado border. She stopped at an intersection of dirt roads; they could see for miles, they simply decided to wait and watch. The Prius couple had been going camping, so the trunk was full of gear. The lawn chairs were just a bonus.

"The Communities, probably." It was Doug, watching the highway through the 300mm lens on the Prius couple's Nikon Df. "We got out. Those things could have made it out once the fences were blown down. And they just started walking."

"The same direction we went?" Jenna asked.

Doug shrugged. "Why not? They had to go somewhere."

"Or maybe they followed our scent." They all stopped and stared at Terry.

"You think they can smell us?" Jenna spat.

"Whoa." Doug could smell a fire starting and he wanted to put it out fast. "We don't know what they can do, except kill us. We can't start speculating over every little thing. It'll drive us all crazy." Doug lowered the camera and handed it to Terry.

Nikki scooped the Nikon out of Terry's hands and focused on the cloud of birds moving slowly away. "But where are they going?" she asked.

Doug raised a hand and pointed to the east. The effort was smooth, easy. For the first time since he regained consciousness in the culvert, he knew he was going to be okay. "Omaha," he said. "They're heading east."

"And how do you know that?" Jenna asked, nudging the back of his lawn chair with her sneaker.

"Honey, I've got a concussion. That doesn't mean I forgot how to tell directions, or how to read. There was a sign." The sun lighted the day again, unattended fields swayed in a soft breeze. The cloud of birds moved over the pack of zombies, casting a black shadow that rippled over the countryside. "What do you make out of those birds?"

Terry shrugged. "I dunno." He dropped a spent can on the ground and lifted another out of the case at his feet. "Why do animals do anything? Food maybe? Those bastards don't have the best table manners in the world, I can imagine they leave a feast behind after they kill something."

Doug nodded. *Yeah, that makes sense. Maybe too much sense.*

"Why Omaha?" Nikki asked.

"I don't think these things are going to a place. They're probably just walking. The one in the lead saw something shiny, so he started toward it.

From what we've seen, these things don't have any higher brain function. They just want to eat. That's the only thing in their heads. They're like a drove of sheep, except dangerous."

Jenna laughed. "A drove?"

"I'm from Paola, Kansas. Fucking sue me."

The afternoon fell silent as they watched as the flock moved east toward Omaha. Sound should have been everywhere. The din of great trucks on the interstate, the hum of farm machinery, the occasional car stereo played too goddamned loud. But there was nothing except for the breeze. In two months, the monsters accidentally born of the antidepressant Ophiocordon had wiped America's volume level clean. The noise of civilization was gone. At least, most of it.

The crack of a can opening broke the silence. Nikki took a drink of sparkling water the Hipsters had in the trunk and burped into her hand. "I think I might know where they're going," she said.

Terry turned his lawn chair to face her. "Where?"

Nikki took another drink and sat silent for a moment, looking across the plains, watching the cloud of birds as it drifted over the fields. The Rockies behind them weren't visible from this far out, from a 360-degree view of where they sat, the entire world looked flat, desolate and lonely. "This whole thing was caused when a pharmaceutical genius noticed a Southeast Asian fungus infected a species of ant, right?"

Doug nodded, his head was still clear. That was a good sign. "That's what we got from the news."

"The infected ants turned placid," Nikki continued, "then they turned into zombies under the control of the fungus."

"I remember reading a story when that Ophi, Ophio–" Jenna started.

"Ophiocordon."

"Thanks. Ophiocordon was introduced. The headline even said 'zombie ants.'"

Nikki sat her can on the hood of the Prius and stood. "The fungus made the ants climb into the canopy in search for the perfect humidity and temperature for it to thrive. Then the ants would die, having served its purpose."

Terry frowned. "So?"

"Oh, my God, Nikki," Doug said, the words coming out slowly. "You think it's doing the same thing to people."

Nikki nodded, her once full black hair flat against her head; it barely moved. "Why not?"

"Then these things might be looking for a better way to make this fungus spread." Doug rubbed his temples. "I think I might be just well enough and just fucked up enough to have one of those beers."

***

Nikki had never seen so many stars. Even if the power had been on in this part of the world, the light pollution in western Nebraska was about that of the night side of the moon. *Was the power on anywhere?* She hoped it was. The Orion Arm of the Milky Way dusted across the sky, Nikki thought she could make out the constellation Scorpio. A low light in the sky traveled steadily westward, a satellite broadcasting signals to machines that couldn't receive them anymore. Nikki shook off a tear and stirred the food.

The four of them sat around a Coleman camp stove Terry had pulled out of the trunk of the Prius, just another part of the camping gear the Hipster couple never got around to using. This Prius was a gold mine. Terry also found a hammer, probably for pounding in tent stakes. He hadn't put it down. A small blue flame on the stove heated Velveeta Shells and Cheese with tuna in a small pan. The Hipsters had packed enough food, mostly crap, for a week, so Nikki figured the four of them should be okay for at least a couple of days. They could camp out here, just close enough to the highway to keep an eye on things; just far enough away nothing would notice them. A little town sat a few miles down the highway, but towns meant people and people meant zombies. Terry set up the tent and Jenna spread out the two sleeping bags into a bed. They could hang out here for a couple of days; by then Doug would be better and they could figure out what the fuck they were going to do.

Hopefully.

"Where's the closest spot that would make the fungus happy?" Jenna asked, eating dried apricots.

Doug plucked an apricot from the bag. "It's got to be warm and humid."

Another beer cracked open. Terry held it in his left hand while he smashed an empty flat with the 16-ounce hammer; he wondered how the weak-kneed Hipster boy was able to swing something that heavy. The tent sat off the road amongst the tall weeds at the beginning of an open pasture, good enough to be hidden, visible enough to keep an eye open for anything dangerous coming their way and close enough to the car to run to it in a pinch. Nikki didn't take into consideration the beer supply; they might have to move a bit sooner.

"Well it's pretty hot and humid in the Midwest," Terry said. "That's for damn sure."

"Yeah, but that's just part of the year. These things were moving east, back toward Omaha," Doug said. "Where is the closest place to western Nebraska that's hot and humid all year long?"

"Texas," Jenna said through a mouthful of apricots. "Houston is a bitch."

"Then why aren't they trekking cross country?" Terry asked. "If they're really following some zombie fungus instinct, they'd just go in the direction that felt right, but these guys are following the highway. Why?"

Nikki shrugged. "I don't even know if what I suggested is right, but if it is, maybe they still have more brain function than we think."

"Then that would mean they're, at some level, solving problems," Doug said.

"Yep. I hope I'm wrong," Nikki said, "or we're even more screwed than we think we are."

Nikki held up a flashlight, another treasure from the Hipsters, as Jenna began spooning mac and cheese and tuna into Styrofoam bowls. "Then we just need to stay where the zombies aren't," she said, sticking a plastic spoon into the first bowl and handing it to Doug. "That should be simple, right? I mean, if they're going someplace hot and humid, we should go someplace cold and dry."

The night fell silent, the hiss of the tiny propane fire the only noise for miles. Then far off a coyote yipped and part of the world became normal again. Jenna finished filling the bowls and Nikki clicked off the flashlight, thrusting the group into darkness, illuminated only by the stars and the waxing quarter moon.

"I don't want to live in Alaska," Terry said, tapping the orange-handled hammer against his leg. "I hate Sasquatch. Can you imagine a zombie Sasquatch?"

Doug shook his head. "Terry, we're not going to Alaska." He stopped and looked at Jenna and Nikki, his face grave. "We're going back to Omaha."

"No," softly spilled from Jenna's mouth.

Another empty can died in a dull crunch under Terry's hammer. "What the fuck, boss? Do you not remember what happened to us the last time we were in Omaha? It wasn't a party, that's for sure."

The camp fell silent. Another coyote yipped in the night, louder this time. A second joined in.

After what seemed like minutes, Doug finally spoke. "I want to know what happened," he said. "And I want to know what they're doing to fix it."

Terry reached back and launched the nearly full beer into the night, foam spraying behind like a contrail. "Jesus Christ, dude. They stuck us in a fucking concentration camp, then tried to kill us – with airplanes. Airplanes with bombs. BOMBS."

The coyotes yipped again; they were closer. "I know this sounds crazy," Doug said, absentmindedly stirring his dinner with the plastic spoon. "But it's the one place we know where there are people. Real, live people. It's the one place so far we've been safe."

"Safe? Dude, are you using the Big Dictionary of Opposites? Because what I lived through is the opposite of safe. If anything, we should go in any direction but east." Terry turned toward Nikki. "Honey, would you hand me another beer. I kinda lost the handle on the last one."

Nikki didn't move, she looked from Terry to Jenna. "Doug's right," she said. "It's our best chance at survival. We just spent the past three days in a culvert; scared shitless one of those zombie things would stumble across it and eat us in our sleep. We're going to spend tonight in a goddamned tent, which, considering all the zombies and those birds who almost caught us on the highway, is just as secure as absolutely nothing." She paused for a moment, looking from face to face, the sound of the coyotes somewhere just beyond the tent. "We have to go back."

"I want a bath," Jenna said, her voice shaking. "I want a good, long hot bath and a meal that didn't come out of a can. But I don't want to find these in Omaha."

Nikki pulled a beer out of the case and waved it in front of Terry. "And you?"

He reached out his left hand; the right one gripped the hammer handle tight. "Toss me that flashlight, babe," he said, his eyes focused on the weeds near the tent. Nikki stood slowly and put the flashlight in his hand. Something rustled in the quiet night; the coyotes had gone silent. Terry slowly sat the hammer in the trunk and picked a can of Armour no-bean chili from a cardboard box in the trunk. He raised his left index finger to his mouth, then lowered it and clicked on the flashlight; a yellow beam stabbed into the night.

A coyote stood about ten feet outside the circle, if four people can make a circle. The beam hit the coyote in the face; it didn't back down. They all saw why. Six more pairs of eyes shone in the night. That was seven 46-pound carnivorous mini-wolves and four people. Terry and Doug had grown up in coyote territory. Coyotes aren't bold predators, they're skittish at best around anything bigger than them and not nearly smart enough to order a giant magnet and rocket skates from Acme. But back in Kansas before the world went to shit, coyotes wouldn't have approached four grown humans this closely. The pack leader, a great, fat beast the size of a medium dog, bared its teeth at Terry. In a couple of short months, they'd lost their fear of humans. Oh, fuck.

Terry pulled back his right arm and snapped it forward, the can of chili without beans hurdled in a straight line toward the lead coyote. It struck the beast in the forehead, sending the canine tumbling backward, yelping in pain. The coyote slowly reclaimed its feet, shook its head and yipped before it disappeared into the night, the pack on its heels. Everyone stared at Terry. "What?" he said. "Who the hell eats chili without beans?" He grabbed the hammer out of the trunk and scratched his back with the claws. "It looks like we have more to worry about than zombies."

They ate their macaroni and cheese in silence.

***

The light came on just before midnight. Doug sat on the trunk of the Prius, the Nikon D*f* with its long lens next to him, but he didn't need its 300mm optics to see the light. It shone in the Nebraska night like a beacon, or a warning. Doug had seen the movie "Alien" at least twenty times; he knew what could happen when people got the two confused – they died. The sign they passed on the highway, about a mile before turning onto Trail Road and stopping where their camp sat right now, read "Julesburg: Pop. 1,227"; the blue attractions sign a quarter mile farther promised the "Fort Sedgwick Museum." Doug hadn't mentioned anything at the time; besides, who wanted to see a museum? The whole world was a museum now. Just more than 1,000 people wasn't very much, most of them were dead. But how many might have stood back up made him nervous.

Despite Jenna's protest, Doug had taken first watch to look for any movement in the scant moonlight, to make sure nothing ate them in their sleep. He had promised to wake Jenna at midnight, then she would wake Nikki at 3 a.m. Terry got the 5 a.m. wake up call simply because he'd passed out in the tent around 11 p.m. and would lay there snoring softly until at least sunrise. Doug's watch clicked on 12:01, then 12:05 and 12:30. He wasn't going to wake Jenna. He wasn't going to wake anybody. That light was a problem, but it was going to stay his problem.

Who's down there? Doug wondered. *And why are you signaling us?* He knew whoever was in the town of Julesburg, Colorado, wasn't signaling them directly. The Prius had flown in on angel's wings. Unless the gas motor kicks in, a Toyota Prius doesn't make a sound. And the highway was just far enough from the town no one would make out a car, unless they had binoculars, or a camera. *Oh, shit.* The night closed in on Doug in a claustrophobic blanket. Any warm feeling of health he'd started to have in the macaroni and cheese evening was gone. His head began to swim, his mouth dry as a drunk's. Somebody was down there in that town and a feeling, nothing more than a feeling, told Doug whoever it was knew they were up here. By the time the sun came up, Doug wanted to be gone.

He slid off the trunk and opened it with a soft click. The Coleman stove was easy to find, but the pan, bottle of water and jar of coffee were stuffed in different boxes and Doug did not want to turn on the flashlight. As he lifted the stove, he clanked the green aluminum rectangle on the side of the trunk and froze. Terry's soft snoring from the tent never wavered. Doug let out a long, soft exhale and rested the stove on the ground behind the car. It fired up easily. He gently sat the pan on the burner, poured in a bottle of Aquafina and plopped down in a lawn chair to watch it come to a boil, then he'd dump in the coffee. Doug was going to stay awake until daylight, until that light was gone, if he had to poison himself with instant coffee to do it.

***

"Doug." The word sounded weak, distant. Sleep. He just wanted to sleep. "Doug." Someone shook his shoulder. Who? Who would do that? "Wake up." Nikki. The voice was Nikki's. Doug pulled open his eyes. Nikki stood before him, he could see her in the dim gray of, what was this? Morning? Her hands were on his shoulders. She didn't smile. What's wrong, Nikki?

"You saw the light," she said. It wasn't a question.

The light? Yeah, the light. Doug nodded. His head felt off center, like he'd stayed up most of the night on only caffeine.

"Is that why you didn't wake anyone up?"

"Yeah," Doug said. He focused his attention on Nikki. "You saw it, too?"

She nodded. "I've been up for an hour. It went off at 6 a.m." She motioned for Doug to grab her hands and he did. "Are you going to tell anybody?"

Doug shook his head; it felt like it was filled with sand. "No." He looked up at her in the darkness, her body just a silhouette. "We have to go back to Omaha. We have to find out what's going on."

"I know," Nikki said, pulling him out of the lawn chair. "I'd rather trust the Army that sentenced us to death than whatever's down there in that town." She started walking Doug toward the tent, an arm across his shoulder to compensate for his ankle in a cast. "You're going to get some sleep, then we're getting the hell out of here."

CHAPTER 5

Donnie stood at the window. He liked standing at the window, the big plate glass covered most of the living room's western wall, the neighborhood he grew up in spread out before him behind 3/16-inch of see-through magic. Mrs. Abernathy's little yellow house sat across the street, Gary Grimes' house next to it, with his sweet tree house in the back yard. Donnie stared at the tree house, its green-shingled roof sagged on the sides; that tree house had seen better days. When had he last played in it? Yesterday? No, it couldn't have been yesterday. He'd stayed inside and taken care of Mother all day yesterday. It had to be the day before, but why did the tree house look so old? And when did everybody get so lazy in their yards? Tall grass and flowers, white Mouse Ears and purple Milkvetch, danced gracefully in the slight breeze that caused the lawns Donnie could see from his window ripple like the surface of a lake. The stretch of West Third Street between Walnut and Maple looked more like a prairie than the neat, well-trimmed Colorado town he grew up in.

The Joy Mission Church at the corner of West Third and Maple rested quietly at the edge of the neighborhood. Didn't anyone go to church anymore? Donnie was sure yesterday had been Sunday; the calendar in the kitchen said so. But the little white church just sat there like a boring, unchurchy lump. Not one car pulled up, not one old lady in a hat walked up those steps and not one annoying child ran screaming from the front doors after the services were over. Mother used to tell Donnie the world was going to hell in a hand basket. Donnie was never sure what that meant, but now, as everything slowly stopped being normal, he thought maybe she was right.

Donnie didn't see many people nowadays, although Mr. Miller from down the street walked by sometimes. Donnie hadn't seen him today, which was fine. He didn't like it when Mr. Miller came by the house; Mr. Miller just staggered down West Third Street, his overalls and blue work shirt stained something awful. It was embarrassing to be out drunk so early in the day. Donnie hadn't seen anyone else in a long while.

Something heavy hit the living room wall. Donnie smiled. It was Mother; she must be hungry. "Coming Mother," Donnie said and walked into the kitchen to slip on his shoes. Can't wear shoes on the carpet, no sir. They have to stay by the back door; can't track anything dirty into the house, especially since the electricity's still off. The vacuum sweeper won't work without electricity. Donnie had tried to call the electric company about the power, but the telephone didn't work either. Neither did the water, but he had bottled water, lots of it and had filled the tub when Mother got hungry. Something in his head told him he might need it.

Donnie unlocked the door and stepped into the back yard; a sturdy six-foot-tall privacy fence kept the neighbor's dirty, dirty dogs off of their property, although he hadn't heard them in a while. Hmm, maybe his neighbors finally got sick of all that yipping and shot those dogs in their stupid little heads. Donnie stopped on the back step, his head cocked to the side. Hey, that's funny. Gary Grimes' dad was in Donnie's back yard. What was Gary Grimes' dad doing in the back yard and why was he tied to the basketball goal with part of Mother's clothesline?

"Donnie. Oh, Donnie. Why are you doing this?" Mr. Grimes wheezed, his voice dry and cracked. "You gotta let me go. You gotta let me go, Donnie. I was getting out of here. Going to Omaha. It's safe in Omaha. Come with me, Donnie." Mr. Grimes stopped, his voice nearly gone. "Please come with me," he whispered.

Donnie looked around the yard. Partial skeletons, rotting flesh still hanging from some of the bones, lay in heaps at the foot of the maple tree and the clothes line poles; a section of rope tied around each. What looked like it may have been Connie Benjamin from down at the Family Market hung limp from the post with the happy purple birdhouse on top. A rope kept most of that mass of bone and flies lashed to the eight-foot four-by-four.

"Why are you doing this, Donnie?" Mr. Grimes rasped. "I've known you all your life. You used to play at my house when you were little. You remember that? You used to play pirates with my boy Gary up in his tree house. You remember?" Tears started flowing down Mr. Grimes' dirty, worn face. "You remember, Donnie? Tell me you remember."

Donnie looked at him absently. He knew this man. He was sure of it. He did play at his house, in that tree house with the green roof, but that wasn't yesterday, was it? "Mother's hungry," Donnie said, his voice hollow, empty.

"No, Donnie," Mr. Grimes screamed, his voice raw. "You can't do this. It's not right, Donnie, it's just not right. Let me go. FOR THE LOVE OF GOD, LET ME GO."

Mother's room opened to the back patio through a sliding glass door. Mother liked lots of glass in her house and so did Donnie. It let in so much light. Donnie wrapped his fist around the end of a pole he'd attached to the door handle to Mother's room and slowly pulled the sliding glass open. Then he quickly stepped back inside the kitchen door as Mother, still in the Sunday dress she'd worn the day she got hungry, lurched out of the doorway and went to say hello to Mr. Grimes. She always looked so pretty in that dress. Donnie smiled as the kitchen door clicked shut, Mr. Grimes' screams almost drowning out the sound. *They must be having fun.*

***

The thumping told him Mother was back in her room. Donnie hesitated; a line of black clouds was approaching down I-80. It hadn't stormed in two months and Donnie wanted to see it rain. A picture on the wall rattled on the next thump. *Boy, she really must be tired. I bet she played hard today.* Donnie walked away from the front window, the black cloud moving like something alive over a spot on the western sky. He went into the kitchen and put on his shoes. Mother liked her house tidy and Donnie was doing his best. His only problems were dust and garbage. Mother had plenty of food for Donnie, mostly his favorites. Cans of SpaghettiOs with meatballs (not with those nasty hot dogs), Campbell's cheese soup, chili, pork and beans, pears and peaches, lined the pantry, although there weren't as many there as there were before Mother got hungry. Donnie knew he'd have to go down to the Family Market sometime to get more groceries. He hoped it was open, but he wasn't sure because parts of Connie Benjamin were in his back yard. He wondered how she'd gotten there. He put the trash in big black bags and threw them in the garage. It was starting to stink in there, but he didn't know when the garbage man would come by his house. It was supposed to be every Thursday, but the man was late, really late.

Donnie pulled on his shoes, unlocked the back door and listened. The pounding had stopped, but faint musical tings came from the wind chimes he'd hung from Mother's ceiling so she'd have something in her room to keep her company. He knew she got lonely in there after Daddy left. Daddy got hungry, too and walked out the front door. Donnie hadn't seen him since. He thought about Daddy sometimes, about the way they played catch in the back yard before the back yard was full of so many bones. How did all those bones get there? Well, life's a mystery.

Donnie slowly opened the door; the air smelled of copper, the concrete under the basketball goal wet with blood. *Where'd Mr. Grimes go?* And why did he leave such a mess in the yard? That was rude. He'd expected more from a neighbor; Donnie hoped Mr. Grimes wasn't rude to Mother.

The wind chimes were louder outside; the soft jingling of metal butterflies and fairies bouncing off each other flowed through the open door to Mother's room. Donnie grabbed the wooden pole on the door and slid it shut. A body slammed against the glass. Donnie smiled as his mother pawed at the door, red streaks of blood smeared the glass; her face was slick with it.

"Hi, Mother," Donnie said. It always made him smile to see Mother, her pretty face gnawing at the glass, foamy, bloody spittle running from her mouth. "Sorry, but I don't want to play today." He pointed at the sky. "Look, it's getting dark. It might rain. I have to go back inside." He waved as he stepped back into the kitchen and locked the door.

***

The car came ahead of the storm; the small silver vehicle weaved around a series of tractor-trailers and SUVs that sat dead on the highway. Donnie used to wonder why the drivers had left all those trucks on there, but the trucks were all just part of his world now. His quiet, quiet world. He rarely noticed them anymore. If it wasn't for the cloud coming, the deep black cloud he stared at through the living room window, he wondered if he would have seen the car at all. *How many cars have gone by while I was feeding Mother, or pooping?* There was something strange about that cloud, but he couldn't figure out what it was, especially when that car cruised by Julesburg on the Nebraska side of the state line and turned off the highway onto Road 187, then he forgot about the cloud. At least for a minute. Donnie hadn't seen a car on I-80 for months; which was fine with him. All the good people were still in Julesburg, even drunk old Mr. Miller; everyone on the highway was bad. The world's going to hell in a hand basket, Mother had said. Mother was never wrong. But Mother didn't talk much anymore, although she always let him know when she was hungry and Donnie was running out of friends for her to play with.

He squinted through the window and thought the car stopped on Road 187, but he couldn't be sure. It was too far away. He had to find out more about Mother's new friends.

Donnie ran to the hall closet and threw open the door, the bang of the doorknob against the wall sent Mother into another fit. *Dang it, Donnie. Mother likes the house quiet. You have to be quieter.* He pushed the family's winter coats off to the side, his blue ski jacket, Mother's long red insulated coat and Daddy's thick beige Carhartt and found the black leather case of Daddy's Jason 10x50 binoculars hanging from a peg in the back of the closet where he knew it would be. "Don't play with those damned things, boy," Daddy yelled when he had caught Donnie in the garage with the binoculars, looking through the next door window into 16-

year-old Vanessa Hagen's bedroom. Daddy snatched the black, heavy spyglass out of his young hands and slid it gently into the hard case. "Those were Grandpa Dooley's. He used those to watch birds, not get a boner. If I ever catch you playing with those I'm going to smack you right into next week." And he walked away, leaving fourteen-year-old Donnie standing alone in the garage with a painfully tight erection.

Grandpa Dooley's binoculars, then Daddy's binoculars, now Donnie's binoculars, had sat on that peg in the back of the closet ever since Vanessa Hagen. *Yeah, they're my binoculars.* Donnie looked around the hallway before he reached into the dark closet and gently lifted the case from the peg, half expecting Daddy, his face pale and crazed, his teeth gnashing, to reach out and grab his wrist with a bony hand and drag him into the depths of nightmares. But Daddy got hungry, he'd rushed out the door growling, yes, growling, running after the little Robinson girl on her bicycle, although Donnie didn't know why anyone would let a little girl outside on a bicycle once people started getting hungry for each other. Daddy chased the Robinson girl around the corner and behind the church, then Donnie heard a gunshot. Probably the neighbors shooting those darned dogs. That's the last time he ever saw Daddy.

Daddy wasn't in the closet. Daddy couldn't be in the closet; he was gone somewhere, probably somewhere important, like Washington, D.C., or New York City. Some place important people go when important things happened. And Daddy was important. He was city manager of Julesburg, Colorado. Donnie's hands shook as he clutched the binocular case to his chest and slammed the door, Mother raising heck in the other room. Donnie didn't try to talk her quiet, it only made things worse.

The sun glinted off the silver car's windshield as Donnie stood looking through the big plate glass window in the living room. He smiled. They were there, not too far from home, people. Bad people. Bad people Mother would like to meet. He pressed the binoculars up to his face and searched for the car. Geez, all that trash on the road. Plastic grocery bags clung to weeds on the roadside, a refrigerator box lay below the road in the scrub, beer cans, a shredded tire and a couple of rotting corpses were strewn on the highway between the stalled vehicles. The bodies didn't make Donnie hesitate in his search for the car, he knew the bad people deserved whatever left them lying in the road. They were the reason the world was going to hell in a hand basket. The landscape bobbed through the heavy binoculars as Donnie swung them around, trying to find Road 187 and the bad people.

There they were.

Four of them. Two men, one with a cast on his left ankle and two women stood at the open trunk of the car. The woman with red hair,

Watch out for those gingers, Donnie, bent over, pulled a canvas camping chair from the trunk and popped it open for the man with the broken ankle. Something stirred in Donnie, something down deep, something he hadn't felt since ginger-haired Vanessa Hagen pulled down her panties all those years ago while he watched through these binoculars. Something Mother scolded him about until late into the night. *You're going to want to play with your pecker, Donnie. Your health teacher at school is going to tell you it's okay, it's natural. But it's not. It's not natural, Donnie. If I ever catch you playing with your pecker I'm going to slap it with a ruler. You hear me, Donnie? I'm going to smack it. It's for your own good. I just want you to go to heaven, baby boy. The path to hell is littered with boys who play with their pecker.* Donnie's breath grew short, his face flush, as he stared at the ginger girl through the binoculars. Mother's voice, Mother's words, were gone. His underwear, baggy white Haynes, became tight as his erection grew. The ginger girl helped the man into the chair, pulled her long curly hair behind her head and tied it into a knot. She leaned forward and kissed the gimpy man. *What's happening? What's happening here?* Donnie held the binoculars with his left hand and pulled at the front of his pants with his right. His penis had grown as hard as his thumb, like it did when he woke in the morning, but he always had to pee in the morning. Donnie didn't have to pee. His hard penis had something to do with the ginger girl and Mother wasn't going to slap it with anything; she was locked in her room. A warm rush filled him when he pulled at the front of his pants. Donnie slid open his brown J.C. Penney's belt, unzipped his Dockers and like he wanted to do when he watched Vanessa Hagen, he took himself into his hand.

***

Darn it, Donnie. Darn it, darn it, darn it. Mother banged on her wall, pictures shook all along the living room side. She wasn't hungry again. No. It was too soon; she'd just played with Mr. Grimes. So, she must know. She must know what he'd just done in front of her pretty pane glass window, into her potted rubber plant. She knew, she darn well knew. But how? Did she smell it? *Did she smell my spunk?* It was Vanessa Hagen all over again. "Those were Grandpa Dooley's," Daddy had scolded him as his penis grew hard watching the neighbor girl slip her pink panties to the floor of her bedroom.""If I ever catch you playing with those I'm going to smack you right into next week." Donnie flinched, but the blow never fell because he was alone. He was bad and alone. A wet spot grew on the front of his khakis when he pulled them up and zipped them. The stain a sign of his weakness.

Through the binoculars, the ginger girl, the bad, bad ginger girl, sat on the hood of the silver car next to the black-haired girl, both men in the camping chairs drank beer. Daddy drank beer; there were still ten of them in Daddy's beer refrigerator in the garage. Donnie had never had one; Mother said they make you stupid. Donnie thought he might just get stupid today.

Something was different outside Donnie's house, something had changed over the minutes, or hours, good lord, it felt like hours, while Donnie shamed himself. The sky was darker. The black cloud, undulating now, covered a large section of the western sky and it was closer. Much closer. He swung the binoculars toward the cloud.

"Oh, dear gravy."

It wasn't a cloud, at least not a cloud formed by evaporated water. Birds, thousands of them, flocked in a flowing mass over Interstate 80 and the baddies on the hill just sat watching them. Why? Why did they stop? Something moved under the mass of birds; good people, about twenty of them like Mother, walked eastward on Interstate 80, moving around the empty vehicles, the sea of birds flapping overhead like a, like a, like a what? *Like a fleet of bombers in advance of infantry.* The sky over Julesburg soon grew dark, the cloud of birds leading the death parade. Donnie lowered the binoculars and watched the cloud flow like a living river over the highway.

The good people moved slowly; they always moved slowly unless they wanted to play with someone. Donnie watched them for at least a half hour or so, he guessed, with the electricity off, the clock on the wall didn't work anymore. The birds kept their slow pace, circling in a rippling blanket overhead. They were miles away when Donnie turned his binoculars back toward the silver car. The bad people were all turned facing the birds. *What were they doing?* Donnie wondered, then nodded to himself, a smile grew across his face. They were hiding. Yes, that's what they were doing. They were hiding. The good people frightened them. The man, the one with both feet, dragged a tent bag from the trunk and walked into a patch of weeds at the roadside. A tent? They were going to stay put for a while. Mother thumped in the next room. *Oh, yes, Mother, don't worry. I'm going to get you some new friends to play with.*

***

The quarter moon shone softly over the Great Plains, but there wasn't enough light for Donnie to see jack shit. At dusk the bad people set up a camp stove and cooked something out of a box, but as soon as the sun set, Donnie's peekaboo world blacked out. "Darn it," he hissed as the last light of the day took away his advantage over these people. Nothing moved. He'd hoped they would have started a campfire, at least if he couldn't see what they were doing, he could see where they were.

Donnie had no idea how many hours he'd sat in front of that big window in Mother's comfy flower print chair watching, waiting for something to happen with the bad people in the silver car. Two, three, 78? Well, Donnie knew it wasn't 78, but time didn't mean much to him anymore. After people got hungry and the garbage man stopped running his route on Thursday, what was the point? But, as Donnie stared from his dark living room into the night, he thought of time again. They wouldn't stay there, living in a tent forever; they would leave soon. There were plenty of empty houses in Julesburg they could live in. Soon after Mother started living in the back bedroom, Donnie had gone down to the Red Rooster Café to get a sandwich and chips and the thing was locked up tight as a bank. Nobody was outside in town; it was like an episode of a scary movie Donnie had seen on the Syfy Channel. The town was just empty. The next day he saw drunk old Mr. Miller, then found Connie Benjamin and caught Mr. Grimes outside hooking a trailer to his pickup. Donnie knew he wasn't alone, but the people he found weren't good like Mother, they were bad. But mostly, the people in town were just gone. The bad people in the silver car might look for some place to stay in Julesburg, but Donnie didn't think that was right. If they were going to do that, they wouldn't have driven onto some country road to camp. They would have driven into town.

He put a hand to his mouth to suppress a giggle. Donnie couldn't see them anymore because they didn't want to be seen. He reached for Mother's Bic lighter she always kept on the end table with an ash tray and a soft pack of Virginia Slims and rubbed his thumb along the sparkwheel, illuminating a few feet of the living room with butane flame. He touched the fire to the blackened braided cotton wick of a candle shoved into one of Grandma Dooley's brass candleholders, the yellow light danced with shadows in the living room. Donnie picked up the candleholder and walked into the kitchen.

The door to the garage, the door Daddy had used to discover Donnie staring at Vanessa Hagen through the window, opened quietly. A waft of warm garbage assaulted Donnie's face as he stepped into the garage; *doody garbage man*. He went to the shelves on the back wall. That's where Daddy kept a lot of his toys. Donnie sat the candleholder on a shelf and grabbed the propane lantern and tucked it under his left arm. Then he grabbed Daddy's deer rifle and slung it over his right shoulder. He didn't need to check to see if the rifle was loaded. It was. Daddy always kept his deer rifle loaded because he never knew when he'd need to shoot a deer, or an asshole. It felt heavier than Donnie remembered, but not too heavy. He grabbed the candle and started to leave the garage, but paused. Daddy's beer fridge sat next to the door. WWDD? Ran through Donnie's head and he laughed. What Would Daddy Do? Daddy would have a beer, then sit in front of the window with his deer rifle and wait for something to happen. That's what Daddy would do. The door pulled open with a click and Donnie stuck his index finger through the plastic ring on a six-pack of Coors cans. But what if Daddy came home? Came home and found Donnie getting stupid? A chill shook him. He stuck the six-pack back in the refrigerator and shut the door. Daddy would be mad.

Donnie blew out the candle and sat it back on the end table where it was supposed to be. The feeble moonlight still illuminated nothing, but that didn't matter anymore. The lantern ignited with a soft hiss and Donnie sat it on a small table he'd moved in front of the window. If he couldn't see them, at least they could see him. He felt good about today, about Mr. Grimes, about Mother's play date and about the parade of good people on the highway. This world hadn't gone to hell in a hand basket. At least not yet. There was still good in this world and Donnie was going to make sure that good was going to stay. He sat in Mother's comfy flower print chair with Daddy's deer rifle across his lap and waited for the bad people to come to his beacon.

CHAPTER 6

Andi woke, her mind screaming. The shrieks of the crows, the moans of the things that used to be human, the words of Polo Man. She couldn't hear Polo Man as she lay on the roof of the Muskogee Motel 6 preparing to blow his brains out. In her mind, their eyes met, although somewhere in her aching head she knew he couldn't see her. 'Help me,' Polo Man mouthed to her in her dream. Andi shot up in the seat of the Army High Mobility Multipurpose Wheeled Vehicle, her breath came in short snips, her face slick with sweat. The piercing morning sun – *of where? where am I? Kansas?* – poured onto her face, forcing her eyes into slits. Andi slowly exhaled. A hangover fuzz filled her head, her mouth as dry as the day after a AΣA party back at Missouri State University. *Go Bears*.

Then the morning hit her, yesterday flooding fully into her mind. The army, the Fence, the poor man just trying to live. The military had placed soldiers all along the Fence, doing exactly what Cotton had told her to do. A man, a person, needed her help and she'd shot him. She'd shot him dead. "Oh, my God," she whispered, her voice loud in the vehicle cab. Andi's hands shot to her face, but couldn't hold in the tears.

You ever shot a man, Bakowski?

"Fuck you, Cotton," she meant to shout, but the energy wasn't there. This wasn't Cotton's fault. *It's not mine either,* she thought, but knew that was a lie. Andi was the one who pulled the trigger – twice.

Something moved in the driver's side window. In one smooth movement that sent empty Bud Light cans rattling across the floorboard, Andi pulled her 9mm sidearm from its holster and leveled it at the bullet resistant window. The glass might absorb a shot fired from a distance, but not from two inches. The deer staring at Andi, a wet nose smear on the glass, threw up its ears and stepped back before bolting across the Walmart parking lot and disappearing into a line of trees, its white tail flashing its warning. Four, no five more deer scattered, following Andi's friend into the thin trees. Andi's breath came hard. *Oh, geez.* A click filled the cab as she decocked the sidearm and reholstered it. With the movement in the window she'd expected a bloody, slathering human monster pawing at her, but it was a deer, a deer that had forgotten man was the superior species on the planet. A lot of species had forgotten this fact, probably even man. She wiped a sleeve across her face and sat still in the hot cab of the vehicle for a few minutes until her breathing slowed and the tears stopped. She didn't have time for this.

Andi had pushed the Humvee in the dark up U.S. 69 that goes (until nature reclaims it) 1,136 miles from Port Arthur, Texas, to Albert Lea, Minnesota. She didn't go either place. She stopped a few hundred miles north in Fort Scott, Kansas, drunkenly swerving as if every lesson she'd sat through in the D.A.R.E program hadn't meant a damn thing. But in her stupor, with nothing else on the road but abandoned cars, she knew she had to make it far enough away from that Fence nobody would come looking for her.

So far they hadn't.

It's hot. Her hand slapped at the door, reaching instinctively for the button that would lower the window, but it wasn't there. The windows didn't roll down, something about safety if the enemy was shooting at you. Apparently, the Army didn't care if you were hot. Andi pushed open the door, a couple of empty beer cans dropped out and clanked against the sun-bleached asphalt. She wondered, just briefly, what Cotton would do to her if she'd driven back to base drunker than a U.S. senator. Desk job, probably. He'd have his excuse to keep her safe. *Safe. What the hell's safe?* The world had come to an end; everyone was just dancing in the mirror. She'd pulled off the highway and into the store lot because a semi sat cold and silent near the back, a school bus between it and the highway. The Humvee fit right in between them, hidden; she was too tired and drunk to run anymore.

Andi reached into the back seat and grabbed an MRE. Through the thick, fuzzy hangover mouth the pizza, the Army's new menu item – it stays fresh for three years – tasted better than the last steak she'd eaten. *When was that?* In May at the White Sands Restaurant back home with Dad? These MREs may be the last pizza on the planet. She realized she'd better enjoy it.

Her head hurt. There were acetaminophen capsules in the medical kit, but she wasn't going to waste them on a hangover. She had food and water in the vehicle, but she also could take care of herself if she got hurt. Uncle Sam made sure his soldiers were ready for anything after the zombie apocalypse, except emergency psychological counseling if you killed someone in cold blood. Andi didn't know if there was anything to prepare anyone for that, but she did know she'd be okay unless the generous Uncle Sam ever caught up to her. She had to ditch the Humvee – and fast.

Andi stepped out of the vehicle, the morning already starting to heat up. Chirps of birds and the drone of insects were the only sounds to break the morning until Andi unzipped her Army-issue woodland camouflage pants and squatted in front of the Humvee, holding onto the bumper. A hard stream of urine hit the dry pavement, the beginnings of cracks spider webbed under Andi's boots. By next summer those cracks would probably be home to grass and weeds. Grass and weeds first, comb-over trees five years down the line. How long would it be before everything was gone? She hoped she lived to find out; then again, part of her wanted nothing to do with it.

Andi stood and buckled up. The first leak of the morning is the best. She felt better already. It was 7:50 a.m. Cotton has known she'd been gone for almost eight hours. Fort Scott was three hours north of Pryor; they might be on her tail right now, that is if Cotton could afford to send anyone after an AWOL private he didn't want stationed at the Fence anyway. Even then, where would they look? Interstate 44 about an hour north of Muskogee (couldn't go south. Uh, uh. That was the Bad Lands), went west toward Tulsa and east toward Joplin, Missouri, a half dozen rural highways along the way could have taken her anywhere. But Andi lay passed out most of that time; anyone could have driven past the Fort Scott Walmart Supercenter and not even noticed she was there; the tan and blue building sat nearly a quarter-mile off U.S. 69. *I could just camp out here,* she thought, but immediately knew that would be a mistake. To be safe she needed to find people; there was safety in numbers. And if she found enough numbers, maybe she wouldn't have to kill anyone ever again.

***

Andi decided to ditch the Humvee here, behind the semi and the school bus; she didn't even have to start it; all she had to do was unload the necessary supplies and equipment and wave good-bye. She felt comfortable in the armored truck – *who wouldn't?* – but the gas mileage was less than twelve miles per gallon and on the road it stood out like a pimple on prom night. If someone was looking for her, she needed to look like a civilian, which meant different car, different clothes, different hair. *Hair?* Andi'd never colored her blond hair, always preferring to stick with what God gave her. But she didn't think God had anything to do with this shitstorm.

Andi slung her weapon over her shoulder and went to the back of the vehicle. There was something she needed; a flathead screwdriver. She slipped it into her back pocket and walked toward the front doors of Walmart. Andi had to find a car.

A gray Subaru Outback sat next to a black Land Rover between the final resting place of the Humvee and the storefront. The owner of the Land Rover, Andi named him Jimbo, was still in the vehicle, buckled into the driver's seat, pounding the window with raw, bloody hands, the man's once-human face taught with anger. No. Not anger, hunger. His arms flew wildly when he saw Andi stop to inspect the Outback, his growls audible through the glass as he beat at it furiously with shredded palms.

"I'm sorry," Andi said softly, the words uncomfortably loud in the silent morning. "I think you're just into girls in uniform."

Andi never considered the Land Rover; it barely had better mileage than the Humvee and was filled to the windows with monsters. She needed something she could drive forever on a tank of gas, because getting gas out of convenience store ground tanks nowadays took a little more effort than swiping a debit card. For that reason, Cotton made sure every Humvee in the unit carried a hand pump, but it still took more time than Andi liked to have her back turned to anything. A 1993 Geo Metro, a three-cylinder marvel that could go sixty miles on a gallon of gas, would be nice, but those were more than twenty-five years old and about as spacious as a Matchbox Car. The Outback was a mini four-wheel drive station wagon that got at least thirty miles per gallon on the highway. It would do, for now. Probably had shit music in the CD player though.

Problem One wasn't much of a problem. If a car was in the Walmart parking lot, chances are its owner was in Walmart with the keys. *But how am I going to find them?* A car's not much good without the keys, unless keys didn't matter. Big Andy taught his daughter more than just how to shoot and skin a deer. She knew her way around a car.

"Sooner or later, you're going to have to know this," Big Andy told fourteen-year-old Andi the day of Grammy Bilton's funeral, a sad smile hanging off his bottom lip. He held a flathead screwdriver between them.

"Why will I ever need to know this?" Andi asked, wishing she had a Pepsi. Every time they visited Grammy, Big Andy stopped by JD's Liquors for a six-pack of Miller Lite and Andi walked out with a stick of beef jerky and a Pepsi. Score. They hadn't stopped at JD's today; today they had laid Grammy Bilton to rest under an oak tree in South Pointe Cemetery.

"Every day somebody gets stuck in a spot they didn't ask for, kiddo," Big Andy said. "This is just in case one day that somebody is you."

Big Andy leaned into the open window of Grammy's old Buick LeSabre and slipped his hand around the steering column. "You know Grammy insisted on being buried with her purse, right?" he asked.

Of course, Andi knew. Grammy Bilton always carried her big, flowery purse full of old peppermints and half-used tissues "because the other half is still good." For her not to have it with her when she went to the great beyond would just seem wrong.

"She left her Buick to your mom and me because you're going to be driving before you know it," Big Andy continued. "Well, I think the keys were still in her purse. We can't find them anywhere." He reached behind him and pulled a standard flat-head screwdriver from his back pocket, gripping the red and blue handle lightly in his thick-fingered hand. "We could just get a new key, but this thing is twenty-five years old with enough miles to get to the Moon. So, this Andi, is my key."

Big Andy shoved the blade of the screwdriver into the key slot and jimmied it until something snapped. He grinned and turned the screwdriver; the Buick fired right up. "That a girl," he said to the dash, then turned toward Andi. "This doesn't always work, but if you're in a pinch, try it. It's easier than trying to hot wire the thing."

"Why?"

He shrugged. "Life ain't the movies, honey." He paused and rubbed his chin, shaved smooth for the funeral, not the graying stubble Andi was used to. "I'll show you that little trick some other time. You about ready for a Pepsi?"

Andi nodded.

"Then get in," her father said, pulling himself from the driver's seat and standing in the leaf-strewn gravel driveway at Grammy Bilton's little white house. Andi started to run around to the passenger side. "Hold on honey," Big Andy said, stopping her in his tracks. "This side." He patted the top of the open driver's door. "You're sitting here."

What? Really? Andi thought she might throw up and pee herself at the same time. "You want me to drive?"

Big Andy grinned. "You're fourteen. I should have already taught you. Besides, JDs is only about a mile down the road. You'll be all right." He stopped and looked sternly at Andi, crows feet pinched at the corner of his eyes. "But I won't be all right if you tell your mother. Our little secret, okay?"

Oh no, oh no, oh no. "Yeah," Andi said and ran around the car toward the open door, slipped on the gravel and grabbed the trunk for balance. Big Andy laughed as he shut the door for his only child, walked around the blue boat and crawled into the passenger seat. It was the first time Andi drove to the liquor store. It wasn't the last.

***

A man in khaki cargo shorts, a blue T-shirt and leather sandals lay like a sun-dried tomato on the pavement next to the Outback's driver side door. Andi bent and cringed as she gently eased her right hand into the man's pants pockets. A melted tube of ChapStick, a pocket knife, lint and seventy-seven cents in change. No keys. *Dang it.* Cargo Shorts didn't belong to the Outback. Andi thought he might belong to the Land Rover, but she really had no idea. She also had no idea how she was going to get into the Outback without keys. She reached out and pulled the door handle. The door clicked and swung open effortlessly. Andi smiled. This was small town rural Kansas, of course the door was unlocked. The doors to half the houses in town were probably unlocked; Andi just wasn't going to open them.

The man's body was uncomfortably easy to move away from the door; Andi pushed the dehydrated human shell with her feet. A plastic Walmart sack sat nearby; Andi didn't bother to look in it, she had an entire store ahead of her, besides, she didn't want to know the last thing this man did in life was buy hemorrhoid cream. She swung the door to the Outback wide, laid her weapon gently on the asphalt, slung her backpack into the car and sunk into the driver's seat. The car wasn't as big as Grammy's Buick LeSabre, but it would do. She pulled the screwdriver out of her back pocket, the blade dirty from use. "This Andi, is my key," Big Andy had told her before he started the car. It started and Andi never learned how to hot wire a car, so she hoped this worked. She shoved the screwdriver blade into the ignition and twisted. Something popped in the steering column and the tool began to turn. Andi held her breath, praying like heck this worked and that this two-month dormant car would– The engine fired. She pinched her eyes tight and smiled, tears leaking from the corners. "Thanks, Daddy."

The stereo fired with it.

"No stop signs, speed limit," blared from the speakers, the monster in the Land Rover next door getting more agitated with the noise. "Season ticket on a one-way ride."

Andi's fingers fumbled with the buttons as the creature pounded harder on the Land Rover's window. "Good thing you're not coming with me," she said, her voice soft in the hot, stuffy car, "or this would be a long trip."

***

The Outback slid to a silent halt right in front of the store. The previous owner had Andi's tastes in music and took good care of the brakes, not a squeak, not a grab. Andi moved the car close to the store because she had no idea what faced her inside. Although with the number of vehicles in the lot (a lot of them pickups. This was rural Kansas), she had a pretty good idea she wouldn't be alone. Andi stepped out of the driver's side, grabbed the weapon from the passenger seat and opened her backpack. Each soldier was issued a sound suppressor just in case gunfire might attract the wrong kind of attention. Alone in (probably) hostile territory, any attention was the wrong kind of attention. The sound suppressor wouldn't work on an automatic rifle forever, but Andi was just looking to live through today.

There were no monsters, and thank God no crows, in plain sight except the thing in the Land Rover, but those undead fungus things could be anywhere. Andi pulled back the rifle bolt. "These are no longer human beings," Cotton told them the night before deployment. *Not human beings. They're crazy, hungry and dead. How does that work, anyway?* The sound of the grunting, snarling human-like beasts, snapping at each other as they ate Polo back in Muskogee, filled her head. They weren't people anymore. She knew that. They didn't have loved ones, they didn't feel pity, they didn't feel anything. *They're monsters.* She pulled a flashlight from the backpack and walked unsteadily to the front door.

Andi hated going to Walmart before the world came to an end; she sure didn't like it now that this building was potentially filled with undead shoppers. Darkness filled the interior of the store as she stepped toward the sign that read "Enter" and right into the sliding glass doors. Her weapon clacked on the glass, followed by her forehead. No electricity. The electric eye didn't work. *Doofus.* She managed a smile. When's the last time that happened? She stared through the glass into the store. At least three of the human monsters milled around the cash registers; she couldn't see much farther. Freaking great. There had to be more. Andi wedged her fingers on either side of the sliding doors and pulled; the doors wouldn't be hard to open all the way, but she just tugged until they opened a few inches; only a few. Andi didn't want to do this, to step into a dark Walmart store, but she needed things to survive, to hide, and they were all inside this store. She exhaled slowly. Showtime.

"Hey," Andi shouted through the crack. "It's dinner time. Come and get it." The three creatures at the cash register, two wearing blue Walmart smocks, looked toward the door, their eyes milk white. A chill ran through Andi. "Come on. I don't have all day." They moved toward her and two more joined them from around the $5 movie bin. Andi clicked on the flashlight and shone it into the store, the powerful beam cut through the darkness. Six, seven, eight. At least twelve of the drooling monsters wandered out of the aisles and started toward her. "Oh, come on. Come on." She waved the flashlight beam in the glass of the door. One woman in a flowery dress, her face crusted with dried blood, followed the light around like a cat. More came pouring from the back of the store. Andi's stomach clenched, her legs grew suddenly weak. *Oh, no.* There were at least twenty-five of them now and coming fast. She backed away from the door, pocketing the flashlight and raising her weapon, the heavy automatic rifle comfortable in her hands. The first creature slammed into the door, its twisted face smeared drool and mucus across the glass.

"Come on," Andi whispered. "Come on." She took another step back as more monsters leaned into the door. Their growls grew louder the closer they got to her; the morning now sounded like Muskogee. The taste of stale beer and Army-issue pizza hit the back of her throat. *No. No, no.* She steadied herself, pressed the stock of the weapon hard onto her shoulder and swallowed. One creature's hand pushed through the crack Andi had opened, forcing the doors a little wider. *No. Not yet.* More of the monsters pawed at the glass, obscuring the rest of the store; they were all massed under the sign that read "Enter," pushing toward her with one thought process in their mostly dead brains. Food. Andi was nothing but food. The doors slid open a few more inches. Andi took a steadying breath, slowly squeezed the trigger ("Squeeze it like you're hugging your teddy bear, honey," Big Andy had once told her) and fired the rifle on full automatic.

Bullets tore through the glass, shards crashed to the ground and glass dust filled the air like a mist under the pounding of fully automatic gunfire, 16 reports every second. The NATO rounds thumped into the monsters, their once-human bodies jerked like this was a dance contest instead of a massacre. Blood and gore splattered the front of the store, the white tiled floor slick with it. Andi released the trigger and the morning was suddenly still.

She waited for ten seconds, then twenty. A minute, then two. "Anybody else coming to the party?" she screamed into the huge, dark building. Nothing. Not a moan, not a growl, not a fat woman knocking over a rack of Junior Miss slacks on its way to rip open her throat. Andi popped in a new clip before she pulled open the second set of sliding doors, the ones under the "Exit" sign and stepped through, her weapon pressed into her shoulder. She clipped the flashlight to her belt and clicked it on; the torn bodies of the monsters lay a couple feet away. There was no way she was walking through that mess. No way.

***

The store smelled. Bad. Not just from the twenty-five or so creatures she mowed down in a spray of gunfire, although the smell of coppery rot was strongest; she could make out the underlying odor of decaying meat and produce from the grocery section and must from the unused store. The still darkness, hot in the Kansas morning, brought Andi's nerves to Alert Level Holy Shit. She knew there were no more creatures in the store; they would have all flocked to the noise. Even the noise of the silenced machine gun (can't make it completely silent. Science ain't magic), would have brought any one of them straggling near the back. She was alone, but there were things in this world more frightening than the monsters. She grabbed two shopping carts and moved back toward Women's Clothes, pushing one in front, pulling the other. The feeling of claustrophobia gnawed at the back of her mind; Andi wanted to get out of there faster than if it were Black Friday in Bentonville.

The cart quickly filled with clothes. Three pair of jeans (practical), a handful of T-shirts, underwear, socks, two pair of Nikes, some nice pumps and a green dress because you never know. She'd need a winter coat eventually, but the Piper hit at the beginning of the summer, winter coats weren't on the shelves. A grin tugged at the corners of her mouth. Winter coats would never be on the shelves. Screw it. She'd find a coat when she needed one. Andi grabbed a Kansas City Royals baseball cap to cover her hair, then moved on to drugs and cosmetics. Acetaminophen, Tums, vitamins, antibiotics, Valium, lotion, ChapStick, isopropyl alcohol, bandages, soap, deodorant, boxes of pads and a package of condoms just in case she met that special someone. It was the hair dye that made her linger. She had always been blond, the kind of blond that almost looked white after a summer in a chlorine swimming pool. Any color would take, it was just— *Eff it.* It's not like she had to weigh her purchase against a budget. She grabbed a box of auburn, brown and jet black and dropped them into the front cart. She jogged through the rest of the store, picking up anything she thought she'd need on the road. Camp stove and fuel, canned, powdered and boxed food, beef jerky and power bars. *Now this is the shopping list for the apocalypse. I should probably write this down. If the human race lives past this year, maybe my grandkids will think it's funny.*

In and out. Her entire shopping experience for maybe the rest of her life took twenty minutes. "No, thank you. I think I can make it out to my car myself," Andi said to the pile of wet, dismembered bodies splayed across the floor near the exit. "And you have a pleasant day yourself."

She packed the car quickly. Andi now wore a pair of new blue Wranglers, bright white tennis shoes and a red T-shirt featuring Old Glory and the word 'Merica. Somewhere to the north a dog barked; it was close. Too close. Andi knew she had to be careful. Stray dogs might be friendly in end of the world movies, but she knew dogs and left alone they didn't get friendly, they got hungry. She grabbed a bottle of water, a stick of beef jerky, a fist full of Led Zeppelin CDs and slowly lowered the Outback's hatch. It secured with a click.

A movement in her periphery swung Andi's head toward the Humvee. *Oh, shit.* A dog, a big mutt, at least part Rottweiler, stood at the edge of the parking lot, its coat matted, its teeth bared. Another joined it, a collie mostly and another and another, both mutts and all big. "Shit," she hissed. The Outback was loaded with enough supplies for weeks, including two cases of Bud Light in the front seat. She already had her pack and weapons, but there were five gallons of water in the Humvee, plus MREs, ammunition, explosives and the gasoline pump. She needed those, all of those.

She slapped the roof of the cab, the "whop" unnaturally loud in the Kansas morning. *Damn it.* She had a weapon, she needed her supplies, she didn't have a choice.

Andi threw herself into the driver's seat and turned the ignition with the screwdriver; the Outback came to life. The door slammed at the car's forward motion when Andi shifted to drive and shoved her foot onto the accelerator, the little car squealing tires toward the Humvee. The dogs ran toward the moving vehicle, teeth bared. She would get to the Humvee before the dogs, but she couldn't get out of the car before they tore her into so much Spam. She glanced at the weapon in the seat next to her. *No.* She had enough ammo in the Humvee to rule the entire state of Kansas, but it would run out sometime. *Save it. Save it Andi.* The lead dog, the big, black alpha male, foam flecking from its lips, bared down on the oncoming Outback. Andi had another weapon, she floored the Subaru.

The lead dog hit the bumper with a bigger thud than she had expected. She'd only run over armadillos and opossums, nothing as big as that dog. She pulled the car to the right, smashing the driver's side door into the collie. The thing went down with a yelp and thumped under the rear tire. Andi turned the car straight and clipped the next dog, a German shepherd and screeched the Outback to a stop. The shepherd trotted away in a limp, a terrier close behind. Andi gave them the finger.

The collie lay in a bloody lump, whimpering when Andi pulled the Outback next to the Humvee and got out. She never heard it.

The ammo and food fit in the Outback, the water jug and pump she bungeed to the roof. Andi slid back into the Subaru and pulled out of the parking lot toward U.S. 69. She knew where she was going. Cotton had mentioned an emergency shelter at an amusement park in Kansas City, Missouri. Worlds of Fun. Big Andy and Momma had taken her there when she was eight. She rode the Finnish Fling six times in a row, a god-awful Centrifugal force ride and threw up her lunch. Andi hoped to God things were better up north.

JULY 29: I-80, WESTERN NEBRASKA, JUST OUTSIDE OF JULESBURG, COLORADO

CHAPTER 7

Terry would have crossed his arms if he hadn't been eating; the plate got in the way. "And, we're doing what now?" he asked, holding a plastic fork with a fist, his new-found hammer friend tucked into his belt like a sword.

Doug sat in one of the canvas chairs looking at Terry, his friend's face pinched and as close to angry as Doug had ever seen it. And he'd seen it drunk and talking shit about alien conspiracies with Mike down at The Corner Bar back home in Paola. This idea was going to be a hard sell, Doug understood that; convincing his friends to go backward, into the arms of the men who sentenced them to death in a concentration camp full of lepers (zombie lepers). They weren't even infected with the Piper, the HG-17 fungus delivered with a seemingly harmless anti-depressant; Col. Corson had to know that. Still, that bastard sent them to the Community anyway. "You'll be relocated," Corson said to them in the bowels of the Nebraska Medical Center the Army unit had barricaded itself inside, surrounded by snipers and a tall chain-link fence. "There are thousands of survivors like yourself living in these safe, comfortable communities until we get this mess cleaned up." Safe and comfortable, sure. Only Corson didn't say he considered them part of the mess. They'd trusted Corson. He was an authority figure. The only authority figure they'd found in this world of the dead and Col. Corson was a goddamned liar. They had all faced unknown enemies since the world had gone to shit; Doug preferred to face the one he knew – and that asshole was in Omaha.

The morning sun sat high enough in the sky it was probably 8 or 9 a.m., Doug didn't know exactly. Although he had only a couple hours of sleep after his vigil, he felt better, much better than yesterday, but he still had a way to go before he was ready to do anything on his own. Like deal with the light. The light in the little town bothered him; it shouldn't have been there. The lone light in the darkness wasn't for some insomniac reading late at night; it was a beacon. And since whoever lit that beacon wouldn't have enough fuel to light it every night in the two months since the Piper started turning people into zombie incubators, it was meant for them. Someone in the little Colorado town just over the Nebraska border knew they had made camp on that country road and that person wanted them to come down and play. If he were still driving the Marstens H3, armed with those survivalist's SX3 shotguns and several M27 light machine guns, he would have taken his friends down there, but all that was gone, taken by the Army in Omaha. Now, with a Toyota Prius and a hammer, Doug didn't much feel like playing.

"We're going back there," he said. A feeling of terror, like feeling something crawly in the arm of a long-unused coat, ran through him. Whoever was down in that little town might be watching them right now.

Terry nodded. He shoveled in another plastic forkful of reconstituted eggs from the Styrofoam bowl and swallowed. "That's what I thought you said." He scooped out another forkful of eggs. "You're crazy," he said, pointing his fork at Doug, a mound of scrambled eggs barely on the tines jiggled, then fell into the dirt.

"It's the only way."

Terry threw the bowl and rest of his eggs into the weeds. "To what? The only way to what, Doug? Die? We did a pretty good job not dying while you were unconscious, but ever since you woke up you've been begging us to let you die. 'Leave me. You'll be faster.' Aaaaahhhhhh." Terry grabbed the back of his head with both hands and walked around the car.

"I'm with Terry." Jenna sat in the other canvas chair, pulled next to Doug's, an empty bowl in her lap. "We escaped from that awful place. The Community. I know it knocked you out, Doug, but don't you remember the bombs? The airplane trying to kill us? Those people in Omaha sent us there." She paused to still her trembling voice. "Don't you remember what they locked us in there with? The bodies, with that fungus growing from their chests? And that man, that thing with the white eyes?"

Cataract Man. Doug was suddenly cold.

"Those people in Omaha did that to us," Jenna said, her eyes starting to tear. "I don't want to go back."

Doug reached over the chair arm and wrapped his hand around hers. "I remember all that, honey. I'm still going. It's the only way we can find out."

"Find out what, dude?" Terry spat, coming around the other side of the car, holding his first beer of the day. There'd be more; Terry made sure they had plenty. "Find out what it feels like to get shot? Or hung?"

"Hanged," Nikki corrected.

"Because I'm sure that's what's waiting for us back in Omaha."

Terry was right. Of course he was right. Any sane person would understand that. Run. Run, run, run. Just run away. Find someplace safe. Doug wasn't sure there was a Someplace Safe anymore, but the closest thing they had to someone knowing that was Col. Corson. "Don't you want to know?" he asked.

"Know what, boss?"

A slight breeze caught Jenna's hair, her auburn curls flowing like a field of flowers. Doug squeezed her hand and smiled. "If there's any hope. I need to know if the trains are going to run again, Terry. I need to know if there's going to be hospitals and grocery stores and a new season of 'Game of Thrones.' I need to know if we should give up hope and just barricade ourselves behind walls somewhere and say 'fuck it.'"

"I'm all for saying 'fuck it.'"

The morning grew silent, the breeze carrying only the buzz of insects.

Nikki spoke, her voice steady. "I think we should go."

"No, baby. No," Terry moaned.

"Look, we don't know what's out there. We're going to run into zombies, but there are things worse than zombies." *Preacherman.* "I've seen them. We have to go back. I'll take my chances with people. The doctor at the hospital, the nurses, even that asshole Corson. They're at least people."

Jenna threw her bowl to the ground and stood. "I don't like this." Her voice shook; tears ran down her face. "Goddamnit. I don't like this at all. I don't want to fight zombies. I don't want to fight Army men. I'm tired of sleeping on the fucking ground." Her knees started to buckle. Doug pushed himself from the canvas chair, putting most of his weight on his right leg. He caught Jenna, her body melted into his. "I'm tired, Doug. I'm just tired."

Terry tossed his empty beer can into the ditch. "Fuck it," he said. "When are we going?"

Doug kissed Jenna's forehead. "Now."

***

The silver Prius cruised east on I-80 in silence. Terry occasionally swerved around an abandoned car or truck, but the interstate was relatively clean. Nobody was driving in the last days; they were too busy dying.

"So, what do you ladies want to listen to?" Doug asked, pulling down the sun visor, a row of CDs tucked into a sleeve on the back. "We have Pete Yorn."

Terry shook his head. "No."

"Do you even know who that is?" Nikki asked from the back seat.

"Nope, but I bet he sings about being in love and losing love and finding love."

"How can you tell that from a name?"

"Simple, honey. I haven't heard of him. If I haven't heard of him, he sings about shit I don't care about."

Nikki slapped him on the shoulder.

"Ben Folds," Doug continued.

"No," Terry said.

"Maroon 5."

"No."

"Dave Matthews."

"No way in hell, dude."

"Are you going to like anything I say?"

Terry frowned. "Depends. Got any Judas Priest?"

Doug fingered his way through the CDs. "Nope. I don't think Judas Priest was one of the owners' favorites."

"Led Zeppelin?"

"In my truck, but it's in Omaha. We'll have Zeppelin when we get there."

Jenna moaned. "Just pick something, will you."

"John Mayer."

"No."

"Abba Gold."

Terry slowly exhaled. "Okay, we've got about five hours to whatever in the fuck we're going to do in Omaha. We might as well enjoy the trip." He held out his right hand. "Boss, would you let me see those CDs?"

Doug slipped the CDs one-by-one out of their sleeves and sat the stack in Terry's hand. Terry hit a button on the driver's door armrest, the window rolled down and he dropped the CDs onto the highway.

"Hey," Nikki said, slapping Terry on the back of the head. "I actually like Abba."

"Sweetheart, you are probably the only person on the planet who can say that."

***

"Slow down, Terry." Doug leaned forward in the passenger seat of the Prius. To get a better look? *Jesus, I'm only 37. Since when did I need the large print apocalypse?* The last road sign he saw read "Elm Creek: 3 miles, Kearney: 15 miles, Omaha: 200 miles." They had to be close to Elm Creek by now. *What the hell went down there?*

"What is it, Doug?" Jenna asked, leaning over his shoulder.

"Smoke."

"I don't see anything, boss," Terry said, taking his foot off the accelerator, the Prius quickly slowed from 80 mph to 50.

"It's just a trail. Pretty faint."

"I see it," Nikki said, pointing over Terry's shoulder. "It's a gray line."

The faint finger of smoke was somewhere ahead of them; it could have been a dissipating jet contrail, but it was too low. "You think it has anything to do with our friends from yesterday?" Terry asked.

Doug shook his head. "I don't know." Where there's smoke there's people. "Could be. But if it is because of them and those birds, they didn't start that fire. They couldn't have." He pulled the Hipsters' Nikon out of its case and put it up to his face, the 300mm lens brought the smoke to him. "Looks like a semi caught fire."

"But how could that happen?" Jenna asked, her voice tense.

"I don't know," he said, "except that it didn't happen on its own."

Terry pulled the Prius to a stop a mile and a half later behind a Jeep Cherokee and the smoking semi blocking the road. Bodies lay in bloody lumps across the highway; the white and blue trailer of the Fleming Foods truck smoldered, smoke from its load of hamburger buns and whatthehellever rolled into the Nebraska sky. "And it's a mess. You see what I see, boss?"

Doug nodded. "There was a hell of a fight here."

"Who won?" Jenna asked.

A man in a camouflage John Deere cap lay closest to the Prius, a bloodstain pooled beneath him. "Not the good guys."

"Dibs," Terry said as he opened the door and stepped out onto the highway.

"Where are you going?" Doug called after him. Dibs? "And dibs on what?"

Terry stuck his head back into the Toyota. "That rifle."

"I'm going, too," Doug said. The passenger side door clicked as he pulled the door handle.

Jenna put a hand on his shoulder. "Oh, no you're not. You can't even walk without help."

A smile crossed his face. "Well, honey, you're just going to have to help me."

The three joined Terry on the highway, Doug's arm around Jenna's waist as they walked toward the truck, the rifle slung over Terry's shoulder. It was a slaughter. Three men, large chunks of flesh ripped from their bones, lay in a wet mess behind the Cherokee; one body still held a 9mm pistol, an M1 lay next to another, the third man had a baseball bat. The rotting corpses of zombies lay strewn among them, the jagged tear of bullet holes in the head of each. But Doug only counted ten zombies – *still hate that word*. There were more on the highway yesterday. A lot more.

"Dibs on the pistol," Terry said, handing Nikki the deer rifle and tiptoeing around the bodies; he reached over and pulled the pistol from the dead man's hand. "Hey, there's a lump in his pants. You think it's another clip, or is he just happy to see me?"

"Inappropriate," Nikki said. "And gross."

Terry grinned, pushed his hand into the man's pocket and came out with a full clip. He picked up the M1 and handed it to Jenna. "What am I supposed to do with this?" she asked.

Terry shrugged. "Shoot zombies."

Doug stood leaning into Jenna in the strangely silent morning, Nikki held a deer rifle, Jenna an old fashioned M1 Garand military weapon; fear crawled over his back. Something was wrong here. Something more than the ordinary wrong, you know, where people turn into zombies and the world comes to an end. He felt like this when they went into Allenville to save Herman Munster's life, unsure, unsteady. People died that day. Doug waved a finger toward the Fleming Foods truck.

"We need to clear this thing out of the way. We'll never fit the car between the truck and the Jeep and the shoulders are too steep to drive on." He pushed a flat, dirty Walmart sack stuck to the highway through the pool under the guy with the John Deere cap. "We need to go fast. This blood is still wet."

"On it, boss," Terry said. "Looks like they set the fire in the trailer. Maybe hoping to scare the things off."

Jenna spat a humorless laugh. "It didn't work."

"The tractor looks fine," Terry said. "If it'll start, I'll move it and see if there's anything else I need to push off the road." He walked around the rear of the smoking trailer and into a horror movie. The shoulder of the highway that sloped down to a ditch was black with crows. The big, fat birds pecked and tore at the meat of the festering zombie corpses strewn across the grass; grizzly bullet wounds decorated their flesh.

"Fuck me," spilled from Terry's mouth. He swung his head around to a sudden movement near the cab of the truck. A zombie stood near the open door holding a leg with a boot on it, a strip of bloody flesh hung from its lips. Terry mounted a shooter's stance, leveled the 9mm on the monster's forehead and gently squeezed the trigger. The pistol jerked slightly and a crack broke the mid day's silence. The zombie's head flew backward and the once-human thing dropped to the pavement.

Crows, thousands of them, flapped into the sky, their beating wings and piercing caws pounded Terry's cries to "run" out of the air. He thought he heard Nikki scream his name, but he couldn't tell. Terry flailed his arms at the murder flapping around him as he forced his way to the driver's door of the Peterbilt. A crow struck the side of his head and almost sent him to the ground. What was once a teenaged girl, her blue Kearney Bearcats T-shirt stained with blood, stepped from around the front of the truck and lurched toward him. *Shit.* He swung the cab door fully open and caught the girl with blond ponytail in the face. It went down in a wet slap. Terry scrambled into the truck and shut the door.

The keys weren't in the ignition.

"FUCK," he screamed.

The apocalypse had come quickly and deadly enough most people forgot their keys were in the ignition, or it just wasn't important anymore. What the shit? He threw open the glove box. Tissues, first aid kit, rubbers, a .38-caliber pistol, beef jerky, everything a trucker needs. He pulled down the sun visor. Nothing. Then dropped his hand to the floor, his fingers ran over an empty potato chip bag, something sticky, thumped into an empty convenience store coffee cup, then grazed a loose pile of metal. It jingled. Keys. Terry pulled himself vertical behind the wheel, fit the key into the ignition and looked at the road ahead. "Oh, no." A wall of zombies, some as decayed as Miss Havisham's cake, some as fresh as a Cinnabon roll, walked toward the truck, the cloud of crows blacking the sky. "Please, God," he whispered. "Please make this thing start." He pushed the clutch to the floor and grabbed the keys, the South Park keychain dangling under his hand. He turned the key. The Peterbilt rumbled to life. Terry knew in a few months most vehicles in the world wouldn't start without coaxing, but now– "Thank you." He shifted into first and slowly released the clutch. The truck ground forward, two zombies dropped beneath it. He grinned as the Prius appeared in the side mirror, Nikki behind the wheel, Doug and his broken foot sat shotgun with the M1. Is that possible? Sitting shotgun with a rifle? And Jenna? He caught a glimpse of red hair flashing between the front bucket seats. They all made it. Terry shifted into second, birds slapped against the windshield like he was in a goddamned Hitchcock movie; he popped it into third. Damn. There are a lot of cars on this road. He caught a zombie on the grill and smashed it onto the rear of a brown Suburban. The monster, flesh starting to rot off its withered purplish face, stared at Terry with white, dead eyes, grinding its teeth and pawing at the hood like it wanted to climb into the cab.

"Fat fucking chance, Fester," Terry said, then laughed. "Whoo-hoo. Catch the Zombie Express." He reached up his left hand and pulled down a cord; the air horn cut a loud path through the day. Although it wasn't daylight anymore, it was twilight under the black cloud of crows. He turned on the headlights just before the Suburban hit a Kearney School District bus that sat sideways in the road, the driver lay slumped in his seat, a yellow spore stain across the windshield, the high school band, in uniform, pawed at the windows; the Peterbilt's headlights shown off their cream-colored eyes, their bloody teeth tore at the glass. The impact jerked Terry in his seat as the Peterbilt peeled vehicles off the road, rolling them both over the shoulder and down the embankment. "Whoo-hoo."

The afternoon sun suddenly broke through the eye of the hurricane of whirling crows, the small town of Elm Creek north of the highway, the grain elevator and white and blue water tower bright in the sudden sunlight. Terry only saw Elm Creek in passing. The highway ahead locked his eyes forward. A score, maybe a hundred once-human creatures, stood on I-80 swaying back and forth waiting for him; a teen in a Burger King uniform stood in front, along with a young mother, her right breast swollen and purple exposed from her nursing bra; she held her infant by one arm. The baby in a Natty Light onesie dangled from its mother's grip, chewing at the air with its toothless mouth as Terry slammed into it. Terry tried to swallow the cotton in his mouth, but his throat was dry as a Nebraska summer. He shifted into fourth gear, the Peterbilt growling as Terry pushed it further into the throng, bodies thumped against the semi's grill like he drove through a cornfield. Wipers spread the blood and gore that splattered the windshield, blue wiper fluid cut it just enough for Terry to see his way.

"Dear Lord in heaven," he whispered. "What am I doing?"

Eleven miles east of Elm Creek, the weak Prius horn blaring as loud as it could, Terry pulled the Peterbilt to a stop on an empty stretch of highway, put his forehead on the steering wheel and cried.

***

The skies over Omaha were blue and free of noise; the white airplane contrails that crisscrossed middle America gone. A United Airbus 320 at Lincoln Airport had been visible from the highway when Nikki drove through the hometown of the Nebraska Cornhuskers; the plane that took passengers on short jumps to Kansas City, Missouri and Chicago would sit there forever. Nobody mentioned it and fifty miles went by, the cab of the car as quiet as its electric engine. Terry sat as if asleep, but his bloodshot eyes were wide open.

"What I wouldn't give to see an airplane fly again," Jenna said, as they approached Omaha under the shadow of an Omaha Storm Chasers billboard.

"We did," Terry said bluntly. "In the Community."

"I mean one that's not trying to kill us, jerk." She winced as the words came out.

"I want to see a train." Doug looked out the window, counting down the mile markers. Omaha was closing in, vestiges of the suburban sprawl popped up in subdivisions and strip malls with Starbucks and Runza Restaurants, stared blankly at the highway. "I remember as a kid in Paola, my dad used to take me up to the railroad tracks just to watch the trains. I loved it. I used to carry around a penny Dad put on the train tracks once. Took us forever to find it."

"Where is it now?" Jenna asked.

A sad grin pulled at Doug's mouth. "Taped onto the glass frame of the first dollar I ever earned back at my muffler and brake shop."

"Sorry to break this memory lane thing up," Nikki said. "But I don't remember where the hospital is. I didn't really pay attention to the roads after the soldiers took us."

"Seriously?" Terry asked, his face drawn and pale since they dumped the truck.

"Seriously. Kind of embarrassed about that," she said. "But right now I need directions."

A big green road sign approached, 126th St – 3/4, 275/92/L St – 2 1/2, Junction 680 – 4. "We've got a ways," Doug said. "I think it's on 42nd." He leaned into the back seat and slapped Terry on the leg. "We all saw what happened back there, man. You saved our lives. Thank you."

Tears formed in Terry's eyes. One broke free and slid down his stubbly cheek. "But that woman had a baby and I could see it gnawing, gnawing on nothing. But it was a baby. Just a—"

Doug squeezed Terry's leg hard. "It was a zombie." *Zombie.* "It wasn't a baby. It wasn't even alive anymore and if given the chance it would have eaten you."

Terry wiped away the tear. "It didn't have any teeth."

A grin crossed Doug's face. "Then things would have gotten ugly."

***

A trio of giraffe walked north on 72nd Street as the Toyota drove overhead. The landscape of the continent would change dramatically if those animals became fruitful and multiplied. Doug doubted the animal rights nut who let all the animals out of the Henry Doorly Zoo was the only person to think of that and as a thank you the bear had eaten him. The thought of the bear hit Doug like a punch in the stomach. He remembered running from the gigantic brown bear and diving at the H3, the 800-pound beast slamming into the door, crushing the bones in his lower leg. Jenna pulled him inside and into the passenger seat. His last memory before passing out from the pain was the great, snarling face filling the window, snot and saliva smearing the glass. He stared quietly as the giraffe bobbed down the road and wondered how many other nuts out there had released zoo animals and how long it would take to fill North America with lions and chimpanzees.

"Sixtieth coming up," Nikki said through a mouthful of the beef jerky Terry had rescued from the Peterbilt.

"Pull over," Doug said.

"What? Now?"

Doug nodded and pointed at a car. "Yes, pull over right there."

Nikki guided the Prius to a stop beside a green Dodge Stratus and put it into Park. Doug looked at the Dodge, no sign of a driver, no sign of passengers. The sun glinted off something in the side mirror; Doug's eyes shot to the mirror, but nothing moved. Jenna rested a hand on his shoulder. "What's the matter?"

Doug took a deep breath. "This is my plan—" he began.

"Mine, too," Nikki interrupted.

"—so nobody has to go with me." Jenna started to protest, but Doug put up a hand. "Please, honey. The idea of doing this scares you and Terry's in no shape to go through with this."

The snap of a beer can opening filled the cab. "I'm better."

"Nikki and I can take that Dodge and you two can just sit here and wait for us."

"Bad idea, boss."

Jenna cupped Doug's stubbly chin in her strong, smooth hand and turned him around to face her. "Doug Titus. You're not going anywhere without me."

"That's right," Terry said. "If one of us does something stupid, we all do something stupid."

Nikki put the car back into Drive and kept going. "Hey," Doug protested.

"Sorry, honey. You're outvoted," Jenna said, leaning into the front seat and kissing his cheek. "But when we get there I might not get out of the car."

***

Nikki stopped the Prius at the corner of 42nd Street and Dewey Avenue, black birds, silent and watchful, lined the electric wires along the crossroads, a swath of the 12-foot-tall chain-link fence the Army built to keep the zombies at bay, lay flattened inward. The hospital grounds were silent, blank windows looked over empty M35 cargo trucks, Humvees with mounted M2 heavy machine guns and the carnage on the asphalt at their wheels. Hundreds of zombies lay torn to shreds under machine gun fire, the bodies of soldiers amongst them ripped into indistinguishable piles of bloody meat.

"I'm not getting out of the car," Jenna whispered.

"I don't blame you." Doug searched for any sign of movement, but there was none. Birds lined the roof of the hospital and the canopy entrance to the emergency room. The machine gun nests at the top of the three-story parking garage were unmanned; crows perched on the .50mm Browning machine guns.

"Looks like there were too many of them," Terry said. "The Army didn't have a chance." He looked into the front seat at Doug. "Still going in?"

Doug nodded. "I have to. Let's go."

Nikki put the Prius in gear and went forward slowly, the wheels thumped over the shredded corpses of the zombies. "I'm going to throw up," Jenna wheezed from the back seat.

"Don't throw up, honey."

"Shut up, Doug. I'm going to throw up."

"We're almost through the worst of it."

The front wheel rolled over a zombie in a brown UPS uniform. "It's coming up."

"Okay," Nikki hollered. "Now." She stepped on the brake and the Prius squeaked to a stop. Jenna threw open the door and emptied the can of cold ravioli she'd eaten in the car near Grand Island, Nebraska, onto the pavement.

Terry patted her back. "You going to be all right?"

Jenna nodded and sat up, wiping her mouth with a Starbucks napkin from the floor. She hit Doug's shoulder. "Thanks for being there to hold my hair."

***

A warm breeze glided across the parking lot as they stood on the pavement outside the front entrance to the hospital; shards of blood stained glass lined the frames of the wide, sliding glass doors blown inward by the horde of hungry dead. They all wore pistol belts peeled off the massacred soldiers, Beretta M9s in the holster, spare clips in the pouches, flashlights clipped to the side. Doug and Nikki both held an M27 infantry rifle, Doug's lashed over his shoulder. Jenna's sat propped against the Prius, the closest a hybrid ever got to seeing some kind of action.

"You sure you're going to be okay?"

Jenna nodded at Doug. He grabbed her and pressed her closely to him. "I love you, you know?"

A tear dropped down her cheek. "I know."

He kissed her deeply, then let her go. "I taste like vomit," she said.

He grinned. "I don't care. I will be back for you."

She grabbed his hand and squeezed tightly. "You bet your ass."

Doug turned and put an arm around Nikki. "Let's get this done before it gets dark."

They walked to the jagged hole in the doors, Doug hobbling on his one good leg. He paused at the door and glanced up at the birds that lined the roof of the parking garage and hospital. "They're still in there."

Terry stole a glance at him. "You scared?"

Doug nodded. "I'd be an idiot not to be. Let's go."

Terry stepped in first, the M27 pressed into his shoulder. He flipped on his flashlight and disappeared. Nikki put an arm around Doug's waist and they too stepped into the darkness.

Jenna picked up the rifle and gripped it tight. She was alone.

CHAPTER 8

Donnie woke slowly, sucking in a line of drool that stretched to his shoulder. "Wake up, sleepyhead." Mother's voice seemed so far away. But she wasn't far away. She was close, just in the next room. "Come on, Donnie honey. You don't want to be late. Mommy's hungry. Mommy needs her breakfast."

"Yes, Mother," he whispered. "I'm coming." Donnie shook his head, trying to work out the cobwebs. Mother? It couldn't be; Mother didn't talk anymore. But she did get hungry. Insatiable, that woman. He forced his eyes open, the morning sun harsh. He sat in Mother's comfy flower print chair in front of the big living room window, where he'd watched the bad people and their silver car all night through Daddy's binoculars. *My binoculars, darn it. My binoculars. Daddy's gone.* The light in the window had long gone dead. Must have run out of fuel. Those bad people must not have seen it or they would have been here, Donnie just knew it.

The living room wall thumped. "Mother?" Yes, she was close by, but she hadn't talked to him; it was just a dream. A dream where Mother still talked and Donnie didn't keep her locked in her bedroom. The wall thumped again, a growl Donnie couldn't understand coming from a human throat, was muffled through the drywall. "I'll go get breakfast."

He lifted the heavy Jason binoculars to his eyes and looked across I-80 toward the quiet country road where the bad people had slept last night, riding in before a wave of black birds and good people. Holy people. This morning something was wrong. The tent the man with both feet put up just last night at dusk was down, the canvas chairs were gone, too, folded and slid into the trunk the man with two feet shut just now. Just right now. Donnie's knuckles grew white as his fingers tried to dig into the unyielding plastic of the binocular barrels. *They're teasing me. They saw the light. They know I'm here and they didn't come down to say 'hi.'* The ginger woman who looked like Vanessa Hagen helped the limping man into the car, but before he sat down, she wrapped her arms around his neck (*and choked the doody out of him*) kissed him. She kissed him right in front of Donnie. *YOU GUNKY. YOU'RE SUPPOSED TO BE FOR ME.* The limping man sat in the car and ginger-haired Vanessa Hagen closed the door behind him. She disappeared into the back seat, her long legs the last things Donnie saw before the back door slammed shut.

He shot up from Mother's flower print chair, Daddy's rifle clattering to the floor, forgotten. *Oh, my God. What's happening? What's happening here?* He dropped the binoculars; the dead weight jerked on the strap he'd looped over his neck. The light was an invitation. They were supposed to come down to the house and be friends with Mother. A smile crossed Donnie's sweaty face. *They're packing because they're coming for a visit. I need to make some tea and set out cookies.* He shook his head. He'd eaten all the Chips Ahoy! in the cabinets. All he had left were those nasty Voortman Chocolate Wafer Cookies Mom liked. He didn't have time to run down to the Family Market. A giggle popped from his mouth; he cupped a hand over his lips to keep Mother from hearing it. She got upset so easily. Donnie couldn't go the Family Market because the checker Connie Benjamin was all chewed up in the back yard. The wafer cookies would have to do.

A reflection of morning sunlight flashed off the window of the sliver car. Donnie looked through the Jason's one more time before he went to fix the tea. Well, he had to do Number 1 out the kitchen door first, but then he'd fix tea and get out the cookies. He just wanted one more look at company coming to pay a visit. The silver car turned onto a side road that went parallel with the highway, then went south on Route 27 toward Julesburg. It was, it was, it was— "NOOO," Donnie screamed. Mother pounded the walls harder. The people in that car were bad. *Bad, bad, BAD.* The silver car turned from Route 27 and onto I-80, taking all of Mother's new friends east, away from town.

The binoculars dropped to his chest again as he brought his right hand to his mouth, his index finger finding its way in like it had ever since he was a little boy. Think, Donnie. *Think, think, think.* Fix this. You have to fix this. Daddy's truck, a 2011 red Chevy Silverado was still in the garage. It hadn't been started since Daddy ran away, but Donnie knew where Daddy kept his keys, on a peg by the door that led from the garage to the kitchen and Daddy showed Donnie how to drive it. He said Donnie was a good driver.

The blows to the wall came harder. A picture of Donnie and his parents at the Garden of the Gods fell and hit an end table, the glass shattered and danced across the short, tight carpet. That was the last trip they had taken as a family, after Donnie had gotten out of the hospital. That would have been his senior year in high school, but he'd missed so much school, too much. People started to change less than a month later. The wall shook. "Shut up Mother," Donnie screamed, then winced. He'd never spoken to Mother like that before. She's going to be angry. Food. Food would make her happy. He had to get food.

Donnie grabbed Daddy's keys off the peg and pulled open the door to the garage, the window he'd used to watch Vanessa Hagen peel down to her panties bathed the Silverado in light. He stopped. The bad people had to come home with him; they had to. *How am I going to make them do that?* The smile returned to his face. He pulled a wooden-handled knife from the cutlery set on the counter that ran from the garage door to the back door, its clean, sharp blade bright and silver in the morning light. He might have to get naughty.

The door slammed behind Donnie as he stepped into the garage, holding the knife in his sweaty hand.

***

The red Silverado stood in the garage like Marty McFly's 1985 Toyota Hilux at the end of "Back to the Future." Not sideways in the garage; that was just stupid, but its presence commanded all the space in the garage like the Hilux, although the garage was made for two vehicles. Mother's Camry was down at Stone Motors because of the stupid Check Engine light. It had been there for two months. Donnie wondered when they'd get finished with it.

He walked to the big rolling door and grabbed the handle. It slid up with a squeal, dust danced in the sunlight. *Need to get some WD-40 on that before Daddy comes home.* The smell of flowers drifted on the breeze and Donnie breathed in deeply. He hadn't been outside the house much lately; well, except for the back yard. But the back yard didn't smell like fresh air and flowers. For some reason, it smelled like blood. Donnie gripped Daddy's keys tightly enough to hurt the palm of his right hand and slowly approached the truck. "Sorry, Daddy," he whispered as he walked up to his father's truck, the one Daddy used to haul him and Mother and all the camping equipment over to McConaughy Lake to fish in the summer. Donnie loved the family fishing trip to McConaughy Lake, but after the year Donnie met that Taylor boy, the trips just stopped.

The driver's door looked as big and heavy as the gateway to Mordor. Donnie reached toward the handle and flinched. "Don't touch my fucking truck." The baseball only bounced off the sidewall, just that one time, but oh, how Daddy had beaten him. *Daddy's not here.* Donnie looked around; he was alone in the garage. He thought he might be alone in the town (except for drunk old Mr. Miller) and Mother. Donnie smiled as another picture fell in the living room. *She misses me.*

"I'll be right home, Mother," he said softly. "With a present for you."

Donnie slipped inside the Chevrolet; the engine came to life on the first turn of the key. *Daddy always kept such good care of his truck.*

Donnie sat the knife on the passenger seat, pulled Daddy's binoculars *Mine, darn it, mine,* over his head and sat them beside the knife, then backed the Silverado into the street. He drove through his neighborhood with the shamefully unkempt yards toward Interstate 80.

***

Donnie was mad at Daddy's truck. It made him think of the Taylor boy at McConaughy Lake and that was bad. The Taylor boy was wicked. Donnie was 14 when Daddy and Mother took him to the lake for the last time. "Let's go into town for pizza," Daddy had said on their third night camping and they set off in the red truck under the wide, blue July sky that was just starting to hint at darkness. Going out for pizza on The Annual Barnett Family Camping Extravaganza was fine with Donnie; Daddy's campfire hamburgers were always black and crunchy.

The upright Ms. Pac-Man video game in the back room of Jimmy's Old Country Pizzeria wasn't retro, it wasn't a reproduction, it was just old, like the rest of the pizza place. Donnie stood in front of the box, two quarters in his pocket, looking at Ms. Pac-Man chase ghosts across the dingy screen. Drink stains and cigarette burns decorated the console. Mother and Daddy sat inside at one of the dozen red-and-white checkerboard tables waiting for their Big Jimmy, a 16-inch deep-dish pie topped with pepperoni, knackwurst, Italian sausage, pork sausage, bratwurst and three other sausages Donnie hadn't heard of. He got tired of waiting and wandered toward the back of the restaurant where he found the arcade; Jimmy was taking too long.

Ancient Galaga, Asteroids and Defender games lined a wall, but it was Ms. Pac-Man that drew him in. It was colorful with happy music. Donnie moved the joystick for a few minutes, pretending he was playing the game before he realized he wasn't alone.

A kid stood by the door that read "Exit." Donnie was sure he hadn't been there when he'd walked in, but sometimes things happened Donnie didn't remember. Kid. The boy wasn't really a kid. Donnie was fingering the quarters in his pocket when he noticed the boy, maybe sixteen, leaning against a Galaga machine, the Plexiglas screen over the game monitor spray-painted with a peace sign. He was tall with a faded Pearl Jam T-shirt hanging loosely off his lanky frame. The kid nodded at Donnie, the smile beneath his wisp of a mustache bent.

"Hey," the boy said.

Donnie just looked at him. He didn't like strangers. Oh, no. Especially not strangers alone. Mother said strangers shouldn't talk to a boy his age, especially when they were alone. Those strangers were wicked.

"What's your name?" the skinny boy asked, his voice smooth and low.

Donnie didn't answer. He didn't move. Ms. Pac-Man's "wagga-wagga" seemed forever away, his parents in the dining area forgotten.

"I'm Kurt," the boy said, then his eyes sprang wide. "You're not from here, are ya?"

Donnie pinched the quarters between his fingers, the metal dug into his skin. *Stranger Danger. Stranger Danger.* He started to turn away from this wicked Strangerboy, back toward the restaurant to wait for the slow, slow, slow Big Jimmy, but the Strangerboy's grin grew wider.

"Wanna see a dead rat?"

Dead? Rat? Donnie had seen dead things. Mice in Daddy's snappy-snap traps, a cat he found behind a bush in the back yard, Aunt Denise in the box at the place where everybody cried. Donnie always expected these dead things to get up and move, but they never did. All except the cat that's belly squirmed when Donnie poked it with a stick. That's where the rat that had been hiding, eating it from the inside. It squirmed out the hole it had made in the cat and disappeared into the bushes. Donnie always wondered what that rat would look like dead.

Donnie nodded. "Yeah."

The boy winked at him and pushed open the door under the Exit sign. "Cool," he said. "Let's go."

The old wooden door moved silently on its hinges revealing the exit, a dented metal slab with a thin vertical glass crisscrossed with wires and darkened by night. A dim wooden stairwell, its steps worn, led upward. The Strangerboy went up two steps and turned. Donnie stood, staring at him.

"You comin'?" Strangerboy asked.

Why's there a rat upstairs? Every movie he'd ever seen with rats, the sneaky, gnawing vermin had always been in the basement, the drippy, moldy basement. "Are you sure there's a dead rat up there?" Donnie asked, his voice high, wavering.

The Strangerboy winked again. Donnie didn't think he liked that wink. "You bet. It's swollen and everything."

Swollen? Like the cat? The Strangerboy went up the steps slowly; Donnie knew Mother would be mad at him, would scold him for being a silly boy, but he followed anyway.

The fluorescent light at the top of the stairs flickered slightly as the Strangerboy topped the stairs and stood on the landing in front of a door to somewhere. He stopped and looked back at Donnie, his smile now almost painful. There was something silly about the way the boy smiled. Donnie took the last few steps slowly, watching the older boy like he might change into some kind of monster.

The Strangerboy seemed tense, nervous. The landing was empty. No people, no pizza, no dead rat. Donnie stepped toward the door.

"Where is it?" Donnie said, pulling his hands from his pockets and reaching toward the knob. "Is it in here?"

The Strangerboy stepped closer. *Too close. Too close.*

He slapped a rough hand on Donnie's shoulder and shoved down, his tall frame stronger than it looked. Donnie collapsed to his knees. He tried to stand, but the Strangerboy loomed over him, casting a menacing shadow in the fluttering glow.

"It's right here, kid," the older teen said, unzipping his pants with his other hand.

What? Donnie stopped struggling, his mind unsure what to do. Strangerboy fumbled inside his pants and slowly pulled out his stiff circumcised penis, bigger than Donnie's and bigger than Daddy's, the only two he'd ever seen. A sudden revulsion rushed through him, but it disappeared quickly, replaced by something. What? Curiosity? Anger? Yes, anger. *He lied to me.* And Mother always told Donnie lying was wrong.

"You're bad," Donnie said, his voice soft. "You don't have a dead rat. You're a liar."

This made the Strangerboy's wicked smile fade. "Don't call me that," he said, his voice no longer smooth, no longer friendly. It was hard. He moved his erect penis inches from Donnie's face. "You knew there wasn't a rat. You knew what I wanted you to do, didn't you? So, go ahead. Put it in your mouth." The Strangerboy's grin returned. "You know you wanna."

Wanna? Thoughts of Mother popped into his head. Mother who sat at the table in the restaurant below and waited with Daddy for the Big Jimmy to finally reach the table. Mother who didn't like Donnie to walk around the house naked. Mother who hated words like "wanna." Donnie suddenly felt sick, like he didn't want the pizza with all that sausage. *Wrong. This is wrong. This is wrong. This is wrong.* He looked up at Strangerboy, past the thing the boy was now pressing toward his lips and saw the smile. The bent smile.

You're wicked.

"Open up. I know you wanna."

Donnie threw his hands out and struck the skinny teen's hips with the heel of his palms. The Strangerboy bent at the impact, a whoosh pushed past his lips. *Doodyhead.* Donnie reached out again, this time grabbing the teen's ankles and pulling the tall boy's weight out from under him. The

Strangerboy flew backward. His head hit the steps first, the thunk loud in the stairwell. The rest of his body followed like a big, meaty Slinky. Oh, what a wonderful toy.

Donnie knelt at the top of the steps, his breath coming in shallow draws. The Strangerboy was bad, he was wicked, he would burn in hell, Mother would say if Mother knew. But Mother could never know of this. Oh, no. He stood and started down the stairs, a hand on the metal railing, the paint flaked with age. The boy lay in a lump at the bottom. He didn't move; his head tilted at an angle that didn't seem right. *He's going to hurt in the morning,* Donnie thought as he stepped over the boy and opened the door to the back room. A kid of about six was playing Ms. Pac-Man.

Donnie stuck his hand in his pocket, pulled out the two quarters, sat them on the console and walked into the restaurant.

"Where have you been?" Mother asked as Donnie approached the table and pulled out his seat. The Big Jimmy sat on the table with one slice out.

Daddy shrugged. "I was hungry, kiddo," he said. "I couldn't wait forever."

The chair squealed against the concrete floor when Donnie scooted it under the table. Daddy had already grabbed another slice, but Mother's plate was still empty, her eyes on him.

"Are you all right, son?" she asked, her elbows on the table, fingers laced before her in a fist.

Donnie didn't look up. Mother's eyes were magic, he knew. They made him tell her things, things Donnie never wanted to tell her. "Yes, Mother. I just lost at Pac-Man and I'm hungry."

"Are you sure that's all, honey?"

But he wasn't going to answer Mother. He slid a piece of Big Jimmy onto his plate and picked it up. *Put it in your mouth,* the Strangerboy's voice echoed in his head. *You know you wanna.* Donnie smiled and took a bite as the little boy at the Ms. Pac-Man machine began to scream.

***

Donnie had never driven on the highway. Daddy taught him to drive on country roads and had once even let him drive on C-138 to Ovid to buy beef at D & L Meat Co. "Best cuts of steak this side of Denver," Daddy told him, as Donnie got the Silverado up to 55 mph. "Yessiree. Don't go anywhere else." He looked at Donnie and mussed his brown hair. "Then we'll stop off at the Gridiron for a quick beer. If you promise not to tell Mom, I'll buy you a Pepsi." Donnie had promised. He hated keeping secrets from Mother, but a Pepsi's a Pepsi and Mom didn't allow that awful sugary syrup into their house. Driving to Ovid and back to Julesburg meant Daddy thought Donnie was grown up, but not just grown up. After he'd spent two years locked inside Sisters of St. Francis Hospital learning why it was wrong to push that bad Taylor boy down the stairwell, Donnie was grown up and safe. Donnie couldn't remember the time he'd been so happy, until the day Daddy got hungry and went away forever.

He pushed the Silverado up to 60 mph on I-80. He knew the bad people in the silver car were going that fast or more and he had to catch them. Wherever they went, Donnie would follow; they had to stop sometime, he would get them and bring them home to Mother. A grin tugged at the corners of his mouth. At least the Vanessa Hagen-looking girl, but Donnie wanted to play with her first.

It was a long way to Omaha. Mother and Daddy took him on vacation there once, to the Henry Doorly Zoo and a baseball game. Donnie didn't remember much, except the drive was long. Long, long, long. He pushed the accelerator a little harder, the Silverado moved to 65 mph. There were vehicles on the road, but not many and they weren't moving. Occasionally he'd see a good person in the cab of one, pawing at the window. Donnie would smile and wave back, but he didn't slow down; he couldn't slow down. Mother was hungry.

Outside Elm Creek, Nebraska, Donnie forgot about Mother. Bloody, mangled bodies of good people lay strewn across the highway, a red smear that stretched a quarter mile marked with the fat tracks of a big truck and the skinny tracks of something small. *The silver car.* Tears ran from his eyes as he slowed the truck to a crawl, those poor, poor people, torn apart by those gunkies in the silver car. He didn't know who drove the truck, but he suspected it was someone from the silver car – *the man with two legs. It had to be* – but he would take care of all of them, all of them. Donnie wiped the dripping snot away with the sleeve of his shirt and mashed at his tears with the palm of his right hand, the left one guiding the pickup through the gore. Large, fat crows looked up at the Silverado as it rumbled by, but only until they understood it wasn't a threat, then they returned to pecking and tearing meat from the rotting corpses. Eleven miles later Donnie found the smoldering Fleming Foods truck and he smiled. They were all back in one car; they'd be much easier to catch.

***

The nurses at Sisters of St. Francis were mean, what Daddy would call "total bitches" if Mother weren't around, which wasn't often. It seemed like Mother was always around, watching, listening and she didn't like Daddy to say bad words.

"Would you like to tell us why you're here, Mr. Barnett," Nurse Karen said like Donnie was an idiot. *Which I'm so not.*

Donnie sat on a white plastic chair placed in a circle with six other teenagers in the same hospital-issue pajamas and slippers. No belts or shoestrings here at St. Francis. Nope, nope, nope. "No," he said, staring at his feet. They seemed small and far away.

"Now, Mr. Barnett." Nurse Karen turned to face him. Nick Cordray, the boy who liked to burn things, made faces behind her back. "You're here to get better. You can't get better unless we talk about what happened." She motioned around the circle. "You have nothing to be afraid of. We're all friends here."

"No we're not," Kelli Patterson, the bleeder said. Kelli sat slumped in her chair, arms scarred with even horizontal lines were crossed over her chest.

Nurse Karen frowned and made a mark on the clipboard she carried everywhere, then looked back at Donnie and smiled. Her smile was even and white, not bent and seedy like that wicked Strangerboy. Marc Taylor. He found that was the Strangerboy's name when the police in a clean black and white car with flashing blue and red lights pulled up to Jimmy's Old Country Pizzeria and took Donnie away.

"Now, Mr. Barnett, why are you here?"

Donnie's eyes went around the room. Nick, Kelli, Tommy Caruthers who got his sister pregnant and Rachel Abbott who got excited in group therapy when she talked about what she liked to do with cats. They all looked at something else, the floor, the ceiling, the barred windows, anything but Donnie. Nurse Karen cleared her throat.

"I didn't do anything wrong," Donnie said. "That wicked Taylor boy tried to stick his—" *Don't say it. Don't say it. Don't say it. Mother will be mad.*

"His what, Mr. Barnett?"

Donnie shifted on the hard plastic seat and looked flatly at Nurse Karen. *Put it in your mouth. You know you wanna.* "He tried to stick his wiener in my mouth." Kelli barked a laugh. Donnie ignored her. "I pushed him away and he fell down the stairs, boom, boom, boom."

The room grew quiet.

"You do know he died, don't you?" Nurse Karen asked.

Yep. Dead. Dead as a cat with a rat. "Yes."

"How does that make you feel?"

Feel? Donnie sat back in the chair and looked at the ceiling. He'd never thought about how it made him feel. How did he feel? "Happy," he said. "He was a wicked boy and I made him not wicked anymore."

Rachel started to clap. Donnie's pills were a different color after that.

***

Something moved in the distance. It wasn't one of the good people, or one of the bad people, it was a vehicle, gliding smoothly from lane to lane to avoid a Casey's General Store tractor-trailer stopped dead on the north side of the highway. Donnie smiled. It was the bad people in the silver car; it had to be. He pushed the Silverado up to 70, the feel of the truck nearly out of control, like riding a bike down a steep hill. He took his foot off the accelerator and the truck slowed back to 55. He didn't want them to see him; he wanted to surprise them and he didn't want to crash. Surprise them. Yes. Maybe get one of them alone, especially the Vanessa Hagen woman. Get them alone and tie them up for the trip back to Mother, or use the kitchen knife if they didn't want to go. The crotch of Donnie's pants grew tight as he thought of sneaking up on the man with one foot, maybe while he sat in front of the camp stove. He'd plunge the big kitchen knife into his neck and paint the night with blood. Then the Vanessa Hagen woman, with her curly red hair, would want to come with Donnie because Donnie could walk. A wave of warmth rushed over him and he pushed his erect penis to the left side as he kept driving. *Yes, that's exactly what would happen.*

He eased the truck back to 65 when the movement ahead of him on I-80 disappeared. Donnie didn't want to spook the Bad people, but he couldn't lose them. As the city of Omaha grew thick with buildings, the silver car, he was certain of that now, pulled off the highway. Donnie slowed the truck to a crawl and watched the car full of bad people drive north on 42nd Street. The sign said so. They were going somewhere. Somewhere special. Donnie knew that; why else would they have turned off the highway. Was it someone's house? Was it someplace with ice cream? He hoped for ice cream. He hadn't eaten ice cream since the stupid electric company stopped giving his house electricity; his Neapolitan melted into a chocolate, vanilla, strawberry mix of goo. He'd had to eat the last of it like ice cream soup. Donnie drove a little faster, turned onto 42nd Street and followed the bad people into the tree-lined streets of Omaha.

The silver car stopped at a hospital. Donnie hated hospitals, but this wasn't Sisters of St. Francis. Could it be worse? He stopped the Silverado behind a blue Dodge Caravan and watched the bad people through

Daddy's binoculars. The silver car sat in front of a broken gate lined with Army trucks; Army men and good people lay strewn across the pavement. *What is this awful place?* Donnie winced as the silver car drove through the ruined gate and over the corpses of the good people. He choked back a scream. Monsters. Those bad people are monsters. Crows lined the dead electric wires that ran to the hospital and sat on the emergency room awning, just watching. The car stopped and the Vanessa Hagen woman leaned out the back passenger door and vomited. Yes. Donnie knew she wasn't like the others. He just knew it. She was a good person, well, a good enough person. He was going to enjoy taking her.

The man with both legs, the man with one leg and the black-haired girl picked up Army rifles and walked toward the smashed front door of the hospital, leaving the Vanessa Hagen woman alone. Alone with the crows. Donnie smiled and put down the binoculars. The knife sat quietly in the passenger seat. Donnie didn't know why, but he kind of expected it to talk to him. He wrapped his fingers around the wooden handle and picked it up. It felt good there, natural. The driver's door of the Silverado opened with a click and Donnie stepped onto the pavement. The Vanessa Hagen woman was going to be his, today.

JULY 29: KANSAS CITY, MISSOURI

CHAPTER 9

Hand-painted signs reading "Survival Shelter" pointed Andi off Interstate 435 toward the Parvin Road exit and to 48th Street. She didn't take the exit. There was a survival shelter there; that was part of Cotton's first briefing. "There's a safe zone set up at an amusement park in Kansas City, Missouri. The high security fence and large area of the park make it easy to defend and it can hold many thousands of people," he'd barked, all the fresh-faced recruits' muscles frozen at attention. "A message directing survivors to the shelter is being broadcast on all Kansas City radio stations. If you find any survivors on your patrol, direct them there." Andi started looking for the radio broadcast the moment she pulled out of the Walmart parking lot and found only static. Something had gone wrong. She'd only been in the Army two months, but she'd learned a few things in those two months. One of those was surveillance. She kept driving.

Worlds of Fun sat north of the Missouri River amongst the bluffs. Andi drove with the window down, the wind clear of pollution; she smiled as she sniffed the air. It smelled sweet. Giant steel-framed roller coasters broke the horizon and pointed toward the sky as Andi crossed the river, the Mamba and the Patriot roller coasters dead and quiet. A herd of about twelve whitetail deer, just like the one Big Andy taught her to hunt, stood at the shoulder of Interstate 435, grazing on the tall grass. Andi slowed the Outback and crawled by them; they didn't move. *We got rid of the wolves and the mountain lions and the bears. Deer may one day rule the plains.* "You're too trusting, Bambi," Andi said. The words came out softly. "It may be your time next."

She crept past the sleek, beautiful animals and accelerated again. Yep, Big Andy trained her how to take these beasts down, how to gut them, how to skin them and how to butcher them. She didn't need the deer yet, she had food for weeks, but when she got hungry, she knew she wouldn't starve.

A few miles down the road, Andi eased the Subaru to a stop between a massive green, yellow, blue and red water tower and the amusement park. From the quiet highway Andi could see the entire park, from the Scandinavia section to Americana to the Orient and the parking lots, mostly empty but one jammed with cars. She opened the door of the Outback and climbed onto the car, sitting crisscross applesauce on the hood, looking through Army-issued binoculars for any movement.

Nothing stirred inside the park, except the slight breeze that caused a ripple in the trees that covered the bluff. *Where are the survivors?* She swung the binoculars to the parking lot. Nothi– Wait. Something moved behind a Thor Motor Coach. Or did it? Andi waited, but the motion didn't reappear. *A dog? A deer?* A monster. A thing that was once a man lurched around the front of the RV and stopped, apparently perplexed by a pickup parked sideways in front of the Motor Coach. One monster, one lone monster had appeared in her sweep of the park. There had to be bodies somewhere, alive, dead, or dead and still walking around, but Andi couldn't find them from the highway.

The binoculars froze on a piece of paper attached to the park's fence, but she couldn't make it out. *Dang it.* This was a survival shelter. There might not be any survivors, but a survivor left a note and if somebody thought that note was important enough to write in a world infested with death, Andi was sure as heck going to read it. Polo Man never got to write a note. She slipped back into the Subaru, turned the car around and took the Parvin Road exit toward the park.

***

Dust covered the windshields of the vehicles parked in the lots. *They've been here a while.* Andi could make out an occasional body slumped in a seat as she moved through the maze of cars, SUVs and motor homes on her way to the front gate; the monster she'd spotted from the highway wandered on the opposite side of the lot. Nothing moved in the vehicles; the interiors of many windows were blasted with yellow spores. *Oh, these poor people.* They died in a bloody mess as a fist of fungus burst from their chests. Andi turned her hips to squeeze between a green Ford Explorer and a yellow Chevy Camaro. If there's anything Andi noticed at the end of the world, it's that people stopped giving a shit about the rules, like parking within the marked lines and thou shall not kill. "Shoot them in the head." *Damn it, Cotton.* The driver of the Camaro's head hung back over the seat, its drying flesh pulled from its face. Andi turned away from the corpse in the bitchin' Camaro and walked on.

Vehicles pointed toward the front gate forming a wedge so tight Andi climbed onto the trunk of a car and walked the rest of the way across hoods, her new tennis shoes squeaked softly as she jumped hood to trunk, hood to trunk. The lone monster Andi had spotted from the highway growled to her left. It had found a way to come closer, but the shambling, white-eyed thing was behind too many cars for Andi to worry about it. Just in case, she'd put a full clip in her sidearm before she stepped out of the Subaru; Andi was taking no chances. She jumped off the hood of a

Ford Taurus and landed with a slap on the cracked, gray asphalt about ten feet from the front gate.

Oh, no. The paper lashed to the fence with zip ties wasn't a note, it was a laminated map, the mark of a black Sharpie circled Omaha, with a line tracing I-435 to I-29, "Shelter Here!!!" written in a woman's handwriting. *What now?* The Army had told her this was a secure shelter, a place where people could get food and medicine and hope behind a 235-acre perimeter of chain-link fence. Cotton didn't say anything about a shelter in Nebraska, but plans must have changed. What now, right? Andi knew what now. She knew her day wasn't getting any better.

Andi raised her face to the sky and shouted, "Hello. Is anybody here?" The words loud in the quiet afternoon. "Is this still a shelter?" The monster's growl grew louder. "My name is Andi and I'm here to join you. Somebody please talk to me." Nothing stirred. Whoever had been here had abandoned this place, this place with the secure fences. *What happened?* "Dang it," she whispered.

Omaha was just north of Kansas City, two hours tops. Andi mounted the Taurus and sat on the roof, the drooling human creature now only twenty feet away stuck between a Ford F-150 and a PT Cruiser. She could pick that thing off with her sidearm easily, but she fished a warm Bud Light from a belt pouch instead. The crack of the can sprayed the 'Merica T-shirt with foam. Andi didn't know the time, but she was pretty sure it was still morning. She never drank much alcohol, even at college, but what the heck? It didn't matter anymore. "What are you?" she called to the monster, the thing's rotting face angry, or maybe just hungry. *Hungry for what? What purpose? These things are dead. Why do they need to eat?*

What information she didn't get from news reports before the world got wonky, Andi got from the Army. It all started with the Southeast Asian fungus Ophiocordyceps unilateralis and ended with people. The ants, the fungus. Infection travelled. What about you?

"Where are you going?" she shouted at the thing that had once been a thirty-something semi-professional. Andi could tell that by the coal black hair, khaki Dockers and blue Oxford shirt; the thing's red tie hung like a tongue, wagging as it shuffled between cars. A black glasses case jutted slightly above his breast pocket, although the creature's glasses were long gone. *Did that affect his vision?* Andi wondered, but she didn't know how they saw through the milky film that covered the eyes of the old ones anyway and this thing must have turned early during the outbreak, popping Ophiocordon for depression, or the massive orgasmic boner it gave him. Handy side effect. It shambled when it walked and the white of its cheekbones showed through the rotting flesh of its face. The monster snarled, those white eyes staring straight at Andi. Earlier victims are fast,

with clear eyes. *Maybe you can only stay dead-alive so long before the ol'
body goes to pot.* This thing's body might break down before it gets where
it's going.

Is the fungus telling it to go somewhere? "Come on," she called.
"Where are you going?" It wedged itself tight between the Explorer and
Camaro Andi had shimmied through, reaching toward her even though
she was cars away. Then it did something Andi didn't know was possible;
it screamed at her. Andi stood and dropped the half-full can of beer.
"Well, I know where I'm headed," she said, her voice dropping to no
more than a whisper. "I guess I'm going to Nebraska."

The hood of a red Hyundai crunched as Andi stepped onto it on her
way back to the Subaru, leaving the once-human businessman wedged
between the two cars forever.

***

Two hours later, a homemade sign, a 4x5 sheet of plywood staked
into the shoulder at the end of a bridge that spanned the Missouri River
and brought Andi into Omaha, read "Survival Shelter Ahead." Another
sign followed and another and another. A large red, spray painted arrow
directed Andi up an exit ramp to Thirteenth Street, a billboard advertising
the Henry Doorly Zoo rose from the off ramp. "Well, folks, I'm here," she
said, pulling off the interstate and onto the Thirteenth Street exit that
curved up to an overpass. Another sign directed her south. A dark, empty
McDonald's, the marquee advertising "McRib Limited Time," sat across
the street to the north. What she wouldn't give for a McRib, or even a
greasy McDouble about now. *If McDonald's has stopped making greasy
things between white buns, the world really has come to an end.*

Andi turned away from the golden arches and followed the arrows
south across the overpass, the four-lane highway stretched quietly to the
horizon, a few cars and two semis sat still. Trees and long berms of tall
grass lined Thirteenth Street as she approached the zoo, a great dome
peeked over the trees. Something was off here. A prickle of worry danced
at the back of Andi's newly-blackened head, her hair cut short with
Walmart scissors in the mirror of the Subaru and dyed in the water of a
creek somewhere north of Fort Scott. There was no good place to sit and
study the area she was being drawn to, she didn't like that. Anything
could be waiting for her at the end of the hastily made road markers.
Anything.

Four blocks later she eased the Subaru to a stop. "What the heck?"

The door release clicked as Andi pulled on it and stepped out of the
car, one foot still on the floorboard, her right hand on the steering wheel.

That's as far as she was going out of this small mobile sanctuary. A great bloody lump lay in the road over a great, rust-red stain, not ten feet from a black H3 and an old red F-150, just across the street from a green-roofed fast food joint named King Kong, a big black gorilla on the sign screaming at a hamburger. "What happened here?" Andi's brain suddenly registered what her eyes were seeing. A bear – *a freaking bear* – lay dead in the street. It was mostly hide and bones, nature and the great brown beast's animal friends picked it clean, but Andi knew what killed it. She didn't need the hundreds of shell casings scattered across the road to tell her it had been torn apart by automatic gunfire. The thing had been ripped to shreds. Andi didn't wonder why a brown bear, maybe a grizzly, lay dead on the streets of Omaha, Nebraska. She knew. Some moron let it out of the zoo; and if some moron let out a bear, what else roamed the streets? Lions? Tigers? Gorillas? It would be just her luck to survive the zombie apocalypse and wind up in the damned Planet of the Apes. Andi slowly sank back into the car, shut the door and rolled up the window.

A makeshift military tent city stood in a parking lot of the zoo, surrounded by hundreds of cars from neighboring states. An RV and a group of Humvees sat on the far side of Tent City. Nothing moved here; it was as dead as Worlds of Fun. "Some survival shelter, guys." A hollow feeling crept over her, as hollow as the pit that opened when Polo Man dropped off the Fence. What if there were no survivors anymore, anywhere? She hadn't seen anyone since Muskogee. Andi pulled the car to a stop and stepped out, gripping her rifle tightly.

"Is anybody here?" she called toward Tent City. Only the sound of the breeze came back to her. "Hello?" The population of Omaha was once close to half a million people. Now it might just be Andi Bakowski. She stepped away from the still-running Subaru and ventured into the smattering of olive drab tents.

The pungent smell of death struck Andi like a punch in the face. The breeze that had smelled so sweet earlier in the day had blown the smell of death away from her as she approached the shelter. *Great shelter, guys.* Now that she walked amongst the tents, the smell threatened to bring up her stomach. Bodies in black bags lay stacked like boxes in a buy-in-bulk store. She wanted to cover her face with her arm and breathe in the deodorant she'd taken from a Walmart shelf, but Andi kept her weapon at her shoulder and walked on toward the Humvees. She wouldn't let her guard down; she couldn't.

A yellow piece of paper lay on the pavement; it stopped her cold. She knelt beside it. "Attention," the laser-printed message read in big bold letters. "In the event of a biological attack or the introduction of a highly contagious disease affecting the public, the U.S. health system may take measures to prevent those people infected with or exposed to a disease or a disease-causing agent from infecting others. The federal government has jurisdiction over interstate and foreign quarantine and may use the military in enforcing quarantines."

So, the military stepped in to put a stop to all this. Just like the Fence she patrolled in Oklahoma. From the looks of it, it didn't work out well here. For the first time Andi wondered how her unit was doing. Guthrie was kind of a jerk, but she liked the guy. Guthrie was dead for all she knew. They all probably were, even Cotton. A pull of guilt yanked at her, but she shrugged it off. No regrets at the end of the world. Andi moved toward the ring of Humvees, her heart hammering, and stepped into a thing of nightmares.

A sea of civilian skeletons covered the asphalt; their clothes ripped as scavengers had slashed and clawed their way to the soft meat beyond. More shell casings littered the ground. Her knees gave way and dropped her to the ground; vomit splattered on the dusty pavement. *These people were murdered.* Murdered by someone like her. Andi's stomach clenched and more MRE and Bud Light vomit danced across the pavement. *What if I'd been assigned here? What if I'd gotten the order?* But Andi knew what she'd do; she'd follow her superior's commands, just like when she killed Polo Man. Tears welled in her eyes; the sound of the poor man's final screams tore at her mind.

The caw from a crow came loud in the stillness of the late afternoon. Andi wiped the vomit from her mouth with the back of her hand and pulled herself up on the side of a Humvee. The crow sat on the roof of a vehicle, staring at her with dead black eyes. Andi had never thought of crows outside old cartoons, but now crows were things that came in great black clouds. They scared the heck out of her. It cocked its head and cawed again. Andi gave the black bird the finger, walked weak-legged back to the Subaru and collapsed in the front seat. "I gotta find someplace," she said, lightly slapping the steering wheel with a hand, eyes never leaving the crow. "Someplace quiet." She grabbed the steering wheel with both hands and looked out over Tent City with its body bags and its murder field. The crow stared back at her. Yeah, that quiet place wasn't Omaha.

***

Andi turned west onto Interstate 80 because turning east would take her over the Missouri River; she'd driven across the Missouri River twice today and it didn't do her any favors. She stopped the Subaru in the middle of the highway three miles from the massacre, her shaking knees made it hard to press on the brake. She turned the screwdriver in the ignition and the engine slid into silence. Andi just stared into the bright, blue day, the sun leaning toward the western horizon. It would get hot in the Subaru if Andi sat there long, the hot days of summer still ran like normal. At least something was still normal. She pulled a water bottle from the back seat and cracked the seal. The world had come to an end. It was over. Everything. Everything she grew up knowing to be true was just gone. She understood that, she just didn't know if she could deal with it anymore. Not after what she'd seen. She opened a bag of Nacho Cheese Bugles, closing her eyes and deeply inhaling the smell of the processed yellow corn meal and ingredients she didn't want to know about. The shelf life timer on Bugles was ticking, just like everything else. In a year, most packaged foods would be expired, in five, everything would be.

"Oh, shit."

Something moved. Andi's eyes shot toward it, the crunch of a mouthful of Bugles filled her ears. An animal jumped on the hood of a Buick Encore sitting probably forever in the passing lane. The animal crouched and sniffed the air. Andi stared at it. It was a monkey. A monkey in Omaha, Nebraska. Who would have imagined a monkey in Omaha, Nebraska? *A crazy person. This is all in your head.* "Shut up," Andi whispered. The monkey leapt from the Encore onto the pavement and disappeared over the shoulder of the highway. The world wasn't getting saner anytime soon.

I'm going to Colorado, ran through her head. She didn't know where that thought came from. She'd never been to Colorado, but she liked the idea. *I'm going to find a cabin in the mountains away from the monsters, away from the survivors, away from everything. A cabin close to a liquor store.* A vision flashed through her head, a vision where she spent the next sixty years living off nature and taking naps – a lot. Andi started to turn the screwdriver in the ignition but another motion on the highway stopped her hand. It wasn't a monkey. The glint of the sun off a windshield flashed in the afternoon. Andi sat and waited as a silver Toyota swung off Interstate 80 East, onto 42nd Street and turned north. Nobody in the car seemed to notice her; they all stared straight ahead, but she saw four people in the car. *Oh, my. People. Real live people. I'm not alone.*

She almost turned the screwdriver again, but as the Toyota drove out of sight on 42nd Street, another vehicle appeared on I-80 East, a red Chevrolet pickup. *Seriously?* Andi hadn't seen a moving vehicle, or a person in the 449 miles from Muskogee, Oklahoma, to Omaha. These two had to be connected. Then why were they driving so far apart? Andi twisted the screwdriver and the car came to life. She whipped a wide U-turn and drove to the 42nd Street exit.

Andi found the red Chevy easily enough. The driver sat in the cab, parked behind a blue Dodge Caravan. A hospital surrounded by a tall chain-link fence was just beyond the truck; at about the distance the people in the Toyota probably wouldn't notice the Chevy following them, if the hospital was their destination. Andi let the Subaru slowly coast to a stop on the roadside about fifty yards behind the Chevy and turned off the engine. *What's happening?* The driver never noticed the Subaru because he was focused on the hospital. Andi pulled the binoculars to her face; the driver looked at the hospital through a pair of binoculars of his own. *What?* The man in the Chevy wasn't with them, he was following them. *Sneaky, sneaky Mr. Peeky.*

The driver's door to the Chevy crept open and he stepped out; Andi slumped low in her seat, but that wasn't necessary. *I could be tap dancing and he wouldn't notice me.* The driver was just a kid, about eighteen, just four years younger than Andi, but it seemed like twenty. He was dressed in khaki slacks, a white shirt and blue tie. *What is this? Nineteen Eighty-five?* He walked slowly, trying to be stealthy like something he saw on television. Andi didn't see a weapon on the boy, but she wasn't taking any chances. The Subaru door opened with a click too faint for Mr. Peeky to hear and Andi slid out, her weapon slung across her shoulder and the sidearm in her hand. She quietly shut the door and followed Mr. Peeky.

The stench of blood tickled Andi's nose as she approached the hospital fence, a section lay inward. It had been pushed down. Bodies of monsters and soldiers – *like me* – littered the hospital parking lot, the pavement a sticky black pool. The boy walked through the mess like he didn't notice the mangled bodies that lay at his feet, or the congealed blood sucking at the soles of his shoes. *This isn't right.* He was headed for the Toyota and a thin red haired woman who stood at the door to the silver car, a rifle lay on the hood of the car. She didn't see him; her eyes were on the hospital. *Where's everybody else?* Dang it. Andi knew where they were. In the hospital, the main entrance to the Nebraska Medical Center a black, jagged hole. *Oh, no.* A murder of crows, their inky black wings glistening in the sunlight, covered the roof of the hospital and parking garage. Andi hoped that wasn't a bad omen.

The abandoned military vehicles gave Andi cover as she went through the hole in the fence and skirted the gore; the taste of copper filled her mouth as she breathed. The boy was about ten feet from the woman when Andi rounded an M35 cargo truck and started toward the car. She couldn't reach the boy to stop him from doing whateverintheheck he had planned. The boy didn't have a gun; she was fairly certain of that; his hands swung empty as he walked and nothing bulged in his pants. Andi slid her sidearm into its holster and shouted, "Boy, am I ever glad to find you guys."

The red-haired woman snapped around and screamed, the M27 suddenly in her white-knuckled grip and pointed at the dead center of the boy's forehead.

JULY 29: OMAHA, NEBRASKA

CHAPTER 10

The tart burn of stomach acid tickled the back of Jenna's throat. *Dear God, not now.* Two people, two people she didn't know, she didn't even know them, had snuck up behind her. Jerks. One, a boy of eighteen or nineteen with a sickly molestache stood about ten feet away, the other a woman with a pistol on her belt and an Army rifle slung over her shoulder about fifteen feet behind that. The woman slowly raised her hands and smiled naturally, her teeth straight and white. The boy dressed like a Mormon missionary – *no 'Ensign Magazine' for me today, thank you –* stood with his arms at his side. A black stain slowly grew on the crotch of his pants.

"You assholes," she screamed. "You scared the shit out of me."

"Sorry about that," the woman said, her voice calm and steady, the solid Midwest accent made her sound genuine. She didn't move. She stood in place with her hands up, palms facing Jenna. *She could have just shot me.* "I didn't mean to." Her mouth slowly pulled back from a smile to a grin. "It's just so hard to meet good people nowadays."

"You're goddamned right." Jenna's stomach lurched and she swallowed. *No more puke, Jenna Mullins. Not right now.* As much as her body threatened to double her over and spill what was left in her stomach onto the parking lot, she stood straight, her arms held the machine gun steady, right at the Missionary's face. "Now where in the fuck are you from?"

The Missionary flinched, his head moved slowly in a nod. Words spilled from his mouth in a low mumble.

"What was that?" Jenna shouted, the M27 pressed hard into her shoulder.

"You're saying bad words," the Missionary boy said, his gaze never leaving the pavement. "Mother's going to punish you."

"Is your mother here?"

He shook his head and gripped his hands over his urine-soaked crotch.

"I'm not with him," the woman said. "I came up from Oklahoma and followed signs to a survival shelter in–"

"Kansas City?" Jenna asked.

The woman nodded. "Yes. Worlds of Fun. It was abandoned, but a map pointed me up here." She looked around then her eyes rested back on Jenna's face. "Omaha's not much of an upgrade."

Jenna looked at the Missionary. "What about you?"

"Colorado," he said in barely more than a whisper.

Oklahoma? Colorado? "So, you two aren't together?" *What are the chances of two random people finding me at the same time? Not very damned likely. Something's not right here. Not right at all.*

"No," the woman said. "I saw both of your vehicles while I was parked on the interstate. I came up here looking for people. I didn't want you to get away."

Jenna nodded, memories of latching on to Craig in Harrisonville, Missouri, flooded her mind. It seemed like years. "I understand the feeling."

"You're waiting for someone? Someone in the hospital?" the woman asked.

Good lord, how long have they been in there? Just seconds? Minutes? Hours? "Three someones."

The woman slowly lowered her hands to shoulder height. Jenna didn't move. She seemed nice enough, or was it just because she was a woman?

"Do you mind if we wait here with you until they come out? I'm looking forward to having people in my life again. Conversations with the inside of my car are getting a little one-sided."

Jenna decided right then she trusted the woman, but something was wrong with the Missionary. He was a mostly grown man, but looked like he still pulled wings off flies. "Sure," she said, nodding her head toward the Missionary. "And you might want to help this guy find some dry pants."

***

Trails of gore streaked the once sterilized white floors of the Nebraska Medical Center like the hospital had been invaded by enormous bloody slugs. Terry's flashlight cut through the darkness as they walked by Admitting, the room behind the half windows in order, like staff had simply left for lunch. A coffee mug reading 'Keep Calm and Call Batman' sat next to a computer that would never hum with the power of electricity again. A violet sweater rested on the back of the chair, a Snickers bar stuck half out of the pocket. Terry moved toward the doorway, but Doug grabbed his arm.

"We're looking for Corson, Terry," he whispered. "Get in, get out."

"But," Terry whispered back. "It's a Snickers."

"We'll hit the next convenience store and get you all the Snickers we can find. But we gotta go, now."

Nikki pushed the switch of her flashlight with her thumb, the white beam merged with Terry's, filling the hallway with light. Color-coded lines ran along the floor. Red went to cardiology, yellow to radiology, blue to x-ray, green to general surgery.

"What are we looking for, Doug?" Nikki asked, Doug's arm around her shoulder, his shattered ankle a doctor in this hospital stuffed in a cast swung helplessly as she helped him walk. Doug tried to keep his weight on his one good leg and off of Nikki; he knew that might help keep them alive.

"Corson," he said flatly. "The son of a bitch who sent us to the Community."

"Got any idea where he is?"

Doug shook his head. "We only saw him in the cafeteria. I sure as shit doubt he's there."

"If he's still alive," Nikki said, her voice barely a whisper.

"Yeah. If he's still alive."

The body of a nurse lay against the wall; an arm torn from his socket lay down the hall, most of the flesh gnawed from the humerus. Nikki threw a hand over her mouth and bit into her palm, the scream died in her throat. "Just keep moving," Doug whispered. They continued down the hallway.

Doorways loomed at even intervals, the darkness beyond them like black painted on glass. Doug was thankful the sunlight couldn't bleed into that darkness; he didn't want to know what was there. Terry threw an arm in front of Nikki and Doug's chests; they stopped. He pointed his light on a sign that hung from the ceiling.

"Cafeteria's that way," he said, pointing down a side hall. "We could try there." The glow of the flashlights was aimed at the sign, but enough hit Terry's face to show Doug he was grinning. "Last time we were there, they served beer."

"Goddamnit, Terry," Doug hissed. "Can't you be serious for one minute? You're not playing 'Left 4 Dead' here. This is fucking real."

"Hey," Terry started, but a sound, a scrape; the subtle scratch of a hard-sole shoe across tiles stopped him cold. "Boss?"

Doug swallowed and pulled the Beretta M9 from its holster. "Get ready." He sucked in through his nostrils; the smell of rot mingled with disinfectant fought for control of the air. He blew his breath slowly from the tight circle of his mouth. "Light up that hallway on three." Doug's heart beat heavily in his chest. He knew if the front of his shirt was visible, he would see his heartbeat. "One." *Oh, shit.* "Two." *Lord, let me see Jenna again.* "Three." Terry and Nikki swung their lights into the hallway, the lines on the floor indicating cardiology and the cardiology waiting room.

A lone zombie, a doctor by his bloodstained white lab coat and Barker Black shoes, shuffled its way down the hall toward them, its right shoulder against the wall to keep itself standing. A short laugh escaped Terry. "Poor bastard." He raised his rifle." Let me put him out of his misery."

Are you fucking crazy? "No."

The crack from Terry's rifle filled the short hallway; Nikki and Doug winced from the explosion. The bullet caught the doctor on the bridge of the nose; the thing's knees buckled and it dropped backward like a drunken frat boy at formal. Terry turned toward Doug and Nikki. "You see, no worries."

The light from Nikki's flashlight sliced into the dark room beyond, the beam glowing off dozens of white eyes. The cardiology waiting room was full of zombies. One of them roared. *Goddamnit.* Doug pushed Nikki into Terry; the force shoved him backward into a wall. "Run. Run damn you," he screamed.

Feet shuffled across tiles and the zombies rushed down the hallway. "Boss," Terry yelled.

"Just run," Doug screamed back.

The sharp, sudden flashes of Terry and Nikki's gunfire lit up the black hallway, bullets tore through flesh and ricocheted off the walls. The light disappeared as Terry and Nikki backed down the hallway, the dead human monsters walking into a rain of gunfire. Doug sank against the wall, the darkness of the interior of the hospital perfect. *What the fuck am I supposed to do now?* He reached to steady himself and his left hand hit the surface of a door. He fumbled in the blackness and found a cold metal handle. He turned it to the right and fell inside.

***

Andi unbuckled the belt of a private who lay half in/half out of a Humvee. His torso was torn and gnawed, but Mr. Peeky didn't need a shirt, he needed pants. "These will be a little big on you," she said, grimacing as she pulled the green camouflage combat trousers off the corpse, its legs starting to turn blue. "Just tug your belt real tight and you'll be okay." She didn't turn her back on Mr. Peeky as the boy slowly dropped his wet pants and tighty-whities. Andi didn't trust Mr. Peeky; privacy was something you earn.

"I saw you spying on them," Andi said, standing straight, her hand resting on the butt of her sidearm.

"What do you mean?" the boy asked.

"You know what I mean. I saw you following them on the highway, hanging back just far enough they probably wouldn't see you. Then you were watching them through binoculars in your truck. What are you up to?"

"I'm not up to anything," he said weakly.

Andi approached the boy; they were about the same height, but he seemed to shrink as she approached. She loomed over him. "I just want to get one thing clear. I don't trust you, but this isn't my show. The woman you were sneaking up on and her friends in the hospital, it's their show. They get to make up their own minds on you." She leaned closer. "But I already have."

***

"We lost Doug," Nikki screamed, the sound of her voice drowned by the roar of Terry's machine gun. Two zombies danced as bullets riddled their chests, then they dropped to the hallway floor.

"What?"

"We lost Doug."

"No we didn't." Terry squeezed the trigger; the tattoo of bullets filled the hall again. Another zombie, a soldier, its helmet hanging over its left eye, fell in a lump. More came, more than Terry could count in the shitty light. He lowered the weapon and grabbed Nikki's arm. "Let's go."

"But we lost Doug."

Terry pulled her into motion and they ran down the hall toward the exit, a gray fuzz of sunlight fighting its way into the hospital led them to the front door. "We didn't lose him. We know right where he is."

"But how are we going to get him?"

The moaning behind them grew louder as the mob pushed itself hard through the corridor; its next meal was getting away.

"I don't know," he said. "I'm not made of ideas."

***

The flashlight click was loud in the small space. Doug slowly spun the light around the room; racks of gauze and tape, blankets, bottles of isopropyl alcohol. A supply closet. Doug exhaled slowly. *Lucky boy.* He leaned against the wall. Without Nikki or Terry to help him, hobbling out of this place was going to be tough, but Corson was Priority Number One. Doug was going to find that son of a bitch, he was going to find him and make him talk.

The sound of gunfire grew farther away, the moans and shuffling of the monsters in the hall became faint as the creatures followed Terry and Nikki, then all sound just stopped. *Go,* Doug thought, trying to will himself into motion. It didn't work. He couldn't move fast enough to outrun, *outhop,* a zombie and if he got trapped between two, he was fucked. He knew that. His light slowly crawled over the interior of the closet as Doug methodically looked through for something, anything. "Well, shit," he whispered. A pair of aluminum crutches leaned against a wall, hiding from Doug's first search behind a rack of blankets. "I guess this is a hospital." He put the crutch pads under his armpits and leaned on them. A bit shorter than he needed, but close enough for now.

Doug listened at the door. Nothing. No moans, no rustling, nothing. He took a deep breath, slowly swung open the door and stepped into the hallway.

***

Terry and Nikki burst from the gaping hole and out into daylight; Terry held his machine gun in one hand, Nikki's hand in the other. A stream of zombies gushed from the entrance. Five, ten, seventeen. Jenna screamed.

"I have this," Andi said and raised her weapon.

"Holy shit," Terry yelled, staring at Andi, the rifle pointing toward them. He pulled Nikki to the left away from this mad stranger by the Prius.

Andi squeezed off a shot, the lead zombie's head jerked back and it fell to the pavement. The others came fast. She shot again and again. Two more. Another. Jenna raised her weapon and sprayed a line of bullets into the oncoming horror. Three went down. Andi knocked down two more with one shot each. The monsters lost sight of Nikki and Terry and ran straight toward Andi. Pop. Pop. Pop. Three bloody corpses dropped to the pavement. The roar of gunfire sent the crows that lined the awning and electric wires cawing into the sky. Three zombies fell to automatic gunfire as Terry stood his ground and shot into the walking corpses. Nikki shot one down. The two remaining ran straight toward Andi. She put a bullet in the head of a zombie in purple nurse's scrubs, its brain exploded from the back of its skull. Then the rifle jammed.

Damn. The monster, a fresh one, ran at Andi, its eyes still clear, foam and mucus ran down its pimply face. Ten feet, five feet. Jenna screamed again. Andi leaned the rifle against the Prius, calmly pulled her 9mm sidearm from its holster and fired inches from the slathering monster's face, the beast's filthy, bloody hands nearly at her throat. The thing lurched back and dropped to the asphalt in a sickening thud.

"Who the hell is this?" Terry shouted.

"Corporal Andi Bakowski, United States Army," she said, reholstering her sidearm. "Nice to meet you."

***

"Where's Doug?" Tears streamed down Jenna's face.

"He's okay," Terry said.

"Well, where is he?"

"He's okay," Terry said again and turned toward Andi. "Where'd you come from?"

"Oklahoma."

"And this guy?" he asked, pointing at Donnie.

"I have no idea."

"Colorado," Jenna said, wiping tears away with the back of her hand. "Now, where's Doug?"

"Inside." Terry glared at Donnie. "Can you talk?"

"Yes," Donnie said, the word barely audible.

Andi walked toward a dead soldier and took the rifle out of its stiff hands. She pulled out the clip and slapped it back in. "You left your friend in there?" Andi said, her voice flat, serious. She pulled back the firing pin then let it snap back with a click. "Let's go get him."

"I'm coming, too," Nikki said, stepping toward Terry. He shook his head.

"No, darlin', you stay here with Jenna." He leaned close and whispered, "keep your eye on that shifty looking guy."

Nikki nodded and wrapped her arms around Terry's neck. "You come back out," she said.

Terry smiled and kissed her. "You just have a beer ready for me when I do."

"Me, too," Andi said and nodded at Terry. "Let's go."

***

Nothing moved in the hallway; it smelled of death. Blood pooled on the floor under the heap of bodies Terry and Nikki had piled up. *Please tell me they got out.* A black line on the floor led to administrative offices, an orange one led to the cafeteria, both led away from the carnage. Doug clipped the flashlight to his sweaty shirt, the light swayed as he swung himself down the hall.

The hospital president's office was luxurious. Doug guessed that was to be expected. A great wooden desk, its surface clear of everything but a layer of dust and a picture of children in front of the Matterhorn at Disneyland. *Children? Grandchildren?* He'd figured if Corson had set up shop in the hospital, he'd be here, but no trace of the military was in that room. No equipment, no maps, nothing. A gunshot, then two. Doug rushed around the desk toward the windows, heavy maroon curtains hung over them like a cloak. He pulled them aside, the late afternoon light almost blinding.

The front parking lot opened up before him.

Jenna. His heart hammered in his chest. She stood at the Prius next to two strangers, one held a rifle up to her shoulder, zombies fell before her. The other stood behind them, looking away. *What's he doing?* The man pounded his fists into his thighs. *What the hell's wrong with him?* Terry stopped running and fired into the mob, three zombies hit the ground. Crows flapped around the window, blocking parts of the scene. The last zombie ran at the woman with the rifle. She dropped the rifle, pulled a pistol and blew out the thing's brains. Doug waved at them, but nobody looked toward the president's office. Why should they? It was under the shade of a tree far away from the action. Terry and the woman with the rifle ran for the hospital entrance.

Doug smiled. "They're coming to get me." His smile faded. "Oh, no. They're coming to get me." *I can't leave yet.* He turned from the window and hopped back into the hallway on the crutches. Doug looked to his left; the sunlight bathed the hallway in gray. The orange line continued down the hall and ended at a set of double doors. The cafeteria. *Well, Terry, you got your way.*

Light bled from the cracks where the doors fit into the frame. Sunlight? He didn't remember any windows in the cafeteria where he'd had his last good meal. Doug grinned. A good meal in a hospital. That's hilarious. He gently took the aluminum door handle and pulled open one door, artificial light poured over him. "What the hell?"

"The generators are still on," a voice said. Doug's head swung toward the voice. The doctor who examined him and repaired his shattered ankle sat at a white table, a wineglass and a plate with a steak, baked potato and broccoli lay in front of him. The doctor popped a piece of medium-well meat into his mouth. "Please shut the door. You'll let in an HG-17."

HG-17?

Doug moved away from the door, the pneumatic bar pulled it shut. The doctor cut another piece of steak. "How'd you get in here? The place is crawling with the HG-17 infected."

"Where's Corson?" Doug asked.

The doctor shrugged and plucked the meat off his fork. "I don't know," he said through a mouthful of food. When the world comes to an end, manners are the first thing to go. "The last time I saw him he was wandering down by Anatomic Pathology."

Shit. "He's a zombie?"

The doctor's face grew blank, then he nodded. "I guess that's what we'll have to start calling them now, isn't it? Yes, he's a zombie."

Doug pulled out a seat and sat down. "That will save me from killing him."

"You didn't tell me how you got in here."

"The doors were open," Doug said. He leaned his crutches against the table and looked hard at the doctor. "I want you to answer a few questions for me."

The doctor took a sip of red wine. "Merlot, my favorite," he said. "I wonder if I'll miss it."

"Look, doc, is this thing curable?"

"The HG-17?"

Doug nodded. "Yes."

He took another sip of wine. "No."

We're fucked. We're all fucked. "How did this happen?"

He dabbed his mouth with a white, linen napkin and looked at Doug. "Ophiocordon, as you may have heard."

Doug nodded.

"After placating the host – and I mean seriously placating - it causes orgasms – the fungus kills the host." He grinned. "They go out with a bang."

"Then the stalks grow."

The doctor nodded and took another sip of wine. "Yes, a sporangium blub emerges from the host's chest and waits for something to pass by to transfer its spores, HG-17. The new host then becomes—"

"A zombie."

"Yes, a zombie."

Doug rested his elbows on the table and clenched his hands. "For what purpose?"

"Who knows?" the doctor said, cutting another piece of steak. "What does any living thing want? To eat and reproduce. The HG — the zombies are going where the spores want them to go, so the spores can continue to reproduce."

"Someplace hot?"

The doctor nodded. "And wet."

"A mass migration?"

"It's possible and soon. I don't know if zombies can survive the winter. The spores can hibernate, but a zombie is dead matter. When it's frozen and thawed several times, it will decompose very rapidly once spring arrives." He ate another piece of steak.

"But someplace like Florida, the fungus will thrive."

The doctor laughed. "Alligators, hurricanes, invasive Burmese pythons, now zombies. I bet tourism is down this year."

Doug rubbed his chin, the stubble rough under his fingertips. "I'm with other people. We can't stay here. Where should we go?"

The doctor frowned and swirled the remaining swallow of wine in the bottom of the glass. "Anywhere there are uninfected people. Set up a colony somewhere far away from these zombies. Given enough time, a lack of hosts will destroy the spores no matter where they are. Do that or the human race isn't going to survive. It's probably a good idea to stay out of Florida."

The doors to the cafeteria swung open and Terry and the stranger rushed in. "I fucking knew it," Terry said, a smile splitting his face. "The cafeteria."

"Welcome," the doctor said. "There's beer in the refrigerator, if you'd like. Cold beer. I would offer you some wine but–" He drained his glass, "–I've just finished it."

"Thanks, Doc," Doug said. "But we have to go."

The doctor nodded. "I'm glad you stopped by."

What? "You're coming with us."

He shook his head, as he cut a large broccoli floret in two. "No."

"That's suicide, Doc," Terry said, walking back to the table from the kitchen. He held a bus tub of beer cans. "There's zombies all over the place."

A small laugh escaped, followed by a cough. "I know." He reached into his shirt pocket and pulled out a small medicine bottle. "The hospital was full of zombies. They'd destroyed the military base here, what the hell was I going to do against them? I didn't want to be eaten by one of those things, so I injected this into my steak and into my wine. I thought it was sensible at the time."

"What is it?" the stranger asked.

"Botulinum toxi. It's–"

"Botulism," the stranger said. "It's the same stuff they use in Botox. It paralyzes your muscles and your lungs, then–" She wiped his index finger across her throat.

"I mean, I wish you would have called first," the doctor said, a series of coughs racked his chest. "I think I'm going to lie down, now. You'd better go."

106

The three left the doctor alone in the hospital cafeteria.

***

"How'd you know that stuff back there?" Doug asked the woman named Andi. They stood on the Missouri River Bridge outside of Omaha, the brown muddy water silently moving beneath them. Doug and Terry had stood on that bridge before, to decide if they should move on to Omaha. Doug knew now that was a mistake.

"I was working on my biology degree at Missouri State when this thing hit," she said. "My mom caught it, then I think my dad did, too, so I joined the Army."

"Then why aren't you with the Army?" Nikki asked.

Andi looked at Nikki, her green eyes welling with tears that threatened to break free. "I was ordered to shoot a man, an American and he wasn't even infected. I never signed up for that."

Doug decided, right then, that he liked her. The other guy?

"What's his story?" Doug nodded toward Donnie who stood next to the Silverado, staring across the water at the Union Pacific steam and diesel engines at a park on the bluff.

Andi shook her head. "I don't know. When I pulled up to the hospital, I thought he was with you."

"He's weird," Jenna said, staring at Donnie. "He gives me the creeps."

"Well we can't just tell him to take his ball and go home," Doug said. "Nobody has a home anymore."

The crack of a beer can, a cold beer can, was loud in the afternoon. "What are we doing here, boss?" Terry took a drink of beer and grinned. He never thought he'd drink a cold beer again. "We should have turned back around and gone straight to Wyoming, or Montana, or one of those damned states nobody lives in and played house for the rest of our lives."

Andi took a beer and rolled the can gently in the palms of her hands. "I was going to Colorado," she said. "The moment I saw the mass slaughter at the zoo, I was going to just hide in the mountains. Then I saw you driving on the highway."

"That sounds good, boss. Colorado?"

Doug stood silently and stared into the swirling brown water, an occasional whirlpool appeared beneath the bridge.

"You still want to find someone in charge, don't you?" Jenna asked.

Doug nodded.

"Well there is no one in charge anymore, Douglas Titus. No one. There are no planes, there are no trains, there are no goddamned breweries open." She grabbed Terry's half-full can and threw it off the bridge.

"Hey."

She stood close and grabbed Doug's head in both hands. "Nothing exists anymore. We need to go somewhere safe and hiding in the mountains sure as shit sounds better than driving into some city again."

Doug didn't move. Jenna slapped his shoulder. "Did you hear me?"

"The doctor said we should find people. That would be the best way to survive this thing. Find people and set up a–" He froze. Something carried through the air. Something familiar. Something Doug thought to be gone, just like Jenna said. A smile pulled across his mouth. "Yes, dear, I heard every word you said, but did you hear that?"

"What?"

The sound turned into a steady roar. It was close. Doug didn't know where, but it was close. "What do you mean trains don't run anymore?"

PART TWO: THE BAD LANDS

JULY 29: MAYDAY, KENTUCKY

CHAPTER 11

A slap broke the silence of the morning. Lazarus stood in the doorway to his home and clapped an open palm on his belly again, the pop loud in the open air. He rubbed a stomach that had started to get out of control and wondered what Gwenny was going to cook for breakfast. What was there to do in paradise, but to eat and sleep, sleep and eat?

"Beautiful," he said and stepped out of the house for his morning walk around town. "Simply beautiful."

First he'd visit the front gate, then the garden, then the greenhouse, before heading off to the Whistlestop Café to see what magic Gwenny had created. He hoped for blueberry pancakes. Yep, blueberry pancakes and sausage. Real blueberries and sausage were getting hard to come by, but a hope's a hope and Gwenny was full of surprises. A grin grew on Lazarus' clean-shaven face as their weekly Saturday romp in her apartment over the post office crept through his mind. Yep, full of surprises.

Lazarus stepped into the warm, muggy morning and shut the front door behind him. He didn't lock it. Nosiree. Nobody locked their doors in Mayday; no need. The town was solid; nothing but love and respect. Jeremy waited for him outside the door. Lazarus' smile grew. What a good soldier.

Dew clung to the freshly cut grass they walked through; the sides of Lazarus' black leather boots dotted with flecks of green. The town looked good, darned good. Everything green, crisp and fresh. His small, neat white house with a neat emerald lawn sat in the center of Mayday, surrounded by other small houses, some ranch, some two story, the face of one covered in ivy. Doc Thomas lived there. Not that Lazarus needed a doctor; he'd come back from the dead.

"What a glorious day, right Jeremy?" Lazarus said, patting the tall, slim man on the shoulder.

Jeremy walked beside Lazarus in silence.

Lazarus. Pretty presumptuous, but who are people to judge nowadays? You could call yourself whatever you darned well pleased. Besides, he'd earned it. A doctor prescribed him Ophiocordon because of depression; his wife had left him for her personal trainer, a woman named Lilith and the man named Tim Hardy was sad, sure. Who wouldn't be? Finding out your wife of ten years now had six-pack abs and preferred a woman named after the Howling Demon to boot? What the heck? Of course, he was sad. The Ophiocordon made him feel better, though. Oh, so much better. So good it almost took him away, to make him a member of the Purpose, but it didn't; it couldn't. As Tim Hardy lay in the recovery room at some silly hospital in Louisville, he couldn't remember the name, he realized he must be righteous; the Piper can't take the righteous. He started calling himself Lazarus at that moment of awakening; he felt he'd earned it.

Tim woke in darkness the day he came back from the dead, sweat beaded his face in a stifling heat, the world around him a complete dark, an India ink stain his eyes couldn't penetrate. The Piper hit Tim hard, the dizziness, the pain; he'd suddenly sat straight up in the hospital bed, blood spewed from his nose and mouth, splattering a screaming nurse and staining red the blinding white sheets of his hospital room. When? Days ago? Hours ago? Minutes? *How'd I get there?* Yes, of course. Tim staggered down Main Street of Mayday, beautiful Mayday, his face pink with fever. The world spun through his eyes and he collapsed on the sidewalk in front of Ace Hardware, the bag from Paulson Pharmacy spilled onto the concrete, a bottle of NyQuil he'd just purchased flew from the plastic sack and bounced into the street. Then everything went black. He woke in the hospital; a pretty blonde nurse hovered over him. Then he closed his eyes and the pretty blonde nurse was middle aged with brown hair. *Was it the same person?* Every time Tim closed his eyes, something new floated before his blurry eyes. Then everything was dark and it was hot. It was so hot.

In the heat, in the black stain, he became Lazarus.

Lazarus reached out to the darkness, his hands pressed against a plastic sheet. *Where am I?* Not the hospital, surely. Dead? Probably not, he was hungry. Dead people – *real dead people* – probably didn't get hungry, at least not for a sandwich. A ham sandwich and a bottle of water; no, a gallon of water, was all he needed. Then he'd be up on his feet and could go to work back at the plastic factory. Lazarus took a deep breath, the hot, sweaty stink burned as it went in. He was in a bag. *A bag. Why am I in a bag?* Lazarus smiled in the darkness. *A body bag. Don't these people know who I am?* The zipper was easy enough to find; it was right in front of his face. He hooked a fingernail over the top of the slider and pulled down, the zipper teeth slowly parted and a dull gray light seeped into the bag. Lazarus pulled the plastic apart with numb, rubbery arms, ripping the sticky wet material away from his face, the cool air outside the bag raised goose flesh. A dim yellow light shone over an empty examination table, the red box letters EXIT glowed behind it over a flat gray door. Other lumpy bags, some still, others twitching like they were full of snakes, lay stacked against the walls. "Hey," Lazarus tried to scream into the dim room. "Hey."

Nobody came. It was a morgue, after all. Lazarus – *Yes, Lazarus. They thought I was dead. I rose from the dead* – pulled his stiff, damp legs from the body bag and swung them over the side of the table. "Hey," he yelled again, his voice a dry wheeze. *No wonder they didn't come. They can't hear me; but they must hear me. They will hear me.* His feet slapped on the cold, hard tile as he dropped off the table. He caught himself on the side of the metal structure, wobbly knees threatening to spill him onto the floor. "I'm coming." His words came out in a hiss. "I'm coming to save you all." Soft, florescent light spilled into the morgue as Lazarus pulled open the door to the hallway and stepped into the world of the living. The screams were glorious.

***

"Come on, Jeremy. Keep up," Lazarus called behind him. Jeremy was a good boy, but a bit slow, Lazarus was certain it was only because his attention tended to wander. The walk to the front Gate was a short one for Lazarus; only three blocks from his house. The garden and the greenhouse were seven from the Gate, the Whistlestop five from that. Thank the Lord for small towns, eh? Thank the Lord? Yes, Lazarus thanked the Lord a lot.

Walter Seidel stood at the big, tin door the hunters rescued from a local barn, affixed to utility poles sunk deep into the ground at the entrance to town and held fast with concrete. Louisville Power and Light had just set up to replace all the old poles from Carlson to Mayday, stacks of the forty-foot wooden posts lined the road between the two towns. Lazarus thanked the Lord for that, too. Some Carlsoners were righteous and were living as members of the town, but most were wicked and dead. The righteous helped bring these poles back to Mayday and sink them into the ground, then string wire woven field fence three high. Sutherlands Lumber up in Louisville had almost enough. The rest of the fence was finished with walls torn from barns the farmers didn't use anymore. No one lived on a farm; they were all in Mayday behind the fence that circled the town like a mother's arms. Yes, thank the Lord for small towns.

"Morning, Walter."

The young man looked away from the fence and Route 64 that led right up to the front gate and into Mayday. A deer rifle hung over Walter's shoulder. One sat at the feet of Gil Haply who manned the Gate with Walter. Gil snored softly in a lawn chair. "Good morning, Mr. Lazarus," he said, a weak smile pulling at his face. His eyes shifted to Jeremy and the smile faded. "Good morning, Jeremy."

Lazarus clapped a hand on Walter's shoulder and squeezed tight. "How's the outside world today?"

"Full of birds," Walter said. "Crows and such."

"Any people come to visit?"

Walter shook his head. "Not today." He tapped a walkie-talkie clipped to the front pocket of his jeans. An identical one hung off Lazarus' belt. "You'll be the first one to know if we have company, Mr. Lazarus. I promise. The first one."

Lazarus eased his grip, then slapped Walter on the back. "I know I will. Good work, son." He rubbed his belly again. *There'd better be pancakes.* "Anything to report?"

Walter shrugged. "I saw a cow. Wandered down Route 64 about five in the morning, then meandered into the Johnson's pasture over there," he said, pointing to a green patch of tall grass a quarter mile down the highway between two stretches of trees, a white farm house and big red barn sat further back on the property. "I would have gotten it," he said, patting the butt of his rifle, "but I didn't want to wake anybody."

Lazarus nodded. "Understandable. The righteous need their sleep. But if you see that thing again, put a bullet in it. I haven't had a steak in a long time. A long time." He tugged at the sleeve of Jeremy's blue plaid shirt. "Come on, boy. Miles to go before we eat."

***

Lazarus wanted to punch George Stanley in the head, which made him squirm a bit on the soft gray couch. Not a righteous thought from such a righteous man. Stanley sat next to him on the "Good Morning America" set, bright, hot lights making Lazarus sweat. He waited through the last commercial break, watching stagehands help some ridiculous chef in one of those tall, white hats prep lobster on a set adjacent to the raised circle where he sat. Under all that heat, the lobster would be as safe to eat as spoonfuls of manure. Lazarus' stomach rolled.

The floor director signaled Stanley; his smile was blinding. "And welcome back to 'Good Morning America.' With us this morning is Mr. Tim Hardy, a plastic factory worker from the small town of Mayday, Kentucky. You're lucky to be here, Mr. Hardy," the show's host said, not calling him Lazarus at all. Georgie boy turned toward the red light atop Camera Three, his eyebrows pinched in faux concern. "In early May, a doctor prescribed Ophiocordon for Mr. Hardy who suffered from depression." Stanley turned back toward Lazarus, the lights drawing great pools of sweat underneath Lazarus' funeral-and-wedding suit. *Holy, moly.* "Ophiocordon is being blamed for a rash of deaths around the country.

Some of those victims have come back to life in a semi-vegetative state in what some people are calling the Zombie Virus. But in this case, that didn't happen. What exactly did happen to you, Mr. Hardy?"

A bead of sweat broke on Lazarus' temple and trickled down the side of his face. *Geez, it's hot.* Stanley looked as cool as a high schooler thinks he is. "Lazarus."

Stanley cocked his head like a little dog. *A Terrier,* Lazarus thought. *I'm looking at a Jack Russell Terrier.* "Excuse me?"

Lazarus took a drink of water from a 'Good Morning America' coffee mug a stagehand had shoved at him before he sat on the gray couch under those horrible, horrible lights. "Lazarus," he said, the word thick in his mouth. "Call me Lazarus."

Stanley didn't try to hide his smirk. "Lazarus? As in Lazarus of Bethany? Lazarus of the Four Days?"

He's making fun of me. He's making fun of me on national television. And these people need to know. "Ophiocordon kills people, Mr. Stanley. It killed me." Lazarus' hands shook, water spilled over the side of the cup. "I came back to life." Lazarus turned toward Camera Four, his eyes trained on the red light. He was on. He was on camera for the nation to see. He could tell his message to everyone. "I came back because I'm righteous." He pointed a shaking finger at the camera. "The Piper is killing us; it's killing us all. If you want to survive–"

Hands grabbed him from behind. One jerked the lavaliere microphone off his lapel, the rest pulled him off the couch and off the set as the stupid chef chopped onions like the entire dish wasn't already prepared and sitting off camera. Before security snatched Lazarus, Camera Three trained on Stanley went live and that little Irish bastard didn't stutter a word as security pulled Lazarus over the back of the couch. It was all one big, choreographed dance. "The man who lived," Stanley said, his white smile never left his face. "Now we're going to see what Chef Steve has prepared for us. Later, Colonel Gary Corson from the United States Army will join us to discuss the military's plan for the worst-case scenario. Survival encampments in Nebraska."

***

Tall, yellow goalposts rose from either end of the garden, the 360-feet by 160-feet plot just inside the tall, wire fence, covered from end zone-to-end zone in flowering plants. Everything from green beans, to tomatoes, to corn and strawberries grew on the field where the Terrance County Bulldogs played just last fall. Nobody in Mayday needed a football field anymore, but they needed food. Cans and boxes wouldn't be around forever. A garden that size wouldn't feed even a small town for long, but after the righteous inherited the Earth, the population of Mayday had taken quite a hit. Only a quarter of the town remained. The town wasn't big, but it was strong. Lazarus meant to keep it that way.

Lazarus and Jeremy stepped onto the cinder track that circled the garden. Mayday might not need a football field, but people still used the track. Old Mac Bronson power walked past Lazarus, his white T-shirt stained with sweat in the humid morning, the temperature starting its uncomfortable climb up to probably near 90 again. "Mornin' Lazarus," the white-haired man said as he moved by. Mac didn't have need for Doc Thomas either, not an ounce of fat on him. Lazarus smiled and waved at the man who'd been his Cub Scout leader years ago. He also thought maybe he needed to do a few laps around the ol' track every once in a while, but his stomach growled and put that thought quickly to rest. Lazarus rubbed his belly and stopped at the home team bench. He propped a boot on the purple, wooden plank where Coach Martin used to gather his Bulldogs for a pregame prayer. *Prayer didn't save you, you lecher,* Lazarus thought. You can't pray to God to help you win a football game, then get caught fondling the backup quarterback in the front seat of your pickup truck and expect to be one of the righteous. Oh, no. That's why Coach Martin is rotting in a ditch off Route 64 covered in branches and leaves.

Lacy Tomlinson stood straight when she noticed Lazarus approach; she waved. Oh, Lacy. Her daddy, Pastor Fry Tomlinson, was one of the first ones in Mayday the Piper took down, spitting blood over the communion table one Sunday morning, his life fluid mingling with the blood of Christ. Pastor Fry staggered from behind the ambo and fell off the altar onto the table, the polished wooden antique, that had sat at the base of the alter of Mayday's United Methodist Church since 1895, tipped over, tiny plastic cups of grape juice and Goldfish crackers scattered across the tight maroon carpeting of the sanctuary. Mrs. Mulroony screamed from the back of the church. The back. Of course, she screamed from the back. This was a protestant church, nobody sat right up front where the Lord could see them; he might recognize them from the liquor store down in Albany.

Lacy came home from Murray State University in Paducah for the funeral and didn't go back. Not for finals. Not to bring home her things. She just came home to Mayday to grieve. She met Lazarus on a Thursday; the grief was short. You know what they say about pastor's kids.

Lacy's hair, tied in a ponytail, lay draped across her right shoulder. She leaned against her hoe, a hip cocked toward him. The front of Lazarus' underwear grew tight; Gwenny was a surprise every Saturday,

Lacy was a predictable Thursday, but Lazarus liked predictable, too. *Is it Thursday yet?*

"Good morning, Lacy." His voice flowed like honey. "How are our crops?"

She spread her left arm slowly open like a game show model showing contestants a refrigerator, an all-expenses paid vacation to Puerto Vallarta and a brand-new car. "Great," she said and bit her bottom lip. "I'm taking extra special care of those lima beans, just like you asked me to."

He grinned. "Thank you, Lacy, darlin'. This town would just dry up without you." *So would my pants.* "You're doing righteous work here, Lacy. Keep these plants alive and you keep the town alive. You remember that."

She nodded, her ponytail bobbing like a child's toy behind her. "I can't forget that," she said. "Now, you get going. I've got work to do." She bent back over her hoe, then turned back to Lazarus. "And order me a sandwich when you're down at the Whistlestop. I'm starving."

Oh, Lacy. Lacy, Lacy, Lacy. So predictable. "Bologna's getting scarce, but I'll see what I can do." He turned and left Lacy to scrape the weeds from the crops on the Bulldog football field. She paused and watched Lazarus walk away, Jeremy at his side. He didn't see her smile melt into a grimace.

***

The pounding on the front door started the day Pastor Fry fell over the communion table. Lazarus pulled his head off a sweat-stained pillow and looked at the clock on his nightstand, the red letters flashed 12:00. *Who the heck is knocking at 12-blinky-o'clock?* "I'm coming," he yelled, the words uncomfortably loud in his throbbing head. The "Good Morning America" goons – *and goons they were* – all but threw him into a commuter Boeing 717 airplane at JFK Airport and he landed at Louisville Regional Airport with just enough time to stop at Rite Aid to buy a bottle of Ten High bourbon and a two-liter bottle of RC Cola. He drank most of it by the time he got home, pulled himself up the stairs to his bedroom and fell onto the mostly-white cotton sheets face first. Then, sometime later, some jerk started knocking.

"I'm coming," he screamed this time. He lurched out of bed and grabbed the doorframe to his bedroom to keep himself from doing what the spinning room wanted him to do, which was vomit and fall to the hardwood floor. The pounding got louder, but Lazarus didn't know if that was outside his house, or inside his head.

It was 2 p.m. on the Sunday afternoon when the people of Mayday, Kentucky, gathered on the front lawn of the man who was just recently Tim Hardy, a plastic factory worker who rose from the dead and stood to watch him open the white front door to his house. Lazarus stood before the town in a pair of bright blue boxer shorts and white Haynes shin socks and talked with the townsfolk about brotherhood.

***

The Motorola walkie-talkie clipped to Lazarus' black leather belt crackled to life as he stepped onto a square patch of concrete where the high school boys used to lift weights outside the locker room door of the Terrance County High School gymnasium. Lazarus unclipped the radio and held it to his face. "What do you have for me on this fine morning?" he said.

Static crackled and Walter Seidel's voice came through strong. "This is Walter," the voice said. "I was just about ready to turn the Gate over to Ken Gundy, but I heard a motor out there. Sounds like it's getting closer."

Yes. "I know you've had a long night, but don't pack it in yet. Put together a welcoming committee and invite our new friends to join us. Have Lois Eller get the old Stinson house ready for visitors." He released the push-to-talk button. *Gundy? No, not Gundy.* Ken Gundy was about as personable as a member of the Schutzstaffel. He hit the button again. "And keep Gundy the heck away from them. They need to want to stay. Gundy will scare them away before you can shut the door behind them."

The walkie-talkie hissed. Walter's voice came back on. "He's right here."

Lazarus sighed. The pressures of leading shouldn't involve people's feelings. Gundy was efficient and cruel when he needed to be. Lazarus liked that about him. Gundy was a good member of the community, but he was dangerous and people immediately knew it. If he greeted a newcomer at the front Gate, these people the town needed would scream away from Mayday faster than Chuck Yeager. Lazarus' thumb depressed the button. "Ken," he began, his voice strong. He knew he had to sound strong with Gundy, or Gundy might snap someday; and when he snapped, Lazarus wanted to be able to point him in the right direction. A shiver ran through him. Something about the man's eyes scared Lazarus, scared him to death. He felt them boring into his head from blocks away. "You're one of my chiefs. You know that, right?"

Static greeted him.

He pressed the button again. "I want you to fall back and watch these people." Crazy man's probably slinging his butterfly knife like a ninja. "I

117

trust you, Ken. You're the head of my new surveillance team. I want you to go all James Bond on anyone who steps foot in Mayday." Lazarus swallowed, wishing like heck he'd grabbed a plastic bottle of water out of the still running refrigerator in his kitchen. Generators were wonderful things. "You're my eyes and ears."

More static. Then someone pressed the button on the other walkie-talkie. "Roger," Ken said.

Lazarus dropped his hand that held the walkie-talkie to his side and looked up at Jeremy. "The end of the world was easy, my friend," he said. "Dealing with people is hard."

"He's off," Walter said, his voice wavering in the static. "Going toward the Stinson house, flipping around that damned knife of his. What now?"

What now? Always questions. Expecting answers. Poop. "The welcoming committee. Get Brenda and Kyle and Kelly. I want these people to love us." Lazarus took a deep breath. "We're friendly people, Walter. Sell it."

* * *

The end of the world came fast; most people didn't know it was lurking just beyond their periphery, creeping upon them in the full light of day. One day the newscasters preached doom and gloom, but what was different about that? Instead of snowmageddon, or the Red Chinese threat, it was a pill. A little pill that caused people to drop to the floor dead, then get back up and walk around until they got where the little pill wanted them to go, then they had permission to die the whole way. The next day the newscasters were gone, the television just static, the newscasters apparently victims of the little pill. As were the police, the fire department, the cashiers at the FoodFair grocery store. Businesses were empty, the people just gone. Well, not everyone was gone. Lazarus walked by Dan Miller who worked the cup machine at the plastic plant. Hmm. He hadn't seen Dan for a couple of days: he called in sick with the flu. His coworker lay on the sidewalk outside the Aztec Movie Theater and Pub, a one-screen movie house that had gone out of business years ago in this small town. Now it was a bar, old "Star Trek" movies rolling across the screen as people got drunk and shot pool. A stalk about two feet long lay flat across his chest, the bulb on the end of the stalk had burst from the inside, a yellow mark stained the sidewalk in an arc. Lazarus walked into the street to avoid the yellow spot.

The front entrance was open to Ferguson Plastics on the outskirts of Mayday. Lazarus crossed the railroad tracks that ran beside the building and up to the front doors. "Hello," he called into the large, corrugated tin building, his voice echoed amongst the quiet machinery. "Anyone here?" He paused and listened; someone was in the building, or something. A squeak, like someone running their hand across an overfilled party balloon came from inside the factory. Lazarus *"None of that Lazarus shit in here, Mister. Your name's Tim,"* stepped through the double doors propped open with bricks and into the factory. He paused and grabbed one of the bricks; it felt like power in his hand. The gray metal door swung softly shut, the other stayed open. "I said, is anyone here." Tim took a tentative step onto the factory floor, morning light streaming in through the windows high on the tin walls. Then he found Mr. Ferguson.

The old man lay on his back next to a blow molding machine, a fine gray fungus covered his face and clothes, a stalk like the one that lay across Dan Miller's chest, stood tall. Tim's feet were rooted to the concrete floor as the stalk sprouted, *it sprouted,* from between the buttons of Mr. Ferguson's white Oxford shirt, a bulb on the end swelled to the size of a softball as Tim watched. "Oh, my God," he whispered. The bulb twisted toward him; the squeaking grew louder. Tim turned and ran out of the factory and became Lazarus again.

***

Lazarus clipped the walkie-talkie to his belt and stepped off the concrete pad. His stomach had growled and the Whistlestop wasn't getting any closer with him standing at the back of the high school. Jeremy didn't follow Lazarus. Lazarus stopped and spun on his boot heels in the gravel. "What's the matter, son?" Lazarus asked. He liked the boy. He knew some of the townsfolk did not, but that didn't matter; what Lazarus says, goes. So, Jeremy stays. Jeremy just stood there, staring at him, his lips twitching to reveal a line of straight teeth. "Are you hungry?" Jeremy didn't move. "Okay, okay. I know, it's time for breakfast." Lazarus beckoned the boy with a wave of his hand and Jeremy took a step toward him. "That's better, my boy." Lazarus started to walk again; he didn't turn to look this time. He knew Jeremy was behind him.

Lazarus walked around to the front of the high school building, passing the clear windows of classrooms that now held food, medical supplies and weapons the hunters had rescued from local stores and surrounding farms. For the town to survive, they needed food and they needed guns. From the moment he found Mr. Ferguson lying dead in the plastic plant, Lazarus knew he had to protect the people who remained in Mayday and that was just what he was going to do.

A six-foot-high wooden fence formed a circle on the front lawn of the school grounds, metal bleachers pulled from the football field sidelines sat around the fence. "We're here, son." Lazarus reached for the latch on the one gate in or out of the Corral, then turned. Jeremy stood at the edge of the ring of bleachers, frozen. Lazarus pulled open the door and stepped through.

"Oh, my God." A woman in a blood-stained shirt sat on the grass floor of the Corral, her arms behind her lashed to a pole, her eyes bugged from a swollen face as she watched Lazarus approach her. "Let me go. Let me go." The words came out in a whisper; tears ran down her face. "Why are you doing this? Why am I in here?"

Lazarus squatted before her and took in her face. It was probably pretty at one time, but the tenderizing process had left it blue and puffy. "I'm sorry," he said, his voice calm, almost friendly. "I just can't."

The woman's head slumped to her chest. "Why?"

Lazarus smiled. "We all have a reason we're here. Some of us are members of this town. We're survivors. When we help each other, we keep surviving. Others are like you. That's important. Oh, yes, that's so important. You are what gives people like my friend Jeremy the strength it takes to reclaim this world of ours." He paused and sighed. This woman did look bad. Yes, very, very bad. "Not even I can change what you are."

She raised her head slowly, staring at Lazarus with pale blue eyes stained with blood. "But you can't do this. I'm a church secretary, for God's sake. I have a husband." Tears began to flow again. "I have a husband."

"Yes, I know," Lazarus said. "He's like Jeremy now. You should be so proud of him." He stood and turned and walked from the corral. Jeremy remained where he stood, shifting weight from foot to foot. "Well, go on. She's not going to get any better."

The woman screamed as Jeremy staggered through the gate, his milky white eyes like a blind man's. Jeremy growled and rushed toward the woman. Her screams split the morning as Jeremy fed on her flesh.

Lazarus turned and started toward the Whistlestop for his own breakfast. He sure loved that boy, but he hated to watch him eat.

CHAPTER 12

The Army woman would have to go first. Donnie knew that. She was dangerous and the main threat to keep him from taking Vanessa Hagen away from these awful people, these Bad People. Donnie stood by Daddy's red Silverado – *funny name for a red truck. Silver-Ah-Doh* – and stared across the river at a park, a yellow Union Pacific diesel engine and a gray steam engine sat atop a bluff, a sign underneath read "Kenefick Park. Welcome to Omaha." Yes, the Army woman first. Donnie smiled. He used to melt Army men on top of the space heater in the bathroom, watching their little legs slowly bend atop the flat green bases and eventually fall. The bazooka man was his first. He watched it until it was a disfigured lump. That made Daddy mad and Daddy whipped him for "making a good goddamned space heater look like shit." But he did it again, this time to the officer with the pistol. Donnie pictured the woman named Andi melting away before him, her skin bubbling and falling away to reveal a six-foot-tall bazooka man underneath. Then that melted onto the highway into a pile of green sludge. Donnie cupped a hand over his mouth. He couldn't let them see him smile. Oh, no. They'd have questions.

Donnie was sure he couldn't melt the Army woman who said her name was Andi, but he could push her. Andi stood holding a beer and leaning against the Jersey barrier; the concrete slab the only thing keeping her from falling fifty feet into the river. Donnie saw himself walking slowly up to the group of Bad people talking about the future, his future. What should we do? Where should we go? Well, they could all go to hell for all Donnie cared. He was going home. Donnie would stand with them for a few minutes listening like he gave a poop about what they were saying, then push Andi over the barrier. A snort escaped his nose. *Be careful, Donnie. Don't let them remember you're here. It will be much easier to make them go away if they don't remember you're here,* his inner voice said, but his inner voice sounded like Mother. He didn't much like to hear his inner voice, even when it was right. Andi was already off balance. All it would take was a good push in the chest to send her plummeting into the swirling, dirty waters below. And if Donnie knew how to do anything well, it was push wicked people.

But then what would I do?

The knife. He'd have to have the knife he took from Mother's kitchen; he'd tuck it in the back of the Army pants he wore. They all had guns, but he could be quicker with the knife. He'd take out the big man next, stab him in the throat, then knock the black-haired girl to the pavement with a rock. Donnie looked around. Nebraska kept its bridges clean; there were no rocks, or chunks of concrete anywhere. What, Donnie? Think, think, think. *Oh, yes. Oh, yes.* Daddy kept a toolbox behind the seat. There'd be something heavy in there, if not a hammer, a big wrench. Yes, that would do it. The girl might not even get up again if he hit her just right with a big chrome Craftsman wrench. That just left the man with one good leg, Doug. Everybody thought Doug was so smart, but he wasn't. Donnie was smarter. Mother always said he was the smartest boy she knew, that must mean he was smarter than Doug, too.

A piece of driftwood, a water-swollen log, moved quickly with the rushing current. Donnie's mind saw Andi thrashing for help in the filthy, brown water, the log coming quickly behind her, then smashing her, smashing her in the head. The grin that pulled at Donnie's face almost hurt. Doug. What to do with Doug? Nothing. Donnie wasn't too worried about a man with a broken foot. Donnie'd just grab Vanessa Hagen who he knew wasn't really Vanessa Hagen, put her in Daddy's truck and go home. He'd even drive over that Doug if the gimpy man limped into the way to stop them. *Babump.* His grin faded. He was still five hours away from Mother and oh how hungry she would be when he got home. There would hardly be any time to play with Vanessa Hagen before Mother demanded dinner. He'd have to play with Vanessa Hagen before he got back home. That's just what he'd have to do. Find a motel on the highway somewhere, or a house, or right in the front seat of Daddy's pickup. Right in the front s–

"Hey, kid." The words sounded distant and under water. "Hey, kid." *Kid?* Donnie turned toward the Bad People; the gimpy man was calling to him. *Kid?* "What's your name?"

My name? My name? "Uh, Donnie," weakly squeaked from his mouth. "My name's Donnie."

"Well, don't you hear that, Donnie?"

Hear? Hear what? He shook his head.

"It's a train."

Train? Donnie listened to the wind over the water. A pink spoonbill someone had released from the zoo flew by. Then he heard it, the rhythmic thunder of a diesel locomotive. Railroad tracks went through Julesburg, going right by the Ford Sedgwick Museum. When trains, mostly carrying grain on the Union Pacific line, roared through town, everyone heard it. This train sounded far off, like a train coming into town, but it never got louder. They all got louder coming into town. This one must be going away.

"Where there's trains, there's people," Doug said. "Let's go find them. I think Terry should ride with Andi."

"Shotgun," Terry shouted.

Nikki rested a soft hand on his forearm. "You are such a dork." She turned toward Andi. "Do you even want to come with us?"

Andi nodded. "There's safety in numbers. All I want to do is be safe."

"Then I'm riding with you, too," Nikki said.

Terry leaned over and kissed her. "Cool, but you must recognize my legal claim to shotgun."

Doug looked at Donnie; the stare sent a shiver through him. "We've got room, Donnie. Do you want to ride with us?"

No. No, no, no, no, no. My knife. The Craftsman. I can't get rid of these Bad People without Mother's knife and Daddy's Craftsman. They're trying to ruin everything. Everything. "No, sir," Donnie said. "This is my dad's truck."

Doug nodded like he understood, but he didn't understand jack diddly doody. "Then follow us, but keep up. We're going to be in a hurry." The gimpy man got into the driver's seat of the Toyota, Vanessa Hagen sat beside him. The black-haired girl – *I'm still going to beat her brains in –* stood by the car walking Terry to the Army woman's Subaru where she gave him a kiss before sliding into the back seat. Gross.

Donnie crawled into Daddy's truck and shut the door. His fingers found the handle of Mother's kitchen knife and squeezed it tightly as he pulled the Silverado behind the cars and followed them closely.

***

"There's something wrong with Donnie," Andi said. She pointed toward the glove box. Terry opened it and found packages of beef jerky. "You know how I found him?"

Terry opened a packet of teriyaki flavored dried meat and handed it to Andi, then opened a black pepper jerky packet, pulled out a piece and handed it back to Nikki. "In a psycho ward?"

Andi didn't laugh. "That'd be funny if it wasn't accurate." She lay the packet of beef jerky on her right leg and turned on the wipers, white streaks of crow shit and wiper fluid smeared across the glass until it was clean enough. "I was parked out on the highway, scared. I was scared. I'd just seen the massacre at the zoo and, yeah, I was so scared." She pulled a bite of jerky off the stick and chewed slowly. "I sat there and saw your car

123

come down the highway, then pull off onto a street. This guy was following you."

Following us? A shiver crossed Terry's shoulders. "No shit."

Andi nodded. "At a safe distance. He could see you, but unless you were looking, you couldn't see him." She took another bite. "Mr. Peeky, that's what I called him, turned on the same street you did and I followed him. He was sitting in his truck spying on that red-haired girl–"

"Jenna," Nikki said.

"Jenna, through a pair of binoculars. He started sneaking up toward her so I got out of the car to see what he was up to. I don't know what would have happened if I hadn't been there."

Terry sat silently, chewing the jerky. "You wanna beer?"

"Sure."

A beer cracked open, Terry handed it to Andi and opened one for Nikki before popping one for himself. "That kid creeped me out from the moment I saw him," Terry said. "He's got that look, you know? Like he's got a head full of squirrels, or something."

"Yeah."

"But what are we going to do about him?" Nikki asked. "We can't turn him loose. He's a baby. He'd be dead in a day."

Good. Andi nodded. "I know. We just need to keep our eyes on him."

The Subaru passed a gigantic wooden Bass Pro Shops building and under modern sculptures that rose over the highway, the kind of sculptures that looked a bit like sailing ships, but not enough for anyone to actually think that with any confidence. Maybe future artists would fall back into realism, if the human race lasted at all.

"What have you all been through?" Andi asked. Terry sat in silence, staring straight ahead as they approached the Lake Manawa exit. Nikki poked his shoulder.

Terry shook his head. "What? Oh, sorry."

"You okay?"

Terry nodded. "Yeah, sure. I was just thinking about Batman." He turned toward Andi, his brow pinched. "What superhero would most likely survive the zombie apocalypse?"

A slow hiss escaped Nikki. "Not this again."

Andi shrugged. "I really haven't thought about it much. Superman, I guess."

"You'd think so," Terry said, pointing at Andi with his beer. "But it's gotta be Batman."

A quick flash of George Clooney in director Joel Schumacher's nippled batsuit flew through her head. She smiled. For the first time in months, Andi felt like she belonged somewhere. Terry didn't seem to care the world had come to an end and Andi liked that just fine.

"Why Batman?"

Terry took a drink of beer, the cold cans they brought from the hospital now bordering on cool. "He's the most badassed of the badassed, he wears body armor and he drives the goddamned Batmobile."

"And he's got a great place to hide to wait everything out."

"Please, Andi," Nikki said. "Don't encourage him."

Terry nodded like a bobblehead. "Yeah, yeah, right."

"But you forgot something important," Andi said. "This apocalypse was caused by an antidepressant."

"So," Terry said through a mouthful of jerky.

"So, who has more emotional problems than Batman? If anybody needs antidepressants, it's Bruce Wayne. He'd be dead in ten minutes."

Terry sat silently for a moment, chewing jerky. "You're right, but wrong. You saw 'The Dark Knight,' right? Batman's not on any kind of psychotropic medication. He can't be. That dude's got some serious untreated mental issues."

"What about Super–?" Andi started, then stopped. Her right hand flew toward the window and pointed to the north. The city of Council Bluffs seemed to be covered in railroad tracks.

"Holy shit, they're everywhere," Terry said. *How come we didn't see them when we drove by here before?* But he knew why; they weren't looking for railroad tracks. *What else have we missed?* What looked like a dozen tracks, some of them just sidings, ran parallel to South Avenue. Andi pulled off the highway onto Harry Langdon Boulevard, then onto South. The train was gone. Long gone.

"How are we going to find that train?" Nikki asked, leaning her chin on the front seat of the Subaru.

"Pull up as close as you can get," Terry said. Andi drove off road, making use of the car's all-wheel drive, through the grassy right of way and toward the tracks. "The trick isn't finding the train," Terry continued, "it's finding the right track."

The Subaru stopped. "Good enough?" Andi asked.

"A red carpet would have been nice, but I guess this will do," Terry said, grinning. He opened the door and spilled out. Where did these things go? Texas? Canada? California? *Hell, one may even go through Paola. I might have flattened a penny way down this track when I was a kid.* He rested his palm on the hot-rolled steel, the metal warm under the summer sun. Terry closed his eyes, concentrating on the smallest vibration. Nothing. He jumped to the next set of tracks and the next. He stood in the middle of the jumble of rails when the Prius and Silverado pulled to a stop beside the road, the Silverado twenty yards back.

"What the hell are you doing?" Doug asked through the open car window. Nikki and Jenna both stepped out of their vehicles to watch Terry.

"Hey, Doug. What superhero would survive the zombie apocalypse?" Terry shouted.

Jenna turned toward Nikki. "What'd he say?"

"He's been thinking about Batman again," she told her. "Don't worry about it."

"No brainer," Doug yelled back. "The Flash."

"Whoa," came out of Terry in a slow breath.

"Makes a lot of sense," Andi told him.

Terry nodded. "Yeah, it does."

"Now," Doug yelled. "What are you doing?"

Terry pointed toward his feet. "I'm looking for the right track."

"What?" Nikki asked.

Terry stepped over the tracks and onto another. He bent to touch it. "If it's vibrating, that means a train just went through," he yelled. "I watched a lot of cowboy movies when I was a kid. Works every time." He moved from track to track, feeling each one, occasionally dropping onto the cinders to rest his ear on a steel beam. After feeling the last one, he walked back toward the Subaru.

"Did it work this time?" Nikki asked.

Terry shook his head. "No. It did not."

***

Pink and orange stained the western sky like God had spilled His drink. Fading daylight cast a warm glow on Terry and Nikki as they set up the tent in a grassy spot across South Avenue, still close to the tracks, but not close enough to get hit with anything that flew off a train. That shit happens; at least it did. Doug and Andi sat in canvas camp chairs around the Coleman stove, pork and beans and Vienna sausages just starting to boil. Jenna sat on the hood of the Prius, a beer can in her hand.

"What's the plan then?" Jenna asked, tossing the empty beer can onto the road, the aluminum clanked until it rolled to a stop into the tall grass on the shoulder. "I'm getting sick of beer. One of you is going to go find me something civilized, like a nice 2010 Sauvignon Blanc, or some shit."

Doug patted her foot. "You okay there, honey?"

Jenna jumped off the hood and punched Doug in the arm. "Of course I'm not okay, asshole. I want to sleep in a goddamned bed. I want a goddamned steak dinner. I want clean clothes." She hit him again. "I want a fucking shower. When am I going to have those things again, Doug? When?"

Doug caught her hand when she pulled back for another hit and drew her into his lap; Jenna struggled like a bad actor. "You'll have those things again, honey. I promise."

"When?" she asked, her voice soft. She gently nestled her head into Doug's neck and wrapped her arms around him.

"I don't know," Doug said, pushing her hair behind her left ear. "I don't know."

She looked up into his eyes. "I still want my 2010 Sauvignon Blanc."

"We'll get it tomorrow." Terry walked into the circle and sat in one of the chairs. "Nikki, Andi and I'll go shopping. We need a list."

"Soap and lots of water," Jenna said. "Oh, and Tampons and chocolate."

"Donnie should go with you." Doug's words cut into the conversation like a psychotic clown suddenly showed up to make balloon demons.

"Yes." Andi turned toward the Silverado. Donnie stood leaning against the grill, staring at them, a Pepsi in his hands. "Hey, Donnie. Come over here."

Donnie just stood, staring.

Andi waved him over. Donnie slowly peeled himself off the grill and walked toward the group.

"Jesus, he's cheery," Nikki whispered.

Donnie came in almost slow motion, like he was walking under water. "Yes," he said, approaching the tent, his eyes never left the ground. "What is it?"

"A shopping trip," Doug said. "You, Terry, Nikki and Andi. There's a bunch of stores back by the interstate. We're going to need your truck. I hope you don't mind."

Donnie's head snapped toward Doug, the whites of his eyes blazed in the dimming light. "I drive," he spat. "Nobody but me drives."

A smile grew on Doug's face. "Of course you'll drive," he said, the words smooth. "You're important to this group, Donnie. That's why we're giving you such an important job. Now, please join us for dinner."

Donnie stood still, the night deathly quiet. Doug motioned him toward an empty camp chair; with the movement of his hand Donnie sat, like Doug had flipped a switch to activate him. Nikki handed out paper plates and plastic spoons and Terry dished up hot beanie wienies and potato chips. They drank beer well into the night, except Donnie; he drank Pepsi. Donnie smiled and he even laughed once, but he didn't mean it.

***

The truck smelled like sweat. Donnie slept in the Silverado, the doors locked and the windows barely cracked. There were Bad People in the world and last night they ate beanie wienies. Nikki and Andi sat in the middle as they drove through south Council Bluffs, squeezed between Donnie and Terry. Andi could feel Donnie's tenseness.

"There's a Mendards up there," Terry said, pointing ahead.

"And there's a Walmart Supercenter that way." Andi pointed east. "What are we getting?"

"We didn't get a list," Terry said, "except all that about the Tampons and chocolate."

Nikki shoved an elbow into his ribs. "And soap."

"Yeah and soap." Terry looked at Donnie. "You need anything, Donnie boy?"

Strychnine and maybe an ax. "No." He stopped, yes; there was something he wanted. Something he really, really wanted. "Chips Ahoy! I want some Chips Ahoy!"

"Walmart?" Andi asked.

"I need to stop at Menards first," Terry said. "I want to pick up a little present for everybody."

PVC pipe, a jar of sealant, shower curtains and a hacksaw. *What kind of present is that?* Andi wondered as they pushed carts through the dull gray store, their flashlights lighting the way. "Anything else?"

Terry pointed at a pallet of gallon water jugs. "That," he said. "We can pick up the coffee can at Walmart."

"Coffee can?"

Donnie wandered the store, holding a flashlight before him, the weak yellow beam more than a way to light his path. It was a signal, a signal for any of the Good People in this store to come out and play. He'd left the Army woman, the drunken redneck and the black-haired girl back at Aisle 9. He now walked down Aisle 17, the line of display toilets should have looked hilarious, but Donnie wasn't in the mood.

"Come out, come out wherever you are," he whispered. The others didn't know what he was doing. Nope. They couldn't hear him looking for the Good People while they were trying to be so quiet. "Come out and pla-ay."

He found tools in Aisle 21, great wicked tools. Axes, double and single blade, sledge hammers, saws. He smiled as he watched himself run a saw through the Army woman's neck, blood spraying across the display of screwdrivers, but he couldn't kill the Army woman here. Nope. The three doody heads were "joined at the hip," Daddy would say. He had to get them alone, one at a time and take care of them with Mother's kitchen knife that sat under the driver's seat of Daddy's truck. Unless he could find some of the Good People to kill them for him. They were here, they had to be.

In Aisle 29, standing in front of a shelf of carpet tacks, he found a man in jeans and a dark blue button up shirt, the word "Menards" on the breast. The tall fellow shifted his weight slightly from foot to foot, his milk white eyes glaring at a box of Grip Fast carpet tacks. "Hi, buddy," Donnie whispered, his heart jumping like a schoolgirl asked to the homecoming dance. A Good Person was here. A Good Person was here to save him, to help him take Vanessa Hagen back to Mother. The Mendards Man turned his head toward Donnie; his nose was missing. Donnie beckoned the Good Person with his hand, palm up, calling the missing nose man like he was a dog.

"Here boy," Donnie whispered. "Come here. It's time to play."

The Good Person lurched toward Donnie, a pricing gun still clutched in its talon-like grip. "That a boy," Donnie said, louder. "Come see what old Donnie's got for you." The zombie growled and reached toward Donnie, the pricing gun clattered to the ground as its arms flew up and he clambered for the fresh meat before him. "Good boy."

The gunshot rang like a cannon in the warehouse-sized building. The sound of a bee buzzed past Donnie's ear and a small round hole opened in the Good Person's forehead; it staggered backward, fell with a slap on the hard-tiled floor and stopped moving at all. Donnie turned slowly. The Army woman – *the darned doody Army woman* – stood behind him, pistol leveled at Donnie's head. "You're lucky I came looking for you, Donnie," the Army woman said softly, calmly, calm enough Donnie started shaking.

I'm so going to kill her first.

***

The solar generator kits, three of them, were the first things Terry set up; the next was a 17-inch flat screen TV and an Xbox. He flashed a green plastic case that read "State of Decay 2."

Doug's eyebrows raised as Terry sat the TV on the ground. "That going to work?"

Terry shrugged. "I don't know, but I gotta try. It's for zombie killing practice," he said. "I gotta stay sharp."

"What about me?" Jenna asked, a well-practiced pout on her lips.

Terry fished in a plastic bag and brought out a long green bottle. "A nice 2010 Sauvignon Blanc, or some shit. Just like you asked."

"Thanks, Terry."

"We also got Tampons and chocolate," Nikki said. "And this." She handed Doug a box labeled 'Motorola Talkabout 2-Way Radio.' "Terry thought you might like these."

Doug took the box and sat it on his lap. "Uh, thanks, I guess."

"I know you're upset about not being able to do anything," Terry said, cutting open the game box.

"Yeah."

"I mean you're stuck in that chair," he said.

"That's okay, Terry. I know–"

"And you can't do much."

"Shut the fuck up, Terry. These are so we can keep in contact when you guys are on a run."

Terry nodded. "Yeah, boss. That's right."

Doug frowned. "I have a broken ankle, Terry. I'm not brain damaged."

The sound of ripping cardboard turned everyone's head to the back of the truck. Andi held up a box of Sweet and Sour Chicken Helper. "We've got boxes of canned chicken and tuna back here, too. Adding a little variety to our diets." He pulled apart another case of food and took out a Chef Boyardee pizza kit. "Pizza tonight."

"But the best is yet to come," Terry said, grabbing the PVC pipe from the bed of the Silverado. "But you can't look."

"Why not?" Jenna asked.

A smile washed across his face. "It's a surprise."

***

The PVC shower stall went up fairly quickly. Terry built it away from camp and had Donnie park the truck between it and the tent. The pipes formed a frame to hold the curtains, two rose above to six feet and were joined with a cross bar. An empty 33.9-ounce Great Value coffee can hung from the cross bar by wire; Terry had punched holes in the bottom of the can with a hammer and screwdriver.

"You just turn over a jug of water in the can, the water comes out here," Terry said, demonstrating the holes. "And, voila, a shower."

"Who says living during the apocalypse can't be civilized?" Nikki hugged Terry's waist.

"Dibs," Jenna said, her voice high and giggly. She pulled off her shirt before she disappeared behind the shower curtain.

Doug had poured the wine by the time Jenna and Nikki finished in the shower. They sat in front of the camp stove in terrycloth bathrobes, Doug trying to cook pizza on a device designed to cook no such thing. Their clothes lay across the hoods of the vehicles drying in the slowly sinking sun. The boys had also picked up a washtub and detergent. Nikki was right, somebody had to stay civilized. Why not them?

"Who's next?" Terry asked, walking into the circle.

"Eww." Jenna turned her head.

"Goddamnit, Terry." Doug waved a spatula at him. "Close your bathrobe. Nobody wants to see that thing."

"Jealous?"

"No, you damned Sasquatch. I'm just scared you'll lose the truck in all that hair."

Donnie tried to laugh, he tried really hard. Everybody else was laughing. *Savages. They're all doodyhead savages.* Donnie'd thought about running away in the night, running back to Julesburg and Mother. It was too hard being around them, these Bad People. He didn't fit with them. But the thoughts of being alone sent his belly into a fit, curling around itself like it was full of worms. He needed to stick with the plan, but the plan was taking too long. "Donnie." somebody said. The word so faint he wasn't sure if he'd even heard it. "Donnie."

He looked up. It was the Army woman. Donnie tried to keep his hatred inside, all bottled up. He couldn't let these Bad People know he knew they were bad. That would end the plan all together. "Yes," Donnie said, his voice squeaky.

"You want to shower?"

They want me to get alone and naked. No, no, wicked lady. You won't get me alone and naked. He shook his head. "No, you go."

The Army woman nodded and walked behind the Silverado to the shower. Nobody saw Donnie's hands in fists because they were in his pockets.

***

"How long are we going to wait?" Nikki asked, looking at Doug, a glass of Sauvignon Blanc in her right hand.

The small campsite across the street from the railroad tracks had grown. Terry, Andi and Donnie had gone on another shopping trip for deck umbrellas to keep them out of the scorching July sun. They'd also eaten well; Doug had whipped up a stovetop canned ham and Velveeta powdered egg quiche, which Jenna said was pretty good for a mechanic. Andi shot three rabbits; they were having them for supper. Jenna covered hers with barbecue sauce to forget what she was eating.

"Looks like we can wait a long time," Doug said. "Except for a flushing toilet, this is almost as good as my house back in Paola."

Nikki drained her wineglass and handed it to Jenna who reached for the bottle. "Yes, we can. But how long should we wait? I'm ready to say fuck it."

Yes, how long? Doug sat back in the canvas chair, a warm beer gripped tightly in his hands. How long? Going back to Omaha, back to the bastards who sent them to the Community to die was his idea. But damn it, he had to know. He had to know why. He had to know if there were other people out there, uninfected people. Nikki had been behind him for that. She was also willing to follow the train. But there was no train and she was nearly finished following him. "I don't know," he said. "We have to stay together. We have to. Maybe I'm wrong." *Maybe the doctor was wrong. Maybe we don't need people. We are people.* "What does everybody think?"

"Safe. I want someplace safe. Safe and away from everything," Jenna said. She'd filled Nikki's empty glass and was working on her own.

"Anyplace but Nebraska," Terry said, burping.

"I was headed for Colorado before I met you." Andi gently pulled the last strip of meat off a rabbit bone and tossed it into the grass. "Mountains and fresh air. Few people also means few monsters."

"Not Colorado." Nikki swirled the wine in her glass. "The Marstens had a circle around Denver on their map. It didn't look good."

"Marstens?" Andi asked.

Doug waved his hand. "Survivalists. Knew their shit." He turned toward Nikki. "Just because Denver's gone doesn't mean we still can't go to Colorado."

"Colorado's nice." The campsite fell silent and everyone turned toward Donnie. He sat in a canvas chair, gripping a Pepsi so tight the sides crinkled, his eyes were level with everyone else's. As he sat, looking at all the Bad People look at him, he dropped his gaze toward the Pepsi can. "I said Colorado's nice. I was born in Colorado. We should go there."

Doug smiled. "Maybe, Donnie. Maybe."

The next morning, they heard a train.

JULY 31: MAYDAY, KENTUCKY

CHAPTER 13

"Thank you for having us to your house," Bryce McKenney said, raising his wine glass in a toast, the Cabernet Sauvignon that half-filled the glass as dark as blood. Lazarus' house was simple. After all, before he rose from the dead he worked at the plastic factory outside town, but since the world fell, it had become the nicest house in Mayday. Lazarus held up his own glass and motioned it toward McKenney before taking a drink and falling back into his meal. McKenney sat at the head of the table; Lazarus had insisted. A medium-well steak and mashed potatoes were in front of him on the china Lazarus' parents got for their wedding. Walter Seidel saw the cow through the gate again; this time he brought it home; the potatoes were nearing the end of their usefulness, but Gwenny peeled off the sprouts with the skins and boiled the Yukon Golds, mashing them with butter and reconstituted powdered milk and it was delicious. McKenney's wife, Tabitha's, steak was well done, their son Kyle's – *what was he? Nine? Ten?* – ground into a hamburger he ate without a bun.

Lazarus smiled at the man, his teeth stained from years of smoking, although he'd given that up when he rose from the dead. Can't tempt God too much. "The pleasure's mine, Bryce." He stopped, his knife in mid-cut and looked up in concern. "May I call you Bryce?"

Bryce smiled back, his teeth clean and white from years of repeated dental visits and daily care. Don't gloss over floss. "Of course."

"How's your new house?" Lazarus lay silverware on the plate and swirled his wine. He'd read somewhere swirling pulls oxygen into the wine and improves the smell. Whatever. Any wine without a screw-on lid tasted awful, Lazarus didn't care what it smelled like.

"It's fine." Tabitha dabbed her lips with a white, cloth napkin. "There's plenty of room for us; too much, actually. How–"

"I don't like the man," Kyle said as he twisted his fork in the potato on his plate and stared at his hand.

Lazarus cleared his throat and sat his wine glass on the tablecloth. "Man?" he asked. "What man?"

Kyle dropped his fork; it rang the plate as it bounced. "The man outside my window."

"Kyle," Tabitha snapped.

A laugh. The faces at the table turned toward Lazarus, who raised his mostly empty wine glass and nodded. "A toast to honesty," he said, the words smooth as soft butter. He turned toward Kyle, his eyes didn't seem to blink. "Now, what man?"

Kyle turned his face from the person, the scary, scary person across the table from him, the scary person who didn't blink. He stared at his plate, the half-eaten hamburger now a rancid lump. "The man I saw standing outside, staring in my window last night."

Lazarus put his elbows on the table and leaned on his fists. "What did he look like?"

Kyle shook his head slowly. "I don't know. I got up to pee and when I came back to the room, somebody was standing in my window. It was too dark to see what he looked like, except he was tall and skinny, like Jay Baruchel."

Jay Baruchel? Who the hell is Jay Baruchel? Jeremy. "It was probably just Jeremy. He patrols Mayday after dark. You know, to keep things secure. He was just checking on you to make sure our newest guests were safe." *And he probably smelled you. Young and fresh and oh, so tender.*

"Well," Bryce said. "He frightened our son. I appreciate all you've done for us, Mr. Lazarus, but we're all terrified. Kyle especially. The past two months have been so hard on him."

Ungrateful bastard. "Of course, Mr. McKenney. I'll see what I can do about Jeremy. It is very nice here in Mayday. The townspeople are friendly and the fence keeps us safe from all sorts of troubles, from zombies, to bears, to the worst of the lot, people. You'll like it here. So will Kyle." He nodded at the boy, whose eyes were still stuck to his plate. "One of our school teachers is even planning to start classes in September for the children left in town. I hope you'll stick around."

Bryce drained his wine glass and sat it on the white tablecloth. "We appreciate your hospitality, we really do; but staying is something we'll have to discuss as a family. We were heading for the survival shelter in Kansas City, Missouri, when we found you," he said. "It was on the radio before the power went down and there's signs for it all along the interstate. We might keep going that way."

Lazarus' smile never left his face. Bryce McKenney suddenly wanted to punch that face, right in the mouth. Lazarus saw this and his smile grew bigger. "You're welcome to stay in Mayday as long as you'd like, Mr. McKenney, but I understand. I understand all too well."

Bryce poured himself more wine and topped of his wife's glass. He motioned the bottle to Lazarus who ignored him. They ate the rest of the meal in silence.

***

Gwenny walked into Lazarus' dining room to the warm glow of tungsten lighting Lazarus' house, one of four places in town kept in electricity with a generator. Ken Gundy had escorted the McKenneys back to the Stinson house where they might just stay up all night wondering why their stomachs hurt.

"If this town is so safe, why do we need an armed guard?" she'd heard the dad ask as he stood on the front step, his voice loud and angry.

"You can never be too safe," Lazarus said, calm dripping off him. Gwenny wondered why the man who never died hadn't gone into politics.

She handed Lazarus a Bushmills on the rocks; she knew what he drank, she knew almost everything about him. Gwenny held a cold Kentucky Bourbon Barrel Ale in her right hand, the slightest hints of vanilla and oak from her first drink still on her tongue. The generators that kept the refrigerators at the Whistlestop running nonstop also produced enough ice to keep everything cold she wanted to keep cold. Lazarus' steaks, that bitch Lacy Tomlinson's bologna, Frog Keller's popsicles and her local craft brew. She had to have something to take the edge off the end of the world.

"Did you get Ophiocordon in the McKenney's meals?" Lazarus asked, not looking up, his attention on the Bushmills.

Gwenny sat her beer on the table and slipped into Lazarus' lap. "Just like yesterday." She kissed his forehead. "How long before they pop?"

Lazarus slipped his left hand under Gwenny's thin cotton shirt and the cup of her bra, her breast firm in his hand. You can fake love, you can fake loyalty, but you can't fake being twenty-two. "They should be ready for the Program tomorrow. I had Ken Gundy get their beds in the greenhouse ready this morning, just in case the kid went early."

The kid. She felt a bit guilty about that. He hadn't experienced life, hadn't had his first kiss and was years away from driving. His biggest accomplishment was Little League. Oh, well. She'd opened an Ophiocordon capsule and stirred the white powder into the McKenney's mashed potatoes like she had in their pancake batter that morning and the fresh bread the day before; but the kid didn't eat his mashed potatoes and he didn't touch the pancakes. The boy had Cheerios for breakfast. She didn't know about the bread, but he had to get some of it. Gwenny knew what the white powder did and she knew these people would die, but it was for the greater good. Lazarus' plan would create an army he would use to take back the world from the chaos caused by the very pill he was using to save it. Then humans could repopulate the Earth. She liked that idea and when that happened, she would be queen. Gwenny laughed as she felt Lazarus' penis harden beneath her.

"It's not Saturday," she said, biting her bottom lip.

Lazarus reached behind her and unhooked her bra. "It is in Australia."

***

Tabitha woke with a cough; it rumbled deep in her chest, like her mother's cough as she stood over the stove in the morning, a Pall Mall between her lips while she fried eggs in the bacon grease she kept in a coffee can underneath the sink. *Oh, God.* "Bryce." She reached beside her, but the side of the bed where her husband had gone to sleep next to her was empty. "Bryce," she said louder, another spasm of coughing racked her lungs. A different 'asm racked her body during the night after Bryce had drifted into sleep. As she lay in bed, the silence of night coming through the open windows broken only by the distant underlying hum of the generators at the high school and the café, Tabitha felt a desire burning in her she hadn't felt for a long time. It built deep inside her as Bryce began to snore, the loud rattle that used to drive her downstairs to sleep on the couch filled the room. Nope, wasn't him. Lazarus? No, no. That man was disgusting. But there was something about him, something raw, something powerful. She lay stiff and trembled on the wooden poster bed staring at the canopy; the near half-moon peeking through the window cast a dull gray light around the room. Tabitha pinched her fists tightly enough to hurt. No, it couldn't be the thought of Lazarus that washed her body in pleasure. But wha– *Oh, my God. Oh, MY God. OH, MY GOD.* Tabitha had always had strong ejaculations during orgasms. That night she had to go to the bathroom and find a towel to sleep on. Bryce never woke.

"Bryce," she said again, her voice no more than a whisper. *"Shit" doesn't even begin to describe how I feel.* Tabitha rolled over and pushed herself to a half-sitting position and she saw blood. A dark red circle of dry crust decorated Bryce's pale yellow pillow. *Oh, no.* "Bryce," she called, louder this time.

Tabitha crawled out of bed, the heat of the late July morning already crept into the little house. *It's hot. So hot.* Her body ached like she'd been in a car accident, her chest screaming from the impact with the steering wheel that never happened. Why? She coughed again; the pain almost sent her to the floor. Dots of dried blood on the hardwood led her from the bedroom into the hallway; Tabitha leaned on the wall as she stumbled forward to keep herself from falling. A new spot appeared on the floor, wet and shiny next to dull rust-red droplets. *What the?* Another joined the first wet spot, then another. Tabitha ran a hand across her upper lip and held it in front of her face. Her skin glistened in fresh blood. "Bryce."

Her husband sat in the kitchen, a cup of cold tea in front of him, a copper kettle sat on a colorful crochet potholder in the middle of the maple surface of the table. *Oh, Bryce.* His face was ashen, the tissues shoved into his nostrils red with blood. She let go of the wall and wobbled on weak legs. She fell against the table; the chair across from her toppled and clattered onto the floor. "Bryce," she whispered. *Thirsty. So thirsty.* Tabitha fell into a chair and reached for him. Bryce grasped her hand in his. *Dear, Lord, he's burning up.*

"I thought tea would help," he said, forcing a smile, the dried blood on his upper lip cracked from the movement. "I should have asked for Mr. T."

Bryce joked when he was scared. He always did and the jokes were always bad. "Look at it this way," he'd told his mother as she lay on a gurney, a nurse prepping her for surgery to remove part of her large intestine, the part that carried a massive tumor. "Now you'll have a semi-colon." His mother, sweet, sweet Momma Bert, didn't think it was funny. Maybe it was because of all the morphine, or maybe it was because Bryce always made jokes at the wrong time. Tabitha knew "Mr. T" was a Scared Bryce joke. He must feel as bad as she did; he sure as hell looked it.

"We need to get to Lazarus. Maybe there's a doctor in town," Tabitha wheezed, the pain in her chest now sharp, like a heart attack. *Not a heart attack. Who's going to take care of Kyle? Oh, my God, Kyle.* "Is Kyle okay?" She tried to push herself up from the table, but the strength wasn't there. Tears burst from her eyes. "I have to make sure my baby's okay." She tried to stand again, but a voice from the hallway stopped her.

"What's goin' on?"

Tabitha turned as quickly as she dared, vertigo threatening to dump her onto the worn kitchen linoleum. Kyle stood in the doorway rubbing his eyes, his red Washington Nationals T-shirt wrinkled from sleep, a drool stain on the left shoulder. Always the left. Kyle's eyes grew wide and his hands dropped to his sides as he looked at his parents and screamed. "Your eyes, Mom. Your eyes."

Tears, they're just tears. I was worried about you, formed in her mind, but died at her throat when a wet, red dot appeared on her forearm. Tabitha raised a weak, shaking hand to her face and touched her tears. She was crying blood.

"Kyle," Bryce wheezed, a coughing fit struck him and a clot of blood landed with a splat on the tabletop. "Oh, God. Kyle, go get that Lazarus. Tell him we need a doctor." Black spots swarmed before his eyes; the kitchen began to spin.

The boy ran to the kitchen door and threw it open. The man he knew as Mr. Gundy, the man who told them to stay close to him in the darkness as he escorted them from Mr. Lazarus' house, a scary man with a military haircut and hard, cold eyes, stood in the doorway. He grinned; the smile looked to Kyle like a snake's.

"Good morning," Ken Gundy said, his voice low and emotionless. "Just stopped by to see if you fine folks needed anything."

***

The world looked like it was underwater. *Where am I? A gymnasium? What?* A basketball goal hung directly over Tabitha's head, the bars holding it to the tall ceiling distorted in her swimming eyes. *God, it's hot. It's so hot.* She reached up to wipe the sweat from her face, but her arms wouldn't move; neither would her legs. *What's happening here?* The pain was worse than a car crash now, like something was building in her, ready to burst out, but not like her orgasm in the night. Oh, no, not at all. That was right. This was something wrong.

"Bryce," she said, although she didn't know if sound came from her mouth. "Bryce, honey. Bryce?"

Neck muscles screamed as Tabitha turned her head looking for her husband. Yes, it was a gymnasium. Morning sunlight from thin windows that lined the tops of the high walls revealed a grinning purple dog painted on one cinderblock wall, the words Terrance County Bulldogs circled it. Conference title banners hung from the rafters. A noise. A familiar humming noise lay under the structure of this fuzzy dream. *Must be the humidifiers.* A dozen humidifiers scattered the floor amongst hospital gurneys and portable heaters, the kind the Redskins used on the sidelines in December. The room felt like a greenhouse. *Why would the gymnasium be a greenhouse?* She tried to squint through her thick vision and saw things that looked like bodies strapped to the gurneys in the distance. *Everything's in the distance.* Things hung from the bodies, things that looked like garden hoses drooped from their chests, over the side of the gurney and ended in a bloomed, wilted flower. Barbells loaded with steel weights sat on the floor around the tables, chains connected to the barbells lay in piles like someone had unraveled a sweater.

A face suddenly loomed over her. She wanted to scream, but had forgotten how. Lazarus. *What was he wearing? A hospital mask?*

"Good morning, Mrs. McKenney," he said, the words distant. "Sorry to hear you're not feeling well."

My family. "My family," came out in a whisper. "Where's my family?"

A smile broke over Lazarus' face She could tell by the skin around his eyes. "They're here, Mrs. McKenney," he said. "Not to worry." He paused, faking a look of concern; the smile faded but didn't vanish. "Well, maybe a little. You see; your husband is dead." Lazarus swung the wheeled table on its wheels and Tabitha's world reeled. Her stomach threatened to come up, but there was nothing in it to vomit.

Bryce. My God, Bryce. Bryce McKenney lay beside her, his face covered by a fine gray mold. "Bryce."

Lazarus stood between them, hiding Bryce from her view. "He gave his all for this town, Mrs. McKenney. You should be proud."

Bryce is dead, wandered her fevered mild, looking for a place to grab hold, but it couldn't. "Where's Kyle?" she asked. "Where's my son?"

This time Lazarus' smile disappeared. "He's fine. Healthy, in fact, which causes some concern." Lazarus sat with one cheek on Tabitha's gurney. "Gwenny said Kyle didn't eat his pancakes. Why didn't Kyle eat his pancakes?"

Pancakes? My husband is dead and he's talking pancakes? Bryce's death sat in the middle of her mind and began to nestle in. "He has celiac disease. He can't eat wheat. No gluten."

Lazarus nodded. "Well, that would explain the bread as well. What about the potatoes?"

Why is he still talking about food? Potatoes? "They were mashed. He won't eat mashed potatoes." *Dry. I need water. So much water.* "Says they look like puss."

This time Lazarus laughed. *That bastard laughed out loud.* "Well, that makes me feel better," he said. "The Ophiocordon was in the potatoes and the pancakes and the bread."

Ophiocordon?

"There's only one man who's ever survived Ophiocordon," Lazarus said, his voice booming now, echoing off the gymnasium walls, "and that's me. Not enough room in this world for two Lazarus. Lazaruses? Lazari?"

"Why did you put Ophi–?" Tabitha's strength was fading and was almost gone.

Lazarus leaned close, his eyes filling Tabitha's vision. "Because I'm taking back the world from those idiots who destroyed it and I need an army." He paused and stood straight. "Looks like you're about ready to join your hubby. You got a little gray fuzz on your cheek."

Tabitha's bowels evacuated in her once white cotton panties. That's all she wore as she lay strapped to the gurney in the Mayday greenhouse. *I shit myself. Isn't that supposed to happen when you die?* "Kyle," came out in a hiss.

"I'm here, Mom."

The words came out so softly she almost didn't hear it. *Is that Kyle? Is that really Kyle?* Tabitha turned toward the sound. Kyle stood next to Ken Gundy; Ken Gundy and his Nazi face. Gundy's arm rested on Kyle's slim shoulder, his fingers around the back of the boy's neck.

"Your son, Mrs. McKenney. You see, Kyle's just fine." Lazarus waved his hand at Gundy. "Take him to the Corral."

"No," cracked in Tabitha's throat. "Where are you taking him? Where are you taking my son?"

Lazarus' smile returned. "He's not yours anymore, Mrs. McKenney," he said. "He's ours."

Kyle tried to break free from Gundy, to run, run anywhere, but he couldn't move. Gundy's grip was like steel. "You see, ma'am," Gundy said. "Zombies like their meat. Oh, surely ma'am they do. But they like it best young and tender and scared shitless. Like this." Gundy pulled back his arm and struck Kyle in the face with his closed fist. Blood flew from the boy's ruined nose as he skidded across the room. This time Tabitha screamed.

***

What a fine day. The blue sky stretched to forever over Mayday as Lazarus made his way toward Main Street and the Whistlestop Café for breakfast. Birds sang in the still morning and his walk smelled of honeysuckle. It felt like a Disney movie, if Disney made movies where stalks of fungus ripped through people's chests and turned millions of people into zombies. Lazarus waved at Layia Carpenter who trimmed the hedges in her front yard. Good to know people still took pride in appearances at the end of the world. He rounded the corner from First Street to Main and said "good morning" to Ted Simpson, just opening the Apple Mart. Nobody bought anything from Ted, nobody had to, because nobody used money anymore. But there was still the need for a good grocery store and Ted checked them out just like he used to, to keep track of inventory. People needed to feel something normal and grocery shopping was about as normal as you could get. A run into Louisville last week filled the shelves of the Apple Market, so, yep, everything was just like normal.

"Good morning, Lazarus," Ted said, his butcher's apron stained pink with blood that just wouldn't wash out. "It was nice to have some fresh beef."

"Sure was."

"There's plenty of farms around here," he said. "Plenty of cattle, plenty of chickens, plenty of hogs and I've got plenty of freezer space. As long as the gasoline doesn't run out, I can keep my generator running for a long time."

Hogs? Why hadn't I thought of that? "Think you could make sausage?"

Ted nodded. "Course I can."

Lazarus slapped Ted's shoulder. "I'll send Walter and a crew out today to find some fresh meat," Lazarus said. "Ted, my friend, this day just keeps getting better."

Yes, a very fine day. Lazarus thought he could have done without seeing Ken Gundy beat the shit out of the McKenney boy in front of his poor dying mother, but she didn't live through half of it. Gundy usually waited until he had them chained in the corral before venting his frustrations on their weak, breakable bodies, but he must have been trying to prove a point. Lazarus didn't know what the point was, or who he was trying to prove it to. That's what happened to Lazarus when he got hungry, he lost all concentration. He just wished Gundy hadn't called his soldiers "zombies." He hated that word and hated what he had to do to the McKenneys, he really did. The people who chanced upon Mayday just wanted to survive like the rest of them; but they were going to leave Mayday and Lazarus couldn't let that happen. This was his town and his world. God had kept him alive for a reason and Lazarus knew that reason was to bring the human race back from the brink of death. The McKenneys needed to be productive members of society and they were. Mom would soon sprout like Dad and create soldiers for Lazarus' army. When Gundy got back from the Corral, Lazarus would send him to grab a couple of filthy Carlsoners to chain to the barbells at the foot of the McKenney's gurneys.

The bell over the door of the Whistlestop jingled when Lazarus opened it and stepped into the well-lit café. The Whistlestop, like the Apple Mart and the high school, was one of the buildings in town that needed electricity, it needed to keep being normal for the people of Mayday. Gary Thatcher, the plumber, sat sipping coffee over an empty plate, a few scraps of waffle stuck to his fork. He talked with Jim Smithy, the director of Mayday's public works and dogcatcher. Mayday didn't need a dogcatcher much anymore, but they needed public works. Gary and Jim were working on getting the water tower back online. The water wouldn't be drinkable at first, but a permanent boil order would take care of that. With water in the toilets and filling bathtubs, things would really seem back to normal.

"Morning, Lazarus." Gwenny stood behind the counter, her powder blue uniform lightly dusted with flour. The uniform was a little low cut for a small-town gravy restaurant; this wasn't a Hooters, but Lazarus didn't mind. He didn't mind at all. "I have a surprise for you," she said and disappeared into the kitchen.

"How's the project going, gentlemen?" Lazarus asked, sinking into a booth next to their table.

"Not bad, Tim," Gary said. "We were having some problems with the pump, but it should be up and running by tomorrow, Sunday by the latest."

Tim? Tim? "That's good work, fellas. But, Gary, I'm not Tim anymore."

Gary gently sat his cracked porcelain coffee cup onto the café table and looked up at Lazarus. "I've known you all your life and your name's Tim. I'm glad the shit that killed everybody else and turned them into zombies didn't kill you, but that doesn't change the fact that your name is Tim. Tim Hardy. This Lazarus stuff is pretentious bullshit. Now, I'm calling you Tim just like your mom and dad called you. Tim."

Lazarus smiled at Gary. Ken Gundy would have to do something about this man, but not now. Not while the water tower was down. Even then, he needed to wait for a while, you know, just to see if the water tower worked. Then Ken Gundy could do what he wanted to him. "Whatever you like, Gary. Whatever you like."

Jim nodded toward Lazarus. "Where's your friend?" he asked, his voice flat.

Friend? "Who?"

"The tall, lanky fellow," Jim said. "The one with the cannibal condition."

Jeremy. Oh, Jeremy. Lazarus hadn't seen Jeremy this morning, which was odd. Jeremy usually waited outside his house for their walk around town, but this morning he wasn't there. Maybe he was still lurking around the Stinson house, sniffing for Kyle. "He had other things to do, but I'll tell him you asked."

Gary and Jim nodded and fell back into conversation. Jim rose from the table seconds later and pulled on his Kentucky Wildcats cap. "Thanks, Gwen, honey," he said and walked out the door, the chime just as happy as when Lazarus came in. Gary left right behind Jim.

"Any time boys," Gwenny said, coming through the kitchen doors, a coffee mug in one hand, a plate of pancakes in the other. She kissed Lazarus lightly when she sat his breakfast on the table. No one was there to see.

Dark blobs dotted the pancakes. "Whoa. What's this?"

Gwenny giggled. "Blueberries. The search party going through the farmhouses found a can of blueberries. I thought you'd like them."

Oh, yes. "I like them just fine, Gwenny. This means a lot to me."

"I tell you what else will mean a lot to you," she said, stepping away from the booth and walking back toward the counter, shaking her hips. Although a cherry pie in the round display case looked good to Lazarus, too, he couldn't keep his eyes off Gwenny's backside. "Today's Saturday."

Took care of business, found future sausage, made plans to kill Gary, had blueberry pancakes sitting right here, Saturday sex. Yep. This was sure going to be a fine, fine day.

CHAPTER 14

I'm losing them. Doug sat in a canvas camp chair, a lukewarm mug of coffee wedged between his legs, the pastel smear on the horizon slowly pushing back the stars. *Goddamnit, I'm losing them. This is Carter's Phillips 66.* They needed someplace to stay and ride this thing out, someplace safe, secure. Doug knew that and he was trying to find it, but they wanted a cabin in the woods, he wanted Mayberry. Nothing good ever happened at a cabin in the woods, Doug had seen that slasher film more than once; but nothing bad ever happened in Mayberry, especially with Sheriff Andy Taylor and Deputy Barney Fife on the job. He sipped the instant coffee that tasted like he'd strained it through his sock and wondered if a cabin in the woods wouldn't be the best choice. *No, no. People. We need people. Safety in numbers.* There were a lot of crazy people left out there, like Herman Munster's Devil Woman; and she attacked them with a fucking tank. They needed to find people, good people, in a group that was too big to be worried about things like zombies, or a single tank. Doug took over watch from Jenna at 3 a.m.; she now lay in the tent next to Nikki, snoring like Fred Flintstone. Doug figured he'd have to get used to that.

"We could always go back to the Marsten house," Jenna had said to him, her arms wrapped around Doug's neck, the sweet smell of her breath bathed his face. *She got into the pineapple.* "They left food, water, electricity, guns. There's Terry's video game, since his idea didn't work. 'Toddlers & Tiaras' on DVR, enough room in that little town for everybody. We could stay there a long time."

Yes, we could. But should we? The little town of Barton, Missouri, was an out-of-the-way speck, no reason for anyone to find them there. But Herman Munster had found them, falling onto the living room window, smearing it with his blood as he slid down the glass, blood that was probably still dried to the window. Jenna was right, the place was well stocked and St. Joseph was close enough for supply runs to last them a long time. There was enough wildlife and wandering livestock to keep them fed. They could live there for the rest of their lives, or at least get directions to Tanelorn, the Marsten's fortress of a summer house in western Nebraska. Doug had found the layout to the house on the Marsten's computer. It was ready for the end of the world; too bad the Marstens died before they got to use it.

"Maybe," he said. "We can talk about it in the morning." He kissed her deeply; the taste of pineapple filled his mouth.

That was at 3 a.m. He was supposed to be on watch, for zombies, for any visitors. Maybe people, maybe coyotes like in western Nebraska, maybe lions. They were just across the bridge from Omaha where some asshole had released all the animals at the Henry Doorly Zoo. Anything might sneak up on them in the dark, but most of his attention was on the Silverado. Nikki, Jenna and Andi slept in the Hipsters' tent, Terry slept under the stars on a sleeping bag from Walmart, but Donnie slept in the cab of his truck, probably with the doors locked. There was something off about that boy. Doug mistrusted Donnie with the same fervor he trusted Andi. Doug didn't know what Donnie was, but there was something about his eyes, they looked like a cheap doll's. Doug wondered if he shook the boy if those eyes would dance in all sorts of directions. If they did go back to Barton, Doug knew one thing; that squirrely kid wasn't coming with them.

Terry rolled over to his side and farted in his sleep. Doug grinned. *What's wrong with me? I'm a grown man and still think farts are funny.* He started to take another sip of the instant coffee, but a rumble stopped the mug halfway to his mouth. The rumble started low, barely audible. If he would have been here a couple of months ago, with the hum of tractor-trailers on the highway and the din of Council Bluffs waking up in pre-apocalypse America, Doug wouldn't have heard the noise until it was almost upon them; but in the dead silence of the fallen world, he heard the source of the rumble miles away.

Train. A fucking train. "Terry," Doug said, pushing himself out of the camp chair and onto his crutches. "Wake up." Terry farted again. Doug limped over to the sleeping bags laid out on the grass between the Prius and the tent and poked Terry with the rubber tip of the crutch. "Get your ass up."

Terry rolled onto his back and looked up at Doug, his face pale in the light of the coming morning. "What's up, boss?" he asked, his voice heavy with sleep.

"Everything's okay," Doug said. "But we've got company coming." The rumble of a train in the distance was louder. No whistle. There weren't cars to warn off the tracks anymore. "You hear that?"

Terry nodded. "Hell, yes," he said, then he noticed Doug's frown. "What's wrong, man?"

Doug looked toward the trucks, concern covered his face. "Civilization's out there. Somebody sent the train; somebody's receiving the train," he said. "There's civilization on both ends. We're going to find running water and movies and kids playing in parks somewhere. It's going to happen. We just have to follow it."

Terry pulled three cans of Armour Chili out of a bag in the trunk of the Prius. "Breakfast?"

***

Carter's Phillips 66.

Sweat ran down Doug's smooth face, the T-shirt under his tan Boy Scout shirt clung to his torso like a drunken prom date. *Way to go, Mike. Way to flipping get us lost.* He swatted at the mosquitoes buzzing around his face when the toe of his hiking boot snagged on a tree root and he splashed into the water of a slow-moving tributary of the Cimarron River in southwestern Kansas. Doug spat out a mouthful of cold water and sand as he pushed his face out of the stream. *Great. Just great.* He looked at the bank; Danny, Mike and Terry stood in the knee-high grass. Terry grinned like he'd just gotten a Christmas present. Danny had his back to the stream, pissing into the trees. Mike stared at him, his face twisted into one big, gigantic, royal fucking I told you so.

"Ready to give up, kemosabe?" Mike Smeltzer was an asshole, but of the four boys vying for Eagle Scout, Doug knew he and Mike had the best shot, which was too bad. Mike didn't deserve it. "Or were you just early for bath night?"

"Go to hell, Smeltzer." *Don't lose your cool. Don't lose your cool. Don't lose your cool.* The boys, who went off in search of someplace to swim – *guess I found it* – were separated from Paola, Kansas, Boy Scout Troop 100 by any one of the 521 square miles of prairie and forest in the Cimarron National Grassland. They were close enough to Colorado to piss on it and hell, Danny may have just done that. They might even be closer to Colorado than they were the rest of their Troop. The low sun bathed the late afternoon in orange light, Doug knew they needed to find help and they needed to find help now. Mike wasn't helping.

"Clever, Titus. Clever," Mike Smeltzer said, his smug smile not yet shit eating like it would one day be when he sold used cars in Olathe. "It's going to be dark soon. We have to get back to camp."

Don't lose your cool. "We don't know where camp is, Smeltzer," Doug said through gritted teeth – *thanks to you and your "we don't need a compass. Just come on."* "The Scoutmaster is probably freaking out about now. We saw a gas station on the highway. Given the position of the sun and Cimarron River we're approaching, that station should be about a mile away. Maybe two. We can call for help."

"We don't need help, Titus," Mike said. "I can lead us back to camp."

"How you gonna do that, Mike?" Danny asked. "Terry wiped his ass on the map back there when he took a dump in the poison ivy."

Terry suddenly stopped grinning. "What?"

"It's buried behind a bush somewhere covered in Terry's breakfast burrito from that shitty truck stop," Danny said. "You want to go dig it up?"

"What do you mean, poison ivy?"

Mike rested his fists on his hips, like smug pricks do and smiled. "Of course not. I know exactly where we are and exactly where camp is. I was just waiting for Aragorn here to shit himself and give up. He's shit himself enough. Come on. Let's go back to camp." Mike turned and walked into the trees. Danny followed.

"Come on guys," Doug said, his olive trousers soaked in creek water. He pointed to the south. "Help is that way." He looked at Terry. "Come on, man. It's right over there."

"You coming Terry?" Mike called from the trees.

Terry shoved his hands in his pockets and looked at the ground. "I'm hungry, Doug. I'm going with them." He turned and disappeared into the foliage.

"Goddamnit," Doug muttered and followed them.

They were lost for two days. A helicopter circling over the expanse of prairie grass and trees spotted them standing in an open field, hungry and dirty. They were ten miles from camp. As Scoutmaster Thomas drove the van east on U.S. 56 toward home, they went by Carter's Phillips 66 where Doug was marching his fellow Scouts to call for help. Given the topography and position of the Cimarron River as the white and red sign boasting "Unleaded $2.39" crawled by, Doug knew they couldn't have been more than two miles from the station when they turned to follow Mike. Fuck you, Mike Smeltzer. Fuck you.

As the sound of the train grew louder, Doug knew this was Carter's Phillips 66 all over again.

Jenna, Nikki and Andi sat on the camp chairs eating chili in silence; the men stood. Doug was too excited to sit, anyway. This was it. The way to civilization approached in the form of a steel arrow. He glanced over his shoulder; Donnie sat unmoving in the cab of his truck. If Doug didn't know better he'd swear it was a mannequin behind the wheel of the Silverado. Did Donnie know about the train? Doug didn't care.

"It's probably a couple of miles away," Doug said. "If it's a freight train, those things go at a clip of about 60 miles an hour; if it's a passenger train, about 80. Either way, it should be here in no time."

"How do you know anything about trains?" Jenna asked. She reached out and touched his hand.

"I've loved trains since I was a kid." He wrapped his thick, calloused hand around her slight, soft one. "I had an HO scale model train set. It's still in my basement somewhere, in a box. Well, in several boxes."

She squeezed the hand tightly. "Is that why you're doing this? So you can play with your train set?"

A smile swept across his face. "Maybe."

"I see it, boss." Terry tossed his empty chili can into the tall weeds on the side of the road and leaned against the Prius. "You ready for this?" A black speck on the track grew larger.

Doug let Jenna's hand slip from his grip and took two steps toward the street that separated their temporary home from the lines of railroad tracks. "Hell, yes." The train. It was almost here. The rumble soon became a steady ratchet of click-clack, click-clack, as the diesel locomotive carrying whothehellknowswhat thundered toward them. Doug knew it wouldn't stop for them because it couldn't. Once an engineer hit the brakes, a freight train took at least a mile to go from What The Hell? to a full stop. Even if there was a cow, or a car, or a busload of orphans on the track, the engineer couldn't do anything but close his eyes and plow through them. All this train could do was carry on, carry on to someplace with people. And all they had to do was follow the right track to civilization. Doug stood alone and watched Carter's Phillips 66 come to him.

"What do we do when it gets here?" Terry asked.

Doug was suddenly five years old, waiting with Doug Sr. in his pickup at the railroad crossing on North Pearl Street in Paola as the orange Burlington Northern Santa Fe engines hauling coal cars thundered past. "Wave, Dougie," Doug Sr. said, his voice low, a Marlboro between his lips, a breeze blowing the smoke out the open cab window. "Wave at the Cabooseman." The Cabooseman always waved from his bright red car at the end of the train, but the railroads started phasing out the caboose by Doug's seventh birthday; technology took the place of human eyes and arms. An EOT, End of Train device mounted on the last car could tell the engineer everything he needed to know. One day the Cabooseman was gone. There were plenty of caboose cars parked on the lawns of small town city parks across the Midwest, but they sat still and locked tight. The train came toward them, probably without a caboose, but somebody had to be in the engine cab running that thing.

"Smile and wave, Terry," Doug said. "Just smile and wave."

Tension engulfed the morning. Council Bluffs, once a city of nearly 63,000 people, now maybe just six, sat in anticipation, the click-clack still in the background. Somewhere to the west, a lion roared.

"Where do you think it's going?" Nikki sat with a white plastic spoon sticking from the middle of the Armour chili can between her knees. Breakfast during the apocalypse had reverted to college.

"I know where it's going," Andi said. She leaned against the hood of the Prius next to Terry. "I wonder where it came from."

I know where it's going? "How do you know where it's going?" Doug asked.

Andi stood straight and walked to the girls past the pile of solar generators couldn't power Terry's Xbox and pulled a beer out of an open case. She cracked it open with shaking hands. "I was stationed in Muskogee, Oklahoma," Andi said. She took a drink of the warm beer, the beer tasting way too good so early in the morning. "The Fence is there, cutting across the country. Sergeant Cotton said the government was close to completing it. It was going across the freeze line of the United States to keep the infected people in." She paused and looked at the faces around her. Good faces. *Call 'em like you see 'em,* Big Andy would say. *Call 'em like you see 'em.* "Zombies. They built it to keep the zombies out. They figured the fungus that caused this whole thing would die when it got past freezing."

"Do you think that will work?" Doug asked.

Andi's eyes met his. "I don't think so. Fungi thrive everywhere."

Terry laughed.

Doug turned toward him. "What's so funny?"

"Fungi sounds like something weird you do with your dick."

Nikki leaned over and picked a Pepsi out of a cooler with no ice; the crack loud in the morning. She stared at Andi. "What did you do at the Fence?" she asked.

The fence. The Polo Man. Andi pushed her bangs out of her eyes. *Damn it.* "I–"

"Train," Terry said, pointing down the track. "Hot shit, a train. It's pretty close."

Andi and Doug turned toward the spider web of tracks coming from the north. The dark speck was now a red diesel engine, the mass of the train stretched behind it, the vanishing point perspective looked like the train would never end, except it did, under a growing black cloud. Doug forgot about Andi and the Fence, as he turned toward the track, just waiting for a train.

"Get ready to wave, boss."

A black, undulating cloud followed the train. Doug shook his head. "This isn't right."

The red and black engines, the letters CN painted across the side in white, roared by, the sound of the metal against metal thundering drown out the day. Doug waved, but he couldn't see the engineer to tell if he waved back.

"Dude," Terry said, leaning close to Doug. "There's somebody on top of the train." There was; Doug almost missed it. A man crawled across the top of the third engine, his yellow shirt and black pants looked like a uniform. The engines flew by and Doug's stomach felt like it dropped right out of his body.

"That's no man," he said.

Terry leaned in closer, his head almost touching Doug's. "What?"

Doug looked at his friend. "That was a zombie," he shouted.

"Oh, shit."

Brown boxcars marked Canadian National followed the engines, black and silver passenger cars with no faces in the windows behind them. "I wonder where all the–" Doug started. Flatcars carrying Canadian military trucks, tanks, construction equipment and armored fighting vehicles answered his question. The people that should have been in the passenger cars, looking as the scenery clicked by, littered the flatcars. Soldiers in green camouflaged combat fatigues crouched in positions around the vehicles, as their C9A2 light machine gun fire tore into the bodies of hundreds of zombies that swarmed over the rear passenger cars like the ants that helped start this mess.

Terry slapped Doug's arm. "Holy shit, dude. They're everywhere." Zombies, shredded by gunfire, flew off the cars as the train rumbled by. Some hit the ground and lay still; others tried to crawl back to the tracks on broken limbs, jagged tips of bone showing through their worn clothing. Jenna was up, her arm around Doug's waist as the horror train drove past. Somewhere, Nikki screamed over the roar of the locomotive.

Then cloud was upon them.

The first zombie to reach the flatcars lunged at a soldier, machinegun fire ripped its legs from its body, blood and flesh painted the armored troop carrier beside it. The momentum from the lunge sent the creature into the soldier who'd fired the weapon and sent them both off the side of the flatcar. They landed in the tall grass. Andi shot across South Avenue in a full sprint before the synapsis in Doug's head could tell his muscles to move. They all followed Andi. Then the train was gone, as quickly as it came. The flashing red light on the EOT waved its own good bye. The cloud was closer, but still far away. Doug knew what it was: crows. Crows following their supper.

Andi pulled her sidearm from its holster and stopped five feet from the soldier. The man lay on his back in the grass, his neck and shirt slick with fresh blood. The torso of the zombie, the thing dressed like a lumberjack – *it may have been a lumberjack* – sat on the soldier's chest, its bloody mouth chomping. "Push it off you," Andi shouted, her sidearm raised.

The soldier held the zombie by the throat with his left hand and pulled up his sidearm with his right. "I got this," he said through clenched teeth as he placed the barrel of his Browning 9mm pistol against the lumberjack's head and fired one round. The monster grew slack; the soldier tossed him off with one arm and lay in the grass, his breath a wet wheeze.

Andi holstered the weapon and knelt next to the soldier. "You have friends here," she screamed over the flapping birds. "You're going to be okay."

The soldier laughed, a splat of blood landed on his chin. "Like hell I am. I'm all busted up inside." He paused to take a breath. "Then there's this." The soldier turned his head slowly and Andi saw where the fresh blood came from. The zombie's teeth had torn open the left side of the soldier's face, blood oozed freely from the wound. "I'm a goner. You can't patch me up. That thing bit me. It fucking bit me."

"Oh, my God," Nikki said, choking back a scream. To the soldier, Nikki looked like she just appeared next to Andi; three girls sent from heaven to bring him home. "I've got to stop the bleeding. I'll be back." She turned to go back to camp for Andi's first aid kit, but she grabbed her arm.

"Zombie bit him."

Nikki stopped trying to pull away and turned back toward the soldier. "But the bite doesn't cause a person to change into a zombie, does it? It's the spores. This isn't a horror movie," she shouted.

The soldier shrugged slightly, the small movement sent tendrils of pain through him. "Shit happens," he wheezed. "Like I said, my insides are scrambled. You can't fix me."

Nikki grabbed Terry and hugged him tightly.

"What's your name, soldier?" Doug asked, leaning on his crutches.

The man weakly swallowed. "Master Corporal Oliver Tremblay." Oliver waved at these new, strange people gathered around him, his Browning 9mm still clutched in his fist. "Would somebody please get me some water? I don't want to go out with a taste like I just woke up from a bender."

"Sure," Nikki said and ran across South Avenue toward camp.

"Where were you headed?" Doug asked.

Oliver coughed, a fountain of blood spewed across his chest. "Dyersburg," he said through a wet, bloody cough. "Dyersburg, Tennessee. The Fence–" Coughing aftershocks sent more blood up. He lay still and sucked in air. "The Fence has made it to Dyersburg. We're supposed to see it built to Wilmington. Wilmington–" His voice trailed off.

"North Carolina?" Jenna asked.

Oliver nodded slowly. "Yes. Then we'll be safe."

Andi knelt close to Oliver. "Where'd the zombies on the train come from?"

Oliver lay quiet, pulling in breath slowly and unsteadily. "The passenger cars at the end," he finally said. "We were in a rush and nobody checked the ones in the back. Once they figured out how to get outside, those bastards were everywhere." Oliver winced as pain shot through his chest.

"What do you need us to do?" Andi asked; her voice wavered.

Oliver tried to grin, but the pain pulled his mouth into a grimace. "Just go away." He sucked in a shallow breath and waved his Browning. "I need to take care of something."

This isn't going to be Carter's Phillips 66, Doug thought. *I'm going to save everybody.* "We're looking for civilization," he said. "Is that where we find it?"

"Dyersburg," Oliver said, the word gurgled in his throat. "People are gathering there."

Everyone, except Oliver.

Andi rose and stood next to Doug. "Is there anything else you need to tell us?"

A smile broke on Oliver's face. "Yeah, sure," he said. "Americans think Canadians say 'eh' all the time, but we really don't, eh?" He coughed again, the pain sent trickles of tears down his cheek. He pulled the Browning up to his mouth. "Now go."

"But–" Jenna started, but Doug shook his head.

The Browning fired before they walked the fifteen feet to South Avenue.

***

Donnie stood watching as the Gunkies took down camp. The shower was the last thing they disassembled and stuffed into the back of Daddy's Silverado. *My Silverado.* He'd heard the train coming in his sleep and sat up in the cab of the truck, his skin slick with sweat from the early-morning heat. He'd slept with the doors locked and the window's shut. Oh, yes sir. He wasn't going to become vulnerable to them. Let them find Mother's kitchen knife and figure out he was going to kill them all. Their deaths were going to be a surprise. They had to be a surprise. Donnie liked surprises.

The Gunkies tore down camp by 8 a.m., the crippled man coaxing them to go faster, to get out of there before the cloud of birds came. Donnie watched it grow in the sky like a swelling water balloon as they worked. The murder would be here soon enough. Murder of crows. That sounded hilarious. Donnie stood in an open field drinking a Pepsi and watched Jenna, the ginger woman who looked like Vanessa Hagen. While the boys Tetrised their home of the last three days into the back of the pickup, she walked along the train track shooting the Good People who couldn't walk anymore. *Good for her,* Donnie thought. *Good for her.*

"You still want to follow the train, dude?" the drunken redneck asked the crippled man.

The crippled man leaned against his crutches and slid PVC pipe into the bed. "You bet your ass," he said. "I'm trying to do what's best for us, Terry." The crippled man looked at the redneck and frowned. Donnie loved to see people frown at each other. So much excitement. "You remember the Eagle Scout candidate's trip to Cimarron National Grassland?"

The redneck looked away. "Yeah. I remember."

"And you remember two days of eating berries and raw nuts before that helicopter found us? Those berries gave you the runs."

The redneck nodded.

"And how far were we away from civilization when everybody decided to follow that fucking car salesman Mike Smeltzer?"

"Two miles," the redneck said. "We were two miles away from that gas station, just like you said."

The cripple reached out and grabbed the redneck by the shoulder. "I'm right now, too," he said. "We're going to be okay."

Donnie walked out of the field and stood between Doug and Terry. "What are you guys talking about?" he asked, the smile on his face plastic.

The cripple turned toward him. "Our future, Donnie. We're going to find civilization."

Donnie's grin never faded as he patted Doug on the back. "And I'm happy for all of us. When are we leaving?"

"As soon as we're packed," the cripple said.

"Great. Just great." *You're all just like the Taylor boy and we're going to have some fun.* His grin grew bigger. "Hey," he yelled toward the soldier, the brunette lady and ginger woman who looked like Vanessa Hagen. "Anybody want to ride with me?"

AUGUST 1: MAYDAY, KENTUCKY

CHAPTER 15

Lacy Tomlinson tasted like peaches; an empty fruit can and fork sat on Lacy's bedside table, the remnant of a late-night snack. Walter Seidel liked that taste and he knew how much the preacher's daughter liked peaches. He held Lacy tight, his hands down the back of her jean shorts, his fingers making dimples into her bottom. Lacy's tongue became rigid as Walter pulled out of the kiss. Moonlight from the back door of her orderly bungalow that sat along the east wall of Mayday, fell across the young woman's face; a pout on her full lips. Walter squeezed harder, grinding her thighs into his. "I gotta go, honey. My shift at the Gate starts in a half hour."

She wrapped her fingers in the back of his hair and kissed him deeply. When she pulled away, she was grinning. "I know. I just don't want you to go. Who's going to hit my tickle spot?"

Lazarus. Every Thursday. Yeah, he knew Lazarus was banging the preacher's daughter, too. But the man everyone thought was their leader didn't know about Walter. Walter figured he'd just shoot the fat bastard another cow, maybe a pig or two. Sure, Lazarus survived Ophiocordon and looked like a total jackass on "Good Morning America," but Walter bet he wouldn't survive his cholesterol level for much longer. "You know I'll be back." He pulled his hands out of her pants and took the beautiful face in a gentle grasp. "I can't get enough of you." He kissed her softly. "I've got a surprise for you."

She smiled; her teeth glowed in the moonlight. "What is it?" she asked, bouncing on her naked toes.

Damn. Walter wished he could see her deep brown eyes, but the irises were black in the gray haze. Her eyes were so pretty. "I was going to save it, but, well, I went hunting yesterday and I found a house off Route 12, on a long lane the other hunting parties hadn't raided."

"Did you kill any, you know? Any–"

"Zombies?" Walter nodded. Yep. A little girl, about twelve years old, maybe thirteen, locked in her room, her parents dead on the front lawn, their remains shredded by predators and scattered in the tall grass. *She ran at me when I opened the door and I crushed her skull with a hammer.* "An old man," he said, shaking his head. "I don't want to talk about it."

She kissed him again, softly, her lips brushing his. "It must have been hard for you." She held him for a moment, her breasts pressing into his chest. Walter thought he could do that all day. "What's my surprise?" she asked.

"A peach tree," he said. "I know how much you like peaches. I picked six Walmart bags full. Some of them aren't quite ripe yet. I'll bring them over tomorrow night."

She threw her arms around Walter's neck and jumped into his embrace, wrapping her legs around his waist. "Thank you, baby. You're keeping me sane." She kissed him again, then pulled back, dropping her bare feet to the kitchen linoleum, her arms still around his neck. "Do you have to go? I want to wake up next to you."

And that's when Lazarus chains me up next to Mac without my shirt. Walter kissed her again and grabbed the doorknob. "I want that, too, but we all have jobs. You tend the garden; I tend the Gate." He pecked her on the nose. "But you get back to sleep." He opened the door; the sound of frogs from Nelson Creek too damned Disney for his taste. "You know I'll be back."

Walter turned to leave, but Lacy grabbed his arm. "I don't want Lazarus," she said. "I want you."

He nodded. "I know. It won't be long." Walter stepped out the kitchen door into the darkness and clicked it shut behind him.

Maple Street ran in front of Lacy's house, the lane once well-lit by mercury vapor lamps that still sat atop light poles, a uniform gray in the moonlight. Uniform save for the deep black shadows cast by homes and foliage. Walter carried the hammer he'd crushed the little girl's skull with; there were no guns in Mayday, except for the hunting parties and the guards at the gate. Lazarus had seen to that. He wanted Mayday to be Beaver Cleaver's hometown, nothing but friendly smiles and school dances. That's why Walter stayed. *Oh, who am I kidding? I stayed for Lacy.* He had twenty-five minutes to go home, change and–

A scrape, a shoe scuffing on asphalt, whipped Walter around, his grip tight on the hammer handle. A figure, tall and lean, stood in the street, teetering unsteadily on its thin legs, waving like tall grass in a slight breeze. That was no man. There were zombies here, Walter knew, for Lazarus' grand plan, but they were locked up in the Field. Only one was allowed to roam free, Lazarus' pet, Jeremy. Walter adjusted his grip, the heft of the 16-ounce Stanley clawed hammer felt good in his hand. *Come on, charge me.* Walter wanted to plant the head of the yellow-handled hammer into the temple of that monster, but he knew Jeremy wouldn't charge him. The zombie was harmless as long as Walter wore one of the special shirts everyone in town wore, a one-foot-square tanned patch of skin sewn into the back. Zombie skin. Zombies don't attack their own.

***

The summer heat started early at the Gate. Walter sat on a picnic table under the bushy canopy of a tulip poplar with a bottle of Aquafina between his boots, sweat pooled under his arms. Gil Haply sat in a lawn chair, scooping rocks off the gravel parking lot and tossing them over at the peeling paint on the walls of the abandoned of the Dairy Rite outside the fence. The burger and shake shack, open since the 1950s, closed in 1994, the building dwindling into a heaping rot ever since. Gil's rocks thudding off the boards the only sound in the early morning.

"Stop it, Gil," Walter said. He hadn't gotten much sleep. The feel of Lacy's skin against his still tingled. His mind wasn't at the Gate; his mind was on Maple Street.

"How long you think this is going to go on?" Gil asked.

Walter unscrewed the cap on his water bottle. A lot of people in town were secretive, a lot of people were down right strange, Gil was neither. Walter never had to guess what Gil was thinking; he always said what was on his mind. Walter liked that. "What do you mean?"

Gil scooped up another rock and held it. "The end of the world? I miss shit, man. Like television and running water. I miss Chick-Fil-A. I know they just served chicken sandwiches, but I like chicken sandwiches."

Just the thought of a basket of waffle fries sent Walter's stomach rumbling. "I don't know, Gil. They figured out what caused the zombies before everything went south, if there's any government left, I suppose they're just trying to clean everything up."

Gil tossed another rock at the Dairy Rite. It thudded off the sagging roof and rolled off in front of the window teenage carhops once picked up their food to take to the cars on trays that fitted to the rolled down window. Walter had grown up in Mayday. His dad used to take him to the Dairy Rite for root beer in frosty glass mugs, sometimes the carhop would bring it over to the station wagon with a scoop of vanilla ice cream floating on the top. Now all the carhops, grown and married to locals, were probably dead, or worse, they were like Jeremy.

"You think the government is still around?"

Walter took a drink of warm water and screwed on the cap. "I don't know that either, but I do know planes are still flying. I've seen contrails and I know they're not taking gamblers to Vegas. They have to be government planes."

"Well, if Army trucks don't come in here and swoop us up soon..." Gil paused and looked around, then turned back toward Walter. When he spoke again, his voice was barely above a whisper. "Don't tell no one, but

I think I'm going to head out. What Tim is doing with those people who come in here scares the shit out of me. I don't want any part of it."

Tim? Walter smiled. "You don't like to call him Lazarus?"

Gil laughed. "Makes him sound like an asshole." He nodded; the grin quickly disappeared. "He is an asshole. A crazy asshole people follow. Those are the scariest kind. I'll give it about a week, then I'm gone."

God, that sounded good. "Where will you go?"

The summer heat sent a line of sweat running down Gil's face. He wiped it off with the sleeve of his T-shirt. "West, probably. Some place with no people. No people, no zombies."

Out West. No people, no zombies, no Lazarus. Just him and Gil and Lacy. That sounded great. Walter stared at Gil, the young man's shaggy blonde head made him look like a beach bum more than a farm kid. These words coming from anyone else in this little town would have scared him because it would have been a test. A test of loyalty to Lazarus. But this was Gil Haply. He'd had a few beers with Gil down at the Do Drop one night and watched Gil take a dump on Lazarus' front lawn on the way home. Jeremy stood by the front door, watching. He trusted Gil more than he trusted Lacy and he trusted Lacy a lot.

"I can get a truck. There are five we use for hunting parties. I can get the keys. They're always gassed up and ready. Rifles are already in the gun rack, boxes of bullets behind the seats." Walter stopped. This was dangerous talk. He looked around, but no one was there. "I'm in."

Gil nodded. "Let's give it a week." He stood and adjusted his Kentucky Wildcat ball cap. "Boss man just turned off Main Street and headed this way with his puppy dog."

The half-empty water bottle crinkled in Walter's grip. "A week?"

Gil nodded. "That'll give us time to collect supplies from the Apple Mart without Ted Simpson getting all suspicious."

Yep. Walter liked Gil a lot.

***

Before the world fell, Walter worked as a reporter for the Tri-County Courier in Carson. He hadn't gone to college in state; he wanted to get out of Kentucky, away from his parents, away from all the people in high school who'd get stuck in Mayday forever. He wanted to leave, more than anything he just wanted to leave. SIU in Carbondale, Illinois, sounded great. Four years later, he was back in Mayday. At least he worked out of town.

"Good morning, gentlemen." Lazarus stopped at the picnic table; Jeremy stood behind him, softly groaning. "Any excitement at the Gate?"

Walter wanted to knock that man down, strip off his shirt and just see how fast his pet zombie could tear off his face. "Nope," Gil said. "I think the deer are getting smart. They're shying away from here. I might have plugged too many of them from this chair."

"I'm not interested in deer, Gil," Lazarus said, patting his belly. "Walter here shot me a cow. That's what I want. Mmm. I think I'll have Gwenny cook me up some steak and eggs for breakfast. You boys want anything?"

Walter shook his head. "I'm not hungry, thanks."

Gil pulled a bag of beef jerky and a packet of peanuts out of a pocket in his cargo shorts. "I'm good."

Lazarus hiked up his belt that had begun to crawl down to reveal a plumber's crack. "Suit yourself," he said and turned to go. "Just remember, this fine food won't last forever. One day we'll be eating nuts and berries."

Walter wrote the first newspaper article on Tim Hardy, the man who survived Ophiocordon. He just went by Tim then. Once the story hit the Associated Press wire, The New York Times featured him on the front page and all the major news networks wanted to talk to the plastic factory worker, he decided he was better than a Tim. When they boarded up the town, Lazarus told Walter this was all because of him and gave him a job on the Gate. Something cushy for a new friend and Walter had thanked him. That was before Walter realized he wanted Lazarus dead.

Jeremy stood under the shade of the tulip poplar tree for an uncomfortably long time, swaying as he looked through the fence toward the Great Outside. Gil tossed a piece of gravel. It thumped off Jeremy's bony chest; the glassy-eyed thing didn't flinch.

"What are you looking at, butthead?" Gil said. Jeremy turned and followed Lazarus.

Walter watched them until they disappeared into the high school. Lazarus had to check on his botany project, the zombie-making machine he had built in the gym. The thought of those poor people Lazarus force-fed Ophiocordon and lashed to tables to lie and wait for their chests to explode – goddamnit.

"Do we really have to wait a week?"

Gil picked up another piece of gravel and chucked it toward the Dairy Rite. It hit the faded glass sign, 'Dairy Rite. Home of the Riteburger.' The glass shattered and crashed to the gravel lot. "No," he said. "We do not. We'll just pick up what we need along the way. We're hunters, right?"

Good. Fuck Mayday. Fuck Lazarus. Fuck Jeremy. Freedom. Sure, the Outside was dangerous, but Walter knew what kind of danger was out there and he'd survived it. "Yeah, we're hunters. Let's leave tonight."

"We got company, dude," Gil said and fell back into his chair.

Walter turned. *Oh, my God. Lacy.* Lacy Tomlinson walked toward them, her hair tied in a ponytail. She carried a paper lunch sack. His eyes shot to the high school, the sun glinting off the bank of windows blinded him from seeing inside the building. Lazarus could be there, staring at him, holding a rifle against his meaty chest, Walter in the gun sight. *What the hell are you doing, Lacy?*

She walked slowly toward him, her head turning left and right as she looked to see if anyone was watching. *Yeah, babe. I'm sure somebody is.* She still wore the jean shorts Walter had his hands down just a few hours ago. She'd changed her shirt, though. She now wore a loose white peasant shirt, a green canvas satchel with gardening tools hung from her right shoulder, Lacy's brown ponytail bouncing behind her. She'd washed her hair, Walter could tell. *Oh, God, I want to smell that hair.* His chest pounded as she came closer.

"Hi," she said softly, her eyes on the ground. Gil had turned his chair toward the Dairy Rite and sat quietly, throwing rocks at the building.

Walter rose to his feet. He wanted to rush to her and crush her next to him, but he stood next to the picnic table, his bottle of water in his hand. "Hey," he said. "Can I help you with something?"

She looked up, her beautiful face flush and pink. "I'm looking for Cal Miller," she said, her voice wavering as she held a paper lunch sack out of her satchel and handed it to Walter. "You seen him?"

Cal Miller? Cal was the Ag teacher at the high school before the Falling. What did she want with Cal? "No. No, I haven't," he said, setting the bag on the table, never taking his eyes off Lacy. "What do you need Cal for?"

Her eyes, her deep brown eyes, stared into Walter's, a nervous smile brushed her lips. He had to have this woman. They had to leave town together, to get away from Mayday, away from that fat fuck Lazarus. Everything would be better if they could just leave. *Goddamnit, Gil. Your idea better work.*

"I think I've got some aphids on the sweet corn. I'd like to have him come take a look at it." She slid her hands into the front pocket of her shorts and mouthed, 'I love you.' "If you see him, send him over."

Lacy coming to him was dangerous. Even if Lazarus didn't see them together, people might and people talk; people loyal to the man who didn't die. She turned and walked toward the back of the high school, toward the garden on the football field. "You bet," Walter called after her. "You bet I will." He sat on the bench and picked up the brown paper lunch sack, just like the sacks his mother used to send with him to Mayday Elementary, with a sandwich, an apple and a juice box. The word, 'Tonight' was written across the bag with a Sharpie in clean cursive. *You bet your ass tonight.* Mom never left a message like that for Walter on his lunch sack, thank God. He reached in and pulled out a peanut butter and jelly sandwich on homemade bread. *I love you, too, babe.* He watched until she rounded the corner of the building and went out of sight.

"That was stupid," Gil said, chucking another rock at the Dairy Rite. It dinged off the hood of Telly O'Leery's Olds Delta 88 that died in front of the building in 1995 and he just left it there.

"What do you mean?"

He turned his chair back to face Walter, scooting it in the gravel instead of standing up. "That girl wasn't here for Cal Miller. She was here for you."

Walter opened his mouth to protest, but Gil cut him off.

"What is this, fucking junior high? It was obvious." Gil took off his cap and rolled the bill in his hands. "That's one of Tim's squeezes, you know? He'll have you killed."

Killed. Walter's throat grew tight. *We have to be more careful.* "But nobody knows."

Gil pulled the hat back down over his blonde curls, his face more serious than Walter had ever seen it. "I do now," he said. "I'm not going to say nothing, but one more screw up like that and somebody's going to know. Then somebody's going to tell the big man and you'll find yourself chained to a barbell in Timmy's science project."

His science project; turning people into zombies so he can take over the world. "I want her to come with us."

Gil nodded. "I'm cool with that. She got a friend?"

***

The sandwich tasted delicious. There are things in this world that are a constant. The morning, the evening. The stars, gravity. Summer, spring, fall, winter. But if winter disappeared for a time, the first snowfall would be the most glorious day of the year. As Walter bit into that peanut butter and jelly sandwich, Peter Pan creamy and Welsh's Strawberry Spread, it was the most delicious food he'd had in months. Walter almost choked on the last bite when he saw Lazarus and Ken Gundy walking toward the gate.

"Shit, dude," Gil mumbled.

"Everything's fine," Walter said, although his hands shook. He stuffed them in the pockets of his Levi blue jeans. "There's a reason for this."

"No shit."

Lazarus and Ken marched across the clean-cut lawn of the high school, Jeremy far behind them. They went past the bleachers that surrounded the Corral and onto the grass that backed up to the parking lot of the Dairy Rite, where teenagers for decades sat on the graffiti-carved picnic table where Walter's Aquafina bottle sat. The paper sack with the word 'Tonight' rested in Walter's right front pocket where he used to keep his car keys. Lazarus and Ken stopped under the shade of the tulip poplar.

"It's getting hot out here, boys," Lazarus said, sweat running down his red, plump face. "Your shift's about up. Gwenny's got a fresh brewed pitcher of sweet tea all iced down. Might do you good."

Gil nodded once. "That sounds fine."

Lazarus smiled; his smile faded as he turned to Walter. "Ted Barrett was out on his morning walk today and said he saw Lacy down here," Lazarus said, his voice flat. "She was supposed to be at the garden. What business did she have at the Gate?"

Holy shit. Sweat already beaded on his face, the stains of the baking sun showed on his shirt, but Walter felt it start to pump. *He knows. That cocksucker knows.* "She wanted to know if Cal Miller's been out here," Walter said. "She said she needs help in the garden. Something about aphids."

Lazarus' hand smoothed back his hair and stopped at his neck, his fingers kneading something underneath the fat. "She knows Cal's down at the Whistlestop for his morning coffee. He is every day." He crossed his arms across his chest. "He's there right now, in fact. Just saw him. He was working on an omelet stuffed with chili. Ever had one of those? It's delicious."

"I haven't," Walter said. His wobbling knees threatened to drop him onto the gravel. He leaned one hand on the picnic table and turned to Ken. "My shift's up. You here to relieve me?"

Ken took a step forward, but Lazarus slapped a meaty arm across his chest. "No. Why don't you go with Ken to take the Carlsoners over to the Field. They've turned."

***

Walter and Ken Gundy walked toward the Field, Walter pulling the Carlsoners behind him, a rope tied around the neck of each like he was walking dogs. They stood in the Green House, chained to barbells, just moaning, their faces blank and Ken dropped a slipknot lasso over each one of their heads. The McKenneys, the mom and the dad, lay on their death beds, spent fungus stalks hanging lifeless toward the floor. Walter wanted to vomit.

A tall wooden fence blocked the baseball field from view, the backstop and light poles the only thing visible from the street. Everybody, even newcomers, could walk freely in Mayday, but they weren't allowed to see the Field. Only the loyal citizens of Mayday knew what was behind that fence and it made Walter wonder where humanity had gone. He sure knew it hadn't gone into Ken Gundy.

Ken pulled out a key from a chain that hung inside his shirt and inserted it into the padlock that kept the Field private. "There's poles free on the infield," Ken said. "Take them there." He swung open the gate and Walter walked through, pulling his pack of zombies behind him. The field's chain link fence, lined with fat, black birds, ended ten yards past third base; Walter slowly walked the freshly turned monsters toward the opening, their eyes still clear, still human. One crow turned to watch as he shuffled toward the opening, its black eyes followed Walter like it knew something. Crows were smart. Maybe it did. He winced when the demon bird cawed, the sound shrill in the quiet morning. Those fucking things were everywhere.

Fence posts had been sunk into the field and set in concrete. The place where the Mayday Little League teams used to play now looked like a pegboard; zombies stood lashed to a dozen poles, their drooling faces slack; black birds perched on some of them, like scarecrows gone wrong. The eyes of some had already turned milky; they were the first, the mothers and sons, friends and neighbors of the remaining citizens of Mayday. The rest were Lazarus' monsters and they were fresh.

Walter hated the Field. He knew he'd have to bathe and change his clothes before going to bed, the taste of the peaches on Lacy's breath and the smell of her hair long gone from his mind. He shrunk from the zombies he slunk by, their rotting, hollow faces gaunt, a soft, mindless moan a one-note Gregorian chant. Three posts stood empty around the pitcher's mound. Walter made his way there, almost bumping into Florence Geddy tied to a post. Her pale green hospital scrubs were stained with blood. Walter figured it wasn't her own.

"I wouldn't worry about them, Seidel," Ken shouted from the gate. "They don't bite much."

Asshole. He stopped at the pitcher's mound and lashed the ropes around the three poles, his eyes nervously dancing between the knots he tied and Lazarus' prize at home plate. The monstrosity stood on its hind legs, the chains around its waist and legs keeping it upright, affixed to the metal poles of the backstop. It was Mac. Walter didn't know what the hunters did to find the lowland gorilla. They must have gone to Louisville on a run and stopped by the zoo. But why? For fear, that's why. The beast was huge, six and a half feet tall and at least 500 pounds. He was pretty sure gorillas weren't supposed to get that big; why did Lazarus have to find a giant? The beast swayed on its hind legs like Jeremy, like the rest of the brain-dead creatures in the Field, its eyes white, its great, furry muzzle crusted with dried foam and blood. Its moan mingled with all the others. Lazarus let Mac play with newcomers in the Corral in front of the high school when the townsfolk started to get antsy. Walter saw this gently swaying beast fully animate when Ken Gundy pushed a fat teenage boy into the Corral, the bleachers filled with the remaining people of Mayday; Mac pounced on him, ripping the screaming boy's throat out with those great teeth and disemboweled him in seconds. The townspeople cheered. That's the night he met Lacy, throwing up behind the high school. "We don't have TV," Lazarus told Walter the next morning at the Whistlestop. "We gotta give them something." Walter couldn't finish his breakfast that day.

He tied a cow hitch in the last rope and walked slowly away from the Carlsoners, Florence Geddy, the birds and the nightmare chained to the fence. Walter wanted to run. He wanted to sprint from that cursed field and never come back, but that would be weak. He couldn't be weak in front of Ken Gundy. That would be like intentionally cutting yourself while hiding from a zombie hoard. He'd smell it. That's one thing he couldn't let Ken Gundy think, he was weak. Gundy was a psychopath.

"Nice work, Seidel," he said, locking the gate after Walter walked through and slipping the long keychain back around his neck. "Most people freak out when we take the monsters for a walk to the park."

"I'm not most people," Walter said. His stomach hurt. *Don't puke, damn it. Don't puke.*

Ken Gundy ran his hand across his crew cut and grinned. Walter had never seen the man grin. "I know that. It's not everybody who can bang the girlfriend of the man who didn't die. I gotta hand it to you, Seidel. That takes some cahoneys."

Holy shit. Walter's stomach clenched. *Gundy knows. Dear God, Gundy knows. No secrets in a small town.*

Gundy slapped Walter on the shoulder. "Don't worry about it, Seidel," the psychopath said. "I won't say anything." Gundy pulled a butterfly knife from his pants pocket and started flipping it in his hand. "I hate that fat bastard. The sooner he's gone, the better."

CHAPTER 16

It rained in Indiana. Doug sat under a shelter house roof in Hoosier National Forest just south of Bedford and listened to raindrops fall in the early morning. He hadn't seen rain in two months and had forgotten how peaceful raindrops were when they danced off leaves; it's not like there's that many trees back home in Kansas. Sure, there were some, but not like this. The light patter of water in the darkness as he sat under the wood-shingled roof of the shelter brought on a smile. How many times had he smiled in the past few months? Not too goddamned many.

Out of Council Bluffs, Iowa, the small caravan made it to Indianapolis before turning south, following the railroad tracks that had suddenly cut toward Kentucky. Stopping for gas and pee breaks more times than he liked. Terry called on the walkie-talkie from Andi's Subaru an hour west of Indianapolis. "It's six o'clock," he said. "I'm getting hungry. Let's stop in Indianapolis for the night."

No, Terry. Jesus. "That was a big city," Doug said. "That means too many zombies."

The walkie-talkie went quiet for a moment, then Terry's voice flooded the cab. "All the better. I've seen too many ugly zombies. We should camp out in a Hooters."

Nikki leaned into the front seat and grabbed Doug's walkie-talkie hand. She squeezed it and depressed the push-to-talk button. "Asshole," she said.

Indianapolis was gone when they got there, buildings just jagged remains, the ground littered with bomb craters. *Jesus. Who'd Indianapolis piss off?* The only landmark Doug could make out was Lucas Oil Stadium, nearly intact on the decimated skyline. He hoped the Colts had a good season. Nothing smoldered, the destruction was old, like a World War II city left as a memorial. They followed the railroad tracks an hour and a half south and turned off the highway and onto a rural road, away from the tracks that were starting to go west again. They pulled off Indiana 37 and onto South County Road 350 West, passing a school bus abandoned on the rural highway, its once bright yellow paint dulled by months of accumulated dust, windows fogged with dirt. If there was any carnage inside the bus, they thankfully couldn't see it. They turned with the signs toward a campground just out of sight of the railroad tracks. A campground with cabins, enough for all of them. Comfortable beds, the view of a lake and no vehicles for miles, vehicles that had owners who may still be wandering around the forest. Doug, Jenna, Terry and Nikki shared one cabin. Andi and Donnie each had one alone. The cars sat parked underneath a canopy of bur oak, eastern red cedar and Washington hawthorn. When the sky began to rumble, Terry and Andi pulled the picnic tables from the shelter house and Donnie drove the truck under the cedar tiled roof to keep their folded camp in the bed dry.

Doug and Terry sat in camp chairs next to the Silverado, just far enough under the shelter roof to stay out of the rain. "Sure we're doing the right thing, boss?" Terry asked before he followed Nikki to bed, everyone else already in their cabins. Doug doubted Andi drifted off to sleep quickly; the Army does things to people. He didn't have a fucking clue about Donnie, who was a problem he knew they'd have to deal with, hopefully before whatever little monster he had crawling inside his head decided to burst out. Maybe they should just drive off and leave him there, in the camp. Maybe– "Nikki's tired of driving. I am, too."

Hell, who isn't? Doug grew up in Paola, Kansas, just like his parents and their parents. He took some business classes at Fort Scott Community College, living with his uncle's family, but two years later he went back to Paola and started working in the Walmart Supercenter garage, changing oil and fixing tires. With a loan from the First Option Bank, he opened Doug's Muffler and Brakes when he was twenty-six and was glued to Paola like a scrapbooker had stuck him there. He was tired of driving, too.

"So's Jenna," Doug said. "She wants to find someplace and just sit."

"What's wrong with that?" Terry took a drink of water; he'd taken it easy on the beer tonight. "Hey, man we got a good thing here. Yeah, the world's gone to shit, but we haven't. We have two great ladies sleeping in that cabin over there." He paused; thunder punctuated the silence like the night was an '80s rock song. "We could just stay here. I saw a sign for Louisville on the way in. We could get whatever we need to keep us alive. We could get solar panels and a DVD player and fish all fucking day and just live. And it could be normal, like we were camping. You know, forever."

Camping forever. *Yeah, but how long before we started to wish each other dead?* People in close quarters always got sick of each other, no matter how much they cared for one another. The zombies wouldn't even have to help. Doug drew in a deep breath, his eyes on his hands.

"Terry, a person can be alone. A person can be alone for a long time. But people need people, or their world goes crazy. We're not enough people to stop that. We're not even enough people to protect each other if something big happens."

"Dude," Terry said. Doug looked up; his friend was amazingly sober. "We have been enough people so far."

Fuck. "But I'm talking big. Really big. It was lucky you got into that truck on I-80 and it was even luckier that it started."

The keys. Terry remembered the keys. They lay on the dirty floor of the cab next to snack wrappers, when they could have just as easily been in the pants pocket of the zombie truck driver trying to eat its way into the cab.

"If you hadn't gotten that truck started and plowed through that hoard of zombies, we wouldn't be sitting here listening to the storm."

"So?"

"So I'm saying we got here on my good looks and your personality." Doug reached into the cooler and pulled out a Budweiser. The crack of the tab drowned out the storm for a decisecond. "What happens when the next truck doesn't start, Terry? What happens when the goddamned dead outnumber us and we're not so lucky? What if we stay here and a hundred come walking through the trees and start pawing at the windows of the cabins because they smell us? What if we only have a handful of bullets left because we used the rest hunting deer and rabbits?" He stared at Terry, his friend's face hidden by the darkness. "If we find a place with people, we'll be safer than we are on our own."

"Depends on the people we find." Terry rose and grabbed a beer from the cooler. "I'm calling it a night. I got the 3 a.m. to 6 shift."

***

Doug realized the rain must have stopped, because otherwise, how would he have heard the branch snap? Something rustled in his sleep. A line of drool from his sagging head to his right shoulder broke as his eyes crept open, the light of the waxing half-moon through the parting clouds glittered off raindrops clinging to leaves. Something moved. Things weren't supposed to move. Wasn't that why Doug was out there, to make sure things didn't move? Whatever wasn't supposed to move moved again. A grin grew across Doug's bristly face. *It's okay. It's just a Boy Scout. I was a Boy Scout. No, no, I was an Eagle Scout. Boy Scouts are just fi– What the fuck?* Doug shook his head to drive himself fully awake as the Scout loomed toward him, arms raised, bottom jaw moving up and down like a machine. Doug's rifle lay on the concrete pad beside him, but his aluminum crutches leaned against his chair. He grabbed one, the other clattered to the ground as he lifted it up and hit the kid, maybe twelve years old, in the middle of that tan shirt and shoved. The small Zombie Scout staggered backward and fell, the trousers Doug knew were olive green under a thick crust of dried mud, kept moving as if the zombie kid didn't know it wasn't walking anymore.

"Oh shit."

At least a dozen of the little monsters staggered out of the trees toward the cabins. Their troop leader staggered with them, the felt campaign hat lay askew on its head, kept there by the strap. The low moan of the zombies in chorus blended naturally with the crickets. The image of the school bus ran through Doug's head. They were coming camping on the school bus and got caught up in all this. They probably started marching for help when they found somebody in trouble. Somebody with a bulbous stalk growing out of its chest. The Zombie Scout at Doug's feet pulled itself up by the shelter pole; Doug pushed it back down, its moan a little louder. If it didn't eat him soon, Doug knew it would scream. The thought of that sound sent terror shaking through his shoulders. His wounded foot pushed the rifle under the Silverado as Doug swung it underneath him, leaning his weight on the crutch.

"Hey," he yelled toward the cabins. "A little help."

The Scout, its sash dotted with badges, pulled itself back to its feet and lunged at Doug who wondered if eating him would count toward its Wilderness Survival badge. The little monster's head lurched to the right as a gunshot filled the morning; its body followed and the Zombie Scout dropped to the wet ground. Andi appeared next to Doug, sidearm raised in a modified weaver stance. "It's not safe out here," she said.

No shit.

"Get to the cabin. We'll leave at dawn."

Doug started to say 'I'm sorry,' but it didn't come out. Andi walked past him firing shot after shot; former Boy Scouts, two probably around the age Doug was when he went for Eagle, fell as Andi pushed bullets through what was left of their brains.

Doug glanced at Donnie's cabin as he lurched toward the door of his, the boy's face, white in the moonlight, was pressed against the glass in, what was that look? Horror? Doug twisted the handle to Cabin No. 5 and nearly fell inside.

***

They pulled back onto South County Road 350 West at 6:14 a.m., the morning summer sun already bathing the day in warmth. Jenna sat shotgun, the military gun belt around her waist growing strangely comfortable there. The road again. All she wanted was a bed and running water and maybe a four-star restaurant. The restaurant was negotiable; Doug's cooking was beginning to taste good, so she knew her palate was probably ruined forever. The bed and running water, however, were not negotiable. The one thing that kept her sanity was Doug's insistence there was civilization somewhere, civilization with soft beds. They'd passed a sign that read 'Welcome to Kentucky,' about twenty miles ago. Jenna hoped they'd find civilization there, although all she knew about Kentucky was bourbon and chicken. Either one would be nice.

"Are we there yet?" she asked through a mouthful of processed cheese from a cheese and spiced sausage combo snack pack they'd picked up at a convenience store outside Indianapolis. The package claimed real cheddar cheese, although the word "real" was put in quotation marks to get around all the potential legal claims that it most certainly was not. Jenna had tried to read the label before she ripped it open, but the words were tiny and besides, what does it matter anymore?

"Is that the way it's going to be today princess?" Doug asked. Doug. Sweet Doug. Jenna knew she'd never have given the tall, averagely handsome man a second look before the world fell. If she walked into his muffler shop in wherethehellever Kansas, she never remembered where he was from, she'd tell him what was wrong with her car, hand over her keys and that would be it until he ran her credit card (okay, her parent's credit card). She wouldn't have looked at his strong hands, or his straight, white teeth, or the cute dimple in his right cheek when he smiled. He was a mechanic; Jenna would have looked right through him. If it wasn't for Doug she might be dead, or worse, all alone in this world of walking nightmares.

She shook her head. "No. I'm just bored."

"Then I've got just the thing for you," he said, punching a button on the stereo. Blue lights came to life. "You can try and find something on the radio."

Yech. She hit the scan button and listened to static run up and down the AM dial. Doug had once heard a recorded message directing people to a safety shelter in Kansas City, Missouri, and was certain another message was out there, somewhere. They just had to keep listening. Jenna never mentioned to him the safety shelter in Kansas City was a death house. Doug knew that well enough.

"Doug," Nikki said from the back seat, a spiral-bound book in her hands, on the cover the California Pacific Coast Highway under the words 'Rand McNally Road Atlas. Terry was in Andi's car again, this time in the lead. 'Just pay attention to what she says and does,' Doug told Terry in front of Nikki, and only Nikki. 'I trust her, but we still don't know her.' Donnie followed in the Silverado. "Are we headed toward this wall the soldier talked about? The one in Dyersburg, Tennessee?"

"That's the plan."

That's your plan, ran through Jenna's head.

"Well, following the railroad has taken us way out of the way. If we stop following the track and hit the major highways, we'll get there by lunch."

"No shit?"

The hiss of wind entered the cabin as Jenna cracked the window and tossed out the junk food wrapper. She fingered the window toggle and the glass closed. "Guys suck at directions," Jenna said. "Universal fact."

"What do we need to do?" Doug asked, ignoring Jenna.

Nikki wiped her finger across the page. "Looks like if we keep going south, we'll run into Interstate 69 South. That's the first step, but the driving will be easier than Bumfuck County Road Slowpoke."

Jenna laughed. She knew she wouldn't have hooked up with Doug before the Falling, but she thought she could have been friends with Nikki. Nikki was solid. Smart, funny, just pretty enough to make Jenna look prettier.

"Terry, Andi," Doug spoke into the walkie-talkie.

"Yes'm, boss."

Doug could count on his dick the number of times he'd seen Terry take something seriously. Just once. This wasn't it. "Change of plan. Nikki found a faster way to Dyersburg."

"Diarrheasburg?"

The brake lights of the Subaru sent Doug's good foot to the brake pedal of the Toyota. He hoped to hell Donnie was paying attention.

The walkie-talkie kicked on again. This time Terry's voice was flat, emotionless. "Doug. I think you need to see this." *Maybe I need to grow another dick.*

Nikki was out of the car first, running to stand next to Terry; Jenna jogged to meet them. "Looks like you got left behind, boss," the 'boss' coming out in a soft hiss. Doug turned as Donnie walked past him. What was that on his face? A smile? Doug limped forward on crutches and joined them at the front of the Subaru. They sat at a T in the road, Tonnies' Shell Repair and Quick-N-Easy convenience store sat dark and quiet at the intersection, weeds grew high around the gas pumps.

They stood in front of a road sign. The sign was innocent enough; a common piece of sheet metal painted highway department green. White letters pointed travelers east ten miles to Carlson, south ten miles to Mayday and farther south 20 miles to Interstate 69. It was the homemade sign painted on a sheet of plywood and tied to the post with bailing wire that had made Andi stop. "Mayday. The Last Safe Haven in Kentucky. Everyone Welcome." And underneath, in letters nearly too small for the brush the artist used, "Help us rebuild the world."

"Well," Nikki said. "At least they spelled all the words right."

Andi turned toward Doug. "This what you're looking for?"

It was, wasn't it? Safe haven. Everyone welcome. Help us rebuild the world. *Yes, that's what I want. A rebuilt world.* "I gotta go," he said, his voice coming out softly and slowly. "This might be it. We might not have to go to Dyersburg."

"Diarrheasburg."

"This might be exactly what we're looking for." The familiar faces held familiar looks.

Terry smiled. "I've followed you this far, boss."

Nikki frowned. "It's better than nothing."

Jenna looked bored.

"So," Andi said. "You're going?"

Doug nodded. "Yeah. You?"

Andi stood in the middle of the road, the brightly painted sign like clown makeup on a pig, Big Andy would say. *Would have said.* Something rubbed her wrong. Maybe it was the Jethro Bodine shakiness of the letters, or the smiley face on the sun. "No. I've followed enough hand-painted signs."

"But," Terry started. Andi put up a hand.

She pulled the walkie-talkie off her belt. "This has a twenty-three-mile radius. If you want to help me clear that service station, I'll back the Subaru into one of those service bays and shut the door. I can camp out here for a while. If it looks good, call me and I'll join you. If things go south, call me and I'll come get you."

Nikki started to protest, but stopped. Andi wore a Gene Holleran look, a look she'd seen on her dad's face more times than she could count. She didn't need to say anything to Andi; her mind was made up. "Okay," Nikki said, her voice loud in the now quiet morning. A crow cawed somewhere, but Nikki didn't pay attention to it. She'd had enough of crows. "Sounds like a plan. If Doug's dream goes to shit, we have backup." She pulled her sidearm from its holster and cocked it. "Let's go clear that service station so Andi doesn't get eaten waiting to save us." She turned toward the former soldier who looked so strong, but fragile at the same time. "If there are any Nutter Butters in the convenience store, they're mine."

***

Donnie kept his fist in tight balls in the green camouflage fatigues the Army woman had stripped off a corpse in Omaha. Donnie'd pissed his dress pants then as the crazy Vanessa Hagen-looking woman leveled a rifle to his face. The Army woman didn't let her shoot Donnie then. Donnie tried to push a grin away from his mouth because he knew the Army woman was going to wish she hadn't tried so hard. Donnie figured his knuckles were white by now, but he couldn't have his hands out for everyone to see them; they moved too much. "You don't ever have to talk, Donnie," Mother had told him more than once. "Your hands tell the story for you." So he kept them buried. Now, if he could just keep the gosh darned smile off his face.

The Gunkies were leaving, all of them, just getting into their little Prius and going away. The drunken redneck and the black-haired lady followed the Army woman into the convenience store; a bird had built a nest in the Q of the Quick-n-Easy sign over the door. The cripple and Vanessa Hagen leaned against the Prius. Donnie stood next to the Silverado and watched them through the dirty glass. Inside the store, the Army woman produced a flashlight and peered into the coolers before going back into the storage room. The convenience store must have been clean, because the blade of light disappeared and reappeared in the window of the service station. A few minutes later, one of the service bay doors rolled up, the mama bird in the Q squawked angrily and flapped away.

The black-haired girl walked out eating peanut shaped cookies from a red plastic package. "All clear," the drunken redneck said and tried to slip his hand into the package. The girl slapped it away. The three walked up to the Prius and stopped before the cripple, like they had to get his blessing, or something. What was he, the friggin' doodie pope?

"You sure you want to do this Andi?" the cripple asked. That man wasn't anything special. He's the one who got them all into this doodie mess to begin with.

The Army woman nodded. "Yeah. I just have a feeling. Probably nothing. Just give me a call, okay?"

Doug nodded.

Donnie was a long way away from Colorado. He knew he couldn't get back there and take care of Mother anymore, but he could take care of these people. "One at a time, Donnie," Mother's voice said somewhere in his head. "One at a time." *Yes, Mother. One at a time.* And the time to take care of one, all alone, had presented itself all in a nice, pretty little package. Mother's long, sharp kitchen knife sat under the front seat of Daddy's truck and nobody knew about it. All Donnie had to do was keep from laughing, then plunge it into the Army woman's back until she stopped moving, just like that wicked Taylor boy when he fell down the stairs at Jimmy's Old Country Pizzeria.

The Army woman got into the Subaru and backed it into the open bay door. Donnie walked past the front of the car as it backed up and grabbed the handle of the second door. Oh, geez, it's heavy. He grunted as he pulled. The drunken redneck appeared beside him and helped him pull; the door slid up easily. *You're next, fatty.*

"What're you doing, Donnie?" the man asked, his jovial face looked stupid to Donnie. All happy people looked stupid.

"I'm staying here with–" he paused. *Can't say the Army woman, can't say the Army woman.* "Andi. If you guys are in trouble, it might take more than one of us to get you out of it." Oh, the words. The words, Donnie, came out like the truth. You're a good boy, Donnie.

The drunken redneck glanced over at the crippled man, whose face told something. What? What was that look on his smug doodie face? Relief? They were glad to have him gone. *Assholes.* Donnie closed his eyes and winced, waiting for the hand of Mother to come crashing into his mouth for saying that word. That bad, bad word. But nothing came. His eyes slowly crawled open; everyone stared at him. This time Donnie did smile; he couldn't help it, the looks on their faces. Fear. They were all afraid of him. Except for the Army woman and she soon would be.

***

The Shell station with its Quick-n-Easy convenience store disappeared behind the thick, green trees around a long, sloping curve before anyone spoke. "You sure she's going to be okay?" Jenna asked.

"Andi?" Terry laughed. "Haven't you paid attention? Andi can take care of herself."

"But that Donnie kid is so, so, so–"

"Creepy," Nikki finished. "That kid smells crazy."

Doug whistled and everyone stopped. "Andi's going to be fine," he said. "And so are we. We'll see Andi again by sundown, after we find out this place is real." He stared out the window. "I hope to God this place is real."

Five miles closer to Mayday they drove by another homemade sign, the smiling sun in the corner a little angrier than the first; Doug shook it off. "Five Miles Closer to Heaven. Mayday, Kentucky." Doug raised the walkie-talkie to his mouth and pressed the button. "Halfway there, Andi. You copy?"

The walkie-talkie hissed. "Loud and clear, Doug. Remember, I won't call you, you call me."

"Roger. Out."

172

Doug looked at Jenna in the passenger seat and shrugged. "It works." He reached and patted her leg. "Everything's going to be fine."

She crossed her arms over her small breasts and huffed. "It damn well better be, Doug Titus. If you know what's good for you."

Doug dropped the walkie-talkie between his legs and pushed the accelerator harder. He wanted this over now.

Mayday wasn't what he expected, but he'd always found out the hard way nothing ever was. A rusting plastic factory sat off the highway next to railroad tracks just outside town. The blacktop stopped at a crossroads, a green road sign pointing to Louisville to the east and Interstate 69 to the west. Mayday sat dead ahead behind tin barn doors. A tall half-assed chain-link fence looked like it might surround the town, that may have been home to about 1,000 people before the world fell; who knew how many lived there now. Doug could make out the high school; light poles from the football field and probably the baseball field rose into the sky. A water tower loomed over the town, although Doug couldn't tell if it was inside the fence or out.

"This is it?" Jenna asked. "What a dump."

Doug slowed the Prius to a crawl. "Don't be too hasty, babe. It has a fence. Fences keep things out."

"And in."

Shit.

The same smiling sun was painted on the barn door, along with "Mayday, Kentucky. We Call It Home."

"What do you think, boss?" Terry asked.

I just have a feeling, Andi said before they left. As he felt the hair rise on the back of his neck, Doug knew he had a feeling, too. A bad one. He slowed to a stop and unbuckled his gun belt. "Leave everything," he said, pulling the military service revolver from its holster and shoving it down the back of his pants like he'd seen in so many cop shows. "If you think you can hide a gun, hide it. If not, leave it. We want to look as friendly as can be." He picked the walkie-talkie off the seat and shoved it down his underwear, hoping the tighty-whities would keep it from falling down his leg.

"I'm ready," Jenna said, then kissed him on the cheek, his stubble rough on her lips.

"Let's do this." Doug pulled the Prius next to a rusted Oldsmobile Delta 88, probably a 1978, put the keys in his front pocket and killed the ignition.

They stepped out of the car slowly, Terry handed Doug his crutches from the back seat. Nikki swallowed hard as she looked at the town from the outside of the chain-link fence. The lawns were all mowed, the houses were freshly painted. Doug said he was looking for Mayberry from The Andy Griffith Show. She took in a deep breath of clean, sweet air and wondered if he may have found it.

Hinges squealed as people behind the fence pulled open the barn doors to reveal a fat, smiling man. He threw his arms wide. "Welcome to Mayday, Kentucky, my friends. Your new home."

AUGUST 1: MAYDAY, KENTUCKY

CHAPTER 17

Breakfast didn't settle well today. A slice of steak next to a three-egg omelet stuffed with Armour chili, a cup of coffee and Tang (orange juice unfortunately off the menu) usually got Lazarus' day off to a fine start, but not today. The front door to the Whistlestop rang when customers pushed it open, the little bell on a string telling Gwenny she had someone new. It rang a number of times since Lazarus sat on one of the padded metal seats at the café; the Whistlestop was busy this morning, but this ring was for Elmer Toss. Lazarus hated Elmer Toss. The tall, lanky man walked in and sat down across from him.

"Coffee, darlin'," Elmer barked and stared at Lazarus, the dangling piece of egg on Lazarus' fork momentarily forgotten.

"You gotta do somethin' about your pet monkey, Tim," Elmer said through a week's worth of beard. Elmer's breath smelled like the floor of the Doo Drop, all cigarettes and stale beer. He turned over the coffee mug in front of him as he heard Gwenny's tennis shoes slap the tile floor behind him. She filled the cup silently and motioned the pot to Lazarus who waved her off.

Lazarus sat the fork on his plate and dabbed his mouth with a cloth napkin. Paper napkins disappeared from the aluminum dispensers on the tables at the Whistlestop once people realized how much more valuable they were for wiping their asses. He sat the napkin on his lap, although he knew he was finished with it. Elmer Toss made him lose his appetite.

"His name's Jeremy, Elmer," Lazarus said, his words coming out slowly and clearly.

"Well, whateverthefuck you call it, it's scaring the shit out of my kids. Standin' outside their windows." Elmer took a long drink of coffee, unflinching at the scalding heat. "Zombies is what's killed this world. Ain't no place for a zombie wanderin' around this town."

From somewhere near the back, someone said, "amen." Lazarus shot a look at the back where eight people sat crowded around two tables and a booth. It could have been Gary Thatcher, or Jim Smithy, or Gil Haply. Hell, it could have been any one of them. *It could have been all of them.* He turned back to Elmer. "Has he et–" Et, et, et. "Has he eaten any of your children?"

Elmer shook his head slowly. "No."

"Then he won't. He won't harm anyone here in Mayday." Lazarus scanned the café; the twenty people packing the room with its black and white checkered tile floor and pie rack on the end of the counter, stared at their plates. Dear Lord, they agreed with Elmer Toss. They agreed with that drunken fool.

Elmer threw back the rest of his coffee and set the ceramic mug down hard on the table. "Better be damn sure of that, Timmy boy," he said, the words coming out in a hiss. Drops of spittle warm and wet, sprayed on Lazarus' hand. "Or I'll have his head."

"Hallelujah."

Lazarus pushed himself to his feet as quickly as he could, the chair legs squeaking against the tile, but Elmer stood with him, his blue flannel chest blocked the back of the café where the hallelujah had come from the mouth of some unbeliever. Elmer pointed a finger in the fat man's face. "His head, Timmy boy. His fucking rotting head."

Elmer Toss walked out of the Whistlestop, the little bell uncomfortably cheery in the cold silence of the room, leaving Lazarus standing alone, his cheeks flush with anger. He scanned the room; no one looked up to meet his gaze.

"What is wrong with you people?" he shouted, his face slick with beading sweat. The room was silent. "I'm trying to build a future here? A future for all of us. A future for the whole goddamned human race. Don't you see that?"

Someone coughed in the back. *No they didn't. Ungrateful bastards. No they didn't see it at all.* The past few months of careful control, of careful planning, of carefully making sure those bastards weren't eaten in their sleep and they didn't even see it. A pain stabbed behind Lazarus' right shoulder blade. *What was that?* Bet it was a pulled muscle from sex with Gwenny. He knew it. It had to be. Better tell her to slow down. "I'm your only hope in this gone-to-hell world," he screamed, wincing at the tug in his shoulder.

He looked at all the people in the back of the room, the ones from the Amen Corner. He would remember them, oh yes, he would. They were all going to suffer with that prick Gary Thatcher. They all were.

"I'm with you, Lazarus," a voice said from near the door.

"Fuck you, Donnally," Lazarus said as he walked by and slammed the jingle-jangle door behind him.

***

Lazarus felt better after a nap. His walk to the Gate was later than usual, but he needed to sleep the morning off. He'd tell Gwenny to take it easy on him next time; that shoulder still ached. Jeremy was gone when he stepped outside his front door for the second time today. Probably for the best. He hated assholes like Elmer Toss, but he knew what to do with them, a slow beating from Ken Gundy (what a good soldier) and a bottle of champagne for a private show as Ken fed Elmer's kids to Mac. One of the first hunting parties Lazarus had sent out after the fence was up and the big barn gate secure, had found Mac wandering in the woods outside Louisville along with a zebra and a pair of gnu, its great bulk on two legs like it had forgotten to walk on its knuckles. Its eyes were clear then, but they knew it had turned. The great black beast just had the look. The men wore vests back then, vests tanned from the skin of the mayor and police chief who'd turned and eaten the city clerk. Poor Carla Evans. Such a nice lady. Keith Young got a rope around the gorilla's neck and it followed him into the bed of the truck like it was a puppy. Lazarus slapped his belly and smiled as he walked toward the gate. Puppies get hungry.

Ken Gundy stood at the Gate when Lazarus approached. Ken always took his shift alone. Lazarus didn't know if it was because he liked it alone, or because everyone else in town hated the sadistic son of a bitch. Didn't matter; Ken Gundy was good at his job.

"Good morning, Lazarus," he said.

Lazarus smiled. He wouldn't trust Ken Gundy with his life, but he'd sure trust him to kill people. He didn't know what Ken did before the Falling, but he liked killing people a lot. "Where's Seidel?"

Ken shrugged. "Home, I guess."

Home? Wouldn't be over at Lacy's by any chance? No. No. If that little bastard were screwing Lacy, it wouldn't be when the sun was up when everybody could see.

"Well, if you see hi–"

Ken threw a hand in the air and Lazarus' words died in his mouth. Yes, Ken Gundy was a good soldier, but he was a dog, a dog that was dangerous when crossed.

A car, a silent car, one of those goddamned hippy hybrids, sat on the road facing the Gate. "It snuck up on me," Ken said quietly. "This is why we need checkpoints on the road. Deer stands manned with armed men with walkie-talkies, so this doesn't happen."

Two people sat in the front seat and at least one sat in the back. No, no, there were two in the back. The car idled, or the engine was off, it was impossible to tell; and the people just sat there. "What are they doing?"

"Talking," Ken said. "Talking about what they want to do; drive on, or come and join our happy little family."

Lazarus put his hand on the walkie-talkie clipped to his belt. Maybe Ken was right. If checkpoints had been up, that walkie-talkie would have already signaled him and he'd know what to do, instead of standing around staring at a car through a fence. The car moved forward, the silence eerie. It parked next to Telly O'Leery's Olds Delta 88 at the Dairy Rite and the doors opened. Lazarus rubbed his belly. Two men stepped out, one a burley blond man, the other a dark-haired man on crutches. Two women followed them, a ginger woman and a serious girl with dark hair. Perfect. Lazarus pulled the walkie-talkie off his belt and fingered the push-to-talk button.

"Billy. Billy, you there?"

The walkie-talkie sat silent. He began to squeeze again when Billy Keck's voice came through. "Yes, sir."

He squeezed the button. "Go find Lois Eller. Tell her to get the Stinson house ready again. We've got company." Lazarus clipped the walkie-talkie back onto his belt and smiled at Ken. "We'll get two of them ready for the Greenhouse," he said. Lazarus felt better than he did at the Whistlestop, much better away from those assholes who thought they knew better than him. "The other two are for Mac. Some of the people are starting to get ugly on me, Ken. I think we need a loyalty rally tonight."

A sacrifice, you mean. Ken stood looking at Lazarus, his arms crossed over his broad chest. "You want me to get the Gate?"

Lazarus raised a finger. Ken knew when to shut up. The fat man changed the channel on the walkie-talkie and talked into it again. "Gwenny. Gwenny darling, come in."

A few seconds crept by before she responded. "Gwen here."

"Gwenny, hun, we have guests. Four of them." He paused, his breath raspy. "Prepare them a special lunch for the Stinson House, then supper at my place, say around 6 o'clock."

A delay. Ken thought Lazarus looked pale today, not that he gave a shit.

Gwenny's voice came back over the walkie-talkie. "How many do you want to turn?"

What was that in her voice? Was that–? Lazarus shook it off. No, it couldn't be disgust. Not from Gwenny. *Must be these damned muscle spasms, not thinkin' straight.* "Two," he said. "Just two."

Another pause. "I can have two regular sandwiches, two special and potato salad on their kitchen table before they get there. Four medium rare steaks and scalloped potatoes on your dining room table by 5:45," she said.

Good girl, Gwenny. I can always count on you. "And bring some cold beer, if you will. These look like beer drinkers." He gave her instructions on who got the Ophiocordon-laced food, then released the button and clipped the walkie-talkie back to his belt. Lazarus waved at Ken. "Whenever you're ready."

Ken Gundy pulled the medieval bar that sat across the two old barn doors and swung one open, the hinges creaked in protest. Lazarus stepped forward toward the newcomers, the ginger woman's arm around the waist of the man on crutches. Lazarus spread his arms wide. *Good Christ Almighty,* Ken thought. *He loves this shit. What a cold bastard.*

"Welcome to Mayday, Kentucky, my friends. Your new home."

***

A lawn mower fired up somewhere in town. Doug hadn't heard a lawnmower since May and it sounded beautiful. A middle-aged woman in a straw hat stood in her lawn watering marigolds from a bright blue watering can; their host, who called himself Lazarus, told her good morning. She smiled and waved. Lazarus kept walking until he turned onto Main Street, past what looked like a grocery store. An open grocery store.

"You might not find everything you want in the Apple Market, but they have enough to get us by," Lazarus said.

Dear God, this was more than Doug had hoped. A town. A real town, enclosed for safety and normal. At least, as normal as the end of the world could be. He looked around; as far as he could tell, this town was Mayberry. He half expected Andy Griffith to come walking down the sidewalk whistling. Doug swung his legs under his crutches as he intentionally lagged behind the group, taking in as much of this town as he could. Maybe there was a doctor here who could take off his cast in a couple of months. A smile broke across his face. Yes, sir. The feeling of dread in the car was still there, festering in his gut, but it was mostly hidden by the smell of flowers and life. Two men, one in overalls, the other in blue jeans and a red flannel shirt, stared at him as he shuffled behind the group and brought the dread up like they'd fished for it. Anger? Hatred? Contempt? What was that on their faces? Doug's pace slowed as he stared back at them. They turned and kept walking, turning a corner and disappearing. It wasn't anger, or hatred. It was fear. What were they afraid of?

He glanced around. More people were stopped in the street, just looking at them. A pretty young woman with a basket of greens in the crook of her arm walked past them, her eyes pinned to the sidewalk. A few months ago, she might have been in college, her future unwritten, now she was here, behind this fence. Doug watched her pass and duck into the Apple Market. *Mayberry, or the Twilight Zone?* The town was suddenly quiet, the lawnmower no longer running. Doug's feeling of peace from just moments ago had devolved into stark terror.

"Are you okay, honey?" Doug jumped, his heart thumped heavily. Jenna stood in front of him on the well-swept sidewalk. A basket of apples and a sign that read, "Take one" sat next to them in front of the Apple Market. Doug didn't realize he'd stopped.

"Yeah, fine." Not fine.

Her smile pulled him back into motion. "Come on. The guy said we have a house, with beds and there's running water." She pulled on his arm. "A shower. I'm going to take one before lunch, then I'm going to take a nap. They have steak and potatoes here, Doug. That's what we're going to have for supper. Steak." She leaned in and kissed his cheek and Doug wondered for the first time how many of those he had left. "You were right, Doug. You were right."

Was I?

"Come on folks," Lazarus said, standing fifteen feet down the sidewalk with Terry and Nikki. "I'm sure you're tired. I'll make sure the generator behind the house gets fired up just long enough for you to run the washing machine. Nothing like a shower, clean clothes, a nap and a belly full of food to make you feel like a brand-new person."

Doug started moving. *You were right, Doug. You were right.* The looks on the men's faces dragged the dread through the acid in his gut. Fear. But they weren't afraid for themselves. *They were afraid for us.* What of the woman who wouldn't even look at them? As Doug caught up with the group, he wondered if it wasn't Andi who was right.

And there was something wrong with this Lazarus. Jesus brought the biblical Lazarus back from the dead. What kind of pretentious asshole would compare himself with a man from the Bible? A dangerous one. The guy looked sick, but it wasn't his pale skin and sweaty face that worried Doug. It was the way he walked, the way he smiled. That man wasn't right.

***

"This place is awesome." Jenna stood in her and Doug's bedroom, a white cotton towel around her torso, another in a turban around her hair. She bent over her foot that rested on a vanity chair, painting her nails red. This house had all the niceties a person could hope for when they really had nothing. Running water, nail polish, deodorant, snack crackers, sandwiches. A nice lady named Gwen served them lunch on the modest kitchen table, the wooden surface had a few scratches, but it was nicer than what he had in his kitchen back in Paola. Gwen passed out roast beef sandwiches wrapped in waxed paper and Styrofoam bowls of potato salad. It tasted like home. A cooler of local craft beer on ice had been sitting on the kitchen table when they walked into the house and Terry was already into his third.

Jenna leaned her elbows on her knee and studied Doug's face. "Something's bothering you. It has been since we got here. What's going on?"

Yeah, what? A feeling? What good's a feeling without facts to back it up? Doug sat on the edge of the bed, his crutches next to him. "Nothing. I'm just cautious. That's all."

She frowned. "Uh-huh. Whatever. Tell me when you're ready. I'm going to go get a box of Ritz from the kitchen." She started to walk toward the door, then stopped. "We can leave any time, you know? That Lazarus guy told us so. I might bitch about the beds, but if you want, we can go to that place in Tennessee."

"I know."

"But if it's in any way less than this, I will never, ever let you forget it."

Doug managed a smile. "I know."

"Then as long as we have an understanding." She walked out the door, intentionally wiggling her bottom like a dancer.

Fuck.

Doug leaned back on the bed, shoved his hand down the front of his pants and pulled out the walkie-talkie. The small device felt heavy in his hand. This town seemed perfect, the place he'd been dragging them to, a rustic paradise full of healthy, smiling people. But the people weren't smiling, except the fat man at the gate, who named himself after a man who rose from the dead. *What have I done?* Doug clicked the push-to-talk button. "Andi. Andi, do you copy?"

Andi responded immediately.

"I'm here."

"How are things at the Quick-n-Easy?" he asked and just as quickly winced. If someone were eavesdropping, he'd just given away their backup's location.

"It's quiet. Donnie's locked himself in the cab of the Silverado. I'm having a Snickers bar. What about Mayday?"

Mayday. That's what this call was, wasn't it? A prelude to a mayday? *Maybe I'm just jumpy.* "Things look good here, but there's something off about it. Like everybody's got a secret they're not telling us."

Silence on Andi's end, then she spoke "What's the plan?"

The plan. The grand fucking plan. Find a place with people, a safe place to protect us from the zombies. That's what this is, right? It even has a fucking grocery store. Doug pushed the switch. "We're having a nap, then supper with the leader of the place, then we're getting a full tour of the town. If things go south, I might not get a chance to call."

Momentary static. "Then don't. If I don't hear from you by 6 p.m., I'm coming in."

That's no good. "There's a guard at the front gate."

Doug could almost hear Andi thinking through the static; she came back and asked for a layout of the town. Doug described what he'd seen. "If there's a fence, there's a weak spot and the town doesn't sound big enough to have guards posted all around it. Let's make that call 5 p.m. If I don't hear from you by then, I come in. I'll be traveling low. Nobody will see me coming."

"Army?" Doug asked.

"Oklahoma. My father was a hunter. A good one. I learned from the best."

Doug grinned. *This girl's daddy wanted a boy.* "Gotcha. I hope I get to see you after an all clear."

"Me, too. Over."

Doug flicked the switch to off and slipped the walkie-talkie back into the front of his pants. His Beretta M9 still sat in the small of his back, pressed tightly into skin by a brown belt his mother gave him for Christmas four years ago. Terry's sat under the front seat of the Prius with an empty clip. Jenna and Nikki had nowhere to put theirs. Doug was the only one with a weapon; what good would that do against a whole town?

Jenna strutted back into the bedroom with a box of Ritz crackers under her arm and a wet, cold bottle of Kentucky Bourbon Barrel Ale in each hand. She kicked the white, wooden door closed behind her, hooked a thumb into the towel around her body and shimmied it off. She stood in front of Doug, her porcelain skin smooth and dotted with freckles. "Hello, sunshine."

She handed Doug a beer and sat hers and the box of crackers on the bedside table. "Don't get any ideas, buster." She stopped and grinned. "No, I think I might want you to get an idea or two. We've got four hours till supper with the bossman and you've got to drop your pants anyway if you want those clothes washed." She stood naked and touched the cold beer bottle to her stomach, slowly moving it up to her breasts.

Fear was for later. He started unbuttoning his shirt.

***

"I know you." Jenna stared at the man who had welcomed them to town. Something about him looked familiar. Damned familiar. She cocked

182

her head and stared at him across the table. She knew that face, for some reason she knew it. *Was he on 'Survivor'? No, not 'Survivor'.*

Doug grabbed her hand under the table and gently squeezed. Keep low, keep inconspicuous, baby. Don't poke the bear. "Jenna, honey. This is rural Kentucky, not New York. It's not like you just ran into Christopher Walken at the deli." He'd felt good during their short stay at the little white house. Lazarus was right. Clean clothes, a nap and food did wonders. He didn't mention sex; that helped, too. Something was different about Jenna. She was wild, never letting him get on top. And when she came, her orgasm was violent. He was sure the whole town knew they'd had sex.

"She's right," Nikki said in the midst of cutting a piece of steak. "I've seen you, too. You were on the news, weren't you?"

Lazarus sat back in his chair and sipped water from a wine goblet. His smile biting, like an eel's. "I'm the man who didn't die."

Jenna slapped the table. "Good Morning America," she shouted. "Yes. Good Morning America. You started screaming about being holy, or something and then you disappeared."

Shut up, goddamnit.

"I saw the raw footage on YouTube." Jenna waved a piece of medium-well meat at Lazarus. "They dragged you off stage."

Doug dropped his right hand beneath the table. The gun sat in his belt, less than a foot away from his fingers. Lazarus took another drink of water and laughed.

"That's what happened, yes," he said, the words came out slowly.

"Then your name's not really Lazarus," Jenna said. "I mean, your parents didn't look at you in the hospital and say, 'we're going to name this baby Lazarus.'" She took a drink of beer and wiped her mouth with a cloth napkin. "What's your real name?"

Doug's hand inched backward. Andi was on her way by now, but she wouldn't be here fast enough.

Lazarus stared at his plate for a moment, the steak barely touched. When he looked up, his face was grave. "My name was Tim Hardy." He sat his elbows on the table and clutched his hands. "I'm no longer Tim Hardy. I survived Ophiocordon, the drug that killed everyone else who took it. They said I was dead. I woke in the hospital in a body bag, but I was not dead. I rose from the dead. I am Lazarus."

Jenna hiccupped, then giggled. *Jesus, Jenna. How many beers did you have at the house?* "Although I appreciate your position, your name's Tim. Tim, Tim, Timmy Tim-Tim. Lazarus makes you sound like a douche." She ate a forkful of scalloped potatoes and sat back in her chair. "I feel great," she said.

Lazarus' face melted into a chuckle. "I'm glad you feel so good," he said. "That means it's working." He picked up a glass ornament from the cloth-covered table and jiggled it. It rang in a high-pitched, crystal chime. A bell. *Who's he calling?*

"What's working, Lazarus?" Doug asked. He looked at Terry. Terry sat slumped in his chair, asleep. He was fucking asleep sitting up. *What the hell?*

"The Ophiocordon," Lazarus said, wiping drops of water from his lips with his napkin and dropping it onto his barely touched plate. "It was in her food." Jenna laughed out loud. Lazarus pointed at Terry. "And his. It's all part of the plan."

Doug's right hand shot to the back of his pants, the hard handle of the Beretta on his fingertips. A figure loomed to his right, coming quickly out of the kitchen into the dining room. The hard man from the Gate. He pulled his arm back and Doug felt his world explode as a calloused fist collided with his jaw. He collapsed onto the floor, the Beretta skittering across the hardwood. Jenna laughed. *Ophiocordon. Holy shit.*

Nikki threw back her chair and ran for the living room and the front door. Ken Gundy, the man at the Gate, launched himself over the table, scattering steak and half-empty beer bottles onto the floor. He landed on top of her, Nikki's breath shot from her chest and she slammed into the floor. She sucked in air, but with the big body on her back she felt like she was drowning. A cord wrapped around her wrists and twisted tight.

Lazarus sat in his chair, his water glass in his hand. He pointed at Jenna and Terry. "Take those two to the Greenhouse and strap them down." He motioned to Doug, then Nikki. "And take them to the Corral for tonight. Tenderize them, but don't break anything. The folks at the loyalty rally like it when there's still some fight in the big show."

Ken grabbed a fistful of Nikki's thick, black hair and started to drag her across the floor of Lazarus' dining room; Nikki screamed and thrashed in his grip. Lazarus laughed. "She's got some spunk, that one. The people are going to love her."

AUGUST 1: MAYDAY, KENTUCKY

CHAPTER 18

The call never came. Andi stood outside the Subaru loading clips; sweat running down her back in the stifling August heat of the abandoned Shell station. Her weapon lay on top of the car next to the quiet walkie-talkie, her sidearm in its holster. The falling sun sent hard beams of light through the high windows, dust danced in the still air. The smell of grease and gasoline dragged up visions of Hutchings' Service Station back home, where Big Andy stood around and drank beer with Mitch and Kelly while Old Man Hutchings patched a tire. Andi would just sit at Old Man Hutchings' grease-stained desk eating shell peanuts from a fifty-pound sack and listen to her father and his friends talk about cars and football. The station closed when Old Man Hutchings died and Big Andy, Mitch and Kelly had to find some other place to drink beer.

Andi shoved the full clips into the cammo gear she wore now instead of blue jeans and a T-shirt, the multiple pockets in the fatigues and the military utility belt made her feel like Batman. She was glad she kept the military gear, although she'd hoped she wouldn't need it again. Andi picked up a tire iron from the concrete floor of the garage and dropped it onto the passenger seat of the Subaru. Quiet meant quiet. If she ran into a monster in the woods, the solid metal tool would ruin a zombie's skull a lot more silently than a bullet. She was going to drive up to two miles from Mayday, far enough away no one in town could hear the Subaru, then hide the car and sneak into town. The trees in this part of Kentucky were thick enough she was sure she could get there without anyone noticing. Andi stuffed four MREs and five bottles of water into her backpack, along with the first aid kit. She clipped the walkie-talkie to the utility belt. Not that it would do her any good. Doug was under radio silence and presumably something went wrong, or he would have called. Andi looked at her watch; it was 5:05 p.m. She tossed the backpack into the back seat and slid her weapon between the front buckets of the Subaru. It was time.

Then the door to the Silverado opened behind her.

Damn it.

"What are you doing?" Donnie asked.

Andi had known she probably wasn't going to get out of the shop without waking Donnie, she just wasn't happy when it happened. The metal-on-metal screech of the sliding bay door, starting the Subaru, everything was going to wake that creepy little man, but she had sure as heck hoped she could skip out without him. Donnie could survive, or not; Andi really didn't care, and that wasn't like her.

"Rescue mission. Something's gone wrong." She held her hands out, palms facing the floor. "Just stay here where it's safe. We'll all be back sometime tonight."

Donnie stamped his foot, his greasy hair fell in front of his eyes and he unconsciously brushed it back with his fingertips. "No," he said, balling his hands into fists. "No, no, no. I'm coming. Two are better than one. Two. We're two. And we're better than one." He shoved his hands into his pockets, his gaze on the floor. "I'm going. Yes, yes ma'am. I'm going. I'm going with you. You can't leave me behind. You can't make me."

Yes, I can, Donnie, but you wouldn't like it. Andi knew if she left, Donnie would follow her and that would mess up everything. "Look at me, Donnie," Andi said, her voice low and stern. Donnie slowly lifted his gaze to meet Andi's. His look was cold, dead. A chill went through Andi's shoulders. "You can come with me, but you have to do exactly as I say. Can you do that, Donnie?"

Donnie nodded like a child.

"I'm probably going to have to shoot some people." *Polo Man. God help me.* "You can't make any noise if that happens. You can't cry, you can't scream. Can you do that, Donnie?"

His head pistoned up and down.

"We're going to have to walk a long way, so you might get hungry and thirsty. I'm not carrying that for you. You'll have to do it on your own. Okay?"

Donnie reached into the pockets of his military pants and pulled out bags of Skittles and a dry package of beef ramen. "I have a Pepsi in my back pocket," he said.

Seriously? Andi took a deep breath and looked at Donnie like he was a kindergartener. "Are you ready?"

"Yes, I am." He jumped through the still open door to the Silverado and sat in the driver's seat.

Andi just stared at him. "We can't take the truck, Donnie. It's too loud. We have to be quiet. We're taking the Subaru."

I know that, doody-head. I just need to get something special. "I'm just grabbing Daddy's binoculars," he shouted from inside the cab. The binoculars sat on the seat, he didn't need them, but he looped them around his neck anyway. Donnie watched as Andi shook her head and walked to the bay door. Donnie reached under the seat; it was still there. His fingers wrapped around the smooth wooden handle of Mother's knife and he pulled it onto the seat, the sharp blade shone in the dull light of the garage. *Oh, yes. Oh, yes. Get them alone, Mother said. I'm getting them alone, Mother. The Army woman first, just like I wanted.* He slid the knife into the right thigh pocket of the Army pants. It stopped with the handle sticking out. *No, no, this won't do.* The Army woman might see the knife and take it away. She was strong, stronger than Donnie, but Donnie knew he was smarter than that dumb old girl from Oklahoma. The garage filled with a squeal as the Army woman pulled open the garage door. Donnie pushed the knife until it cut through the bottom of the pocket and the handle disappeared under the camouflage flap. The blade scraped his leg on the way through; Donnie could feel a trickle of blood, but he didn't mind. The pain felt good, it made him feel more alive. He knew he just needed the Army woman to turn her back at the right time and the knife would taste more blood.

***

The sun sank just behind the trees when the wooden door to the Corral opened. Doug sat on the grass, his arms tied to a wooden post behind him, Nikki across from him tied to a similar pole, her jaw swollen. Doug still tasted blood. The man threw open the door, the hard man who appeared in Lazarus' dining room like a storm and beat them onto the verge of unconsciousness as Terry slept and Jenna giggled, the Ophiocordon in their system already taking over. Lazarus lead Terry and Jenna away (Jenna, sweet Jenna) to God knows where and this asshole half dragged them to this wooden cage, this Corral outside the high school. Bleachers and lights surrounded the six-foot-tall wooden fence. A Roman Coliseum for rednecks.

The hard man pulled someone else into the enclosure, a young man in his late 20s maybe. "What's going on, Ken?" the man asked.

The man he called Ken put a hand on his shoulder. "You remember how you're fucking Lazarus' girlfriend?"

A panicked look washed across the young man's face, his body tensed. "You said you didn't care. You said you wouldn't tell anyone."

The young man winced as Ken applied pressure to the grip on his shoulder. "I don't care who you're fucking, Seidel. I really, really don't. And I'm good to my word. I didn't say anything about it. It's just–" He turned Seidel around to face him, "–that fat bastard figured it out on his own. He might be crazy as shit, but he's not dumb. Besides, it's a small town, Seidel. There are no secrets." Ken leveled a blow to Seidel's midsection; the man's wind forced out in one sudden rush. He collapsed to his knees. Ken kicked him in the ribs with the heavy work boots he wore. Something cracked. Seidel let out a sharp, high-pitched cry. Doug stared at Ken; that bastard was enjoying this.

"Now," Ken said, pulling out his butterfly knife and flipping it open. He tugged Seidel's shirt taut and stuck the blade through, ripping the side open. He pulled the rest off, leaving the man shirtless. "That's better, Seidel." He grabbed the man's arm, dragged him to an empty pole and lashed his hands behind him. "There's a loyalty rally at sunset." Ken grabbed Seidel's chin in his big, meaty hand and pulled it up; their eyes met. "And I'll make sure that pretty little Lacy is here. It'll be a lesson for her to keep her legs together." Ken dropped Seidel's face and walked out of the arena, shutting the big wooden door behind him.

"We gotta get out of here," Nikki said, her voice thick through her bruised, puffy face. She pulled at her bonds, but they were lashed tight. "You think Andi's coming?"

Doug looked at her through his left eye, his right one swollen shut. "She'd better be."

***

The Subaru fit nicely behind a barn just off the rural highway. Andi did her best to brush the tracks from the overgrown grass with a leafy branch, but the marks remained. If someone were looking hard enough, they'd notice a vehicle had just driven through. That was okay; Andi wasn't sure either of them was coming back. She tossed the branch into a brush pile that lay against the barn and pointed Donnie across the highway.

"There's railroad tracks that run parallel to the blacktop," she said slowly. Andi didn't know how smart Donnie was; the boy was off, that was for sure, but a lot of times stupid and crazy looked the same. She didn't want to take any chances with him. "The trees should shield us from the road. We're going to take that past town and try to get in from the back. Do you understand?"

Donnie nodded. Andi didn't like the boy's eyes. They were dead, like a rat's.

"I just need for you to keep up with me and please keep quiet. Please."

Donnie nodded again and reached into a pocket and pulled out a bag of Skittles. *Oh, my god. This boy's going to kill me.* Andi slipped the backpack over her slim shoulders, tucked the tire iron into her belt and held her weapon at the ready. "Let's go."

Nothing moved on the highway. Weeds grew in the cracks on the unkept asphalt like a patchy beard on a high school boy. Andi crossed the road and disappeared into the trees and underbrush on the other side, Donnie followed closely behind. Saplings that would grow to cover the railroad tracks in a tunnel of branches sprouted along the right-of-way. Soon nature would cover the tracks, the ties and rails buried in plants. Andi stepped onto the tracks, military boots crunching on the dark red and gray granite stones scattered along the railroad bed. She stepped off the stones and onto the ties and motioned for Donnie to do the same. The next few hours, she knew, were all about silence. The less noise they made moving and the less she talked with that creepy little man the better.

"It's really quiet out here. That's good, right?" Donnie said through a mouthful of candy.

Andi turned to him and whispered. "Donnie. You can't talk. Say nothing. We have to be quiet, like ninjas. You know what ninjas are, right?"

Donnie smiled, his head bobbed up and down.

Good. "Ninjas are silent and deadly and that's what we have to be, silent and deadly. Now, if you have to pee, stop to eat, or anything else, tap me on the shoulder. Just don't say anything. Do you understand?"

Donnie gave a thumbs up. Silent but deadly. Donnie liked the deadly part. *Can I be silent but deadly? Yes, stupid Ms. Army woman, I can.*

***

"I'm sorry, Nikki." Doug said, leaning into the pole he was lashed to, a bloody streak on his face now a hard brick-red crust. The early evening sky, dark in the east, the first few stars visible in the blue, was streaked with pastels in the west.

Nikki had worked her way to standing and pulled at the rope that bound her hands, trying to untie it. "What?"

"I'm sorry. This is my fault. Everybody wanted to sit tight. I pushed to find a place with people." He stopped; a cough racked his chest. Ken had caught him in the ribs with the toe of his boot. Something didn't feel right in there. He spat on the grass; it lay in a small glistening pool, a streak of crimson stood out like the bloody trace of a chick in a country fresh egg. "Well, I sure found people, all right."

Nikki's fingers slipped off the tight knot. She kicked the ground. "Goddamnit." She looked at Doug, her face starting to show its bruise. "Stop sitting there feeling sorry for yourself, Douglas. I need you here, now. We need to get out of here, now."

Doug looked up: tears rimmed his swollen eyes. "But Jenna, Terry."

"Pull your shit together, mister. Stand up and work on those knots. We can't help them if we're dead."

The man Ken called Seidel pushed himself to his feet. "She's right. I don't want to die here while that crazy asshole watches." He started feeling for the knots behind his back. A short laugh escaped his lips. "I was leaving tonight. Me and my girlfriend and a friend. We were getting out of this craziness."

"We still can," Nikki said.

Seidel stopped struggling with the knots and looked at Nikki. "Lazarus is insane, you know?"

"We kind of figured that one out on our own."

Seidel shook his head. "No. I don't mean crazy; I mean fucking insane. Do you know why you're here?"

Nikki didn't know. All she knew was she was eating lunch, then Ken showed up and beat the shit out of her. "No."

"He's making an army." Seidel took a deep breath, the pain in his ribs made him wince. "He takes people in and feeds some of them that zombie anti-depressant."

"Ophiocordon."

Doug moaned.

"Then he puts them in the high school gym he's turned into a hothouse. He chains people up to them and when the fungus grows–"

"Zombies." Nikki started struggling with the rope that held her to the post. *What the fuck?* "He's intentionally making zombies?"

"That's his army. Once he gets enough he's going to march across the country, killing everyone who doesn't join him."

That idea hit Nikki like Ken Gundy. "And us?"

"We're part of a loyalty rally. The whole town shows up to see what happens when you don't support the cause," Seidel said. "He's going to let his pet zombies in here and they're going to eat us alive."

***

Light filtered through the trees that lined the railroad tracks on both sides. The silence, broken by occasional doves flapping into the underbrush, seemed like Bilbo's travel in "The Hobbit," complete with goblins. They were out there and they were just as deadly. Andi walked under a branch where a fat eastern gray squirrel with a bright white belly sat chittering at her. In another time, in another place Andi would have put a bullet through that squirrel, cleaned it with a pocketknife and roasted it over a fire just for Big Andy. But she wasn't in that place anymore; she missed that place.

About a mile or so down the track, Andi stopped and threw up a hand to Donnie. She had no idea what the little creep was doing, but he walked right into her, almost knocking her to the ground. A zombie stood on the tracks. The tall figure, a farmer probably by the Key bib overalls and once white T-shirt that hung off its decimated frame. It swayed back and forth, oblivious to the world. This wasn't the same track the Canadian army was traveling on. It couldn't be. This zombie had been there a while. Morning glory vines had grown over the track and wrapped around its legs. Donnie opened his mouth, but Andi slapped an index finger to her lips and hissed, "Shhh." Donnie closed his mouth and stepped backward, his eyes dropped to the tracks.

Zombies moved. That's what they did. They moved and they fed. Why the heck, Andi wondered, did this farmer stay in one spot long enough for weeds to grow around its legs? It didn't make any sense. Andi's hand moved to the tire iron and she started to step forward, to end this affront to nature, when something moved in the trees. Another zombie. *Oh, no, two.* A woman in a business skirt and jacket and a teenager in a skate punk T-shirt and jean shorts, flanked the farmer. One stood on each side of the tracks, softly moaning in the underbrush. They couldn't pass the farmer zombie without getting too close to the ones in the brush. Andi pulled binoculars from the backpack. The zombies hidden in the brush on the right-of-way were tied to trees, leashes around their necks. The farmer was lashed to a post driven deep between the ties, its face slack, a great wedge had fallen off its jaw revealing a row of solid yellow teeth. Andi lowered the binoculars and slid them into her backpack. The town didn't need human guards. It had plenty of protection and Andi knew how to deal with them. These monsters had taken her parents, her country, her world. They were the ones who really took the Polo Man.

She drew the tire iron and advanced on the farmer. The thing's head shifted toward the sudden movement, its milk-white eyes trained on Andi. It moaned; the low plaintive wail, like a sad dog, started to rise. The zombies on the right-of-way joined it. Andi broke into a run; if she didn't end that now, it would grow into a scream and the whole town would know she was there. *This was brilliant.* Andi raised the tire iron as the zombie farmer pulled against its rope, its jaws chomping up and down, its arms outstretched. She dodged to the right and brought the tire iron down on the monster's head, the cast metal crushed through the thing's skull. It dropped toward the ground and stopped, arms askew, held in a half stance by the rope. A puppet without a master.

Donnie grunted. Andi turned; Donnie knelt on the railroad tracks, a fist in his mouth. *What are you doing?* Andi snapped her fingers and Donnie looked up, drawing his knuckles from his mouth. Blood trickled down the back of his hand. The look on his face was what? Shock? Pity?

No, Donnie was angry. *Why would he be angry? I'm the one who should be angry.* Andi waved him on. Donnie still knelt on the tracks, staring at the monster dangling from the post, its brains a bloody gray mass oozing from the crack in its skull. Andi grabbed Donnie's shoulder, forced him to his feet and pulled him into a jog.

The day drew darker the closer they grew to town. Andi knew Mayday was there, just through the trees. She stopped Donnie at a break in the foliage; a blacktop road lifted over the tracks from the main road and disappeared through the trees beyond. A large tin building, a factory of some sort, stood between them and the town. Andi squatted, looking through the binoculars. It was just like Doug had described, the Gate and the high school beyond. There was some movement on bleachers arranged around a wooden enclosure in the front grass of the high school. Something was going to happen tonight, some kind of festival, or game, or death march. She moved the binoculars. A man stood at the Gate, looking inward, not out. Too much was going on in there and too little was going on out here. *We've got to hurry.* Andi started to move, then stopped. The Prius sat next to an old Oldsmobile in front of an abandoned drive-in. She tucked the binoculars away and motioned Donnie to his belly. They crawled in the cinders with their heads down, hidden from the eyes of the town. When they cleared the blacktop road and the darkness of the trees again claimed the tracks, Andi pushed herself to her feet and broke into a run. Something was happening in town and she didn't like it. She didn't like it at all.

***

Jenna woke in semi darkness. *What happened?* Her panties were wet. *Good God, it wasn't a dream,* she thought. *I came. I–* The day flooded back to her in random splashes. She felt great after lunch. There was something about that sandwich and the potato salad, that made her feel so good, like she was drunk, but drunk and horny. Sex with Doug was, *oh God, oh God, oh God.* A rush suddenly built deep inside her. *Dear God, not again.* Heat poured through her face, her torso, her thighs, it built like a pressure inside her and when it went, when it *oh God, oh, God, oh God.* Her orgasm shook her, a gush of fluid shot from her, soaking the bed beneath her. *Bed? What bed?* She looked around, her breath coming in spent wheezes. She was in, where? A basketball goal hung over her head. *A gymnasium? A high school gymnasium?* She tried to roll over, to get out of this bed, but she couldn't. Jenna's eyes looked down along her body; she lay on a hospital gurney. Her wrists and ankles were tied down with straps. "Where am I?" stumbled from her mouth; it was no more than a whisper.

"Jenna?"

She turned her head. Terry lay in the bed next to her. Oh, Terry. "Are you okay?" she asked.

He grinned. "Not as good as you are," he said. "I caught that. Your little orgasmaplosion." He frowned. "You know what's happened to us, don't you?"

She nodded. What else could it be? Euphoria. Uncontrollable orgasms. She watched Doug beaten and she did nothing but laugh. *Oh, Doug. Doug.* She wanted to cry. She felt like she should cry. That was the appropriate response, right? But she couldn't. The Ophiocordon wouldn't let her. "We've got to get out of here."

Terry raised his wrists as far as the leather straps would allow. "Don't see how. Unless the cavalry shows up pretty soon, I'd say we're fucked."

Cavalry. If Doug didn't call Andi by 5 p.m., she was going to come and rescue them. How silly is that? One woman against a town? But she was in the Army and she could talk Batman with Terry. Jenna had watched Andi clear a parking lot of zombies, march into the hospital in Omaha and bring out her Doug. Andi could do it.

"Doug didn't call Andi," she said. "The cavalry might come."

***

More zombies. They stretched out through the trees, tied at regular intervals, forming a barrier around Mayday, forcing travelers to go into town one way, the Gate. The back side of the town was going to be the weak spot and why not? Only a crazy person would try to get in that way. Andi grinned, raised the tire iron and waded into the woods. She rushed each human monster before their moan could rise into a scream, a mom, a man in a suit, a guy in a once-white bathrobe, stained red around the neck, a county deputy. She pretended they were all the monsters that ate Polo Man. The tire iron crashed into skulls, the sentries dropped to the leafy forest floor, their nervous system twitching, then growing slack. After about twenty yards, Andi broke into a clearing, panting, sweat soaked her hair. Donnie ran toward her awkwardly, tears running from his eyes. He started to speak, but Andi cupped a hand over his mouth and shook her head. Donnie shoved his hands into his pants pockets and stepped away from Andi like she was Death.

A swollen waxing half-moon sat high in the sky, casting a yellow light on the clearing. A tall, grassy field opened before them, revealing the patched together fence that encircled Mayday. The fence surrounded the football field; garden crops grew on the gridiron and stopped at the back of the high school. The fence was bolted into the back brick wall of the school, the building itself part of the border between the town and the lands beyond. Cotton had told the unit these were the Goodlands. Andi had seen for herself that was garbage talk. These were the Badlands just as much as those south of the fence that ran east to west through Oklahoma.

Two old metal and wooden bleachers, probably made by students in shop class back in the '80s, sat in the grass. Andi motioned to Donnie. He didn't move. *What the hell is wrong with him?* Andi stepped closer to Donnie and whispered.

"Hold yourself together, Donnie," she hissed. "We're going over that wall and on top of that roof. You and me are going to push those bleachers on the left. Get on the right side, grab hold and push. It's on skids. We're taking it to the wall. You got me?"

Donnie stared through Andi, his soulless eyes black in the near darkness. "You killed them," he mumbled. "You killed them all."

Killed? "Killed who? Who did I kill?"

Tears started to run down his pimply face. "All those people back there. Those Good people. They were just standing there and you crushed their skulls."

Good people? "Donnie. Those were zombies. You're hysterical. I want to slap you, I really do, but that's noisy. We have to be quiet. Take a deep breath and help me push that bleacher up to the wall. Afterward you can go hug all the zombies you want, but not before we save our friends." Andi stood still, the sun finally gone from the sky. Donnie's eyes were black now, like in a vampire movie. Suddenly, yellow light bathed the night; it came from the other side of the high school. Andi grabbed Donnie's shoulder and pulled. "Please."

The bleacher slid easily in the tall grass. The metal frame clanged against the brick, but Andi was sure no one in Mayday heard it. The noise rising in the town from the other side of the high school bordered on rabid fans at a Friday night high school football game. She climbed the wooden steps and jumped to catch the lip of the roof. Her hands hit brick, grabbed hold and she pulled herself over.

"Help me up."

Andi looked over the side of the wall. Donnie stood on the top step of the bleacher, his arms outstretched, his face pleading. He couldn't climb up himself. *What the heck could he do?* Andi stood on the roof, looking down at the boy. *I should leave him. He's just slowed me down.* But Andi could picture the little man screaming for her, begging her to help him onto the roof. The cheers from beyond the school were growing into a roar, but if Donnie got loud enough, he could ruin everything. Andi sank to her stomach and draped an arm over the wall.

"Grab my arm, Donnie. I'll pull you up."

Donnie jumped and clasped his hand onto Andi's. She grabbed Donnie's thin, bony forearm and pulled him onto the roof. Donnie fell on his ass. "Thanks," he said.

Andi stood in a crouch. "Yeah." The roar from the crowd grew louder. "Come with me," she said. "And stay down."

Light bathed the school lawn in yellow. Andi dropped to the tarred surface of the flat roof and took the binoculars from the backpack. At least a hundred people were in the bleachers, some sat quietly, looking away from the ring in the center, but most stood, looking inward, chanting something Andi couldn't make out. *Were they saying "Mac"?* Telephone poles were sunk in the ground in a ring around a tall wooden fence, topped by lights scavenged from the football field. The lights, powered by a gas generator, pointed down into the ring. She trained the glasses into the enclosure.

"Holy shit," she wheezed.

Doug and Nikki stood near the walls, tied to posts along with a man he didn't know. A fat man stood in the center of the ring, his arms spread for the crowd. The man shouted something, something Andi couldn't make out. She didn't care what he said. Doug and Nikki were strapped to poles. He meant to kill them. *No.* If someone was going to die tonight, it was going to be the fat man. Something moved to the fat man's right outside the enclosure. Andi swung the binoculars toward the movement and her mouth went dry. A man. A man walked through a worn path in the grass holding a leash in one hand. The long leather strip dragged the grass behind him, then rose to the neck of a beast. *That's not possible.* A gorilla, its cream-white eyes gleamed in the artificial stadium light. The thing was enormous, looming a good foot and a half over the man who escorted it. The simian walked unsteadily on two legs behind the man toward a door in the fence, a door that would lead them into the enclosure, to Doug and Nikki. A small cloud of flapping, black birds hovered behind it. Andi thought of Pigpen from the "Peanuts" comics, but Pigpen wasn't a reanimated corpse.

She dropped the binoculars and unshouldered the weapon, tossing her backpack onto the tarred roof. "Turn around, Donnie," she said. "You may not want to watch this." Andi pulled her weapon into her shoulder and took aim at King Freakin' Kong.

Donnie stood over Andi, the glow from the stadium lamps bathing them in a soft light. The kitchen knife he pulled from the side pocket of the Army pants shone bright in the night. He dropped to one knee and plunged the blade into the Army woman's back.

CHAPTER 19

The lights stung Lazarus' eyes. He stood in the center of the Corral, surrounded by the good people of Mayday and he couldn't look at them. This was his show and he couldn't see his people. The pain in his back had returned. *Damn Gwenny and her reverse cowgirl. It's gotta be good old-fashioned doggie from now on.* Sweat ran down his face.

"We all know about my plan," Lazarus said, the words came out slowly, like his tongue was suddenly too big for his mouth. *Is it nerves?* he wondered. "The plan is our future. Our way to reclaim the world." He paused to swallow, his mouth dry as a hangover. He wished he'd brought a bottle of water with him, but that might show weakness. If Lazarus couldn't afford something, it was to look weak in front of the good people of Mayday. He's the man who didn't die; you don't survive by being weak. He stretched his right arm toward the three people lashed to poles behind him. "These people you see here came to end the plan, to end Mayday." A few boos rang out from the crowd. *Yes, they're still my people.* "And you know what happens when someone is against our town?"

"Mac," someone yelled from the audience.

Lazarus smiled. "Who wants to see Mac?"

A cheer rang from the stands.

"Who wants Mac to rain justice down on these outsiders?"

The chant started low, but slowly rose. "Mac, Mac, Mac, Mac."

These fine citizens, who shopped at the Apple Market, ate at the Whistlestop, mowed the lawns and kept Mayday beautiful, were working themselves into a frenzy. Lazarus knew they would. They always did when it was time for the show. He wondered if the good citizens of Rome chanted and foamed at the mouth when criminals were thrown to the beasts, like Caspian tigers and leopards. It was the Christians who got all the attention, but Lazarus knew Christians were rarely fed to anything. It was the common criminal that faced the fangs of the beast. Those Romans sure knew how to keep order and so did he. The town needed a little reminder every once in a while about who was boss. *It's me. I'm boss.*

"Then welcome the beast from the forests of a far-away land. Mac the Magnificent."

Ken Gundy pulled open the gate from the outside, spilling the directional light over him and the beast. Mac stood behind him, towering over the thick, menacing man like an adult over a child. A cloud of crows followed Mac and lighted on the poles that loomed overhead. Ken tugged the rope and gently pulled the oversized gorilla into the full light, the beast's once sleek black fur matted, crusty with dried mucus and blood. It moaned as it lumbered through the gate, any semblance to the quick, strong noble beast it once was, gone. It was a fucking monster.

"Is anybody hungry?" Lazarus yelled. As if on command, Mac's bellowing moan split the night, drowning out the cheers. The audience grew silent. It was time for the show.

*＊＊

The pain was more than anything Andi had ever felt. The kitchen knife easily sliced through her shirt and plunged into the flesh of her back. Andi bit her lip to stifle a scream. The world swam. *Donnie.* Why didn't she see this coming? The boy was unhinged. Andi turned a few inches, new pain tore through her torso, a hiss escaped her lips.

"Donnie, you little bastard." He stood over Andi and pulled at the knife. It didn't move. *Stuck on a bone you shit.* Andi moved a hand to her sidearm, every inch tearing new pain through her chest. "I'm going to kill you, Donnie," came out in a whisper.

Donnie squeaked. *Of course, he squeaked.* Andi's fingers fumbled with the holster.

"Run Donnie," his mother's voice spoke in his head. Donnie shook it, trying to dislodge the voice he knew wasn't there. *Not now Mother. I'm doing so good.* The voice came back, louder. *"Run, Donnie, or you can't finish your work. You can't kill the gunkies. Then you can never come back to me, baby boy. You need your Momma, yes you do. Now go."* The Army woman's fingers were on the pistol grip. The lights from the arena shone on the roof and glistened off a pool of blood forming under the Army woman. Donnie grinned. *I stuck her real good, Mother. Real good.*

"My job here is done." Donnie released the knife handle and ran to the edge of the roof. He gripped the side and dropped out of sight.

*＊＊

"What's going on out there, Terry?" Artificial light filtered into the gymnasium through a few small windows. The rhythmic chanting of 'Mac' deadened by the thick brick walls, but the engine-like moan sat in the night like a ticking clock.

"I don't know. But something's got them all worked up."

A metallic clank sounded from somewhere in the school. Jenna and Terry lay quietly in the stifling heat of the gym, sweat beading on their bodies. Terry thought it felt like a goddamned greenhouse. *Why the hell's it so hot in here?* A moment later one of the gym doors opened and a woman looked in. Her hair, bobbing behind her in a ponytail, and half her face visible; the rest of her hidden behind the swinging wooden door. Terry'd only seen the fat man and the asshole who punched Nikki since they came to town. A feeling squirmed inside. What was that? Anger. The drug had started to wear off. Who was this person? The woman pushed the door open further and stepped inside. He hadn't seen her before, or had he? Was this the woman who took a basket of greens to the grocery store? Looking nervously around the gym, she approached Jenna and loosened the straps on her legs.

"Who are you?" Jenna asked.

The woman, maybe twenty-two, looked at Jenna, her face grim. "My name's Lacy." She undid the leg straps and worked on the leather around Jenna's wrists. "Your friends are in trouble," she said. "They're in the Corral with Walter."

"Who's Walter?" Terry asked.

"My boyfriend. Lazarus is going to kill them all. We have to stop him."

Lazarus. *Tim. Tim, Tim, Timmy Tim-Tim.*

"And how are we going to do that?" Terry asked. "Sounds like the whole town's out there."

Jenna sat up on the bed, her pants wet, the musky scent of her orgasms hung in the air. Lacy moved to Terry. "There are guns in the science room," Lacy said. "It's padlocked, but I brought this." She patted a 16-ounce Stanley hammer stuck in her belt. It was Walter's. She removed Terry's straps and helped him up. "Can you two move?"

Jenna pushed herself onto the floor, her legs weak, but she stood. "Yes. Terry?"

Terry was already on his feet. "Yeah. I can make it."

A gunshot cracked and the night exploded in screams.

***

King Kong wobbled fully into the light on its short hind legs, its deep moan the only thing Andi could hear, except for her own heartbeat. *Stupid Donnie.* The knife had punctured a lung; she was sure of that. It had collapsed; her breaths came in shallow wet flaps. Andi felt like she was drowning. The little shit had cut into an artery, as well. The growing pool of blood too much for her to stay alive. *I'm bleeding out. I'm bleeding out.* Pain lanced Andi's body as she inched closer to the edge of the roof and steadied her elbows on the brick ledge. The simian monster swam in her vision, but it was big, damned big and black. A good target. She had to take it out before it ate Nikki; before it ate Doug. As Andi's strength began to fade, she felt sorry for Doug, who just wanted a home, who just wanted safety and had found this damned place. Andi pulled the scope to her eye like she had with the M24 Sniper Weapon on the roof of the Motel 6 in Muskogee. *When did it get so damned heavy?* The big, black figure loomed large in the sights. *'Just one shot Andi,'* Big Andy said. Where did that come from? *'Just one shot is all you need. It's all you ever needed.'*

"What? Daddy?" Andi's words were less than whispers; they died as they left her lips. "I gotta do this, Daddy."

'I know you do.' Was that a worn boot that rested on the brick ledge next to her? Andi didn't dare look, to take her eyes from the sight of the weapon. There was a monster, a monster that should be in Africa beating its chest and running on its knuckles. She had to shoot it. But she was so sleepy. *'No,'* Big Andy said. *'You have to kill the monkey.'*

But it's not a monkey, Daddy.

'You remember the first day I took you hunting?' Big Andy's words were loud, but strange. Like he was talking inside a glass bowl.

Andi took in a shallow breath. Flap, slap. Flap, slap. Her world was a world of pain. She grimaced. "I sure do, Daddy."

'You remember the first time I took you deer hunting? You got one, remember? On your first try, with your first shot. You got a doe. You shot her for me. And you only needed to pull the trigger once. You remember?'

Sweat ran into Andi's eyes. She couldn't wipe it out; she couldn't let go of the weapon, because she knew she'd never be able pick it up again. "I do. I do, Daddy," she whispered.

'Then get that big ape for me.' Big Andy's voice was quieter now, like he was farther away.

Don't go Daddy. Don't leave me here.

'Shoot it, Andi. Shoot it for me.'

Andi concentrated on the black, hulking figure approaching her friends, concentrated on keeping her body steady as she gently squeezed the trigger.

***

Nikki screamed as the monster lurched toward them, its milky eyes glaring. The bullet crack momentarily sucked the sound out of the night like a balloon pop, followed by Mac's crows cawing and flapping into the night. The great, lumbering simian, with its zombie eyes stopped, a red, runny hole appeared just above its right eye and a bloody mass of brain and bone blew out the back of its thick skull. Its eyes lolled and it staggered backward, its big stupid head not sure what had just happened.

"No," Lazarus whispered as the great black ape tottered on its short, thick legs and dropped like a safe to the grass of the Corral floor, grass that had drunk the blood of all the other unbelievers Mac had made pay for their sins.

"Andi," Nikki whispered, then turned to Doug who stood, pulling against his post, looking more alive than he had in hours. "Andi's here."

Screams filled the night. Ken Gundy stood in the doorway of the Corral; his head scanning the buildings close by. There weren't many tall enough for a shooter, except for the high school. The sound came from the high school, didn't it? There was no grassy knoll like in the Kennedy assassination, so there was no question here. It didn't come from the stands, there weren't guns in Mayday anyway, at least that average citizens could get their hands on.

"Go to the high school," he yelled into the night as townsfolk scattered into the darkness. "Get the shooter. Get the shooter." No one stopped. Lazarus stood over Mac in a daze.

Ken Gundy turned and looked toward Walter Seidel. The fucking punk stood, pulling against ropes Ken knew damned well he wouldn't be able to untie. Ken tied those knots himself. Seidel wasn't an average citizen; he could get his hands on guns. So could that goddamned slacker Gil Haply. Who was out there? Ken stepped toward Walter, his fists bunched. "I'm going to break your spine." He took a step, then dropped to his hands and knees. Lacy stood over him, the Craftsman hammer clenched tightly in her hand.

"Lacy," Walter screamed. She ran to him and cupped his bruised face in her hands.

"Oh, no. What did they do to you?"

"Just get me out of here, baby."

Lacy went behind Walter and pulled a pair of pruning shears from her back pocket. They easily cut through the rope. Walter grabbed Lacy and kissed her deeply. No peaches, but her breath tasted like home. He took the shears and cut Nikki loose, then Doug. Lazarus moaned from a stack of fat over Mac.

Walter looked at Doug. "Can you walk?"

Doug shook his head. "Not very fast."

Walter looped an arm around Doug's waist. "Let's go." They took two steps and stopped. Jeremy stood at the gate, its face no longer placid. There was blood in the Corral and Jeremy smelled it. Its mouth opened and shut like one of those grinning toy monkeys pounding cymbals.

Walter looked down at his naked chest. Ken Gundy had taken away his shirt, the special shirt with the patch of zombie skin. Now he was food.

"Lacy," he yelled and threw the shears; they landed near her feet. "Cut off their shirts."

She nodded and grabbed the shears. Suddenly, Ken Gundy rose in front of her. Blood ran down his scalp from the hammer blow. He groaned something unintelligible and stepped forward. Gundy. Lazarus' security man. She hated the way he looked at her as she worked the garden, staring like he wanted to eat her. She sometimes saw him outside at night, standing under the big elm tree in her yard, staring at her house. Always staring. He was the reason her Walter was here. Lacy froze. His eyes glazed as he stumbled forward.

Nikki pushed Lacy aside and leveled a kick between Gundy's legs, her tennis shoe smashed into the man's testicles. Gundy groaned and dropped like the gorilla. She plucked the shears from Lacy's hands and pointed to a foot square leather beige patch on the back of Gundy's shirt. "This it?"

"Yes," Walter shouted. "Get the leather."

Gundy moaned as Nikki sliced into the fabric, cutting away the leather patch. She kicked him in the head. Lacy kicked the back of Lazarus' knee and he toppled on top of the rotting carcass of Mac. He screamed as she grabbed the back of his threadbare shirt and ripped off the patch of skin. Nikki stepped in front of Walter and Doug, holding the shirt in front of her like a shield.

"What is it?"

"Zombie skin," Walter said. "They don't attack their own."

Nikki's stomach threatened to come up. She winced and swallowed, the taste of stomach acid sour in her mouth. *What kind of fucked up place is this?* Lacy stepped next to her holding the great expanse of Lazarus' shirt toward the zombie.

Jeremy shrieked and rushed forward. Nikki winced as the monster staggered past her. Lazarus screamed again as Jeremy fell onto him, ripping into him with its strong, yellow teeth.

***

The chants outside were now screams. Lacy ran outside the school after the gunfire exploded in Mayday, leaving Terry and Jenna standing in the sweltering wet heat of the gymnasium. There were guns here in the school, in some room. Lacy (was her name Lacy, or Lucy?) said so, but whateverthehell room they were in was locked. She had a hammer to break the lock, but she took it with her. Terry shook his head, but the fuzz wouldn't budge. "You okay?"

Jenna tried to smile, but it wouldn't come. "Yeah. Let's go."

Light poured into the hallway from the large front windows. They staggered to the front doors and pushed their way through. Outside was chaos. People ran from the circle of lights that shone above the wooden circular fence surrounded by bleachers they saw when they came to town.

"What the hell's going on here, Jenna?" Terry asked, but Jenna was silent. He turned to her, her face pointed toward the roof. "What's wrong?"

Jenna turned toward him, tears rimmed her eyes. "Oh, God, Terry." He slowly looked up.

"Andi."

Corporal Andi Bakowski lay on the ledge of the Terrance County High School roof, head hung over the side, a line of blood ran from her mouth. Andi was dead. "I think Andi just saved our asses, Terry," Jenna said. Terry just stood, staring at the still figure dangling unnaturally off the brick wall. He'd just had a beer with her this morning. Jenna pulled at Terry. "We have to go."

She dragged him with unsteady legs toward the Corral, most of people from the stands now gone, some lay on the ground crying. Screams still rang through the night, but they were farther away. Four figures moved in the Corral gate and started walking toward the high school.

"Doug," she yelled. "Terry, it's Doug and Nikki." Jenna dropped his arm. "They're alive. They're alive." She ran toward them in a half trot, her spinning head threatened to drop her to the ground with every step. "Doug," she screamed.

Doug pulled away from Walter and hobbled forward, catching Jenna in his arms. Her hair smelled like strawberries. "Oh, Doug. I thought I'd never see you again." She kissed his bruised face. "I was so scared."

Walter wrapped his arm back around Doug. "We can do this later," he said. "We gotta go now." He pointed toward the west side of the high school. "There are trucks parked in the Ag shop parking lot; the keys are just inside the shop door."

"Is the door locked?" Terry asked.

Lacy put the Craftsman hammer in his hand, the head stained red with Ken Gundy's blood. "Break the window."

***

Artificial light poured over the back of the school and onto the patch of high grass beyond. Donnie giggled as he bounced down the old wooden bleacher seats like a kid and jumped into the tall grass that had once been a lawn where the FFA students judged cattle and sheep. He'd stuck that doody-head. He'd stuck her good. He spun in the tall grass, arms stretched wide, like Julie Andrews in that mountain singing movie with all the Nazis. His mother loved that movie, but he didn't understand it. There was much too much singing for a war movie.

The half-moon stood out in the sky like a spotlight, the stars bright and clear, almost as clear as the stars back home in Colorado, but nothing could ever be like that. Donnie felt so close to the stars of home, he could almost reach out and grab them. The moon bathed the forest behind the grassy field in enough light the trees were gray and the paths through them, made by people or deer, were easy to find. The rifle crack split the night, killing the roar of the crowd, as Donnie stepped into the tree line. The sudden sound froze his steps.

He stood at the edge of the forest, listening for anything. Screams, far away, burst into the night. A smile split his face. People were suffering. Why did that always make him so happy? When Gordie Tomlin fell off the slide in kindergarten onto the gravel bed of the playground, the crack of bone as loud as a handclap, Donnie laughed. Kindergarteners stood around Gordie as the little boy with a crew cut and short pants screamed, his arm jutting in a strange way, like it had two elbows and Donnie just laughed. He was still laughing when the playground teacher ran over and carried Gordie inside to the nurse. He hoped those people in town had broken something, too. That would be funny.

Something moved about twenty feet into the trees. Not much, just enough that Donnie noticed it. He stepped slowly into the trees and stopped, waiting for his eyes to adjust to the dimmer moonlight that filtered through the branches. The figure didn't move so much as it swayed. As Donnie stared at it, his eyes found arms and a shirt. A thin beam of moonlight reflected off something round and shiny. *Glasses.* It was one of the Good people. The Army woman – *dead as a doody-head. Dead as the Taylor boy* – found the Good people standing on guard in the trees to protect the town, then she killed them. She smashed them in the heads and killed them, but not all of them. Donnie stepped forward slowly; the soft moans of the Good person grew louder as the screams from the town grew faint, then stopped altogether. The Good person was a man in a white shirt and tie, his clothes just like Donnie wore before that stupid Vanessa Hagen-looking woman made him wet his pants. Now Donnie wore Army woman pants. If there's anything Donnie regretted from his trip with the Gunkies, is that he didn't get to play with the Vanessa Hagen woman. Maybe there was still time.

"Hi," Donnie said, standing about four feet from the Good person. The Good person stood fast, a rope tied him to a tree. The man in glasses reached out to Donnie like he wanted to play. Donnie had played this game with Mother lots. He ducked under the Good person's clumsy grab and continued down the path. "You'll get me next time." Donnie chuckled and skipped down the overgrown path. He didn't know where he was going; he was just going away, happy.

***

The truck started on the first try. Walter told them Lazarus wanted the four pickups always ready to go. A Dodge Grand Caravan sat off to the side; the McKenney family's last ride. The 1997 Ford F-150 Walter picked held a five-gallon water jug in the back, a full gas can, enough food in the tool chest for four days in the woods and three rifles on the gun rack in the back window of the cab, loaded and ready to take down anything that fat fucker might want to eat. Two dented wooden baseball bats, Louisville Sluggers, sat in a bucket welded to the floor of the truck bed. More weapons at the ready. Walter sat behind the steering wheel, Lacy pressed next to him like they were in high school. Jenna squeezed in next to Lacy and Doug pulled himself slowly into the passenger seat.

"Our car's outside the gate," he said and patted his right front pocket. "I still have the keys. Let us off there."

Walter opened his mouth, but his words died under a pounding on the roof of the cab. "We can talk all day long later," Terry said. He stood in the bed of the truck, hands on the roof of the cab. "Let's go." Nikki put a foot on top of the back tire and prepared to hoist herself into the bed.

"Yeah, let's go," Lacy said, then screamed. A man limped from around the side of the high school; the stadium lights bathed him in silhouette.

"Aw, fuck," Doug spat.

Ken Gundy walked toward them, his shirt torn, his face awash with blood, his breathing heavy. Gundy's left arm lay slack beside him, a chunk missing from the deltoid; he held a piece of rebar in his thick right hand. "You fuckers," he hissed. "You goddamned losers. You've ruined everything. Everything."

Nikki dropped off the tire. "No you don't," she said and grabbed a baseball bat from the bucket. She gripped it in both hands. This man had beaten her, dragged her by her hair and tied her up to die for sport. *No you don't.*

"You need to just die." She rushed Gundy, who pulled his right arm back for a swing. The Louisville Slugger caught him in the neck and he staggered, the rebar fell into the grass. "Just," Nikki screamed as she pulled the bat back and slammed it across Gundy's forehead. He fell backward, his skull dented from the blow. "Fucking." She pulled back again and caught Gundy on the chin as he pitched toward the ground, it moved to the right like Elmer Fudd had just shot Daffy's beak and it spun around that stupid duck's head. "Die." Gundy's body hit the ground and twitched. She hit him again, his skull making a flat, squishy sound. Nikki reached back to hit him again, but Terry grabbed the bat and wrestled it from her grip.

"TCB, baby," he said and dropped the wet bat on top of Gundy's chest.

"What?" she said, her breath hard and heavy.

Terry turned Nikki toward him and pulled her in close. "Elvis had a ring," he said. "It read TCB. That meant Taking Care of Business." She fell into his arms and wept.

Doug stepped out of the cab on his good foot and held onto the door for support. "Move now, cry later. Get in the back."

The truck moved smoothly over the well-trimmed grass of Mayday, Kentucky, light from the Corral still running. Walter suspected it would run until the generator ran out of gas. He stopped at the Gate, the big barn door loomed like the one on Skull Island. Terry jumped from the truck bed and landed on the pavement of Main Street that led from this damned town. He lifted the ten-foot-long two-by-six, tossed it into the weeds and swung the door wide.

Terry walked back to the pickup and helped Nikki down. "I think this is where we get off," he said. "Doug?"

Doug opened the door and got out. "Yep. Thanks, but we're all on our own." Jenna helped Doug walk toward the Prius, the lights flashed and the car chirped when he hit the remote's unlock button. Terry and Nikki followed them.

"Where are you going?" Walter asked out the open window of the truck.

Doug stopped and looked back at Walter. "Dyersburg, Tennessee. There's supposed to be an army there." He stopped and looked at Jenna. She smiled at him. "I'm not going to ask you to follow us," he said. "I've fucked up everything else before now. But that's just where we're going."

Doug dropped into the driver's seat of the Prius and Jenna sat next to him. Nikki sat on Terry's lap in the back and Doug started the car. A sign outside Mayday said Interstate 69 South was 10 miles west. He turned the Prius around and went west, over the railroad tracks and through thick fields of corn and cotton that would never be harvested, the headlights of the Ford F-150 behind him the whole way.

***

The game got old quickly. An old grandma lady leaned toward Donnie against the strap that held her to a thick walnut tree, her moan loud and hungry. *Well, if you knew you were going to be out here so long, you should have brought a snack.* Snack. Donnie had snacks, but she wasn't getting his Skittles, no way. He reached into a pocket in his Army pants and pulled out the packet of beef ramen. He held it up to her.

"It's all I have, lady. Take it. It'll make you feel better." He tossed it toward her. The package struck her old saggy chest and fell to the forest floor. "Ungrateful," Donnie spat. "That's what you are, ungrateful. And I'm not playing with you." Other moans started in the darkness. He looked at the grandma lady, chomping at him like a monkey eating a banana. Donnie walked up to her, ducked under her arms and kept walking. "Good-bye, grandma lady. I hope you learn some manners."

The forest slowly began to brighten, individual leaves now visible on the branches that hung low over the path, the twisted limbs of hawthorn trees a maze in the canopy. Then the trees began to thin and Donnie stepped into a clearing. The moon had moved, ever so slightly, its bright light filled the clearing of high grass that looked to Donnie like a soft bed. Donnie breathed in the cool air of night. He just wanted to lie on that bed of grass and roll, then stare at the stars and dream of a world of Good people, a world without Gunkies. He stepped into the wonderful clearing and knew he wouldn't be surprised if this weren't the Hundred Acre Wood and Pooh Bear and Piglet came out and took him on a hunt for Heffalumps. He all but danced into the tall grass, then he realized he wasn't alone. A lone figure stood in the middle of the clearing, tied to a post, just like he'd found Mr. Grimes tied to a post in his back yard in Julesburg. He stepped forward and the figure moved.

"Hello," Donnie said. Whoever it was didn't say a word; it just stood there, waving at him. Donnie stepped forward.

Grass high enough to brush his thighs parted when he walked toward the mysterious figure on the post. It didn't move. *Did it ever?* It didn't talk. *Who are you?* he wondered. Detail came as he stepped closer. The figure was a woman, a beautiful, beautiful woman. Her thick black hair was pulled back in a red ribbon and fell onto the shoulders of a red and white dress, the same red and white Sunday dress Mother wore back in Julesburg, Colorado. "Mother?" he whispered. More detail became clear as he approached, the wedding ring Daddy gave her glinted in the moonlight. The dried, crusty blood on her face that had soaked under her chin made a pretty red necklace on her dress. "Is that you, Mother?"

'Of course it is, Donnie honey. Come to Mommy.'

"Mother?" But how did she get here? *I'm a thousand miles away from home, Mother.* Donnie stepped closer on weak legs. *'Mommy missed you, honey.'* Of course she did. Of course she missed her baby. Donnie threw up his hands and ran to her. "Mother," he yelled, his mouth twisted into a smile, a real smile.

She's here. She's really, really here, he thought as he ran to her and threw his arms around her. Her arms found him and her nails tore through his shirt and into his flesh, blood squirting from the wounds. "Mother?" he wheezed and looked into her face. The eyes were wrong; the nose was wrong. This wasn't Mother. Donnie screamed as the zombie ripped his cheek from his face.

PART THREE: THE BLEAK LANDS

CHAPTER 20

By the position of the sun, it had been up for hours. The once cool morning breeze that slowly drifted through the slightly cracked Prius windows during the darkness, now carried with it thick humidity. Doug stirred in the driver's seat, sweat beading on his face. He turned toward the passenger side of the Prius; the door sat wide open and Terry stood just outside, pissing onto an asphalt parking lot. The splatter of urine loud in the – *whatthehell time is it?* – morning. Terry's butt moved in circles. *Where are we?*

"Hey, Terry," Doug said, his voice gravelly from sleep.

"Just a minute, dude," Terry said and swung his ass in a tighter circle, then pumped his hips to the left.

"What the hell are you doing?"

Terry shook his penis, zipped his pants and climbed back into the passenger seat of the Toyota. "Pissing a picture of SpongeBob. Didn't work out so well. Not my medium. I'm a better artist in snow."

Doug reached to his left and grabbed the seat's recliner lever, his body screamed in pain as the seat popped up, a heavy weight he couldn't see pinned to his chest. *Fuck you, Ken Gundy.* "Where are we?"

Jenna stirred in the back seat. Doug pulled down the rearview mirror; her head rested on Nikki's shoulder, a hand on Nikki's right breast. He smiled. It was going to be fun watching them wake up.

"Dawson's Creek," Terry said.

What? "That's a TV show, with that guy who never did anything else."

"Urkel?"

"No, Vandersomething."

"James Van Der Beek." It was Jenna.

Doug looked back into the mirror. Jenna and Nikki both sat straight, Jenna's hand now nowhere near Nikki's breast. He'd missed it. "Every Tuesday night," she said, wiping her forearm across her cheek. "Sue me."

"This isn't Dawson's Creek. What is it?"

Terry sat staring out the front window, the pickup from Mayday parked in front of them, empty. "Not Dawson's Creek. I think the sign read Dawson Springs, or something. Close enough." He pointed at the truck. "Where are those new people?"

Doug looked ahead. They were gone. *Who cares? We're all dead anyway.* "They couldn't be too far." He unlatched the door and stepped out, putting his weight on the car door. The vehicles sat in the lot of a gray building with a blue roof, a yellow sign that read 'Dollar General' stretched over two glass doors. The Toyota and the Ford truck were the only vehicles in the dusty lot.

"People must have left town early." Nikki stepped out of the car. Nothing moved but the leaves on the tall green trees that dotted their view of Dawson Springs. The slight breeze brought nothing to them; no smells, no sounds. The town was quiet as a visitation. Nikki pointed at the various businesses that stretched down the main street; only two cars sat in plain view. She nodded to Doug and turned toward Terry who was just stepping out of the Prius. "Nobody's here. That's a good sign, right?"

Yeah. A good sign. Finding people had been the goal for Doug, the only goal. People were supposed to be a safe haven, protection, they were supposed to mean a place to sit back and relax and drink lemonade on the front porch. He'd just killed Andi and probably Donnie with that belief. That Lazarus asshole had exposed Jenna and Terry to Ophiocordon, the shit that started the zombie plague. They might be the dead walking right now. It was all on his shoulders. He shifted his weight on his good foot to look at Nikki, pain lanced through his ribs. If Jenna and Terry died, it was all on him. *My fault. My damned fault.* People were poison. He didn't want them anymore.

"Yes, Nikki, it's a really good sign."

"I think we should hang out here for a while, boss." Terry put his arm around Nikki and gently kissed her bruised face. "You two are pretty banged up. I think we could all use a little rest."

Rest. Yeah, rest. All of the late, great Warren Zevon's songs sat in silence in Doug's record collection back home in Paola. 'I'll sleep when I'm dead,' played for Doug now. *Yep, Warren, if I start acting stupid I'll shoot myself. I probably should have done that already. I've been an idiot.*

"There's a motel just down the road."

Doug followed Terry's eyes. Yes, there was. A little two-building mom and pop motel with a tin roof right across the street from the First Christian Church; all the doors were on the outside. "You want to go check it out?"

"Whoa, whoa, whoa." Jenna rested a hand on Doug's chin and turned his face back toward hers. "Shouldn't we all go together?"

No. I'm not risking your life anymore. Doug shook his head. "It's a motel. We'll look at the register before we unlock any rooms. We'll be fine."

Jenna kissed him. "Damn straight."

Sunlight flashed off one of the two glass doors of the Dollar General Store as it opened and Lacy and Walter stepped out. Lacy cradled a handheld shopping basket under her arm, Walter carried a bag of charcoal in the crook of one arm, an aluminum walker in the other. Walter smiled as he saw the group standing outside the car and cocked his head up; the universal small-town wave.

"Looks like they went shopping for breakfast," Jenna said and reached into the car to pop the trunk. "I'll get the chairs. If we're going to eat shit from a box, we might as well be comfortable."

***

Grilled Pop-Tarts, instant mashed potatoes and Sunny D tasted better than it sounded when Lacy emptied the contents of the basket onto the hood of the truck. The walker was for Doug. "I know it's not going to work as good as crutches," Walter said. "But it's better than nothing. The old lady in the back of the store didn't need it anymore."

A sad grin washed across Doug's face. Yep, most people didn't need anything anymore. *What was grandma buying when the Ophiocordon took hold? Toilet paper? Cat food? Toys for the grandkids?* He looked at the light metal walker, designed for geriatrics to shuffle from place to place, two tennis balls slit across the middle were affixed to the front legs. He'd hoped a doctor in Mayday would remove his cast when the ankle was healed. Now he was just going to have to guess.

"Thanks. Let's hope I don't need it for long." *The old lady didn't.*

Terry stood from the camp chair and dropped his paper plate and water bottle into the black, Hefty garbage bag Lacy had brought from the store. Keep America beautiful. He reached into the open door of the Prius and pulled out his gun belt, the 9mm snapped into its holster, the clip reloaded. "You ready, boss?"

Yeah. I'm always ready. Doug used the walker to pull himself out of the chair.

"Where are you going?" Walter sat on the Ford's tailgate, a half-eaten unfrosted blueberry Pop-Tart in his hand. Lacy sat next to him, her arm on his thigh.

"To the motel down the street. Terry and I are going to find us a place to relax for a couple of days."

Walter hopped off the tailgate. "I'm coming with you."

Doug shook his head. "No, we can handle it. We need you guys to go back in there and stock up on supplies; everything we'll need for at least a week." *A week. Did Terry and Jenna have a week?* "We need a man in there, or the girls will forget the beef jerky."

Terry pulled the second baseball bat out of the back of the truck. The first one was still back in Mayday covered in Ken Gundy's brains. "Ready, boss."

Really, Terry? Are you ready? For what? Are you worried about the Ophiocordon in your system? I sure as fuck am. Terry slipped the bat into the back seat of the Prius. No smiles. Terry always smiled. *Yes, he is.* And so was Doug.

***

Brand new black asphalt covered the parking lots of the Dawson Springs Motel. Two long, thin buildings stretched back from Arcadia Avenue, faux brick covered each building from the concrete sidewalk to the level of the doorknob of each white door and gave way to off-white vinyl siding. Each doorknob had a keyhole. Fucking A.

Doug parked the Prius in front of the motel office. Yes, the motel was only a few blocks away from Dollar General Store where the rest of their party was picking up baskets of canned chicken and Tampons, but as Mr. Finch, the high school driving instructor at Paola High School hammered into the class's brain, always leave yourself an out. Terry pulled Doug's new walker from the back seat and carried it around the car. He couldn't get too far away from his out.

A large window framed by forest green shutters looked out onto Arcadia Avenue, the oval red and blue "open" sign dim, probably forever. Terry stood outside the window, his face pressed to the glass. "Nothing, boss. The office is clean." Doug looked down the street, he'd turned off Interstate 69 onto U.S. 62 at 2 a.m., too tired and beaten to go any more; the little town of Dawson's Creek – *damn it, Terry, Dawson Springs* – small, quiet and off the Interstate enough anyone following them from Mayday probably wouldn't find them here. The moon painted the town gray last night as Doug drove into the Dollar General Store parking lot with the Prius' lights off; the Ford behind him following suit, hoping the taillights didn't betray them to the evil in that town. There had to be evil. There had been evil everywhere else. But as he stood, leaning against the aluminum walker, its wheels and bright, greenish-yellow tennis balls resting on the dark black asphalt, everything was quiet. No once-human monsters trudged toward them from down the street, or from behind the Dr Pepper machine on the side of the Tobacco Shack next to the motel. They had found no evil here. Not yet.

Terry knocked on the other side of the big glass. He was already inside. He launched himself over the counter, sliding on his ass like a 1970s TV cop across the hood of a car; a bowl of motel matchbooks fell to the floor. He dropped behind the counter, then popped up holding a handful of matchbooks, grinning like he'd just won a prize at a carnival *Lucky winner, every time. You want the stuffed monkey, son? Or how 'bout the commemorative Def Leppard mirror?* Terry stuffed the matches in his front pocket. Doug shook his head and walked inside.

The smell of must and disuse permeated the little office, a layer of dust rested over everything, the walls covered in wood paneling and reprints of nature paintings. Douglas Titus Sr. had pulled Mama Titus and Doug Jr. into tiny out of the way motels just like this on every family trip. Mount Rushmore, the Great Smokey Mountains, Dallas for the Great Kennedy Assassination Conspiracy Tour, all had wound up at a place like this motel. No Holiday Inns for the Titus family, only places with a good chance of a taxidermied animal in each room.

A rack of keys was mounted on the wall behind the office counter, each key on a key ring with a green diamond shaped plastic key tag, probably with the name and address of the motel on the front. Terry flipped through a ledger on the counter. No computer in this office. Nosiree. This was Mom and Pop all the way.

"Anybody checked in?"

Terry stopped flipping pages and slapped his index finger on the paper ledger. "Yep. Last entry has a check-in date, but no check out. Only one." He looked up at Doug and grinned. "Tom and Carol Murphy, 14775 Walnut Street, Kansas City, Missouri."

KCMO. "Welcome home, Terry."

He turned and pulled a key off the rack. "They're in Room 27." Terry dropped the key in his breast pocket and pulled three more off the rack. He handed them to Doug. "Forty-one, forty-three, forty-five." Terry picked the Mayday baseball bat off the office couch where he'd tossed it and dropped it onto his shoulder. "Why don't you go air out those rooms for us, boss. I'll take care of the Murphys."

Doug started to protest, but stopped. What was the point? He took the keys. "Sure."

Terry stopped at the brochure rack, grabbed one of each and slipped them into his back pockets before following Doug out of the office.

***

Room Twenty-seven sat facing the Tobacco Shack, a gray building with a sloping blue tin roof, quiet beer lights hung in the long plate-glass windows. That was Stop Two, Terry hoped; Stop One was Room Twenty-seven. Terry wrapped his fingers tighter around the electrical tape on the handle of the chipped wooden baseball bat and walked down the row of open, blank windows; the ten-year-old blank television sets, pressboard cabinets and tightly made beds vivid in the morning sunlight. Room Fifteen, Seventeen, Nineteen. All the window shades were pulled back, the rooms waited patiently for visitors who would never come. Twenty-one, Twenty-three, Twenty-five. Terry pulled the bat off his shoulder and stepped in front of Room Twenty-seven in a hitter's stance.

The Murphys were home.

Terry's feet melted into the concrete walkway that crossed in front of the window, his dry tongue glued to the roof of his mouth. Tom Murphy stood on the other side of the glass, his white, glazed eyes looked directly at Terry, then its head turned and it looked into the sky. The zombie shifted its weight from foot to foot, a soft moan vibrated through the glass. Tom's white Oxford shirt still clean and crisp, his black tie (like he was dressing for a funeral) hung untied on either side of the collar. Carol, poor Carol, lay across the bed on the orange comforter in a charcoal dress, her chest burst open, the stalk of fungus that infected good old Tom – *Honey. Honey. What's wrong? What hurts? I'll go get a doc–* lay limp and spent over the bed.

Terry pulled back the bat, ready to swing through the glass and beat Tom like Nikki had beaten Ken Gundy to death less than twelve hours before, but he didn't. Zombie Tom just stood there, like Terry didn't exist. Zombies didn't act like that. They acted like the teenage girl in the blood-streaked Kearney Bearcats T-shirt out in Western Nebraska. It had come at him as he tried to get into the tractor-trailer to run it and a pack of zombies over. It had wanted to eat him. The monsters at the hospital in Omaha were just like the cheerleader chick. Tom Murphy wasn't at all. Tom had seen him. This zombie had fucking looked right at him, then turned away. The barrel of the Louisville Slugger rapped softly on the window of Room Twenty-Seven as Terry tried to get Tom's attention. Tom turned his head toward Terry, considered him with its dead, cataract eyes and turned away.

What is– But the thought died. Tom didn't want Terry because he was one of them. The Ophiocordon that bastard Lazarus had fed him had changed something about Terry, something Doug and Nikki couldn't see, but Tom could. See? Or smell maybe, or just feel, like the way a room felt when somebody angry walked in? But Terry knew he wasn't going to be like Tom, with its shiny white eyes and flesh starting to rot from its face, waiting, just waiting for food to walk by this window. Terry was going to be like dear old Carol, lying on the bed with her chest burst open. Terry wasn't a zombie; he was a zombie maker. That's what Lazarus had wanted. *How long do I have left before I'm like her? How long does Jenna have?* Jenna was a lot smaller than him and the drug had hit her harder. He pretended to sleep while they were strapped to the hospital beds in the high school gym hothouse, but he was awake, painfully listening to Jenna's moans as orgasms racked her body. That was one of the side effects. Excessive orgasms. Jimmy Fallon made jokes about it on "The Tonight Show." *If that's what happens, who wouldn't want to be suicidally depressed?* But she didn't sound like she was enjoying it, she sounded miserable.

"Terry?" Doug stood at the corner of the building, his face pinched. *Yeah, dude, I get you. What the hell am I doing?* Terry opened his mouth when Tom burst into a flurry of action, slapping the glass with the palms of its long-nailed hands, its mouth pounding open, shut, open, shut. The sudden movement sent Terry back a couple of feet. *How long have I been here?*

"Well," he said softly, trying to smile and failing miserably. "I found them."

Doug walked closer, Tom's slaps turned into a pounding. That window would go soon. "Are you okay?"

Terry nodded. "Yeah, yeah. I'm fine, dude. I got this. Just stay back." He pulled the key to room Twenty-Seven from the front pocket of his shirt and slid it into the lock. "Here, kitty, kitty," he whispered as he turned the knob and threw the door inward.

The thing that was Tom Murphy, just some guy from Kansas City here for a funeral, or a wedding, or something, lunged out the door and found the barrel of Terry's Louisville Slugger crashing into its face. The skull caved in with a sickening sound, like Terry had pulled a Gallagher and smashed a watermelon instead of a zombie. Tom staggered back and Terry stepped forward, putting the bat against the monster's chest and pushing it back into the room. Tom fell onto the bed, half over his wife and lie still, its ruined skull leaked red fluid onto Carol's pretty charcoal dress.

"Sweet dreams, guys," he whispered. Terry reached toward the curtains and pulled the drawstring, the pale blue flower print sealing the Murphys in their new home.

***

On the second day in Dawson Springs, Walter and Lacy found Riverside Park. It was close enough to walk from the motel where they'd spent an entire night in peaceful silence, but that would have meant not having an out in an emergency. Doug wouldn't have that. The vehicles sat under the shade of the thick oak and hickory trees that lined the banks of the Tradewater River, between a two-deck wooden baseball stadium and the main street. Doug, Jenna and Nikki sat in camp chairs, Walter and Lacy on the tailgate of the pickup. Terry hovered over a Dollar General charcoal grill that sizzled with brook trout fillets. A fishing boat on a trailer behind a long silent Toyota 4Runner provided the fishing poles, a nearby garden the worms and fresh tomatoes. Fishing felt good, normal. Doug, Terry and Walter sat on the bank, lines in the water, while the ladies made potato salad with relish, mayonnaise, reconstituted potato medallions from a box of scalloped potatoes and powdered eggs courtesy of the former Hipster owners of the Prius.

Doug lifted himself out of the canvas chair. "Anybody ready for another beer?"

Walter jumped off the tailgate. "I'll get it for you."

Doug waved him off. "I've got a broken ankle, I'm not an invalid."

Nikki raised her right hand. "I'll take one, Doug. Thanks."

"Terry?"

"Nope," he said. "I'm good."

Doug nodded and walked slowly to the river. He hated to admit it, but the walker really did help him get around. He figured it would get him through the next month or two until he could take off his cast and walk on his own again. The beer was another thing. Terry hadn't had one yesterday, or today. *That's not like him.* Something had happened to Terry at Room Twenty-Seven; Doug just didn't know what and Terry wasn't talking.

What was left of a case of beer sat cooling in the river. Doug pulled the piece of rope that kept the beer from floating away in the current and lifted a six-pack out of the water. Dawson Springs had enough for them to live here for a while. Food, water, shelter. They'd have to move out of the motel and find someplace with a wood stove, or fireplace come winter, but they could make it. They *would* make it. But Dyersburg sat in the back of Doug's mind like a rat, gnawing at his conscious thought. He couldn't make it stop any more than he could make a rat stop gnawing. He'd have to kill it to make it stop. Laughter broke from the circle of people he'd found himself with and it sounded good. He smiled and walked back to his chair.

"Well," Lacy said. "How about that baseball stadium?"

Terry pulled a brochure from his back pocket and unfolded it. "This was once the spring training facility for the Pittsburgh Pirates." He flipped a fillet with a wooden handled spatula. "The original stadium was destroyed in a flood in the 1930s. Hall of Fame shortstop Honus Wagner used to play here and fish right in that river."

"That's what I'm going to name my first baby," Jenna said. "Honus."

Terry started scooping grilled fish onto paper plates and passed them around the circle. "The brochure said Babe Ruth played here once, too."

"There's another name for you," Nikki said. "Babe."

"Totally."

Doug opened a beer, his seventh this afternoon. His head floated on a bed of alcohol, just like at a family cookout back home. He hadn't thought of his dad or his sister for months; they were probably all dead anyway. "What do you guys think of this town?" he asked through a slight slur.

Jenna dropped a spoonful of potato salad on her paper plate next to the fish; she shook the spoon to break off a potato stuck to the plastic silverware. "I don't think there are many zombies."

"We don't know that yet." It was Lacy, sitting on the tailgate, a beer between her knees. "They could be everywhere for all we know."

"But there aren't any birds," Nikki said. "Those big black ones. I think that's a good sign."

Yes, it was. Where ever they'd seen zombies since they'd escaped the Community, they'd seen those fat black crows, clouds of them. Doug took a long drink of Budweiser. They were close enough to St. Louis for Anheuser-Busch products to dominate the shelves of the Tobacco Shack. He pulled down the beer and smiled; this was it. Home.

"I'm ready to stay here," he said. "At least until next spring. Maybe if we ride out the winter here, whoever's still in charge will have fixed things by then."

Terry eased himself into the open camp chair, a small piece of fish on his plate. His stomach hurt. The news reports leading up to the Falling were a bit light on early symptoms, just the ones right before their chests exploded. Bloody nose and screaming pain. *It's just nerves. It's Tom Murphy's fault. It's all his fault.* Of course, the news probably did tell most people. Terry knew he was probably just too busy playing video games.

"I'm good here," he said, Tom Murphy's slack face stared at him; it stared right at him and didn't react. "If we can find a couple of generators we won't even have to move out of the motel." He glanced down at his plate; he didn't want his fish anymore.

Doug turned to the pickup. "We just want to be together," Lacy said, wrapping her arms around Walter's shoulder. *Jesus Christ, what is she? In high school?*

He finished his beer and dropped the empty can to the ground. It rattled against gravel the park's grass had already started to reclaim. "Excellent." He blinked hard. *Probably one more will put me down for the night.* He plucked another from what was left of the six-pack at his feet and cracked it open. "So it's agreed. We're new residents of Dawson's Creek."

"Springs, dude," Terry said. "Dawson Springs."

Yeah, he's right. "Ha. Dawson Springs." Doug raised his beer, his smile fading from his stubbly face. What he had to say next wasn't going to go over well. "I'm going to Dyersburg," he said. "Tomorrow. All by myself."

"What?" Jenna snapped, her voice sharp and loud.

"Whoa." Terry sat his plate on the ground, hoping no one noticed he didn't touch his food. "I don't think that's a good idea, boss."

"Damn straight." Jenna got out of her chair and stood in front of Doug. "I don't know what's going through your head, but whatever it is needs to stop. We're safe here, you're not going off on some half-assed, half-assed." She stopped, words fumbling in her mouth. "Half-assed man-stupid dangerquest. I need you here."

Doug raised his hands, palm first, to Jenna. "Honey, honey, everything's okay. I looked at a roadmap. It's two hours from here. I'll get up, eat breakfast and be home by lunch."

"Why Dyersburg?" Walter asked. "What's there?"

"A fence," Terry said. "The government built a fence across the southern United States and it goes through Dyersburg. We met a Canadian soldier who told us there were people there, some kind of a stronghold."

"And if I don't go, it will make me crazy." Doug held his beer in both hands, looking up at Jenna with watery eyes.

She frowned. "You're drunk."

He nodded. "I know, but I came up with this plan when I was sober. I'm going, honey. I have to. I really have to." He patted her hand. "I'll be okay."

"But," Jenna started, but Terry interrupted.

"He'll be okay because I'm going with him."

"No," Nikki spat. "Have you two lost your goddamned minds? We have to stick together."

"We will, babe," Terry said. "As soon as we get home tomorrow at noon."

"Count me in," Walter said. "I can help. I've been to Dyersburg. My aunt lives there. Well, she lived there."

Lacy threw her arms around his shoulders, tears already starting.

"So you three men are just going to leave us here by ourselves?" Nikki was standing now, her arms crossed tightly across her chest.

"You forget," Doug said. "We all saw you swing that baseball bat. You girls can take care of yourselves."

"You are all fucking idiots," Jenna screamed and turned away from Doug. He didn't see her face, but Terry did. Doug probably thought she was crying and turned to wipe tears from her eyes, but it wasn't her eyes that leaked. She pulled at her nose with the index finger and thumb of her right hand. It was bleeding.

CHAPTER 21

They drove in silence. Calvert City, Benton and Mayfield, all dead, at least from the highway as the Prius drove by; no movement at all. Doug wanted to honk, just to see if there was life anywhere other than in the cab of this Japanese hybrid car, but he kept his hands at ten and two. The Prius used hardly any gas, but if he woke something evil – something living – this car wasn't going to outrun anyone. The highway ran through green, gently sloping hills, farmland showing in patches between stretches of forest. Few abandoned vehicles dotted the highways of Western Kentucky. The people here were either better prepared than they were in Missouri and Nebraska, or they all died at home. A green highway sign riddled with bullet holes read "Fulton – Twenty-two miles; Dyersburg, TN – 74 miles." It disappeared behind them as fast as it came.

"We're halfway there, dude," Terry said. Doug thought his friend had been asleep in the passenger seat; maybe he had been. "You still sure about this?"

Sure? Hell, no. I'm not sure. "I'm not sure about anything anymore. I just know I have to see if the government is still around. If anybody's found a cure for this thing, that's where we'll find it."

"You mean a cure for me and Jenna?"

My best friend and my girlfriend. I killed both of you. I'm sorry, Terry. I'm so sorry. I can't stop looking. I just can't. "Yes."

Terry stared out the window; cumulus clouds dotted the bright, blue sky like cotton balls glued to a kindergarten art project. "It's not your fault, Doug. You need to stop pretending like it was."

"But I–"

"Cut the shit. You didn't make any of us go with you, we all chose to. We're all grownups and could have bailed on you at any time, but–" Terry turned back toward Doug. "But we didn't. You didn't give us the Ophiocordon, some asshole did. Now get your shit together. Don't bail on us."

"What do you mean?"

"I mean this. We go back now and everybody will be happy."

Abandoning Dyersburg meant abandoning hope. Doug shook his head. "I can't, Terry."

"Then put your foot into it. I miss Nikki already."

***

Walter leaned into the front, his chin almost resting on the back of the bucket seats. "I miss French fries. Greasy French fries pulled out of a stainless-steel fryer by a kid with pimples, then covered in salt and served in a cardboard bucket."

Terry grunted. "Oh, God, what I wouldn't give for a basket of Sonic fries. But me, I guess I miss my Xbox the most." He popped Doug on his bicep. "How 'bout you, boss?"

What did I miss? Mowing the lawn? Opening my muffler shop in the morning? Watching "Archer"? Running water? "Baseball on the radio. I miss turning on the radio and listening to the Royals lose."

"Boss, that may be the most boring thing you could have said."

Walter sat back and laughed.

The road never changed, just asphalt, trees and weeds. The last sign read, "Dyersburg – Five miles." If this town was a haven, a hub of activity, Doug figured they should have seen something different, something busy. Military Humvees, helicopters, caravans of civilians looking for shelter, anything; but the stillness of U.S. 51 remained a constant.

Terry pointed to an exit ahead. "Take Business 51."

"What good's that going to do?"

Walter leaned back into the front seat. "It takes you right downtown. The railroad tracks are close to there."

The railroad. Lying in the grass with a zombie clawing its way toward his chest, the Canadian soldier Oliver told them the train was going to Dyersburg. "People are gathering there." *Like hell they were.*

The town looked deserted. Blank houses and storefronts stared at the Prius as it cruised slowly through town, windows down. The streets were silent as they were vacant.

"How big's this town?" Terry asked, his hand out the window, making an airplane.

"About 17,000 people," Walter said.

"You think there'd be somebody here, right? I mean, somebody probably lived."

Maybe they were smart and got out. Doug stopped the car and listened, the electric motor of the Prius silent in the morning. "I don't hear a thing. Maybe that Canadian soldier was messing with us." *But he wasn't. People gathered here, but they were gone now.* "Which way are the railroad tracks?"

Walter pointed south on Main Avenue. "Just go down to East Court Street. It goes right to them."

They never made it that far.

Military vehicles, Humvees and Bradley fighting vehicles were scattered over downtown Dyersburg. Bodies of soldiers, hundreds of them, lay strewn across the blood-streaked pavement, the remains of thousands of zombies were piled high. Crows covered the bodies like flies, pecking, tearing flesh off humans and zombies alike. *Dear God.* A tank with a red maple leaf painted on the side had crashed into the wall of a bank. The train made it here. Fat fucking lot of good that did.

Doug drove through the bodies, the path a maze. "They were here," he said, his voice trailing. "But they lost." He tried to swallow, but it caught in his dry throat. "We lost." The Fence Andi had told them about, the Fence that split the country in two, lay on East Court Street in twisted wreckage. The monsters had come through. *They were here, but where are they? Where the fuck are they?*

"Stop the car, boss." Terry's voice was urgent. He grabbed the steering wheel. "Stop the goddamned car."

Doug pushed the brake pedal and slipped the transmission into park. "What's going on?"

"Oh, shit," Walter whispered, but Terry was already out of the car. Doug and Walter followed. They'd found the residents of Dyersburg.

Animate rotting corpses stood swaying in a factory parking lot on the south side of the Fence. A thousand human monsters, maybe 2,000, maybe 5,000, filled the lot; their cumulative moan the soundtrack to madness. A blanket of those damnable black birds roosted on the factory roof, the roof of the Citgo Food Mart that sat at the edge of the parking lot and on a tanker truck parked next to the pumps. The hoses were still in place; the driver dead; he never got a chance to unload.

"This is bad," Walter said. "This is real bad."

No shit.

"There are so many of them," Doug said. "It looks like the Fields of Asphodel."

Walter turned toward Doug. "What's that?"

"In Greek mythology," Doug spoke absently. "It was a place in the underworld where the souls of normal people went, people who didn't do bad things, but didn't do great things. They just stood forever in mediocrity, waiting."

"Sounds boring," Walter said.

"Boring as shit." Terry slapped Walter's back. "Doug, turn this car around and get ready to book it." He took a step toward the fence.

"What are you doing?"

Terry stopped and looked back. "Something stupid."

***

He couldn't believe Doug let him go that easily. That wasn't like him. When Terry told Doug he was going to travel the Midwest with these migrant workers he got drunk with, Doug offered him a job and stability. Doug always bailed out Terry's ass, but Doug wasn't Doug anymore. He was beaten. It was Terry's turn.

Terry stepped over the destroyed chain-link fence, wincing at a slight jingle, but the hoard of waving bodies didn't move. They didn't even notice him. Tom Murphy wasn't blind and neither were they. *I'm not a threat. I'm not dinner. I'm just part of the big old happy family.* He broke into a jog and stopped at the Citgo tanker. Doug had already turned the Prius around. Good. Terry turned to the tanker and tried to remember back to high school.

Doug was the reason he got his second job, but Debbie Pimberton was the reason he got his first. Sweet Debbie Pimberton who wore her long blond hair in a ponytail when she worked at Casey's General Store making pizzas, a piece of chewing gum in her mouth, always Extra wintergreen. Terry wanted to taste that gum on her breath, but he couldn't talk around her. Every time was like–

"You going to buy something, or what?" Casey's manager Maude Stapleton asked, snapping Terry out of a Debbie-tight-shirt trance. Maude was a big woman who filled the space behind the cash register like Jabba the Hutt.

No, I'm not going to buy anything. "I'm here to–" *Fuck if I know what I'm here to do.* Debbie looked at teenaged Terry from behind the pizza counter and smiled. *She smiled.*

"You're here to what?" Maude didn't lean across the counter, she couldn't. That would take physics that hadn't been invented yet. But to Terry she loomed like a Sasquatch. He hated Sasquatch.

Terry smiled back at Debbie. It was simple math. *Debbie worked at Casey's. If I worked at Casey's, I'd see Debbie more and, and, and what, dumbass?*

"Well?" Maude bellowed.

I don't know.

"I'd like to fill out an application."

Maude shrugged and pulled one out of a folder next to the cash register. "Here," she said, shoving it at him. "And spell your name right."

Debbie's family moved a week later, but Terry got the job and watched the gas guy fill the underground tanks every time.

He looked at the parking lot of zombies Doug had called something fancy. The Fields of Ass Models or something. The zombies hadn't noticed Doug and Walter either, maybe the Prius was too far for their cataract-glazed eyes to see. *Just stay put, guys.* Terry fumbled with the vapor recovery line, but got it open. He wasn't sure if he needed it open, but he was sure he didn't give a rat's ass if gasoline fumes escaped into the atmosphere. There were so many more things to worry about, like feeding the hungry and balancing the federal budget. *Ha.* Something scraped. Terry's head jerked forward; a zombie had taken a step from the pack. It stood about twenty feet away, looking at him, its head cocked like a curious dog.

"Move along, nothing to see here, pal," Terry whispered as he worked.

The thing shifted its weight back and forth as it stared in Terry's direction. *But is it looking at me?* He unlatched the hose from the tanker and pulled. It dropped onto the parking lot. The zombie moved forward another step; a crow atop the tanker cawed. Terry slowly dragged the hose as far from the truck as he could before laying it on the ground about ten feet from the monster, his hands shaking. The brass valve fitting slipped from his weak grip and dinged off the parking lot. Terry winced at the noise and froze. The zombie didn't move.

The parking lot sloped downward, toward the mass of swaying bodies. *Thank God for the Tennessee hills.* He lay the hose on the asphalt, slowly walked back to the truck and reached toward the delivery valve. The first zombie was ten feet away, the next thousand were twenty, a tanker full of fuel was right behind him and a fistful of motel matchbooks made a bulge in his front pocket. His hands began to shake as he stared at the dead that had ripped apart an army from two countries. *How am I going to light this without killing myself?* He looked back at the truck, the tanker, a silver bomb shining in the morning light, loomed large over him. *Terry boy, you didn't think this through.* The zombie in front of Terry moaned. *Fuck it.*

He released the valve. Gravity pushed and 1,100 gallons of 93-octane premium gushed from the hose, the gurgling liquid spread out quickly, rushing downhill toward those dead fuckers. Terry took a few steps back and watched the gasoline spread. It would reach them in–

Something bumped into his shoulder, sending him off balance. Crows squawked and took flight, their black, greasy wings beating the air over his head. Terry caught the side of the tanker and turned. His bladder let go, the warm liquid streamed down his right leg. A zombie had bumped him, its flesh hanging off its arms in strings, the thing more bone than meat. *It didn't see me.* Another walked by. Terry turned; a line of them came from behind the Citgo station and crowded past him. *Where the hell are they going?* But he saw, first toward the noise from the metal valve hitting the pavement, now toward the rushing liquid. Terry smiled. *This is going to work.* The gasoline reached the first zombie, then began to soak over the feet of thousands beyond.

He ran through the oncoming dead, ducking the arms that weren't trying to grab him, but Terry knew he might scream if one of those rotting hands wiped across his bare skin. He didn't know what those assholes would do if he screamed. What was once a woman, a bride, stepped around the back of the Citgo, her wedding dress still mostly white, though blood clotted on her chest. Terry's breath came hard as she approached. This was the one. He fished a pack of Dawson Springs Motel matches from his front pocket and held it in his shaking hands.

Oh, shit. Oh, shit. Oh, shit. Gasoline catches fire. Terry knew that. He was a mechanic, for Christ's sake. That's how the internal combustion engine worked. Gas goes in, spark plug makes it go whoosh, the expanding gasses make the pistons move, car go vroom. But movies and 1970s TV cop shows all taught him gas tankers explode and he was going to light a match. Briday the Thirteenth staggered forward, but not toward him, those milky white eyes didn't notice him. He pulled a match from the book that read along the base of the matches, "WARNING: Close cover before striking." *Babe, I got other things to worry about.* He scraped the head of the match across the striking surface and it sprang into flame. Terry held it under the fine lace train that dragged behind the bride zombie. The match went out. *Fuck.* She waddled closer to the tanker. *Goddamnit.* Terry pulled out another match and struck it. The match flared to life. He held it higher up the train, moving forward with the zombie. The white material crackled to life and Terry stepped back. Orange flames danced across the back of the dress as the zombie dragged herself closer to the gushing gasoline.

Terry turned and ran.

***

The Prius was five blocks away when the tanker exploded; the shock waves sent the little Japanese car skidding across the street. "What did you do, Terry?" Doug screamed.

Terry pulled himself upright in the seat, grinning. "I lit a tanker truck on fire."

"You did WHAT?"

He looked behind them; the entire downtown was burning; human figures stumbled around the flames, then fell to the pavement, consumed by fire. "I think I got rid of that pesky zombie problem in Dyersburg."

Doug slammed his hand on the steering wheel. "That was the stupidest goddamned thing you've ever done."

"I know."

"I mean it was really fucking stupid."

"I know."

"And you smell like gasoline and piss."

"There's a good reason for that."

Walter bent over and pulled a six-pack of beer off the floor. "Does anyone want one of these," he said, his voice shaky. "Because if you don't, I'm probably going to drink all of them."

Terry patted his shoulder. "Go for it."

"I mean, that was really, really messed up back there." Walter's words came out slowly, like his mouth wasn't sure what was rattling around his brain. "The dead Army guys, all those zombies, the explosion."

Terry picked another six-pack off the floor in the back and sat it on Walter's lap. "Knock yourself out." He turned to Doug. "Hey, you want to stop and get something nice for the girls?"

"Fuck you, Terry."

***

The thin finger of smoke grew for the next hour before it was lost in the distance. It would act as a beacon, that much was certain, but a beacon for what? Terry lay in the back seat and pretended to sleep, his stomach in the grip of something bigger than him, something that grew inside. The Ophiocordon. It had to be. *When's my nose going to start bleeding like Jenna's?* Jenna. She might be dead already. What's going to happen to Doug when she goes? And she's going to go. *He's fragile now.* Doug's strength had kept Terry out of trouble; it had given him a job and a friend. *Doug's been a lot of things, but he's never been fragile.* Terry didn't like to see his friend broken.

Terry sat up slowly, the pain in his stomach just short of lancing. He swallowed and took in a deep breath. *Oh, God. It's getting close.* He slapped Doug on the shoulder and pointed out the window; a Chevron station sat just off the interstate at an intersection with a rural blacktop. "Pull over here, dude."

"What? Why?"

"Just pull over."

Doug stopped the Prius in front of the gas pumps and Terry got out slowly. He came back with chocolate bars, a box of graham crackers and a bag of fat marshmallows. Terry dropped them in the back seat and climbed in beside them. He couldn't eat any of that, not with his stomach, but he needed to get them. He had to.

"I told you we should bring back something for the girls. They were really pissed." A peace offering? Or a good-bye present? Probably both.

"S'mores?"

Walter mumbled something in his sleep, but they couldn't make it out.

"Girls like S'mores," Terry said. "That probably sounds sexist, but you tell me it's not true."

By the time the exit sign for U.S. 62 to Dawson's Creek – *Springs, Dawson Springs* –appeared on the side of the highway, Terry's insides were burning. He had to get out of the car before the bulbous stalk erupted from his chest and he killed them all.

Doug guided the Prius onto Arcadia Avenue and pulled to a stop in front of the Spring Motel. "What the shit?" Nikki and Lacy sat on the sidewalk in front of Jenna and Doug's room, the light gray concrete a stark contrast with the new black asphalt. He threw open the door and hobbled as fast as he could without the walker that sat locked in the trunk.

"What's wrong?" he yelled. "Where's Jenna?"

Nikki turned her face toward Doug, her eyes bloodshot, her bruised cheeks wet with tears. "She's sick, Doug. She won't let us in." Nikki pushed herself to her feet and ran to Terry who stumbled out of the car and leaned onto the brick and vinyl exterior motel wall, his face as gray as an old movie. "Terry." He held his arm in front of him as she approached and shook his head.

"Stay back, darlin'," he said, his words coming out in a thick wheeze. "I love you, Nikki. I love you like I never loved anything in my life, but you gotta stay back."

She stopped, her body shaking. "Terry," she whispered, the word dying in the still afternoon air.

"She wants to see him," Lacy said, pointing at Terry.

Doug pounded on the door. "Jenna," he screamed. "Jenna. I have to see you, baby." His forehead thudded, a headache formed under his skin like a thunderstorm, tears ran from his eyes. "I have to see you."

Walter made his way out of the Prius, the smell of beer hanging off him like a cloud. Lacy took his hand and squeezed. "She's sick. It's that stuff Lazarus gave her."

Rage filled Doug, a rage that couldn't be answered. Lazarus was dead, eaten by a zombie the people of Mayday called by name. He couldn't make the fat man pay for his crimes; Lazarus, Tim, was already dead.

"The door's not locked," Lacy said, shrugging her shoulders. "You could just go in, if you want." Doug reached for the handle, but suddenly

Nikki was there. She grabbed his arm and pulled hard, whipping Doug around to face her.

"You know what happens," she said. "The fungus, that stalk that grows out of people on Ophiocordon. It might be in there already, on Jenna, waiting for you. You can't go in."

"But–" he started, but Nikki grabbed his other arm and pulled him closer.

"She knows how you feel, Doug." The bite in Nikki's voice had disappeared. "She knows you love her. You showed her enough." Doug's legs gave and he collapsed to his knees on the concrete. Nikki dropped next to him and held him tightly.

Terry shuffled toward the motel room door and slowly wrapped his big right hand around the silver knob. He turned toward Nikki. *Beautiful Nikki.* "Afraid I was gonna leave without giving you a good-bye kiss?"

Nikki looked at him, her head pounded from crying. "Star Wars again?"

Coughs pounded his chest. Terry wiped his mouth with the back of his hand and winked, his eyes puffy and jaundice. "You're perfect for me, you know?" he said. "I'm a lucky guy." He turned the knob and pushed the door open.

"I love you," she said.

Terry smiled through the pain. "I know."

Nikki smiled back as he opened the door and walked inside the room where Jenna was dying. "Asshole."

***

The room smelled. *Is this what the zombie fungus smells like?* Jenna sat on the bed, still unmade from her and Doug's sleep the night before. *Damn housekeeping,* Terry thought. *We'll have to fill out one of those comment cards. Pearl ain't gonna like this.* The comforter was the same orange as the one the Murphys of Kansas City, Missouri, were spending their forever on over in Room Twenty-seven. Jenna leaned on one arm, her complexion slick, waxy; blood streaked her face. She could fall over at any moment.

"Hey," Terry said. He walked into the room and shut the door behind him, sliding the deadbolt in place with a click.

"Your nose is bleeding," she said.

Terry touched his face; it was wet, his fingertips red with blood. "Well, it's about time." He coughed again and spit a blood clot on the blue carpet. No need for manners anymore, you're among friends. He staggered closer and sat on the bed. "You know what caused this, right?"

She nodded. "The Ophiocordon Timmy-Tim-Tim put in our food. I'm not stupid, Terry."

He slid his arm over her shoulder, the weight of it felt like he was wearing brick shirt. "I know you're not."

She leaned into him, her face hot on his shoulder. "We're going to turn into one of those things."

"Zombies?"

Jenna coughed. She felt so small in Terry's arms. "No, goddamnit. One of those fungus things that Aliens out of your chest." She put her arm around Terry and squeezed. "I don't want to do that."

Who does? The pain in his chest felt like something was stabbing him from the inside. It was coming soon enough. Nikki had told him about the fat businessman when she was a waitress at Hooligans back home in St. Joseph, Missouri, when this all started back in, what was it? June? The guy had just finished a medium rare steak and baked potato; she'd stopped at his table to drop off the bill and he spewed blood across his plate and onto the seat beyond. He stood up shaking before he fell to the floor. The man stood again, but he wasn't a man anymore, he was something else. The fungus stalk came later, but in the restaurant it was just blood, like the blood that ran from Jenna's nose and Terry's. He opened the holster of the 9mm on his gun belt and slowly pulled it out. He sat the Army-issue pistol on his lap and moved his hand safely to the orange bed cover.

"I've been going over this since I woke tied to that hospital bed in Mayday." The gun felt heavy on his leg. That was good. A gun was a tool to do a job, like a wrench, or a hammer. Tools were supposed to be heavy. "We're fucked." He moved his hand and rested it on the cool metal of the pistol. "You know, I did something stupid today."

Jenna laughed, a spot of blood dropped from her lip onto the orange comforter. "You do a lot of stupid stuff."

Terry smiled. *Yes I do.* "I lit a gasoline tanker on fire. There were thousands of zombies just standing around and I walked down to them and let the gasoline fly." His finger wrapped around the grip of the 9mm. "You know why I did that?"

Jenna shook her head, the once bouncy auburn locks flat against her face.

"Because the zombies didn't care about me. I walked through them and they didn't even move." Terry hefted the pistol in his right hand. It was heavy, so damn heavy. "That's because I'm one of them now." He wiped his left wrist across his eyes. Tears. *Why tears? Why now?* He pulled back the steel slide barrel with a snap, which pushed a bullet into the firing chamber and held the pistol in front of his face.

Jenna grabbed the barrel of the 9mm and pulled it to her mouth. "Me first."

**

A gunshot exploded inside Room Forty-three. Then another. Doug screamed and beat against the now-locked door. Nikki dropped to the pavement, tears pouring out of her swollen eyes. Lacy patted her shoulder, but none of it made a goddamned bit of difference.

OCTOBER 1: THE GULF COAST OF MISSISSIPPI

CHAPTER 22

The gulls were loud today. The white and gray sea birds, wings spread, coasted on the cool ocean breeze, hanging in the sky like a baby's mobile, their high-pitched calls dancing with the crash of the surf. Doug hadn't seen crows for a month or so. *Thank God.* The sun dropped low somewhere behind the dunes, its fading light glinted off the water like God had tossed handfuls of gold coins on the waves. At another time, screaming, laughing people ran across this beach and played in the gray waters of the Gulf of Mexico. They would have lain under big, colorful umbrellas, their children lathered in sunscreen building sandcastles and eating ice cream they bought from a vendor. Dads would fish beers out of red and white Coleman coolers while watching girls in bikinis anonymously through reflective sunglasses. Those people were dead and the beach was quiet. The surf crashing onto the sand the only sound outside of the gulls; the once-busy highway beyond the beach as quiet as this land was a thousand years ago and probably as quiet as it would be thousands of years from now.

Nikki, the Army doctor and Andi had been worried the zombies were attracted to heat and humidity. So far, they'd been wrong. Doug's little group – *always getting smaller, thanks to me* – hadn't seen a trace of the fungus monsters for weeks.

Doug sat in a beach chair under an umbrella like a tourist, as he had most of the days since they'd quietly left Kentucky; Jenna and Terry locked forever in the Spring Inn, a warning spray painted on the white door in bright red letters, "Infected." Doug hadn't gone into the room, neither had Nikki. The gunshots told the story well enough.

Doug's feet stretched out before him. The heel of his bare right foot sat in the warm sand, his left foot, the cast itchy and rank as hell, lay on a one-by-six. The board was new on the beach. Nikki brought it from the shed behind the beach house where Walter and Lacy had set up, leftovers from construction of the deck that looked out over the ocean. A fifth of Crown Royal sat in the sand next to Doug's chair.

"Keep it still." Nikki knelt over the board, tin snips in her right hand.

"Are you sure about this?" Doug asked.

"No, that's why I brought the whisky," she said.

Doug had worn the fiberglass cast on his left ankle since July 17 in Omaha because some moron had let animals out of their cages at the

Henry Doorly Zoo. He was lucky; the infected brown bear had really wanted to eat him; it didn't get the chance. An Army doctor who was now dead set the broken bones and layered the cast on while Doug lay on a gurney in a morphine haze. That was fourteen weeks ago; Nikki said his ankle had had enough time to heal. She'd broken her ankle once, so she was the medical expert out of the three people he knew who were still alive and that was good enough for him.

"Is this going to hurt?" he asked.

Nikki shrugged. "Maybe, but the whisky's not for you."

She gritted her teeth and squeezed the tin snips. The sharp blades sliced through the fiberglass cast, cutting a line less than an inch long. Nikki sat the snips on the board, unscrewed the cap on the Crown Royal and took a drink, her face pinched as the whisky went down. "This is going to take longer than I thought."

She offered Doug the bottle. He took it and tilted it slightly toward his lips, the amber liquid glowed in the setting sunlight as it ran through the short neck of the bottle. "Have you ever–" He stopped and coughed.

Nikki snipped another inch through the cast. "Lightweight."

Doug wiped his lips with the back of his hand and laughed. "I'm more of a beer guy," he said. "Terry could drink whisky." He paused. His friend had been gone for two months. He still missed him. Doug smiled. "He could pour whisky into the bottle cap and snort it up his nose."

Nikki slapped his leg. "Uh-uh."

Doug took another drink. "It's true. He won a lot of bets with that."

She moved the tin snips deeper into the groove and squeezed again. The stench of fourteen weeks of dying skin and fermented sweat wafted up. She pulled her head away. "Oh, dear God."

"What's the matter? Can't take it?" Doug grinned. He knew Nikki could take the smell. Hell, the smell was nothing. That woman was tough enough to take anything this Fallen fucking world tossed up then laugh about it afterward.

She coughed. "You know I can take it." She shoved the snips in farther and clipped again.

Fifteen minutes later, Doug's cast lay in the sand in pieces like discarded bits of shellfish, his leg from mid-calf to his toes as pasty-white as an Englishman's. He took another drink of the high-end Canadian whisky and sat the bottle, crafted to look like jewels in a crown, into the sand.

"The breeze is cold on my leg," he said. "It's good to feel something down there I don't have to scratch." The alcohol was working on him, his head light, his face warm. The world had gone tits up. Friends and lovers had died and here he sat on the beach drinking booze. Something wasn't fair, but Doug knew he couldn't do anything about it.

"I might help you down to the water so you can try and wash off some of the dead skin and funk," Nikki said. "But I'm afraid you'll kill the fish." She took another swig; the bottle was nearing half empty.

Doug was more content than he'd been in a long time. The nine-hour trip to Mississippi had been rough. They'd seen a few zombies, dodged a roadblock set up by some assholes who ran screaming when they saw all the automatic weapons and faced a section of highway washed out by what was probably a flash flood, but they wanted to experience a warm winter and have the ocean at their back. They got it. The water was one less place to worry about.

"Jenna would probably like this," Doug said, the sound of his words flat in his ears. Jenna was already starting to be a memory, a memory that would eventually fade. He didn't even have a fucking picture of her. How long would he remember her face? "She seemed like a spring break sort of person."

Nikki rested her hand on Doug's leg, her lips curled into a smile. "I think she was. She was in a sorority in college."

"Really? I didn't know that. Never thought I'd date a sorority girl."

The sun was low now, sinking over the land behind them. Stars would be out soon, something Doug never got tired of seeing.

"Would Terry have liked it here?"

Terry. Doug laughed. "Probably not. He was more of a lake and gravel road guy." He stared out over the dark gray waves rolling in, the gulf more like a living thing than a body of water. "He'd probably say it was too big."

Nikki took another drink of whisky, sat the bottle down hard in the sand and screwed the cap on tight. 'Terry.' Her mother's voice, a voice from so long ago, resonated in her head, 'He's gone. Let it go.'

It's hard Mom. It's so hard.

"Walter and Lacy asked us over for dinner and cards tonight," she said, looking up at Doug.

They'd abandoned the Prius in Texarkana, the deer that stood in the middle of the highway as Doug topped a hill crushed the grill of the Toyota like it was a cracker, but the fat doe tasted delicious. They kept strips of deer steak in the refrigerator of the American Coach Heritage RV they took from the dealership as they drove south, eventually hitting the beach. Walter and Lacy found the house and they stopped to put down shallow, shallow roots. Doug and Nikki stayed in the massive RV, in different beds.

"I'm shit at cards when I've been drinking," Doug said.

Nikki laughed. "You're shit at cards when you haven't been drinking, but I think we should go."

I think we should go. Well, so do I. "Let's get me down to the water first. I can't drag this stinky thing into somebody's house."

Nikki picked up the Crown Royal bottle and helped Doug from his chair. "You're going to have to work that leg," she said. "It's going to be a while before you're back to normal."

Normal. There is no normal. "I know that, doc. I need to get this thing working if I'm going to hunt down solar panels and batteries." He rested his left arm around Nikki's shoulder for support as they walked slowly toward the receding tide. "That'll give us a steady flow of electricity. And I wouldn't mind constant running water. I need to—"

Doug's voice dropped into a void; his leg frozen in the sand.

Nikki stopped walking. "What's the matter?"

Doug stood looking out over the gulf, small waves rolling toward them.

"Hey. What's going on?"

There was something out there, something new. Something Doug hadn't seen in the past two months of staring into the sea drinking himself to sleep, thinking about Jenna lying dead in a Dawson Springs, Kentucky, motel. Beneath the clear, sharp stars unbleached by city lights, was something he hadn't expected.

Nikki grabbed his shirt and shook. "Talk to me."

"There's a light," he said, his voice soft and far away. "There's a light out there in the gulf."

Nikki slowly released her grip on the shirt of the only person on planet Earth she could trust and stared into the night. A yellow pinpoint of light shone on the horizon.

"What's that mean?"

Doug took the bottle from her hands and lifted it to his mouth, tilting his head back and taking a long swallow. He handed the Crown Royal to Nikki and wiped his mouth with the back of his arm.

"It means the hard part isn't over yet."

ABOUT JASON

Jason Offutt grew up on a farm near the town of Orrick, Missouri. In his life, he's been a farm hand, journalist, photographer, bartender and the mayor of a small town. He's also a nerd. A Dungeons and Dragons playing, "Star Trek" watching, conspiracy theory believing nerd.

Jason's books include the novels, "Bad Day for the Apocalypse" and "A Funeral Story," the collection of short horror "Road Closed," the parody survival guide, "How to Kill Monsters Using Common Household Objects," the humorous travelogue, "Through a Corn-Swept Land: An epic beer run through the Upper Midwest," and the paranormal titles, "Haunted Missouri," "What Lurks Beyond," "Darkness Walks: The Shadow People among us" and "Paranormal Missouri." Jason also writes a weekly syndicated humor column.

He lives with his family in Northwest Missouri where he teaches college journalism and keeps humanity safe from the inevitable invading Martian space army.

SEVERED**PRESS**

f facebook.com/severedpress
twitter.com/severedpress

CHECK OUT OTHER GREAT ZOMBIE NOVELS

Z BURBIA
by Jake Bible

Whispering Pines is a classic, quiet, private American subdivision on the edge of Asheville, NC, set in the pristine Blue Ridge Mountains. Which is good since the zombie apocalypse has come to Western North Carolina and really put suburban living to the test!

Surrounded by a sea of the undead, the residents of Whispering Pines have adapted their bucolic life of block parties to scavenging parties, common area groundskeeping to immediate area warfare, neighborhood beautification to neighborhood fortification.

But, even in the best of times, suburban living has its ups and downs what with nosy neighbors, a strict Home Owners' Association, and a property management company that believes the words "strict interpretation" are holy words when applied to the HOA covenants. Now with the zombie apocalypse upon them even those innocuous, daily irritations quickly become dramatic struggles for personal identity, family security, and straight up survival.

ZOMBIE RULES
by David Achord

Zach Gunderson's life sucked and then the zombie apocalypse began.

Rick, an aging Vietnam veteran, alcoholic, and prepper, convinces Zach that the apocalypse is on the horizon. The two of them take refuge at a remote farm. As the zombie plague rages, they face a terrifying fight for survival.

They soon learn however that the walking dead are not the only monsters.

SEVERED**PRESS**

 facebook.com/severedpress
 twitter.com/severedpress

CHECK OUT OTHER GREAT ZOMBIE NOVELS

VACCINATION
by Phillip Tomasso

What if the H7N9 vaccination wasn't just a preventative measure against swine flu?

It seemed like the flu came out of nowhere and yet, in no time at all the government manufactured a vaccination. Were lab workers diligent, or could the virus itself have been man-made? Chase McKinney works as a dispatcher at 9-1-1. Taking emergency calls, it becomes immediately obvious that the entire city is infected with the walking dead. His first goal is to reach and save his two children.

Could the walls built by the U.S.A. to keep out illegal aliens, and the fact the Mexican government could not afford to vaccinate their citizens against the flu, make the southern border the only plausible destination for safety?

ZOMBIE, INC
by Chris Dougherty

"WELCOME! To Zombie, Inc. The United Five State Republic's leading manufacturer of zombie defense systems! In business since 2027, Zombie, Inc. puts YOU first. YOUR safety is our MAIN GOAL! Our many home defense options - from Ze Fence® to Ze Popper® to Ze Shed® - fit every need and every budget. Use Scan Code "TELL ME MORE!" for your FREE, in-home*, no obligation consultation! *Schedule your appointment with the confidence that you will NEVER HAVE TO LEAVE YOUR HOME! It isn't safe out there and we know it better than most! Our sales staff is FULLY TRAINED to handle any and all adversarial encounters with the living and the undead". Twenty-five years after the deadly plague, the United Five State Republic's most successful company, Zombie, Inc., is in trouble. Will a simple case of dwindling supply and lessening demand be the end of them or will Zombie, Inc. find a way, however unpalatable, to survive?

SEVEREDPRESS

facebook.com/severedpress
twitter.com/severedpress

CHECK OUT OTHER GREAT ZOMBIE NOVELS

900 MILES
by S. Johnathan Davis

John is a killer, but that wasn't his day job before the Apocalypse.

In a harrowing 900 mile race against time to get to his wife just as the dead begin to rise, John, a business man trapped in New York, soon learns that the zombies are the least of his worries, as he sees first-hand the horror of what man is capable of with no rules, no consequences and death at every turn.

Teaming up with an ex-army pilot named Kyle, they escape New York only to stumble across a man who says that he has the key to a rumored underground stronghold called Avalon..... Will they find safety? Will they make it to Johns wife before it's too late?

Get ready to follow John and Kyle in this fast paced thriller that mixes zombie horror with gladiator style arena action!

WHITE FLAG OF THE DEAD
by Joseph Talluto

Millions died when the Enillo Virus swept the earth. Millions more were lost when the victims of the plague refused to stay dead, instead rising to slaughter and feed on those left alive. For survivors like John Talon and his son Jake, they are faced with a choice: Do they submit to the dead, raising the white flag of surrender? Or do they find the will to fight, to try and hang on to the last shreds or humanity?

www.ingramcontent.com/pod-product-compliance
Lightning Source LLC
Chambersburg PA
CBHW020103180626
46812CB00006B/2452